Beyond the Beyond

Trapped

Michael P. Andre

This book is a work of fiction. Names, characters, places, and incidents are fictional. Any resemblance to any person living or dead is coincidental.

DEDICATION

I dedicate this to my wife and family.

ACKNOWLEDGEMENT

I want to thank Saima and my sister, Joanne, for their editing assistance and Amazon for their cover picture.

OTHER BOOKS BY THE AUTHOR

First Born of the Moon - And Other Stories (2015)

Healer - And More Stories (2017)

Heroes of the Empire - Doom (2018)

Trek (2019)

Contents

1.

Erica, Jiao, Dan, Roche, and Raj had concluded their day at school on this beautiful Tuesday the second week of the start of fall classes for grade eleven. Jiao and Dan, and Erica and Roche, were dating friends. Raj had no girlfriend but was jealous of Roche because he and Erica had been playmates from childhood and he had fallen in love with her.

The friends remained at the high school to support Roche during his football practice in the field behind it. When the practice finished, he went into the school to change back into his clothes. When he returned, he joined his friends and they left for home.

Within minutes, the sky began to spit rain.

Roche said, "We'd better hurry, we might as well keep as dry as we can."

About five minutes into the walk, Dan had an idea. "Maybe we can cut through Mr. McGregor's farm. That should cut off a couple of minutes."

"It'll be darker than taking the road," Jiao advised.

"It's not that dark yet, so we should be okay," Dan responded.

"Mr McGregor doesn't like kids cutting through his farm."

Roche heard their conversation and added, "I think that's a great idea. Mr. McGregor sold the farm."

"He did? Where did you hear that?" Erica asked.

"My dad was talking about it a few days ago. You must have seen a for-sale sign in front of the farm a few weeks ago, so you must have seen it was for sale. Well, he sold it about a month ago and has already moved out. There's nobody there now. My dad's sure investors bought it. There's talk they might be turning it into a new development."

"So, that means we can cut through it without problem," Dan concluded.

"Okay," said Roche, "the rain's picking up a little."

Dan led the way off the road and up the driveway to Mr McGregor's former house. As they passed it, they spotted the boarded-up windows. "I guess you were right, Roche. Nobody is living here now. Maybe we can pick up the pace a bit and we'll be home in no time."

They trudged on at an increased speed through a small grove of trees.

As they neared a small opening on their right, Dan saw the glow of a dim light out of the corner of his eye. He turned his head to it and said, "Hey, what's that over there?"

Everyone swung their head in the same direction. They all stopped to look. About twenty metres away, they could see a rectangular-shaped light about two metres above the ground.

"It looks like a light in the middle of nowhere," Dan said. He started to go toward it.

"Aren't we supposed to be going home?" Erica roared, so they could all hear.

"It's only going to take a second to check it out. There shouldn't be a light in the middle of those trees, usually, there's nothing there," Dan responded.

"Maybe it's a campsite and we'll be bothering whoever's there. Let's get back home before the rain picks up."

Dan stopped and turned around. "It won't hurt to look. There are five of us."

Roche agreed. "Let's go girls. It won't take long."

The girls looked at each other.

Jiao said, "Guys, I'm getting wet."

Dan had already started walking with Roche close behind him. The three others hastily followed behind.

"We're almost there." Dan urged them on. The light grew brighter as they approached it.

They came to a halt only a few metres away. "So, what is it?" Jiao asked.

"Holy crap, I don't know. It looks like an open door – a rectangular door of light with darkness all around it," Dan said, as he walked closer to the source of the light.

Suddenly, everyone heard a muffled bump and Dan yelled, "Ouch."

"What happened?" Roche asked as he stopped his advance.

"I hit something with my foot."

Roche looked down, "But there's nothing there."

"Well, I hit my foot on something," Dan responded with an air of certainty. He edged his foot forward and it stopped.

Roche saw it. "What the . . ."

"I think we should get out of here," Jiao advised quickly.

"I double that," suggested Erica.

"Curiouser and curiouser," Roche said. He lowered his hand and felt the surface of something. It was solid, although it looked as if nothing was there. He felt a little more. "It feels like stairs up to the opening."

"Well, it isn't just a door then. It's got stairs, only we can't see them."

"Let's get out of here fast. If it's solid as you say it is, I don't know any technology on Earth that can be solid and you can't see it. I know we have stealth planes but you can still see them. Come on Jiao, let's lead these idiots out of here," Erica said boldly.

Dan countered. "Come on girls, we only want to look. Whatever it is, this is fascinating. You don't want to go back by yourselves; the boogiemen might catch you. This is a lifetime opportunity to explore this thing. If you want, I'll go in first. If no one is there, we can decide what to do next. If there's someone inside, then we'll skedaddle."

"Or you'll be captured!" Erica stammered.

Dan carefully climbed up the invisible stairs to the opening and looked inside. "Hey, it's a room, like a spaceship's control room. I don't see anybody here." The opening to the door was less than two metres high. He began to pull off his backpack.

"What're you doing?" Jiao cried out.

"It's a small opening. I can leave my backpack outside."

"No, you can't. What happens if whoever owns this comes back? We may need to run and you'll end up leaving it behind."

"Okay, what the heck," Dan said resignedly.

Dan adjusted his backpack, bent down a little, and stepped into the opening. Roche quickly followed.

"Hey girls, come see this," Roche called out.

The girls looked at each other with terrified looks on their faces.

"No way, forget it," Erica said. She looked at Raj. "So, what do you think? Are you a hero too, or do you want to go back home with us?"

Raj paused to collect his thoughts. He did not know what he should do. He was curious about this possible spaceship but terrified at what might happen if the owners were inside, or even if they were outside and caught them in their ship. Would they be friendly, or angry? If he left with the girls and something happened to Dan or Roche, he would never forgive himself . . . although, if something did happen to Roche, he would have Erica to himself . . . but he put that thought immediately out of his mind. He finally blurted, "I'm caught in the middle here but we can't go without them. We'll be safer if we stick together. If whoever owns this thing comes back, they'd split us up. They may even catch the three of us on the trail home. We'll have strength in numbers."

Erica was disappointed. She wanted to convince everyone to get back onto the trail home. She turned to Jiao, "What do you think?"

"It looks as if Dan and Roche want to explore this thing; I don't think they're going to change their minds. I'm with you. We've got to get out of here but maybe if we give them a minute or two, we can still get out okay."

"Well, if you guys want to look, I'll just take a peek from the door and keep my eyes open in case someone comes," Erica said nervously.

Raj and Jiao scurried into the door.

Erica climbed into the doorway and took a quick look around. It looked like a control room of some sort, she thought. She could see why the boys would be curious. She was curious too but would not have had the nerve to satisfy her curiosity on her own. She was terrified.

The ceiling was less than two metres high. Dan and Roche had to slump over to keep from hitting their heads on it. Raj and the two girls were comfortable with the height. That meant that the owners of the vessel were small in stature.

Several places along the walls looked as if they had doors to other rooms. Erica thought of what would happen if one of them opened and somebody or something came out. They would likely panic and dash out of the spacecraft. She turned her head to the outside. If the occupants were there, she could warn the others but the clearing was not very large. She would likely not see them until they were quite close to this thing. And what would she do? She was the only one who could likely get away but then, she would have to walk home alone to get help. She shivered at the thought.

Raj, Dan, and Jiao examined the instrumentation console in the centre of the control room while Roche examined each of the six doors along the inner circle of the spaceship. All the doors seemed sealed except for one that opened at his approach, then closed again when he passed on to the next one. After he tried all the doors, he went to the one that had opened and looked inside briefly.

"This looks as if this is some kind of storage room," Roche said. "It has some cases and other stuff inside. If you guys have finished, we'd better get out of here."

Suddenly, Erica heard some crackling sounds coming from the bushes outside. Someone or something was approaching the ship. She quickly ducked into the room and put her back to the wall beside the door to hide herself from the noise outside. She said in a muffled tone, "Somebody's coming, let's move – now!"

Roche raced to the side of the door and gingerly poked his head out quickly, then pulled it back. "Shit," he said quietly but loud enough for the rest to hear. "I can see one of them; they're too close for us to escape without being seen. I don't think it saw me. Should we rush out and run like hell?"

Everyone froze. They had only split seconds to decide.

Dan suddenly whispered loud enough for the others to hear, "They might have guns, let's hide in the room Roche found." All of them bolted toward the door. It opened and then closed when they were all inside.

2.

The ship's captain stopped and peered at the light shining from the open door into the deepening darkness of the evening. "Shit, we didn't leave the portal open." He walked up the stairs and looked inside. "Where's Grog?" he asked.

"He's not inside?" his first officer asked.

"No. He knows he's not supposed to do that."

"Well, we're isolated here."

"Yes, but he knows the rules. It's all right to leave the ship for a few minutes but he must close the portal. We don't even want insects or other animals getting into the ship, let alone the indigenous people."

They stepped inside.

"I don't like the odours on this planet," the first officer said.

"Every planet has its own smells."

"It smells as if some of those outdoor smells already got into the ship."

"I know; it doesn't take long. This is your first trip out. You must acclimatise to different smells and make it a habit to follow the rules. It should be automatic. The technology of the people on this planet is advancing quite quickly now. We can't let our guard down. We must always have our cloaking shield on and leaving the door open defeats the whole idea of keeping our activities, and even our existence, unknown to local advancing aboriginals. You stay here and record what we've done. I'll go find Grog."

The captain left the ship and closed the portal. He pulled out his communicator and slowly turned until he located the beacon he was trying to find. Looks as if he went back to the farmhouse again, the captain thought as he started to walk in that direction.

Soon, he was at the back door of the farmer's house. Someone had removed the lock from the door. The captain opened it and called, "Grog?"

A voice inside replied, "Yes, Captain?"

"Come here."

Within a couple of seconds, Grog was by the door. "Sorry sir, I wanted to take one last look at this house. The owner didn't leave much behind, so there's not much to find."

"We know that. You should've stayed in the ship."

"It was boring sitting there waiting for you. I thought I'd take one more look around here."

"That's okay but you left the ship's portal open."

Grog blanched. "It was? Isn't it supposed to close by itself?"

"Remember, we had turned it off to move in those specimens. Nobody reset it; another error. I shouldn't have to look after every detail of what should be routine activities."

"I'm sorry, sir. I guess I'm too excited to be here and see for myself what's happening on other planets. I've always dreamed of being an explorer."

"Well, part of exploring is following a routine. If our actions don't become automatic, accidents can happen which can cause a gross inconvenience to us, or end up with one of us killed. I'm sure you don't want to be responsible for anything happening because of your neglect."

Grog hung his head penitently, "No, sir. I understand, sir."

"Okay then, cover your tracks in the house before you leave. When you're done, replace the lock on the door and get back to the ship."

"Yes, sir, I'll be right behind you."

"Sweep up your outside tracks, too. I don't think we need to stay here any longer and, right now, I've been standing here getting wet. We have to leave."

The captain turned and left.

Grog looked at where he had been and could see no signs of tracks inside, so he left, replaced the lock on the door, and started walking to the ship using a brush he had to erase his tracks in the grass.

When the captain arrived at the spaceship, the portal opened and he entered and sniffed. "There's still a smell in here."

"It was stronger before but it's almost gone."

"Hmm."

The door opened for Grog and he entered.

"Okay, men, log in your findings and we'll stay until it gets a little darker. This time we don't need landing lights on, as we're just flying up and out. We'll stay invisible until we're an undetectable distance from this planet."

3.

There was a dim light inside the small compartment the teens were in. The girls huddled together terrified, while the boys tried to decide their next course of action.

"We're in a pickle," Raj whispered.

"Yeah," Roche whispered back facetiously.

"Come on guys, let's not panic. I think we're as terrified as the girls are but we'll have to be strong. If we are, they will be, too. We don't know how soundproof these walls are, so we'll have to keep talking quietly," Dan said.

"What are our options?" Raj asked.

"Yeah, let's start with that," Dan suggested.

Raj started. "We could go to the door, it opens, and we give ourselves up to the aliens. Hopefully, they'll let us go."

Dan added. "We could wait and see what happens, maybe they'll leave the ship again and we can get out of here. The aliens will be none the wiser and we'll be free."

Raj responded, "That's possible. They might sleep when we do and not go out again until daylight."

"Or maybe not; they might be nocturnal."

"But if they're not, another choice may be to wait awhile and escape when they're asleep."

"Yeah, those are all good options. So far, we're not hearing much from the other side of the wall, so we might not hear them go out again and we won't know if they've gone to sleep. How can we find out what they're doing?"

"I wish we knew how long these aliens will stay here. They might move to another location on earth, or move off it then we'll be in trouble."

"Well, if it's to another place on the planet, that really won't be too bad. We can find our way home."

There was a light glow beside Erica for several seconds then it went out.

Erica interrupted their conversation. "Why don't we phone our parents and tell them where we are? They must be worried about us by now. I just tried but can't get a signal. My battery seems okay, though."

Everyone pulled out their phones and tried to get them to work. There was lots of murmuring then Raj affirmed, "Okay guys stop the noise. I don't think it's our phones. The walls of this ship appear to be blocking our phones from getting a signal to make them work."

Dan concurred. "That must be it. Our families are going to be worried by now. Whenever we get out of here, we're going to have a lot of explaining to do."

"I wonder if we should give ourselves up," Jiao said nervously.

"Their ship was invisible to us, so they don't want to let people know they're here. Now that we know they are, they might not want to let us go because we'd tell others," Dan replied.

"We could tell them we won't say anything."

"If you were an alien, would you take that for a response? Our parents are going to be asking questions. Are we going to say we thought we'd play in the rain for a while, especially without telling them we'd be late getting home?"

There was silence for several seconds.

"So, we're stuck with doing nothing," Erica said. "We can't sit here and do that. We're twenty minutes late. Soon, our parents will be looking down the roads for us and they don't know we took a shortcut."

Dan got up and walked to the wall by the door but not too close to trigger the door mechanism. He placed his ear on it. Everyone said nothing while he listened.

Minutes ticked by.

Dan finally said, "I can't hear a thing – nothing."

Raj said, "Maybe they're not moving."

"Yeah, but do you want to sit beside the wall listening forever for them to move? The wall may be almost soundproof. If it won't let our phones work, maybe it doesn't let sound out either," Erica replied.

"We're doomed," Jiao said, almost panicking.

"Maybe we should turn ourselves in and face the music like Jiao said," Erica responded with some assertion. "Let's take a vote."

The boys looked at each other.

Roche said, "I'll be willing to go first. Maybe I can start by turning myself in, while you guys hide. That way, we can find out more about the owners. If they're friendly, everyone can come out and we can go home. If they're not friendly, you guys can figure out what to do next."

The others nodded in agreement and scrambled behind the crates and other stored materials. When Roche could see everyone was sufficiently hidden, he walked to the door. Nothing happened. He tried to slide it in the direction it had opened earlier.

"Well, you guys can come out. The door's not opening," Roche said in frustration.

"Did you try sliding it?" Erica asked.

"With everything I had."

"Let's all try it together," Erica suggested.

Everyone moved to the door, pressed their hands on it, and heaved. Nothing happened.

They stood back and looked at the door.

Raj stepped forward and began to slam his fist against it. Soon Roche joined him. Their fists gave a slight thud sound but it was evident that the soft noise was not transmitting through the door.

Erica screamed and Jiao followed then the others. They continued for almost a minute then stopped and waited. Nothing happened.

"Well, that exhausts all our immediate options," Dan said, his voice quivering.

For long minutes, they stood where they were staring at their only way out.

Raj finally broke the silence. "It looks as if we're stuck here."

"Where's the washroom?" Jiao asked seriously. "I don't think any of us went before we left the field."

"Yeah," replied Raj, "We'll all need to go some time, plus, if we stay here awhile, what about food and water?"

"I think everyone had a water bottle in their packs but they may not be full," Jiao said, "We all ate our lunches, so that's gone."

"I think I still have a couple of chocolate bars," Erica replied.

"I may have some snacks," Dan added.

"I may have something, too," Raj said. "We should ration our water and food. We can live without food for quite a while but without water, we'll only last a few days."

"Right now, we'll be able to move some of the crates around to give privacy for going to the bathroom but we'll have to do it on the floor, as there's nothing to put it in. It's going to stink in here after a few hours," Dan said. "Come help me, Roche."

The two of them slid some of the crates over to one corner leaving an opening at one end. They gathered in the opposite corner and sat on the floor. Jiao and Erica huddled together shivering with fear.

Suddenly, the sole light in the room winked out.

Raj looked up at the ceiling in a daze, as he remembered the dream that he had the previous night. Was that a premonition?

Soon after, they were all thinking in dread of their predicament, the few days leading up to this day, and how this was all going to affect their friends, family, and school. They clung to the hope they could escape the next day.

4.

The Friday before the teenagers' encounter with the spacecraft, each of them awoke to a bright sunny day.

Roche got up first and did his regime of exercises on his barbells and toned his muscles to rock-hard masses. He looked at his biceps in the mirror and flexed them proudly and headed to the shower. When done, he saw that he was behind schedule, so he grabbed his phone and headed downstairs for breakfast.

Raj awakened, raised his groggy head, looked at his clock then rolled over to go back to sleep – until he remembered what day it was and it was a school day. He had to get up. Rather than wait for the alarm to go off, he reached over and shut it off. He sat up, grabbed his phone, turned it on, thumbed a few times across the screen, then tapped in 'I love you. He sighed and put the phone back down, so he could get ready for the day.

Erica woke up when her alarm went off but was still tired from working hard on her math homework the previous evening. She opened her eyes and shut it off. She thought it was a good thing that tomorrow was Saturday, so she could sleep in. She wished that math wasn't so hard, as she could have used the extra sleep.

She crawled out of bed and looked in the mirror. "Gee I look awful," she mumbled. She picked up her phone and noticed only one text from Raj. "Boy, he's a pest. Why can't he leave me alone," she whispered in disgust. She deleted it without responding. She created a text for Roche saying 'I love you' then sent it and began her morning routine.

Jiao got up quickly, opened the blinds in her bedroom, and gazed at the rising sun. She peered out at the sky. She smiled at the bright blue cloudless expanse. It is a beautiful day, she thought. She went over to her bedroom, picked up her phone, and sent a text to Dan that said 'I love you. She put the phone down and scurried to the shower to prepare for school.

Dan opened his eyes, rolled over, and spotted the ray of sun shining in from the corners of his blinds. "Shit," he said quietly. He got up and raced to his phone. He quickly turned it on and noticed Jiao's text. "Damn, she beat me again. Maybe I should send a text to her before I go to bed," he muttered but he knew it would not count. She would know he was cheating by the time of the text. He breathed a loud sigh, then sent off an 'I love you too'. He went back to his bed, sat down, and began to get ready for school.

Raj, as usual, was the first one out of his house. He wandered over to the neighbourhood mail kiosk to wait for the others. He noticed the slight discolouration of the leaves. It was fall and cool this morning. He hated winter and was not looking forward to going through another one. His parents had moved from India when he was an infant. They spoke Hindi at home but life in the streets in his youth and later in the school gave him an almost accent-free English, unless he was overly excited or angry then he would speak an almost unintelligible gibberish of neither language.

He stood patiently for the others to arrive. He had lived in this neighbourhood for six years, only one year after the developer had built the first houses in this new location just outside of the suburbs of Ottawa, Ontario. His father was an engineer in charge of software development.

When Raj was in elementary school, he could use the school bus from this location but high school students were no longer eligible, as they could walk to school within thirty minutes. Some parents of the neighbourhood drove their teens but five youths from the estates were content to walk there and they had formed a tight-knit group of friends.

Erica arrived next. She slowed to a crawl on her last few steps to the kiosk when she saw Raj was already there.

"Good morning," Raj said cheerily. He knew she was rarely in a good mood in the morning for some reason, particularly when she saw him.

"Good morning," she grumbled back.

"Nice day today, isn't it?"

She looked up at the sky and responded, "Yeah, I guess it is."

"Well, it could be raining," he said trying to cheer her up. He tried to imagine her in a bright yellow dress. Today she wore black jeans, a black shirt with a black jacket. Her only change sometimes was a black skirt with black leggings. He thought her black hair and over-coloured face made her look like a vampire. He hated black but, to him, she made black look beautiful.

"Why are you staring at me?" She cut into his thoughts. "You're always staring at me, so stop it."

"Ah . . . oh, sorry. You're just so beautiful," he shot back.

"Yeah, great," she said with an air of disgust.

He pulled his eyes from her and could see Jiao and Dan coming up the street hand-in-hand. They were chatting together as they walked.

Jiao's family were recent immigrants but she had learned English in China while she was quite young, so she was very fluent, only a slight Cantonese accent betrayed her recent arrival to North America. She was short and pretty.

Dan was head over heels for Jiao. His ancestors had lived in the province for a century or more. They were the first people to move into this neighbourhood. When Jiao moved in a few years later, it was love at first sight – at least for him. His constant attention to her had grown to make her love him back.

She was more familiar with oriental boys and it was a bit of a cultural shock for her at first, particularly with the school system. She was taking classes in subjects she had learned years ago in the schooling system in China. Even though local the school had her skip a grade, her parents had to challenge her with additional course material and encouraged her to develop her skills with the violin.

Before Roche left home, he quickly picked up his phone and read the text from Erica. He smiled. Since he had met her, he always got that text in the morning. He put his phone away, grabbed his pack, and hurried out of the house over to the kiosk.

When he arrived, Erica leaned her head back – her signal for him to bend over and kiss her.

The contrast between Roche and Erica was extreme. He wore a tee shirt, light jacket, and blue jeans and was over 193 centimetres tall to her 157.

Roche obliged her with a quick kiss on her lips. Like Jiao, Roche was also a recent arrival to the neighbourhood moving in the same summer as she did.

With the group assembled, they trudged off to school. Dan and Jiao led the way then Roche and Erica. As he was the odd person, most of the time Raj trailed them all. He loved being behind though because he could watch Erica walk. With each step, her hips gently swayed from side to side – his great seduction. He would only tear his eyes away when he found his mind wandering too much.

When Erica's family moved in a year after he did, she attracted him from that first day. He thought she was the most beautiful girl in the world and they became fast friends. But they were children, and when Roche moved in two years ago, she drifted away from him and fell in love with Roche.

Raj's feelings for her were beginning to change around then – from one of a child to something deeper but it wasn't mutual. Since she had been going out with Roche, he could only watch her from a distance. He had seen her transition from a young girl into what he considered a rather weird gothic figure. Weird or not, he loved her but she could only be with him in his rather passionate dreams.

Erica glanced back. She spoke quietly to Roche, "I always feel his eyes boring into me. I wish he would lead, or at least be in front of us."

"Don't let him get to you," Roche whispered in return.

"But he still sends me an 'I love you' text every morning. I've asked him to stop but he just keeps doing it."

"Do you want me to stomp on him or something?"

"No, but maybe if you talked to him . . . He's just so creepy. He's always looking at me."

"He knows you're with me."

"That's why he might stop if you talked to him."

"He isn't doing any harm."

She glanced back again.

"Is he still looking at you?" Roche asked.

"He isn't, now."

"Then see, you might be imagining it."

"I'm not imagining it," she said crudely.

"Okay, just keep walking." He slowed his pace.

She noticed it and began to slow, too.

"I said keep walking."

She quickened her pace, as he fell slightly behind then he sped up and re-joined her.

"What the hell were you doing?" she whispered.

"Well, all Raj can see is your back, so I was taking a look from his viewpoint."

"You mean you've never seen me from behind yet!" she replied, surprised.

"Well, yeah but I was taking a more careful look."

"Why did you do that?"

". . . Because I wanted to put myself in his shoes."

"That was dumb."

"Not really."

"No, that was stupid."

"Not that stupid. From his perspective, I'd say you have a nice ass."

"What!" she grumbled, trying to keep her voice low. ". . . Boys . . . is that all you guys can say? Is that all you guys can think of? So, it's going to make me feel better to know that he's admiring my nice ass." She rolled her eyes with disgust. "I particularly don't want him behind me then. You've got to talk to him," she said sternly.

Raj was watching them from behind wondering what was going on with Erica and Roche.

5.

The teens arrived at school and sorted out to their classrooms.

At noon, Roche, who usually had lunch with Erica, sat beside Raj without saying hello.

Raj was shocked and glanced at Roche quizzically. For several minutes they ate in silence. He wondered why he sat beside him without acknowledging him. He could no longer bear the quiet and finally asked, "What's up, Roche?"

"Ah, nothing much."

They continued eating.

Raj, hating the silence, asked, "What's going on? Usually, you eat lunch with Erica and, when we do sit together, we talk about something. Today you're quiet."

Roche kept eating in silence.

"Have you two had a fight or something?" Raj asked hopefully.

"No."

"Well then, what?"

Roche finished his lunch and crumpled up the paper and plastic wrapping material. He turned to Raj, "Erica wants you to stop bothering her."

"What do you mean?" Raj asked, puzzled.

"I mean stop bothering her."

"Bothering her? Me bothering her! How could I bother her?"

"Don't send her text messages. Don't walk behind her. Don't look at her. Don't talk to her. Maybe just stay away from her."

"But we walk together to school and back! You don't want me to walk with you guys anymore?"

"No, I don't think she means that but walk in front of us. Either you can lead us or walk with Jiao and Dan, I don't care but that's what she wants. Look, this isn't new, Raj. I know she's gotten mad at you before. I know you like her but right now she's with me, okay? That's how it is. Erica's not the only girl in school."

"To me she is," he blurted out.

"You're being stubborn. She isn't interested in you – at all."

"Not interested."

"You're a fool, Raj. If you like Erica, you'd respect her wishes. If you want a girlfriend now, then find someone else," he said with firm emphasis. "Cut her from your mind. Give her some slack and leave her alone." Roche got up and left the table.

Raj sat in shock. Roche had suggested this to him before but he seemed so firm about it this time. Surely, Erica could find a place for him in her heart. Roche wasn't the guy for her; he was. How could he make her understand? Maybe he could send her a note and tell her – but he already had many times in e-mails, tweets, texts, and Facebook.

The reality hit him that maybe all she did with them was delete them without reading them. If she could understand how much he loved her but if Roche was telling him the truth, his messages were all for nought. He didn't want anybody else. He only dreamed about her.

He picked up his phone and began a text, thought better of it, and put the phone back into his pocket. He sullenly got up, dropped his lunch scraps into the garbage can, and plodded off to his next class.

On his way out of the door, he accidentally hit his arm against the arm of a younger girl walking in the opposite direction. Several books slipped from her hand onto the floor. She bent to pick them up. He was going to continue to class but thought better of it and bent to help her. He finally glanced at her to see that she was Indian, like him. She smiled and said, "Thank you." But he looked beyond her, said nothing, stood up, and was on his way to class again.

Jiao had a free period at the end of the day and had chosen to spend it studying in the library. A girl sat beside her and said, "Hi," in a low voice so nobody in the library could hear her.

Jiao turned her head to the voice. She looked at the attractive Indian girl wearing a dress topped by a sweater and replied, "Hi."

The girl appeared to be very nervous and said with a quivering voice, "My name is Amisha and I'm new to the school. I saw you walking into school with your four friends." Out of nervousness, she sat quietly, afraid to say anything else. The mood was so tense Jiao had to end the silence.

"Well, glad to meet you. Welcome to our school. My name's Jiao. How can I help you?" she responded cheerfully.

The girl moved her mouth wordlessly.

Jiao tried again to set the girl at ease. "New students are sometimes nervous for the first few days, so take your time."

Jiao wondered why the girl would want to talk to her in the first place. She had never seen her before or, at least, had not noticed her. Amisha looked as if she was two or three years younger than she was. She stared into the girl's eyes and realised what this was all about.

"My four friends and I live not too far from school, so we walk here every day. There's Roche, he's the big guy, Erica, Dan, and . . . Raj."

"Raj," Amisha repeated softly as she looked nervously at the table.

Jiao beamed with a smile, as she confirmed her suspicion.

"Yes, Raj. Um . . . is he why you came here to talk to me?"

Amisha was ashamed to look up from the table.

"I'm not going to bite you. If you want to talk about Raj, I've known him for a couple of years, so I can tell you something about him, if you want. There's nothing secret about him."

Amisha raised her head and slumped it down again. "I noticed you walked to school with him."

"Raj is a nice person. He's, um, not tied down to anyone . . . It's complicated."

"Complicated?" Amisha glanced up again, puzzled.

"Yeah, it's too hard to explain. I don't think you need to hear it all. Would you like me to introduce you to him?"

"Oh, no, no, I don't know what to do. I just thought . . ." Amisha got up and quickly left the room.

Jiao scratched her head in confusion then went back to her homework.

At the end of the school day, the group assembled one by one. Raj led the way back home deep in thought. How could he make Erica love him?

6.

A chant of "Jiao, Jiao, Jiao" coming from the room next to hers awakened Jiao. It was Saturday and she had to get up. Her little brother, Huan, was calling her. She threw her covers off and wandered into his room. Her mother was likely awake but always elected to stay in bed and let the children have their special morning together.

Jiao liked the arrangement, except when she opened the door, she knew she had to change his diaper. She loved her brother but she hated changing his diaper, especially when the solid stuff filled it.

"It's stinky in here, little guy. Do you like giving me this surprise in the morning?" she asked.

"Stinky, stinky," he called out.

"Shush, Huan, you're going to wake Mom and Dad," she said to quiet him.

She pulled him from his bed and placed him on the change table. She opened the diaper and cleaned him up.

"Boy, I'll like it when you go to the bathroom yourself. I hate doing diapers," she said aloud.

Huan squirmed on the table anxious to get off and play.

She put a clean diaper on him and put the dirty one in the diaper pail. She dressed him and plopped him on the floor. She sat down and pulled out a child's book. He waddled over to her and sat beside her. She read him the story then they played with building blocks.

After about an hour, her mother came into the room to tell them their breakfast was ready. She went to pick him up but Huan called out, "Jiao, Jiao, Jiao," and he reached out to his sister.

Jiao picked him up, cuddled him, carried him to the kitchen, placed him in his chair, and fed him. After that, they played together in the early afternoon. The rest of the day she reserved for her homework.

After supper, Jiao primped and prepared for her regular night with Dan when they went to a movie, if there was one that interested them, or to a fast-food restaurant for a snack. Jiao always wanted to pay her share.

Jiao's father had offered Dan to use his car for the evening, so Dan walked over to her home.

When he arrived, Jiao opened the door and proudly showed him the keys to the car. "Here you are, Dan."

Before she closed the door, Dan saw her father in the background and called out, "Thanks for the use of your car."

He could see Jiao's father nod and smile.

When they settled into the car and pulled out of the driveway, Jiao asked, "How was your day?"

"Pretty dull, I was trying to catch up on homework. I've got a book to read and an essay to write about it. The teachers don't waste time to get us started for the year, do they."

They were soon at the theatre. They enjoyed the movie.

Halfway home, Dan stopped the car off the side of the road and they chatted about school and some of the funny things that happened during the week. They cuddled for a while and Dan gave her a gentle kiss. She kissed him back and, for a few minutes, they continued kissing. Dan began to slide his hand toward Jiao but her hand shot out to catch it. Dan wanted to kiss her again but she pulled her head back.

"I think we should stop," she said reluctantly.

Dan pulled away his hand. He closed his eyes and rested his head on the headrest until he could regain his composure. His breathing finally returned to normal.

"I
love you, Jiao."

"I know. I love you too but there's a time and place for everything. Now's not the time and certainly this isn't the place. As I've said before, you don't show your love by what you do for yourself but what you do for others. As Confucius said: 'he who has control of his senses, controls his life.'"

"Did he say that?"

"I don't know. I just made it up for this occasion and the meaning of what I said might have been lost in the translation. One of my uncles and grandfather always tossed out sayings by him. They probably made them up."

They chuckled together.

Dan sat quietly in deep thought.

"What are you thinking about?" she asked.

"Nothing – just trying to stay cool. It's hard to sit quietly beside a beautiful young woman. We'd better not be late, or our parents will start worrying," Dan said.

He sat behind the wheel, started the car, and pulled back onto the road. "I want to make sure we always get opportunities to have a car to go out."

She sighed, "Yes, my dad is always worried about me."

"He probably remembers what he did when he was a kid," Dan said while smiling.

She smiled and said, "Probably but who knows, maybe he was as saintly as he says he was. Those were different times."

"What does your mother say about teens and sex?"

"She doesn't say much, particularly about things like that. They both get jittery when any conversation sets out in that direction. My mother and father are rather old-school. They didn't get much exposure to Western culture; not like our generation."

They arrived back at Jiao's house. He parked the car in the driveway, opened the door, and stepped out. They walked to the door of the house. Dan handed the car keys to Jiao.

"One kiss to say goodnight?" he asked.

Jiao smiled, puckered her lips, closed her eyes, and leaned her head back slightly.

He gave her a gentle kiss and then backed away.

She opened her eyes, puzzled. "There's not much passion in this one," she commented.

"I can see your dad peeking out of the corner of the window. After your little speech, I'd better be good."

She smiled knowingly, turned, and went inside while Dan said goodnight and headed back home.

Inside, her father was waiting for her in his study. He called to her softly.

Reluctantly, she entered and returned the car keys.

"So, did you like the show?" he asked in Cantonese.

She sat in a chair beside him. "Yes, the acting and storyline were very good," Jiao responded cheerfully.

"I saw you kiss at the door," he said with some hesitation.

"That's not the first time you saw us kiss, Dad," she said with a more sombre tone.

"Well, yes . . . but how serious are the two of you? Do you love him?"

"Yes, I guess I could say I do. He's a nice guy, Dad."

". . . but are you being, ah . . . a good girl?" he asked in an embarrassed whisper.

She smiled, "If what you're asking is, are we having sex, Dad, then, no."

Her father's face turned red with embarrassment at her use of the word.

"I'm grown up, Dad. You'll have to trust me, okay."

"I never thought I'd see the day . . . Jiao . . . why can't you meet a nice Chinese boy?"

"When we were in China, I'd have thought the same thing. We're in Canada. Where am I going to find a nice Chinese boy? There are nine Chinese boys in our school. Only three are close to my age and I'd never want to get to know them, let alone date one of them. Dan came along and he's a swell guy. He's kind, gentle, and considerate. He's also very mature. I love him, Dad; Chinese or not, I don't care. He's a wonderful young man. I wouldn't trade a hundred Chinese boys for Dan."

Her father sat in silence for several seconds, then agreed. "I know Dan . . . I agree he's a fine young man. I guess I can't expect you to choose any less. If you love him, then what's there to do? You're young yet and may change your mind in time. It happens. Love grows and wanes. Families move, a budding love snuffs out, and a new love is found. It's part of life and growth."

Jiao leaned over, kissed her father's cheek, and said, "Thanks, Dad, I'll take that as your approval," and she happily bounded up the stairs to get ready for bed.

Her father sat quietly for several more seconds. His young girl was growing up. She was budding into a beautiful young woman. He sighed, smiled then slowly climbed the stairs to bed.

"Get up, lazy head," Erica's mother said as she shook her daughter,

"It's almost eleven."

Erica opened her eyes. "Ah, Mom can't I just stay in bed a little longer? It's Saturday, isn't it?"

"Sometimes I think that, if you didn't have an alarm clock, or me, you'd sleep all day."

"Okay, give me time to wake up," Erica said as she started to rise.

"Remember, we'll be picking up Katelyn at the train station today."

"Yeah, I know, I have plenty of time."

"You never have enough time. Why don't you dress normally? I got you that nice dress at Christmas and you've never worn it."

"You know I don't like blue," Erica whined.

"Yeah, I know. You don't like blue, or any shade of yellow, orange, pink, red, green, purple, brown, or white . . . have I missed a colour? Oh yes, I forgot black, the only colour you like. It's your current statement."

"It's not a statement, Mom," she said unconvincingly.

"You dress like a zombie and put your makeup on like a zombie. What's happened to you in the last couple of years?"

"I'm not a zombie, Mom," Erica said as she rolled her eyes.

"I'm trying to respect you, as you but what happened to the little girl I once knew? You used to like colours."

"I'm not a little girl, Mom. Nothing's happened. I like black, okay?"

"Okay . . . okay. What am I supposed to say? We used to talk. I miss that," her mother said, exasperated, as she left the room and closed the door.

Erica got out of bed and checked her phone. Her eyebrows raised as she mumbled, "Well, well, well, no message from Raj. Either he's not up yet, or Roche's little talk worked."

She was happy, yet a little disappointed. She had received the texts for months and now, she didn't get one. It was strange. She could not even remember when the texts started. "Well," she muttered quietly, "I hope that's over with. I wish Roche would send me little notes like that." She put down her phone and began her morning routine.

Before she knew it, she was at the train station with her mother and father to pick up Katelyn who had her only university class on Monday cancelled. Her sister had then decided to make a trip home for the now-created long weekend.

They welcomed Katelyn at the station. Her father picked up her bags and drove them home.

For the rest of the afternoon, the three women went shopping.

Before supper, while Katelyn unpacked her suitcase and opened her new clothes, the sisters had a chance to talk.

"How are you doing at university?" Erica began.

"Good, I find the third year is my best year. I feel more relaxed."

"Yeah, you seem to be. Is it easier?"

"No, harder but I'm used to the routine. I've learned to plan and not put things off. I know my way around the university and have good friends who help. I just got comfortable. How are things with you?"

"Okay."

"Still with Roche?"

"Yeah."

"You know, I don't understand what you see in him. I admit he's a hunk but that's it."

"You told me this before," Erica replied in a huff.

"He's an okay guy, and he likes you but after all this time, I don't think he loves you – know what I mean?"

"I love him. He's cool, nice, and accepts me as I am."

Katelyn held up the new dress she bought and held it over her to look in the mirror. "Next party, I can put this on. What do you think?"

Erica paused to watch her admiring herself in the mirror and responded, "It's pretty; looks good on you."

Katelyn swung around and held it up to Erica. "It's a little long on you but that'd be great on you, too."

"Not interested," Erica responded.

"You could glam up you know. You don't need to dress the same way all the time, even if it's just jeans and a shirt."

"Did Mom send you in here to talk to me about this?" Erica sighed.

"No, why? Is she on your case?"

"Not all the time but enough to annoy me."

"And I'm annoying you?"

"No. Why can't people accept me the way I am?"

"You don't think people accept you?"

"I don't think everyone does."

"Like Mom?"

"Especially Mom but there are others."

"Maybe that's why you do it."

Erica's eyes bulged and she raised her voice, "See, that's what I mean. I can't be myself; everyone wants to fit me into a little hole and

I'm dressing like this to annoy people or something!"

Katelyn smiled and stayed silent.

"I was hoping you'd be on my side," Erica lamented.

"I am on your side. I don't have to dress like you to be on your side. I can still say what's in my head and be on your side. You're my little sister. You don't have to be like me – perfection;" and she rolled her eyes with a smile while she said the last word. "You can be yourself."

". . . and I am," Erica affirmed.

"We all go through various phases in our teens. I went through stuff but I just kept them inside. I love wearing pretty clothes. They make me feel happy and that's what I needed at the time. Wearing black would have been too depressing for me.

"You have two guys interested in you. I had some too, but in the end, they weren't interested in me. You'll probably have similar experiences. You'll find that there are plenty of fish in the sea. I've met a few interesting guys at university. Those are the ones you should wait for, as they're much more mature.

"So, don't think that Roche or Raj will stick around forever. However, I don't know about Raj . . ." she paused, "he has liked you since we moved here, now I think he has serious feelings for you, so please let him down easily. He's known you too long to hurt him."

"I like Raj but I guess I've outgrown him. I just don't love him," Erica said almost apologetically.

"I think you should keep him as a friend. He'll always be there for you."

"Right now, he's too there for me."

"I know but go easy on him."

They spent the rest of the day as a family and went out for supper.

Roche spent his day first doing his stretches and exercises then to his homework.

Even though it was Saturday, Raj got up early and went to his phone. He checked it. "Nothing new, I hardly get anything from anybody," he mumbled. "Other people brag about how many friends they have and how many likes and tweets." He thought of sending Erica a text message – or anything – but remembered what Roche had said and thought better of it.

He too, was busy with homework. Late in the afternoon, his mother poked her head into his room.

"How's your homework coming along?" she asked.

"Okay."

"Doing anything special this evening?"

"No."

She paused for several seconds then said, "I was talking to Missus Singh this week. She has a daughter almost your age."

"So? Who's Missus Singh?"

"I met her at the grocery store. They're new in town."

"I'm not interested."

"So, you're still hung up on Erica?"

"No, I'm not hung up on Erica."

"You've known her for a long time but you know she's grown up. She's got other interests."

Raj thought of those swaying hips and sighed, "Just leave me alone, okay."

"I don't like your moping around the house all the time."

"I have homework to do."

"Yes, now but you wasted your whole summer not doing anything and I think it's Erica."

"Just leave me alone, okay?"

"There are other girls in the world, you know. It's not good that a young man like you focuses his attention on one girl, especially one who's dating someone else and has no interest in him."

"Mom, just let me do my homework, okay."

Reluctantly she closed the door and left.

In the evening, Raj stayed up to watch a movie with his parents. He got himself ready for bed and checked for any texts on his phone. There were none. He settled under the covers, sat up on his pillow, and opened the drawer of his night table. He pulled out a handful of pictures and thumbed through them. Every one of them was a picture of Erica that he had taken on his phone. He sighed, smiled, returned the pictures to the drawer, closed it, turned over, and nestled in for dreams of his true love.

7.

Raj sat up in bed, looked at his phone on top of his dresser, and ignored it. He thought back to when he had awakened in the night. He had dreamed of Erica. He was chasing her but she kept running away. She was always out of reach. He could never run fast enough to catch her. Then he woke up and had trouble getting to sleep again.

He thought of the dream. Was that the way it was always going to be? Was he never going to convince her that he was the right guy for her? He hung his head in frustration. Was he supposed to do nothing? How was she supposed to know that he loved her if he couldn't tell her? He wanted to run over to his phone and send that text he had often sent Erica but held back. If it was bothering her, he would have to stop. He wanted to make her happy.

He slid out of bed and got ready for church.

Later that morning while some of the families clustered around the doorway after the prayer service to talk to friends, Raj approached Jiao and asked, "Can I talk with you for a minute?"

Jiao looked puzzled. Raj had never done that before. Why did he want to talk to her? "Ah, okay," she responded cautiously.

"It's kind of private, can we move away from the group a little?" he asked.

"Ah, I don't know. What do you want to talk about?" She frowned.

"Let's go over there," he replied pointing to a shady area under some trees not far from where they stood.

"Okay, it's not going to be long, is it?"

"No, I want to ask you a question."

When they got to the trees, Raj said, "Please keep what we're going to talk about secret. I'd be embarrassed if this got out. I know I can trust you above everyone else."

"Well, what's the big secret?" she asked impatiently.

"You're a girl, right? So, you'd know girl stuff and how they'd feel and everything."

"I'm not a girl psychologist."

". . . but you're a girl, so you can give me advice about girls."

"Okay . . . where is this going?"

"You know I like Erica, right?"

"I think the whole world knows you like Erica."

"I've been sending her 'I love you' texts for quite a while."

"Like, duh . . . the whole world knows you've been doing that."

"Not the whole world," Raj said dejectedly. "Am I making a fool of myself?"

"Maybe to her. Don't tell anyone but I think it's cute." She smiled and continued. "You know, though, that she only has eyes for Roche, so what you're doing is impossible," she said with emphasis.

"So, you think I should stop?"

"Probably, it seems to be annoying her."

"But how do I let her know I love her if I don't keep telling her?"

She thought for several seconds then replied, "Maybe you're looking in the wrong direction. You want a girlfriend but the one you want is not interested in you and can't love you back. Why don't you get to know other girls in school? I'm sure there's a princess out there to find. I really can't help you because you're so fixated on Erica."

"Well, she's the most beautiful girl in the school."

"That's my point. Until you get your eyes off her, no other girl in school is going to consider you. They'd always feel as if they were in second place. I know one girl who's got her eyes on you."

"You do? Who?" he asked puzzled.

"I can't tell you. It wouldn't be fair to her. Until you stop your silly impossible fixation on Erica, you're on your own. I know you say you love Erica but she doesn't love you. She doesn't hate you either but you're nothing to her. Roche is her guy. Now, until they break up, you're not even on her radar and maybe never will be. I don't know how else to tell you. You want my advice but you won't take it. Leave her alone and stop sending messages. That would make her feel better but you've got to break your stupid fixation for your sake . . . There, I did it," she said in earnest.

He stood there, stunned. He did not know what to say. At least, he got confirmation to leave Erica alone for now but to stop loving her! He didn't dream of other girls. How could he do that? He remembered the same advice Roche had given him.

"Well, I guess, thanks," he said sadly. The whole world was crashing in on him.

"Are you okay?" she asked him.

"Yeah, I guess so. You gave me more advice than I was ready for. It wasn't a surprise, I suppose."

"I see our parents looking around for us, so it's time to go. You know, if you ever need help again, we're friends, so you can count on me but I must be honest, okay? I don't want to hurt you, just follow your star, not hers."

He hung his head and went to where his parents waited for him.

His mother looked at him and said in Hindi. "What's the matter, Raj? Why are you so glum? What were you two talking about?"

"Oh, nothing."

"From the look on your face, it was as if it were slapped."

"I wasn't hit."

"No, that's not what I mean. She must have said something that offended you."

"Oh, no, just kid stuff."

"Are you interested in her?"

"No."

His mother looked at her husband and shrugged.

His father muttered, "Kids!"

That afternoon, Erica and Jiao were finishing a school project in Jiao's bedroom.

"There, I think that does it. How does it look?" Erica asked.

"Looks good, the pictures stand out on the display board. I think we should split up the presentation. Do you want to go first, or should I?" Jiao responded.

"You can, the history part at the start is best done by you; I can do the explanations, the close, and answer the questions. Of course, if I look at you, you'll know that I think you should answer that question."

"Okay."

They quietly packed up their supplies and cleaned off the desktop.

"I heard you went to a birthday party last week," Jiao queried.

"Yes, Jane's. It was fun but sometimes girls get into some weird conversations. When we were supposed to be watching a movie in the basement they kept talking about their boyfriends."

"Yeah, I find that, too."

"But why do they get so graphic? Do girls do some of that stuff, or do they make it up? It was embarrassing."

"You have a boyfriend."

"Yeah, but I'm not going to talk about him to other girls. There were six other girls there and none of them were virgins. I mean, so what? Is that something they should talk about? It's as if they were proud of it. I felt so uncomfortable. I felt like the odd person out. They even asked me about my private affairs and I said it was none of their business then one of them put me down. I wouldn't be surprised if they're making things up to be in a certain group. Wouldn't it be funny if they never did what they said, just to appear cool!"

They laughed.

Erica sat quietly in deep thought.

To fill the silence, Jiao asked, "What's got you so silent?"

"Nothing, I'm still thinking of the party. It made me feel a bit sad actually . . . and ashamed."

"Oh?"

"It reminded me of what happened a few months ago. I guess I can trust you. You're one of my closest friends . . . I broke down."

"What do you mean?"

"With Roche."

Jiao looked at her, surprised. ". . . And you're ashamed?"

"Yes, not so much when I did it but afterwards."

In the following silence, Jiao sat thinking, trying to be correct in what Erica was telling her. "You're talking in riddles. I don't want to make wrong assumptions here. Maybe you shouldn't talk anymore."

"Maybe but sometimes it's good to get things off your chest. I have no one to tell it to and unload."

"Maybe it's good to forget it and move on."

"Can I tell you a secret, although I guess it isn't one if anyone else knows?"

"Not if you're going to feel bad, or be uncomfortable."

There was a long pause of silence.

Finally, Erica confessed. "Roche had been bugging me to take our relationship to the next level. A few months ago – it just happened. I didn't plan it. It just happened.

"I thought it would be wonderful and, maybe if I did it, Roche would stop bugging me about it but everything went so fast; in a few seconds, it was over. It was so animalistic; nothing like what you see in the movies. There was nothing romantic at all.

"And everything has changed. For one, I was so terrified. For the first time, I was happy and relieved to have my period that month. For days after, Roche was pressing to keep doing it. Heck, you do it once then the floodgates open. I was so stupid. It took me so long to convince him that was it. I wasn't going to do it again.

"He's almost back to normal but this cloud always hangs over my head but it can change so much. I want to be friends with people. I'm not ready to commit that much to anyone. I love him and want to keep him and maybe someday we'll get married, or something but right now I just want to be me. Why does everything have to be so complicated?"

Erica started to cry and Jiao reached over and held her tightly until she stopped and reached for a tissue to wipe her eyes and nose.

"Sorry, I made a fool of myself." Erica sobbed but soon composed herself.

"I guess you had to get it out. I won't tell anyone. He hasn't told anyone has he?"

"Not that I know of. I don't think he would. He knows how upset I was."

"I hope he won't. Boys are sure a handful, eh?"

"I hope you have a better time with Dan."

"I've got a good handle on him. He knows the limits. He's a pretty good guy."

"Roche is a nice guy, too. I guess it's normal for them to try; those dammed hormones, too much testosterone."

Both smiled then rolled up their display to get it ready for their presentation on Tuesday.

There was a little tapping on the door.

"What was that?" Erica asked.

"I know exactly what it is," Jiao said, as she walked to the door and opened it.

A sudden bellowing began, "Jiao, Jiao, Jiao," while Jiao's baby brother shuffled into the room.

Jiao picked him up and hugged him. He reached up and tried to slip his finger into her nose.

"This is his latest craze. He sees holes in our noses and wants to stick his finger into it." She started to giggle, as she kept twisting her head from side to side to avoid his finger.

She noticed a powerful odour fill the room. "That means he needs to be changed. When I'm home, he wants me to do it, which my mother finds funny, as she knows I hate changing diapers."

"These are the moments when I feel lucky to be the youngest child," Erica chirped. "I'd better pick up things and get going. I'd hate to delay your favourite activity."

"Yeah, sure. Want to help?"

"No, thanks. I'll pass up the fun," Erica said as she collected things and left Jiao on her own.

Erica walked home and said goodbye to her sister, as she would likely sleep in the next morning and prepare for her ride back to university.

That evening, Raj settled himself in bed. It had been a long tiring day helping his father around the yard getting it ready for winter. He had already checked his phone for messages. He opened his night table drawer to look at his pictures. He placed them back into the drawer and sat thinking about his recent discussions with Roche and Jiao. Was Erica beyond his reach? Was she that serious about Roche? Was there anything he could do to make her change her mind about him? Did he have to bide his time? Waiting was going to delay his chances to convince her that he was the best person for her.

Wait . . . that's what he was supposed to do. Should he bother with any other girls? One of the girls in school supposedly was interested in him; but who? He thought about all of them and one by one he rejected each one. He loved only Erica.

8.

It was a bright sunny Monday morning when Raj stepped out of his house. He walked to the group's familiar meeting point by the postal kiosk to await the arrival of the rest of the gang. He had resolved to follow Jiao and Roche's advice and do everything Erica wished. He would walk in front of her, although he would miss the gentle roll of her hips as they swayed from side to side with each step. He would not send her any e-mails or do anything else she wanted. If that would win her heart, that was what he would do.

His thoughts distracted him until Jiao and Dan walked up hand-in-hand.

"Beautiful morning today," Raj greeted them.

"Sure is," Jiao replied.

Within minutes, Erica arrived. She looked behind her to see if she could see Roche but he had not left his house, yet. She turned around and looked at Raj who was looking at her.

She felt uncomfortable and looked at the ground and then off into the distance.

Dan and Jiao watched them amusedly. They could see the tension between them.

Jiao finally sliced through the silence by saying, "I hope Roche is not going to be late today."

Erica countered. "I don't think so. He didn't send me anything to say he was going to be late."

She looked back down the road and spotted Roche leaving his house. "There he is," she said more spiritedly.

All eyes were on him, as he began to run toward them. When he arrived, he drew a breath and said, "Sorry I'm a little late. We'll still have plenty of time for us to get to school on time."

There was not enough time for much conversation, as they walked quickly toward the school. Raj was in front of the group with Dan and Jiao and enjoyed brief chats with them along the way.

The school activities were uneventful that day. Raj had lunch at school alone but sat so he could occasionally glance at his one true love sitting with Roche.

On the way home, there was more time to talk.

Jiao asked Dan if any lights had awakened him around one o'clock in the morning.

Dan responded, "What do you mean, lights?"

"I thought I saw some bright lights outside. At first, I thought it might have been lightning but it lasted longer than lightning would. I got up and looked out the window but saw nothing."

"Maybe you had a bad dream."

"I don't think so," she said.

Dan thought for a moment, "The only things that would make light in the neighbourhood were a car's headlights or maybe a plane but neither would be very bright."

She responded, "The light seemed brighter than headlights but it didn't last long."

Raj interjected, "I sleep soundly, so I wouldn't have seen anything like that. I can sleep through an earthquake."

Jiao was starting to doubt herself. "Well, maybe you're right and it was part of a dream. Maybe a neighbour was out late in their car. Anyway, it doesn't matter, it went away."

When they got close to home, Roche and Erica increased their pace to catch up to the other three.

Erica said excitedly, "Roche said he's having football practice tomorrow at about five. Are any of you interested in joining me to watch?"

The other three nodded in agreement.

Jiao responded, "Yes, maybe that'll be fun."

Erica added, "It doesn't make sense to go home then go back out, so maybe we can bring an extra lunch and just hang around after school until the practice starts."

There were nods of agreement all around.

"Okay, so tell your parents what we're doing. We can walk home after the practice, so nobody needs to pick us up. We're not sure when the practice ends anyway," Erica concluded.

Each person separated to go to their homes.

After supper, Jiao and Erica got together at Erica's house to practice their presentation for the next day. It was past nine when they finished. Jiao thanked Erica's mother for cookies and milk and left for home.

"From what I overheard, it sounds as if you've got a good presentation put together," Erica's mother said.

"We're having a lot of fun, too. It's a dull subject but we thought we'd put some humour into it to keep people awake. Too bad parents don't get to see our presentations."

"Yes, I'd take some time off work to see some of them, if they'd let us. So, how's it going at school, so far?"

"Good."

"Everybody getting along?"

"Yes."

"How about Roche?"

He's doing okay. He's having his first football practice tomorrow and we all want to stay and watch. It starts at five o'clock. We thought we'd bring an extra lunch, stay at school, and come home after the practice is finished."

"What time is it going to end?"

"We're not sure; I guess it'll be about two hours long."

"Well, hopefully, it won't go on too much after that, as it'll start getting dark. Do you want a ride home? You can call me when you're almost done and I can pick you up."

"No, we're not far from home. We can walk. I'll phone you when we leave, so you'll know we're on our way."

"Okay, I'll make you an extra lunch." She paused for a few seconds. "How about Raj; is he still bothering you?"

"No, he's not."

"Good."

"He's a nice guy, Mom. He's liked me since we moved here. He thinks I'm the most beautiful girl in the world." She paused for a few seconds to reflect on what she had said, realising that Roche had never said that about her, except for the comment on having a nice ass. "Eventually, he'll find a girlfriend of his own."

"I hope so."

"It's getting late; I should get ready for bed. It looks as if I'll have a long day tomorrow."

"Okay, sweetheart, come see me before you get to bed, so I can give you a nice bedtime kiss."

Erica turned and headed for her bedroom.

She undressed and, for a while, stared at herself naked in front of her mirror. She twisted herself around to get a look at the back of her. Nice ass, she thought as she shook her head, then mumbled – "boys".

She got into her pyjamas and crawled into bed. She had occasionally thought of Roche's lack of voicing any feelings of love towards her but it rose into her thoughts again. She wondered why Roche had never said he loved her. She had told him she loved him many times before. He was kind to her, she knew they were going steady and, as far as she knew, he was faithful. She also knew that he did not talk much and she had used that as an excuse. He never showed much emotion about anything. That was the way he was. She would have to settle for that.

"So, what's your plan for tomorrow, Jiao?" her mother responded to her in Cantonese after Jiao told her about the plan to stay at school until later the next evening. "Are you sure you don't need a ride home?"

"No, we'll be okay. We'll be walking together, so we'll be safe."

"But the forecast says there's a chance of rain tomorrow."

"It's only a sixty per cent chance, okay; and they're light showers, Mom, not rain, so we'll be fine. We won't melt. I'll give you a call when we head back home."

Her mother regarded her with a worried look on her face.

"You worry too much, Mom. There are five of us. Roche is with us, so he'll be able to scare away any boogiemen or zombies that might attack us."

Her mother frowned.

Jiao scooted upstairs to get ready for bed.

"Have you got all your equipment ready for tomorrow?" Roche's father asked as he opened the door to Roche's bedroom.

"Yeah, Dad; all my gear is in my bag. I haven't forgotten anything," Roche responded from his bed.

"Okay. Mom packed you some extra food, so that should fill you until you return. It's nice your friends will be there to cheer you on."

"It's not a game, Dad, just a practice."

"I know but it's nice they give you this kind of support. Mom said you didn't need a ride."

"Yes, we're walking together."

"I'm going to work early tomorrow, so I'll be out before you get up. Have a nice day tomorrow."

"Same to you, Dad."

His father said good night and left the room.

While Raj looked through his pictures of Erica, he had a thought. He got out of bed and picked up his phone then walked back to his bed. He thumbed through his video list and opened one up. It was a video of Erica he had taken a few days back when he was following the other four to school. He watched her hips sway from side to side as she walked. Their movement captivated him.

He closed his eyes and they watered with tears. If he could not have her, what could he do? He sighed, turned off the phone, and placed it on his night table. He put his pictures back in the drawer and flopped down on the bed.

He thought again of the other girls he knew. One of them liked him; but who? She could be someone he did not know. Jiao said she knew someone but didn't tell him her name. He closed his eyes and quickly drifted into sleep.

9.

Roche woke up, raised his head, and looked at his clock. It read four-thirty. He had planned to get up at five but thought he might as well get up. He wanted to impress his coach and do a higher level of exercise than usual to get him in shape for what he planned to do at the practice that evening.

He slid out of bed, yawned, and got into his exercise clothes. He shut off his alarm and tiptoed out of his room and down into the basement to do his workout.

About an hour later, Erica woke up sleepily and stretched her arms in an extended yawn. She looked at her clock and switched off the alarm. "Time to get up," she mumbled. Today was her presentation with Jiao. She had put their poster by the front door to make sure she did not forget it on her way out. She jumped out of bed, quickly grabbed the project's prompt sheet, and read it again. She closed her eyes and began her speech. She flew through it with ease. She smiled and said aloud, "Excellent, I'm good to go."

She went to her phone, checked for any incoming texts, sent off her typical 'I love you' text to Roche, and put it down to start her morning.

Dan raised his head from his pillow and glanced at his clock. He slid out of bed and ran to the dresser. He picked up his phone and saw that he had no new texts. A large grin grew on his face as he quickly sent off a text to Jiao saying, 'I love you'. "I beat her, I beat her, I beat her," he mumbled excitedly. He got his message of love off to Jiao before she did this morning. "That'll be one for the record book," he whispered proudly as he began his morning routine.

Jiao opened her eyes and sighed. She got out of bed and opened her window shade a crack to look outside. The sun was just rising into a slightly reddish, partly cloudy sky. She went to her phone, turned it on, and read Dan's text. She smiled warmly. She was happy he had beaten her that morning and wanted him to beat her sometime. She thought it would keep their love alive. She brought the phone gently to her chest, hugged it for a few seconds, pulled it away from her, and tapped into her phone, 'I love you too'.

Raj had had a tough night with a particularly unnerving dream. In it, he was alone and had entered a room which was dark and gloomy. Even when he struck a match there was nothing to see. He groped around the room and felt nothing but smelled the stench of human excrement and urine. Then, he woke up hot and clammy with his eyes wide open in terror.

It took a while to get calm and realise that he was in his dark bedroom, the smell was gone, and everything was okay. He lay in bed for many minutes until his alarm went off to shake him out of his stupor. He shut it off.

He remained in bed for a few minutes then rose and started his day.

Despite his slow start, Raj was the first to their meeting spot again. His spirit rose when he saw Erica walking toward him.

She could see him waiting and slowed her pace. She stopped a few meters away from Raj and turned to look back at the houses behind her. Nobody else was visible yet. She slowly turned and continued her way to the kiosk.

"Good morning," Raj said to her, trying to gauge her receptiveness to the conversation.

Erica looked behind her again then looked at him and said, "Good morning," like an automaton.

"A little cloudier today than yesterday but beautiful nevertheless."

Erica looked at the sky toward the east to stare at the rising sun. There was still rosiness to the view.

"When it's red like that, it's supposed to mean that there might be rain ahead for us." Raj continued.

"That's the forecast but not until tonight," Erica responded without really looking at him.

"I wish you wouldn't be so uncomfortable around me. I know you were angry at me for sending you text messages but I won't send you them anymore. I hope that doesn't mean we can't be friends."

Erica finally looked at him and saw sadness there. She lowered her head to stare at the ground for a few seconds then looked at him again. "I didn't know I was making it seem as if we couldn't still be friends but I didn't want to lead you on. You act creepy sometimes."

Raj looked a little surprised at her statement. "Creepy, did I seem creepy to send you those texts?"

"You wouldn't stop. I've been telling you to and you kept on sending them. I know how you feel about me. Maybe I can't change that because it's the way you are but that doesn't mean you have to keep it up if I ask you to stop. I couldn't get through to you that I love Roche. I want you as a friend but you always seemed to want more and I can't give you that. You have to respect me."

"I'm sorry. I didn't want to make you feel uncomfortable. I've stopped bugging you."

"Yes, I know but it took so long for you to do it. I don't know if we can ever be just friends because I'll always know what you feel for me."

"Well, I still want to be your friend and I promise just to be that."

Erica smiled at him. "Thanks, Raj."

Raj hung his head and stared at the ground then raised it and said, "I'm your friend and I'll be there whenever you need me."

Erica looked behind her to see all the other teens on their way to join them.

When everyone had gathered, they were off and Raj spent the rest of the trip chatting with Dan and Jiao about the dream he had that night.

Later that morning, Erica and Jiao gave their presentation and got a nice applause from their classmates at the end of it.

The teacher first gave a little debrief and got feedback from the audience. The part they liked the most about the presentation was the added humour. After that, the teacher had a short private talk with Erica and Jiao separately.

The teacher told Erica that she was well prepared, her pace was good, and the content was excellent. She also projected her voice well, and the teacher could hear it at the back of the room. She constantly looked directly at the audience, so she got an A plus.

When it was Jiao's turn, the teacher told her the same general comment, however, she informed her that her voice was somewhat low, so sometimes she had to strain to hear what she was saying. She often did not look at the audience. That was likely due to her shyness. So, it was an excellent speech but Jiao should try to practice her delivery. The teacher gave her an A minus which is still an excellent grade. She told her that the two of them had set a high standard for the other presenters that year.

Lunch hour came and all the senior students filed out of their classes. Most of them took their lunches to the gym that served as a lunchroom or bought a meal there. Raj entered the lunchroom and spotted Erica and Roche. For the first time, he sat so he could not see her. He wanted to give Erica space from him. To keep her as a friend, he wanted to show her that he would respect her and give her room to be herself without his looking at her and intruding on her. He could see Dan and Jiao not too far from him but their table was almost full.

He felt out of place, as many of his schoolmates had paired up or formed small groups. He felt alone. The only girl he felt anything for was not his to have. Was this what his dad was telling him about being a teenager – all fired up and ready to go but not knowing what to do and how to do it? He had not had siblings to share anything with, fight with, or learn how to socialise with his peers. Sometimes, he felt as if his life was crushing him. Things did not always happen the way he wanted them to.

He sat at an almost-empty table, started opening his lunch bag, and pulled out his sandwich and drink. He poked the straw through the top of the drink and took a sip. He heard a rustle in the chair beside him. He turned his head to glance at who was sitting there. It was someone he had not noticed before in school, probably a more junior student – a girl. She was wearing a pretty white skirt and a yellow sweater.

He turned his head back to his juice box and took another sip. He picked up his sandwich and took a bite. He looked at Jiao and Dan who were talking cheerily to each other. He dared not turn around and look at Erica and Roche. There was nobody he knew at his table.

He sighed and turned his head back to the young lady on his left. She had her lunch spread out before her and was beginning to eat. He glanced up at her head covered with long black hair that flowed over her shoulders and down her back. Her face was a very light chocolate colour – his eyes widened as he realised that she appeared to be Indian!

He turned to his lunch again and continued eating. He had not seen her before, although the senior and junior students had little chance to mingle at the school because their classes were on different wings and their schedules for arriving, leaving, and lunch were different. This approach also reduced crowding in the lunchroom.

When he almost finished his last sandwich, he turned to her again. She had almost finished, too and was packing up while she was finishing off the apple she was eating.

He turned his head to his last bit of sandwich. His mind froze. Why was she there? He wanted to at least say hello but that might seem improper. She was a junior. He swallowed his last piece and drank the last bit of juice in the container. He crumpled up the plastic wrapper and juice container for the garbage can.

He sat frozen. He wanted to get up and leave but he wanted to stay and see what she would do. If she left, then that was it but if she lingered . . . he didn't know what to do.

He could sense her still there. He was afraid to look at her. As the seconds ticked by, he tried to amuse himself by looking over at Dan and Jiao.

They had spotted him and were now staring at him. Jiao leaned over to Dan and said something and he smiled.

Raj was nervous and glanced around at some of the other tables. A lot of students had already left the room but many were still lingering and talking to their neighbours. There was nobody left at his table except for the girl.

Raj looked at Jiao and Dan. They were still looking at him. Now, he was very nervous. The girl beside him was still there. He dared not embarrass himself by glancing at her again. He saw Jiao lean over to Dan and say something to him again. Dan nodded his head and the two of them got up and left the room.

Raj twisted his head far to his right where Roche and Erica had been but they had left.

He remained there. It seemed to be a battle as to who was going to leave first but it could not be. There were lots of reasons why she would still be there. He turned his head slightly to the left so he could see her in his peripheral vision. Her empty lunch bag sat on the table beside her. She had a book on the table and was reading it.

There was nothing to it. She was reading a book, probably one of her textbooks. Many kids did that, so why was he thinking like this? There was nothing unusual about her lingering there a few minutes to quietly study, or read a book.

The lunch period was almost over and they would have to head out to their respective classrooms. He guessed that she probably had a free period at this time and had decided to have her lunch now instead of her usual time. That was it. That was simple. He felt relieved and thought of getting up and getting ready for his next class.

Something held him bolted to his chair. He tried to picture her again . . . her long black alluring hair, her beautiful oval face. Then he stopped himself and mentally erased that thought. She was a junior.

He could say hello, he thought. They both had something in common; the same culture but what would he say; just hello? Was that enough? If she was interested, would she not say hi first? But in his culture, girls did not usually initiate communication with boys. Would he look forward to doing it?

So, it was up to him then. If he did not do it now, he would lose his chance. Then he had another thought that she might still be sitting there because she had another spare period and he was wasting his time thinking about this.

Out of the corner of his eyes, he could see her beginning to close her book. She was going to leave. His opportunity was slipping away.

Then, resolved, he turned his head gingerly to his left. She had closed her book and was reaching for her crumpled lunch bag. It was now or never. She was getting ready to leave. He mustered up his courage and said in Hindi, "Hello."

Her hand moved away from her bag while her head began to turn. It seemed like an eternity for her to turn her head toward him. Her eyes sparkled as their eyes met. They were an intense dark brown. Her lips parted in a wide smile and she said in English, "Hi, that's Hindi, isn't it?"

"Oh, yes, it is," he stammered.

"I don't speak Hindi but I've heard it from time to time, so I know what it sounds like and I can sometimes make out what's being said. Our family came from India when my father was very young with his parents and he has rarely spoken anything but English since then."

He pulled the frog from his throat and responded, "I was born in India and my father came here just a few years ago. We speak Hindi at home mostly." He could see the clock on the wall. They would have to go soon and he didn't want to. She wore no makeup but she did not need any. She was so beautiful just the way she was and her voice was that of an angel.

"You don't normally eat at this time, do you?" Raj asked more confidently.

"No. I have a free period and decided to eat now instead."

They stared into each other's eyes.

Raj forced his eyes from hers and looked at the clock again, now getting nervous. He wanted more time with her.

She continued. "I could eat here again next week if you'd like."

Raj's heart jumped. He could meet her again! He could hardly mouth the words, "Umm, yeah . . . we can plan to meet right here again . . . sure. I'd better get off to my class or I'll be late, though."

She got up, smiled, and said, "See you again next week." She turned and walked away. As she was about to leave the room, she turned her head to him and smiled.

His heart melted but he shook it off, trying to be realistic. He got up a few seconds later and quickly walked to his next class. He did not have time to think. While walking, he suddenly realised something and said quietly, "Shit, I didn't get her name."

Then it struck him. This was the girl he bumped into yesterday. He had not taken much notice of her, so he could be wrong but . . . there were very few Indians in this school.

During the class, he was very distracted. He kept wondering if she was the girl he had met earlier or if was she also the one Jiao had talked about. But Jiao would not likely know the juniors, or would she? And what was to say that she had sat beside him because she had something in mind? There was nobody in the other seat beside her, so she had deliberately sat next to him but maybe she did not want to sit next to the other person only one seat from her.

That was it, it was not intentional, it was more like, serendipitous. He was beginning to realise that he was making much more out of his encounter than what was there. She probably was super social and smiled at everyone. So, was there another girl who was interested in him?

10.

When classes concluded, the teens met on the front steps of the school.

Roche suggested that they go to the rear of the school where there were a few picnic tables. They went there, sat down, and ate their meals. The boys broke off and practised throwing and catching the football Roche had brought with him. The girls sat at the table and watched them.

"It's clouding over. I hope it doesn't rain until the practice is over," said Jiao.

"It's not supposed to. When it comes, it should only be a light rain, so we'll be okay," responded Erica.

"That was a good presentation we put on today, eh?"

"The teacher was very impressed and the kids seemed to like it. We got a nice applause."

"Yeah, they liked the humour we put into it. That was a good idea you had."

"I found the subject boring without it."

"Yeah, I guess you're right. Roche sure likes football, doesn't he?"

"It's his favourite sport. I'm not into it but he keeps me informed about who beat who, who the best players are, and all that stuff. It just goes over my head."

"Dan likes football too but he likes baseball better. He isn't very into sports to play it though. He prefers tinkering with computers and playing video games. He has asked me to play some of his games with him but I just do it for him. Maybe he likes beating the crap out of me."

"I guess so. They can get their testosterone high that way. They can beat you up without laying a hand on you. Roche likes playing computer games, too – the active shooter games."

As the practice's starting time neared and some of the other team members were starting to arrive, Roche put away his ball and entered the school with Dan to change into his practice clothes.

Raj sat down in the bleachers and waited for the other players to arrive. Other than a couple of adults, probably parents of some of the players, there were no other youths that he could see.

He was thinking about his day; non-descript except for the girl who sat by him at lunch. He felt a bit upset because he had waited so long to talk to her and never got her name. Now, he probably had a whole week before he would see her again. He did not even notice if her hips swayed when she walked, he was just mesmerised by her long flowing hair then when she turned and smiled at him. Did that mean anything, or was she just being friendly?

Oh, how complicated life had become for him. It seemed only weeks ago that he did not like girls, except for Erica. Somehow, she was different. She was the first girl he liked. At first, he considered her as another boy but liking her had now grown to something more – much more. He hardly understood what was happening to him. He sometimes wondered if he could make all this go away. He had read the story of Peter Pan and wished he could be like Peter and not have to grow up.

Jiao startled Raj from his stupor by sitting next to him. He turned to look at her and asked, "Where's Dan?"

"He'll be along in a minute or so. He thought he would stay for a while with Roche to help him with his gear."

"Oh."

"Everyone else should be along shortly. The practice won't start for a few minutes."

There were several seconds of silence then Jiao sliced through it. "How'd your day go?"

"Fine, how was yours?"

"Good. Erica and I gave a presentation this morning and it went extremely well. Our teacher liked it."

"What was it about?"

"A historic event – about the politicians meeting at Charlottetown to unite Canada. It was kind of boring, so we tried to dress it up with some humour, not about the event itself but some funny effects some of the decisions could have on us in today's world – things they couldn't have foreseen at that time."

"Hmm."

"Anything interesting happen to you today?"

"No."

"How about at noon?"

"Nothing much," Raj responded.

"Dan and I were looking at you looking dumb with that girl sitting beside you. You saw us. We could see you noticed her. You had such a dumb look on your face."

"Why should I look dumb? Some people say I look like that all the time," Raj replied.

"We finally left because you looked so uncomfortable. You looked almost embarrassed."

"Why do you say that? Is she the one you said was interested in me?"

"I'll never tell you. Maybe she's not," Jiao said coyly.

"She sat beside me. There was lots of room in the cafeteria, so why did she sit right next to me?"

"She can sit where she wants. You're drawing a lot of conclusions you know. So . . . you never said anything to her?" Jiao

"Why?"

"We could see you, dummy. You glanced at her and that's when you started to look dumb. She looked as if she was minding her own business."

"She was."

"Why were you looking so strange then?" Jiao asked.

"I thought she had nice hair."

"You thought she had nice hair!" Jiao exclaimed incredulously.

"Yes, I saw it was long; even longer than Erica's. Most girls have much shorter hair."

"And that would embarrass you!"

"No, you were staring at me."

"That's why we left. We thought you'd continue to sit there looking dumb."

Raj looked down at the empty bleachers below him and turned his head toward her. "Don't tell Dan and especially Erica but I did say hello to her."

"That's nice. It's better than sitting there looking dumb. Like I told you, you should keep your eyes open for other girls. If you find the right one, then she can at least love you back."

"She's got a nice smile."

"She smiled? That's a good sign but don't do anything stupid though, or you'll chase her away. You have a way of doing or saying things that make you out to be somewhat weird."

"I do?"

"Like, duh! Just look at what you've done with Erica and I've seen you with other girls. If you think you're going to do something weird come and talk to me, okay? Although, I wonder if you even know when you're being weird."

"Probably not, or I wouldn't do it. I feel so uncomfortable with girls. Most of them I don't care for, except for Erica. She was one girl I could feel comfortable with, until the last few months."

"Yeah, but you shouldn't show your nervousness. Be friendly with everyone and maybe some might get to like you. You'd have more friends. All the friends you have are the four of us but there's more to the world than just us."

"You know me."

"Yeah, but if you get to meet more people, then you might like them and they would like you. They'd know you as we do."

Raj eyed the bleachers again. He knew she was right. He turned to her and said, "Thanks Jiao. You're a good friend."

"Thanks . . . when you're a friend with somebody, you'd do anything for them. You can be a good friend, Raj. I know if I needed help, you'd help me, so you're a good person. Let other people know you're a good person. Don't hide yourself from the world."

Raj looked at her eyes and repeated, "You're a good person, Jiao."

Dan walked up to the bleachers and sat on the other side of Jiao. He leaned over, looked at Raj and said jokingly, "Hey, trying to steal my girlfriend?"

Raj looked at him and smiled.

Within minutes, Erica rushed up and sat on the other side of Raj and said excitedly. "The players are coming out."

They looked toward the back of the school and, in one bunch, the players ran onto the field. The coach began putting them through their paces and watched each player carefully. Within the next two practices, he had to trim six players from the team.

At first, Raj was watching the guys on the field but there was a slight breeze that blew past Erica to him. Erica used no perfumes but Raj could smell that familiar scent of her hair. Maybe it was the shampoo she used but it was more than that and it drew him from his concentration on the field to what he was picking up from her.

He wanted to lean over, grab her in his arms, and bury his lips into hers. He had trouble putting her out of his mind. What was it anyway? Why did he sometimes react like this?

He had to get her out of his mind. He had to let her go. She was Roche's girl. She loved Roche, not him. She would never change. He had to break the bond he had with her. He tried thinking of the girl he had met that afternoon but that wonderful alluring scent kept wafting gently to his nostrils, tearing his insides out.

He thought of moving to another place on the bleachers but that would not look good. What would the others think? He wanted her to be there. He liked being beside her but being beside her gave him thoughts he should not have. He had to put them out of his mind. He had to focus on the boys on the field and not her.

Out of the corner of her eye, Erica noticed Raj fidgeting and glanced over. Raj was looking at the boys on the field. She returned her eyes to Roche on the field but she could sense something out of order. She had rushed to the bleachers and sat down beside Raj without thinking. She had sat beside him many times before but not so much in the last few months, though.

She regretted the act. She knew she had an animalistic effect on Raj, so why had she not considered that and sat somewhere else? That was thoughtless. It would not be good to move now though, or Raj might think she was shunning him. They had been friends for so many years and she did not want that to end. Why did so much change over the past year or so? She still liked him – he was a good friend to have but why had he changed so much? Why did he have to fall in love with her – or was it only infatuation and he thought it was love?

She made a mental note never to sit next to him again. Maybe she should not sit beside any male. What was it with males anyway, or was there something about her that aroused them?

She wanted to get up and move but decided against it. Some girls have trouble getting a boyfriend and here she was with two who were interested in her. She also knew other boys who were interested in her and would approach her, if she and Roche broke up. Did they like Goths, or was it something else? She was smart and was not ugly, so those traits were with her, or was it her "nice ass"? Was that her only asset? She giggled quietly at the thought of the words.

She thought back to when she first met Raj. He was the first person she met when their family arrived in their community. They got along great. To her, he was a sexless playmate and sometimes the brother she did not have.

Her mother had tried to dampen their playing together. Erica had not understood why at the time but now she did. But after a few years, he seemed to like her more than she did for him, or at least in a different way. He was a little weird and awkward at times but she knew his parents had been very protective. She knew him well enough to realise his good qualities and they were many. To her though, he remained as he had been and she could not picture them as a romantic pair – you love your brother but you would not want to marry him.

But now, both were growing up. She knew that she attracted Raj but what about Roche? She never knew where he stood. If he loved her, he never said it. With Raj, he could never stop saying it. She knew though that love rejected would eventually end up with Raj finding someone else. If Raj found someone else and Roche dumped her, what would she do? She'd have to settle for one of many other possible suitors. Where would that leave Raj in the hierarchy? She did not want to think about it. One step at a time; Roche was hers now and she did not want to think beyond that.

She was getting a headache thinking about everything. She was always doing things for people. Even with Roche, she had wished that he would have said he loved her after their big evening together but it never happened. She had given everything, and for what? In a way, she was feeling sorry for poor Raj sitting beside her. She now wished she could satisfy his wildest dreams but that was weird. She was not ready for anything like that. Roche was a handful himself. She sighed again and wanted to run away somewhere and cry.

Jiao noticed the nervous silence on one side of her. She looked at them. They looked normal but she sensed much more than that. She looked down at Raj's nervous hands and heard his breathing. She leaned toward Dan and said quietly, "I wish I could read minds."

Dan leaned forward to look at Raj and Erica then leaned back. "Why? They look okay," he whispered.

"I don't think so."

"Why?"

"They're too quiet. She should not have sat beside him."

Dan leaned slightly forward, took another look, and pulled back again. "What I see are two people watching the football practice and you see the same people doing who knows what with each other! I'm amazed at your sense of perception. You've been watching too many romance movies on TV."

"I haven't seen one."

"You have a vivid imagination then."

"I'm just guessing. Raj is a very sensitive person and I suspect he may pick up Erica's pheromones."

"Her what?"

"Women have a cycle and give off different scents during it. Dogs can pick them out but humans lost that ability in their distant past. I think Raj can detect them."

"So, Raj is hot for Erica and she thinks he is and both of them don't know what to do about it."

"I guess that's a good synopsis."

"Why don't you think like that with us?"

"Whoa, boy, it's them, not us."

"Why not us? I can think of making out with you and you can do the same and we'll see if we're as quiet as they are."

Jiao ribbed him with her arm, sighed, and said, "Down boy, I'm sorry I brought it up."

Dan shook his head.

Almost two hours passed and the practice was winding down. The two coaches were talking together about the quality of their players.

The head coach looked down the list of candidates. "I can see these four boys as probably the weakest players." He pointed to them with his pencil. "What do you think?"

The assistant coach looked over the list and said, "Yes I agree."

"We can tell them today that some of them won't make the team. In my estimation, that leaves these four we can leave for a decision next week." He pointed to four others. "We can keep two and let the last two go. The rest appear to be solid."

"I agree; now, what about placement?"

"I guess we could leave that for next week."

"Yes, but it would give some indications for us to put together a test plan for next week."

"You have a point." The head coach agreed.

They went over the pros and cons for several players and agreed on who would be good linemen, backs, and receivers.

The head coach then said, "I think it's clear for most guys where they should go but I'm not sure about Roche."

"Yeah, he could go anywhere. I think our best bet is to see how things go next week and we can firm up positions. If we find a weak spot, we can put him there."

"Yeah, I'm not sure about a quarterback or a line back and Roche should be able to slip into either position."

"That sounds good."

The head coach looked at his watch and said, "It's getting late. Let's inform the four boys who didn't make it this week and clear the field. It looks as if it'll rain soon."

The coaches informed the four weakest boys of their decision then closed the practice and packed up.

As soon as the practice ended, the girls phoned home to tell their parents they would soon be on their way and began their walk that would never take them home.

11.

Jiao's mother, Liling, looked at her watch again and said to her husband, Zixin, "They're now ten minutes late."

"Jiao said they'd be leaving soon. They may have been delayed," Zixin responded.

She looked outside the window and did not see any sign of the teens. "She always called us, if she was going to be delayed."

"Don't worry, she'll be home soon." He got up and peered out the window then went to the door, opened it, leaned out, and looked down the street. He was also becoming concerned.

Five more minutes passed. Liling called Jiao's phone with no response.

Zixin looked again out the window and the door then said, "Call Helen and I'll go and find her. I'll be back in a few minutes."

"No, I can call her from the car. Two eyes are better than one. I'll confirm Erica isn't home and ask Helen to look after Huan, after all, he's in bed asleep and won't be a problem. I know she'll do it. She'll be anxious about Erica, too. She can call the boys' parents to see if they've heard anything."

They put on jackets, jumped into the car, and were quickly on their way. She made the call to Helen and confirmed that Erica also had not arrived home and she had tried to call her. They watched each side of the road intensely for the teenagers. They were almost at the school when Helen called them back to say that she was looking after Huan and had called the other parents. Nobody had arrived home and they could not reach the teens by phone. Helen was going to call the coach.

They arrived at the school but, except for the security lights, the site was dark and deserted. They left the car and looked around the back of the school, with no results. Another call came in from Helen saying that she had talked to the coach. He saw the adolescents at the practice and had seen them leave the grounds and walk down the road. Shortly after, he left with a few other kids to drop them off at their homes but he went in another direction.

They finished their search around the school grounds' perimeter in case the teens had returned to the school. They tried the doors but found them locked.

"Everything's normal," Zixin said. "If something was wrong, and they were in the school, they would turn on some lights. The strange thing is that all the kids have cell phones. Why have they not called anyone?"

"Maybe we should call the police," Liling suggested.

"Well, let's make a good search first."

They spotted some lights approaching and a car soon pulled into the school parking lot. Erica's father, John, jumped out of the car and called out, "You haven't found them?"

Jiao's parents shook their heads.

John ran back to his car and pulled out two flashlights. "Here, take this flashlight, Zixin. The kids started walking home, according to the coach, so we'll start with that. I'll take the left side of the road and you take the right. Their normal route is to follow the roads home. Let's see if there's any sign of them along the road."

It took over forty minutes of slowly walking along the road with their flashlights before they ended at their community.

When they arrived at Zixin's house, the rest of the parents listened to their report and were not happy they had not found the teens.

"I think we should call the police," Liling said.

There was a lot of murmuring from the rest of the parents.

"Could they have taken another route home?" one of the other parents asked.

"Where else can they have gone? You didn't find them at the school?" another parent asked.

"They always take the road," Liling responded.

"Okay, then. You checked the sides of the road and around the school grounds. There are five of them. They're not kids. They all have phones. At least one of them would have called, if they ran into any problem, so how can they be missing?" Roche's father challenged.

"Good question. For all five of them to have disappeared doesn't make sense," Zixin answered.

"Where else can we look?" a voice sounded from the group.

"Even if they took a shortcut, they should be home by now," was another response.

"Maybe they got lost," Liling said anxiously.

"How could they get lost? They've lived and played around here for years. It's as if they vanished!" Roche's father countered.

"But they still had their phones, so why has not even one of them phoned?" Helen trembled as she responded.

"I think we should call the police. We might need their help to find them." Zixin said to try to cheer up the group of nervous parents.

"Well, there don't seem to be any other options," Helen said. "We need to find them. If they're lost, I hope they stay put, so we can find them more easily."

Zixin called the police and informed them of the facts.

While they waited for the police to arrive, Jiao's mother put on some coffee and tried to calm the other parents as best she could.

Forty minutes later a police car pulled up their driveway. The officer got out and Liling opened the door, as he rounded the top step. She welcomed the officer into the house.

The officer could see the apprehension in the parents' faces, as he entered the family room where they were sitting nervously. He introduced himself and, for the next twenty minutes, he gathered and recorded the facts as the parents knew them. He got the names and contact details of other people who had been at the practice that evening. He also got the missing teens' phone numbers.

"We'll also call the phone companies. Often, we can locate an individual that way," the officer added.

He sat silently for a few minutes to make sure he had all the details then said, "Well, thanks for all this information. I think the best thing for all of you to do is return to your homes and we'll take over from here. They haven't been gone for long. It might be that they made a wrong turn somewhere, are too embarrassed to phone, and might turn up here sometime tonight. It's dark, so it's going to be hard to find them. I'll go back to the office and phone some of these names to get any other details I need. If the kids turn up, please call our office right away. If you don't call, we'll call you to confirm their absence around ten tonight and we'll decide what to do from there. I hope they'll be home soon but please stay calm. There must be a reason for their absence."

The police officer left the worried parents behind.

Liling watched him drive off then closed the door. For a while, they remained together until one by one they left to go home.

The officer drove slowly onto the rural road and peered out his windows as he drove toward the school. As he pulled into the school's parking lot, he thought to himself, while the windshield wipers pulsed slowly, that the walk was less than thirty minutes; a very short distance to get lost. The girls had called home to say they were on their way, so the teens should not have gone anywhere else. He got out of the car and looked around the grounds. He got back into the car and out of the rain.

In case the teens unlikely had gone into town, he cruised around for a few minutes and went to the office to call the people who had been at the football practice. He wrote out his notes, called each teen's phone number, and got no response. He sat quietly for several minutes and called the headquarters of each phone's service provider. He phoned the principal of the school, informed him of the situation, and asked him to meet him at the school well before classes started. He phoned Zixin at ten to inform him about what he had done and found nothing.

Liling invited all those who were taking time off work to come over the next morning. None of the parents got much sleep that night, if any.

12.

Early in the morning, a police car pulled up to the school. Two officers got out of their car, went to the front door, and talked to the principal standing in front of it.

He opened the school and the police searched inside.

They searched the school grounds, got into their car, and slowly drove along the road to the development. They remained in their car while they phoned in their results. The police went back to the schoolground parking lot and waited.

About an hour later, a police van arrived. The trainer took out two dogs from the back of the van while the lead trainer walked to the cruiser and talked to the two officers. When the conversation ended, the two officers got into their car and headed back to the development.

When the officers arrived at the door, a handful of people greeted them.

As they entered the family room, Liling asked, "Have you found anything?"

The senior officer replied, "We have two officers at the school with some dogs, so we're going to begin to track them down. Their scent might be hard to detect after the rain we had last night but it was only a light rain and the dampness is in our favour. We'd like someone to provide us with an unwashed article of clothing from one of them. We'll use that to scent the dogs. Right now, there'll be many smells around the school with the kids who play around there every day, so something specific can get them started in the right direction. When you get it, please use this bag I have with me. Pick up the item with these tongs I have, so we'll only have that youth's scent on it." He showed the parents how to put the article in the bag.

Jiao's mother took the tongs and bag and quickly found an unwashed shirt of Jiao's in her bedroom. Following the police officer's instructions, she put it into the bag and handed it to the officer.

"Should everyone provide some clothes for you, too?" Helen asked.

"No, not right now; we can collect them later if needed. The teens would likely have stuck together. I'd appreciate it if everyone could save a piece of clothing in case we need more. Here are more bags and tongs for you to use." He handed them out to the parents.

"Can we help with the search?" Zixin asked.

"Not right now. We don't want to confuse the dogs with too many scents. We might need help later if we don't have any luck but for now, just try to remain calm. We'll handle it from here. Hopefully, we'll find them very soon. From what you've said all of them had phones with them, right?"

"Yes, everyone," Zixin answered.

"Were they fully charged?"

All the parents looked at each other and nodded in the affirmative.

Liling said, "Jiao puts her phone into the charger overnight and they don't use them often during the day because they're at school."

"Just checking; it seems strange no one called if anything happened to them."

Liling said, "That's the first thing we thought of."

"I called most of the people you said were also at the practice last night and drew a blank. They had all seen them at the practice but only the coaches stayed long enough to see them begin their walk. They didn't see anything they thought was suspicious. Everything appeared normal; they were all together talking cheerfully.

"Anyway, thanks for your help, I'll take this over to the other officers and we'll keep you informed of our progress. We have two of our best tracking dogs on their trail. If they're lost, we'll find them."

They turned and left the house.

As they walked away, the junior officer said, "This is rather odd, isn't it? These days, kids can still get lost but most of them have phones, so we can easily find them; but five teenagers who have phones and can call for help, and don't? Heck, there were five of them!"

"Yeah, it does seem odd, unless maybe they're embarrassed about it. We should soon get a response from the phone companies."

They got into the car and headed back to the school where they turned the shirt over to the lead dog trainer.

The trainer removed the shirt from the bag and wafted it in front of the dogs' noses. He followed them as they sniffed around the school grounds.

The junior officer looked around the school himself, while the other officers talked.

"How are the parents taking this so far?" the lead trainer asked.

"They're worried," the senior officer replied.

"So, no news from their side?"

"None; they're as baffled as we are."

"Well, the dogs should pick up something soon. The kids were at the practice back here and all the scents overwhelmed the dogs. Now that they have one scent, they can be more specific in their search. You can see that they sniffed around the stands of the park, so they, or at least the young lady, must have been on the bench and touched the school door. Let's see what the dogs find before the kids start arriving for school."

They watched as the dogs walked up the front door of the school and back around the side. After more sniffing in one direction along the road and the other, they seemed to be confident to go in the direction of the development.

The senior officer turned to the junior officer and said, "You stay here with the car and we'll keep you informed."

The lead trainer said, "Okay, they've got the scent now but it's on both sides of the road. That's because the kids must have followed the rules of the road when walking to and from school."

They walked slowly with the dogs until they reached a small roadway that turned off to the right.

"Oh, oh, there seems to be a problem here," the lead said.

"What do you mean?" asked the senior officer.

"The dogs have picked up three trails, one on each side of the road, plus one that seems to be down this laneway. The dogs seem more interested in the trail that leads into the lane than on this side of the road which might be older, perhaps the day before. The teens walked down the left side of the road and crossed it onto this lane."

"This leads to what used to be Mr McGregor's farm," said the junior trainer.

"Hmm, the dogs are looking at us for guidance."

The trainer and lead consulted together for a few minutes.

The lead said to the trainer, "We're going to break up. I'll take my dog and follow the trail up this lane and you can take the other one up the road to the development. That way we can make sure we cover both angles." He looked at the senior officer and suggested, "Maybe you can get the van brought to this site in case we need it."

The senior officer called the junior officer and said, "Lock the car and drive the van to the junction of a laneway. We'll likely not be very far from it when you get here. It looks as if the kids took a shortcut to get home, probably because of the rain."

"Okay, sir," the junior officer responded through the phone.

While the trainer took one dog up the highway, the other two officers began to follow the dog along the lane of an old farm. The dog soon arrived at the old deserted house but walked right by it. She walked along a lightly travelled walking path into some deep grass and a wooded area. She stopped, walked in circles for a while then veered off the path into a small clearing. Again, the dog walked in circles and soon headed back in the direction they had entered but it turned around, sniffed some more, and kept ending up wanting to walk back along the incoming trail. She whined a bit in confusion.

"So, what does that mean?" the senior officer asked.

"Believe it or not the trail ends here," the lead said.

"Maybe they left the way they came and continued down the little path."

"The dog would have found a continuing scent there."

"Well, that's impossible. Let's take him back there and check."

"It may mean though that they followed the same way back to the road and went home, although they never arrived home. I'll call my partner and see where he is."

He got on his phone, talked to the trainer, and said, "He's almost at the turn-off to the development. The van is at the lane entrance."

The senior officer squinted at the brightness of the sun and looked around. "Take the dog back to the trail again and confirm if the teens didn't go back to the trail and continue their shortcut home."

The lead trainer led the dog out of the clearing.

The officer looked around the clearing and peered at the ground. He bent down and looked at the grass. He tried to identify any footprints but the rain had not been enough to soften the ground to detect any depressions that a foot might have made. He dropped to one knee soaking his pants in the process. His eyes peered at the grass. It had almost recovered from its previous compaction by the spaceship and the surrounding grass leaned slightly away from the centre as it had landed and taken off but the officer could still notice it. He raised his hand and scratched his cheek.

He got up, walked to the outer edge of the clearing, and carefully examined the brush around it. In a couple of spots, he noticed bent or freshly broken twigs, or taller grass leaning in such a way as one would find if someone had moved through it.

He looked back in the centre of the clearing. The teens' trail ended off to the side of the centre. Had there been a circular tent here? What had diverted the teens from their walk home? And what happened to them? If someone abducted them, Jiao's trail would have led somewhere else. The dogs would have picked up her scent, as they moved her from here to a vehicle.

The lead trainer returned with the dog and said, "There is only one scent trail. They did not go back to the trail and continued home. The only thing that makes sense is that they went back to the road the same way they came but I would have noticed it in the grass. It's only bent in one direction. We've messed it up with our activities but it was clear when we first came here."

He contacted the trainer with the other dog. The trainer had completed his investigation. The trail led back to her home. Other scents of course went to some of the other homes but they were all within the neighbourhood.

The senior officer contacted the officer in the van and asked him to pick up the trainer and dog then park the van by the old farmhouse and have that dog follow the scent to confirm what the other dog had found. The junior officer would follow the trainer and bring a camera with him.

"Yes, sir," the junior officer responded.

"Look around here and see if you find anything – anything that might seem strange to you," the senior officer said.

The lead carefully walked around the site, sometimes looking closely at the grass or the shrubbery surrounding it. He straightened up and said, "The grass where you're standing looks as if it's recovering from being compressed as if something were on top of it; something possibly circular. Outside of the compression, the grass appears bent outward slightly – maybe the wind might do that. In a few areas around the clearing, it appears as if there had been somebody or something walking or travelling through the grass or shrubs . . . I guess we'd better take some pictures. When the other dog gets here, I would like to use one of the bent or broken twigs to give any new scents to the dogs and we can investigate these new clues."

"My thoughts exactly. Once we get some pictures and collect some of the twigs as evidence, let's find out more about where these other people or persons have been. The teens couldn't have vanished into thin air. Maybe we could find out if there was more than one other person here. Whatever occurred, happened so fast that none of the kids could use their phone, so there would most likely have been more than one individual."

In about fifteen minutes, they could hear the approach of the second dog and his trainer. Within seconds, all four police officers were at the site.

The senior officer said, "It looks as if we all came to the same conclusion." He explained the plan to everyone and soon they had photographed the grassy site, the broken twigs, and the walked-over areas.

The trainers used the twigs to scent the two dogs and soon they were moving around the area to track where the other people had been.

Two of the trails ended at the farmhouse.

The senior officer examined that site with the junior officer. He said, "Looks as if it might have been broken into but it was well done. They put the lock back on the door. It was almost as if they had a key. These guys were real pros. I don't know why they would bother to put it back together so well. Let's try to get some fingerprints."

The two of them worked methodically at dusting the area around the lock but could not find anything meaningful. The senior officer questioned, "Was this guy wearing gloves? Some of the smudges look as if there was something there but we can't get a pattern. Go over to the truck and get some gear and let's see if we can find anything inside."

They broke into the house and soon were dusting any obvious places. They found nothing that looked fresh. The fingerprints they obtained were only of one person and they thought it was likely the farmer but they would have to confirm that.

"Well, that does it for this area. There's not much dust in here to get footprints. The farmer only moved from here a couple of weeks ago. We have no prints, no blood; nothing that would tell us what happened or who was involved. Let's go back to the trainers and see what they have."

They left the house and fixed the lock as best they could. By the time they finished, the trackers were heading to the van. The head trainer called over. "I guess we can go back to the kennel and get something to eat. We've had a full morning."

The senior officer asked, "What did you find?"

"There likely were three of them – although the dogs had problems with the scents. We've mapped each of their trails for you on a map we made of the site using different colours. They didn't go too far from the site. Two of them went to this house and three of them went close to the development. There seemed to be three because we tried the dogs on twigs from several sources and found their distinctive routes. They all originate from the clearing. We found no tire tracks or anything that would show a vehicle was around. It's odd. No vehicle had travelled to the clearing which seemed to be the centre of everything. Do you think they could have used a helicopter?"

"I can ask the people at the development if they heard anything that night. How about a balloon?" the senior officer proposed.

"Maybe but I've never seen a balloon around here. It's the best guess we have at this point."

"After lunch, come back here and finish any work that needs to be done. I'll investigate if any balloons have been around here lately as well as helicopters. I'll talk to the chief and see what ideas he has. We should have information from the phone companies soon. When that's done, I'll meet you back here and see what we have then I'll have to meet with the parents and inform them about what we found. They're not going to be happy. How would you like to be told that your kids disappeared?"

They led the dogs back to the truck and headed out. They stopped at the school and the two officers got out of the van, gathered up their equipment, and loaded it into the trunk of the squad car. They too headed back to town to have lunch.

13.

Liling had an array of food and beverages on the table and everyone helped themselves to it. The group that had consisted of all the missing teens' mothers and Roche's and Jiao's fathers had grown to include other mothers from the neighbourhood and two nannies. The nannies and three of the mothers had set up a large play area in the backyard and were looking after the preschool children and the infants. It had become a supportive community gathering.

Roche's father grabbed his second sandwich and said, "We haven't heard yet from the police. I wonder what they're finding."

"They said they'd notify us as soon as they found anything," Zixin responded. "I guess we have to be patient."

"Yes, but it's noon and they haven't found anything yet. Surely the kids can't be that lost!"

There was silence for a while. It was soon cut by Liling's toddler in his highchair crying out, Jiao, Jiao, Jiao . . .''

At about two thirty in the afternoon, the police officers drove to Liling's house and knocked on the door.

Liling opened it and asked excitedly, "Oh, hi, is there any news?"

The senior officer responded, "Unfortunately not, may I come in?"

"Oh, yes, certainly, please do," she said as she opened the door wider while making a welcoming gesture.

The officers walked into the family room. The senior officer looked at the distraught parents' faces and noticed there were many more people than there had been in the morning.

"Do you want us to talk only to the parents of the lost children, or include all these other people?" the senior officer asked.

"We're a community, so everyone should know what you say," Roche's father said.

The other parents nodded their assent.

The officer introduced himself and his partner and said, "We've used our tracking experts and our best tracking dogs to determine the missing youth's whereabouts. So far, we haven't found them. We've been using Jiao's shirt so far but we'd like to use the collected clothing from the other four youths to assist in our search."

"We have them in these labelled bags," Roche's father said. He leaned over to a corner on the kitchen countertop, grabbed four bags, and held them out to the officer.

The senior officer took the bags and said, "Thank you, we're doing everything we can to find them and maybe these other clothes can shed more light on the situation.

"Just for our information, did any of you hear or see anything the last two or three nights – like lights or any kind of noise?"

Everyone either shrugged or made negative gestures.

"Why do you ask?" Roche's father enquired.

"Just trying to close any loopholes."

"Can you tell us what you've found so far?" Helen questioned.

"Sorry, we'd rather wait until we get further along in our search. We'll give you a report later in the day."

"They were only walking from the school to our houses. That's not more than thirty minutes, how can they get lost in that little distance?"

"I know you're worried. I have kids too and I know how I'd feel in your situation. We're doing everything we can to find them."

"Maybe we can help," Roche's father commented.

"We're trying to keep our dogs focussed, so it's best we keep it like this for now. I'll be back later to fill you in."

There were questioning eyes staring at the senior officer who wanted to say that they had found the kids and they were okay but they still had a lot of work to do. In the silence that followed the conversation, the two officers turned and left for their car. They drove the articles of clothing to the trackers and used them to follow the scents of the other four teenagers.

14.

The senior officer returned to his office, contacted a few key people in the appropriate provincial offices, and found no evidence that there were helicopters or balloons in the area that night. He began to write the report.

Later in the afternoon, he received the report from the trackers. The other youths had followed the same path. All the teens were together when they disappeared. The teens did not make any of the other three trails.

He looked over the reports from the cell phone providers. The boys had not turned on their phones that day, as they were at school. The girls had kept theirs on. Jiao and Erica made one call to their mothers at about the time the football coach said the practice had finished. Minutes later, contact ended and GPS data showed they were near the clearing where the dogs lost the teens' scent.

When he finished his report, he handed it to the chief of police, who immediately skimmed its contents and looked at the pictures taken at the scene.

"Are you sure about this?" the chief asked, surprised.

"We followed each kid's trail. They disappeared as a group."

The chief slammed the report on the table. "How are we going to report this to the parents? How can we tell them their kids seemed to have disappeared – vanished?" he said in frustration.

"I know, this is a tough one. We can get pictures of the kids and put out an amber alert but further searching is futile. The dogs would have tracked them down. Their trails end in a clearing in a small wooded area on farmland. There was no evidence there was a vehicle there. If a truck or car were there, it would have made quite a noticeable path but there was nothing. All we have are slightly bent grass where something round may have been and trails of three other individuals leading to and from that clearing. So, I'm guessing that maybe some unknown individuals abducted them but we don't know. Maybe the other individuals had been there the day before or earlier that day, and are unrelated to this incident. I suggest we send the evidence we gathered of the three other individuals for DNA testing.

"Something must have diverted them from their walk home, perhaps the thing that caused the grass to bend but it was unlikely a helicopter as it would've left other evidence that it had landed there. It was unlikely a balloon because people would have seen it and there were no reports that anyone saw one in the entire city. It could have been a large round tent but the site would have had evidence of poles and pegs and at least one vehicle to carry the equipment, plus the dogs would have found a scent trail leading in and out of the site.

"But if they ran into a problem, why didn't they phone anyone? There were five of them. They weren't little kids. If the three other individuals were abductors, how could they successfully abduct five of them? One of them, Roche, was a large athletic guy. Surely, he would've put up a fight. There would've been some evidence of a struggle in the grass, or we would've seen blood, or some other signs, like torn pieces of clothing, hair, or a backpack left behind. The teens would've left a scent trail if someone dragged them to a car or truck parked by the farmhouse or side of the road. There would've been mixed scents with the other individuals but the teens' trails and the other individuals' trails did not mix except in the clearing. I'm stumped.

"What can we tell the parents? I guess we must tell them what we found and maybe they'll understand. They may ask that they search, too and I guess we could let them.

"The dogs don't lie though. The teens' scent trail ended in that clearing. The dogs would've found them if they had gotten lost. It's as if they were scooped off the planet."

"Now you're talking silly extra-terrestrial stuff. There must be other logical explanations," the chief exclaimed.

"We have what we have. I don't believe in flying saucers and I'm not going to change, now. The trackers said that the dogs reacted strangely to the other individuals' scents found on the twigs and grass samples. They said it was like handing them a banana or a flower to track."

"It's getting late. We'd better get out to those families and inform them of what we have. I'm going with you and take the lead. Feel free to add any other details and answer questions that I can't answer," the chief said as he got up from his chair.

They arrived at Jiao's house and knocked on the door. Liling opened it with a sullen look on her face.

The two officers entered the room. The senior officer noticed more people in the room now, probably more neighbours and parents who were home from work.

The officers told their story. There were lots of questions but many they could not answer. The families wanted more done. They could not believe the teenagers could disappear with so little trace of how. They asked many questions about the dogs and how they could lose a scent. In the end, everyone sat dumbfounded. Liling was holding back tears.

The chief asked for pictures of the missing teens and offered to issue a missing children bulletin to local, provincial, and federal law enforcement agencies and the public. He was also willing to help the families put together search parties if they wished. When the officers finished the session, they left.

There was quite some turmoil in the room for a while after that.

For the next few days, search parties were set up but, of course, they never found the teens. The DNA tests conducted on the samples of grass and twigs found no identifiable human DNA.

Almost every day for the next few weeks, when Jiao's brother woke up in the morning, he cried out "Jiao, Jiao, Jiao . . ."

15.

Raj opened his eyes. The darkness enveloped him. Without sun, moon, or stars he had never awakened to such blackness. At first, he lay puzzled but, as his awareness grew, he realised what had happened – yesterday was real. It was not a dream, or was he still asleep and this was his dream? Then the smell of urine reached his nose. He had had a dream about this the night before; a nightmare. Was he having another one? What day was this? Then he remembered, that yesterday was Tuesday, so this was Wednesday. They had been at Roche's football practice then found, and went into, a spaceship. He was in the spaceship! The rest of the gang was with him.

He reached out and, not too far away, he softly felt another body not far from him. So, this was it. It was real. It began to sink in. He quietly felt around and found his cell phone in his pocket. He opened it and the bright light shone and blinded him for a moment. He tried to dial out. He was not getting a signal. Nothing had changed from last night. It was almost seven o'clock. He quickly closed it again. He could not use it as a phone anymore but now it had become his only source of light in this small compartment in the ship.

He tried to get back to sleep but ended up staring out at the darkness in his new reality as it permeated his thoughts.

"Was that you, Raj?" a whisper that sounded like Erica's broke the silence.

"Yes, you're awake, too?" he whispered back.

"I was almost awake when you opened your cell phone. At first, I thought I was in some sort of weird dream but I guess it's true."

"Yeah, I thought I was in a dream too but I guess this is real."

"The ship seems to have a little vibration."

Raj listened intensely and put his hand on the floor. Erica was right; he felt a small vibration. He had not felt it yesterday. Did this mean that something on the ship was making it – some sort of machinery? Then he had a horrible thought. "I hope this doesn't mean we're moving," he whispered.

"You mean like off the planet?"

"I don't know."

"I think you guys went to sleep quite quickly. Jiao and I were talking for a little while last night. We felt the floor rumble a bit and we were pressed to the floor for a few minutes."

"That might be acceleration," Raj replied. "They may have taken off. If it's still vibrating, my guess is we're in space."

"Why? Are you thinking they'll land again soon?"

"I hope they do, then maybe they'll land in another area of Earth and we can hopefully escape."

"Well, it's been over seven hours since we felt the acceleration."

"Then, that's bad. They would've landed back on Earth sooner than that. Now, it depends on how fast they can fly this thing. We could be stuck in here for days, or weeks, even if they can fly faster than the speed of light."

"If they take that long, we'll starve to death."

"Or die sooner of dehydration."

"Aren't you the optimist," Erica said sardonically.

"Maybe try to go back to sleep."

"I have to go to the bathroom."

"You can use your cell phone as a light but don't use it for anything else and use it sparingly. Don't waste your batteries trying to phone out. I tried and there's no signal."

"Okay."

Seconds later, the light of her phone lit the blackness. He could see her get up and walk to the corner of the room and behind the boxes.

She was soon walking back to their sleeping corner. She sat down and the light went out. Over the next half hour, the others woke up and, in their turn, went to the opposite corner of the room.

The girls told the rest of the boys of the acceleration they had felt in the night.

By the light of one of the phones, they gathered the food and water they had into one spot near the opposite corner of the washroom area. They moved around them the things they would need over the next few days, including tissues and paper for toilet paper. Then it was dark again.

Raj said, "I propose we not have breakfast. We won't be too hungry right now but we'll get hungrier as the days go by."

"What's the best way of rationing the food?" Roche asked.

"I don't know," Raj replied. "We'll have to eat as little as we can and spread out the food fairly. At lunch, we can break off small equal chunks of our chocolates. There are five of us, so it won't last long. Same with the water; we'll have to drink a mouthful of water two or three times a day. We won't be too bad for the first two days but after that, it's going to get bad. I think we might last a week. We'll be getting headaches and weaker. If we don't land before that, we'll have to decide on what to do or we'll get too weak to do anything. We won't even have much paper for wiping ourselves, so use it sparingly. After that, we'll have to use pages from our school notes and textbooks."

"What can we do to get out of here?" asked Jiao nervously.

"I don't know."

"They can't hear us in here, so how are we going to let them know we're here?" Erica asked.

"Over the next day or two let's think of some options," Raj replied. "Let's get through that long. We'll be okay until then."

On the first day, they ate a very small portion of their food at noon and nothing at supper.

The next day they ate breakfast and supper. They talked about their times together and even talked of the funny things that had happened in their lives to cheer themselves up. By the end of the day, they noticed that the room was cooler. It had been so gradual that it was Jiao who brought it to everyone's attention. She had had a rough night trying to sleep because of it.

By the third night, Erica slept close to Jiao to help her stay warm but by the fourth night, Dan slept on the other side of her and they shared the extra clothes that Roche had in his pack.

By the fifth day, three of them had headaches and a general lethargy was overcoming them. Even with taking small gulps, their water was gone. Three of the phones had no more power. The lack of food and water was exacerbating the effect of the cold on them.

By ten that morning, Roche said, "Two things we didn't factor into our plan are the complete lack of light and the cold. The remaining phones aren't going to last very long. I think we should do something. Without that light, we won't be able to see anything and that'll reduce our options. We've got to get out of here. I don't think Jiao will last another day of cold."

"How?" asked Erica, shivering. "Nobody has any new ideas."

"We tried yelling and we even banged on the door," said Roche.

There was silence after that.

"Another thing we didn't factor in was the smell. Our noses have gotten used to it so, although we might smell it a bit, it must reek in here. My dad once told me that he regularly worked in a sulphur laboratory at university for his Master's program. The first day he walked into the lab, it smelled like a skunk had been there but after a day or two he smelled nothing and thought maybe the smell had gone away. He only remembered it when visitors would mention it when they entered the lab. It must smell awful in here," Dan said.

After about fifteen minutes, Raj said, "Whatever we do has to be much more forceful than yelling or banging."

Silence resumed then, after a few more minutes, Raj said excitedly, "The boxes . . . the only thing we have left to us are the boxes. One of them is very heavy. If we could all lift it and drop it, that would make a much larger bang than just hitting the wall with our fists. Unfortunately, the gravity here is not as strong as on Earth. That'll make it lighter for us to lift it off the ground but it would reduce the impact it would have on the floor. That's the only option left to us. If that doesn't work, we're done. I think we have enough strength to lift it but we have to do it, now."

The option excited the rest of them.

Roche responded, "Okay everyone, let's get it done."

One of them turned on a phone to provide the light and they all followed Roche to the largest box in the room.

Erica asked, "What happens if we break what's inside it?"

Roche answered quickly, "Who cares? If we have a choice of breaking what's in the box and living, I vote for living."

"Maybe there's food and water inside one of these boxes," Dan said.

"How are we going to open them to find out?" Roche asked. "We don't have any tools. These boxes are not going to be easy to open without tools and, even if there was food and water, we'll all freeze to death."

Erica added. "If they do hear us, they might kill us when they find us here."

Raj responded, "I guess that's the risk we have to take. We'll die here in a day or so. They might kill us but they might understand our predicament and give us water and food. The last option won't happen unless we let them know somehow that we're in here. It's the only hope we have."

Roche sighed loudly and grabbed the edge of the box. "Okay everyone, put your hands around the top frame of the box, I'll count to three, and everyone lifts at the same time. Then I'll say drop and we let it go. Dan, you go on the side opposite to me, and Raj, you take the side on my left, Jiao and Erica, take the side on my right."

Everyone got into position.

Roche counted, "One, two, three."

The group strained and soon lifted the box off the floor.

"Let's lift it as high as we can," Roche suggested.

The box rose higher.

"Drop," Roche called out.

The box thumped to the floor, hard.

"Okay, let's do it one more time," Roche ordered.

Everyone grabbed the box again.

"One, two, three."

The box rose again.

"Drop."

It fell hard to the floor.

"Do you guys want to do it one more time?" Roche asked.

Erica responded, "How about let's wait and see what happens? That box is heavy. My arms are tired."

"Okay, that's fair but if nothing happens in a couple of hours, I think we should do it again," Roche responded. "This is our last chance to get out of here."

They returned to their living quarters and huddled together with the extra clothes over them to hold in the little heat that remained.

16.

The first officer raised his head from his instrument panel and said, "Did you feel that?"

"What?" Grog asked as he stopped reading a schematic chart.

The officer looked again at the panel and pressed a few keys. "There, see!"

Grog stood up, leaned, and looked at the monitor. "Hmm, it seems like some kind of vibration in the ship."

"Did you feel it?"

"No, did you?"

"It wasn't much to feel. You were sitting and may not have felt it. I was leaning on the panel and I felt it more through there."

"What could cause that?"

"I'm not sure," the officer said, as he studied the signal on the monitor. "It happened twice, with a slight pause between the two." He thought some more. "If it was one, I would say something hit the ship's hull but two? We're in hyperspace, so there should be no physical objects."

"Can we locate the source of the vibration?"

"I can run it through the computer." He asked it to determine where the shock waves originated. Within a few seconds, the response came. He looked at the screen carefully and said, "You won't believe this but it came from within compartment three."

Grog turned his head toward the door of the compartment. "All we have stored in there are some spare parts. We have the samples we collected from the earth in compartment one." He suddenly remembered he had left that door unlocked while he had left the ship when they were on earth. It was impossible that anything was in there though, as there were no sizable animals in the ship's vicinity while he was away. He asked the officer, "Can you confirm that?"

"I don't have to; the vibration came from compartment three," the officer said definitively, as he could see the event log showed that the door had been unlocked while the outer hatch was open when they were away from the ship on Earth. He peered into Grog's eyes. "You left doors unlocked and the strength of the vibration would indicate a very large object hit the surface in there."

The officer asked the computer to scan the compartment.

"Here, look at this," the officer said as he looked at Grog and pointed to the screen.

Grog leaned over to look at the screen again and turned pale. There was not one animal in there but five and the shapes were humanoid and huddled close together in one corner of the compartment.

"Well, Grog, your carelessness has complicated things further. I don't know how they could make the vibrations they made but we have several humans aboard and we're well on our way to Bracha. There were no humans within a kilometre of the ship while it sat in its landing spot but the fact remains, they're here and unless they're carrying lots of food and water, they're probably very hungry and thirsty." He looked at the compartment's temperature and added ". . . and cold." He sneered at Grog, "The only thing we can do is wake up the captain and tell him what we've found."

"Can't we eject them into space and get rid of them, so the captain won't know we had them?"

"We could but we won't. The computer keeps a log of everything that happens here. He'd find out about it. Did you turn off the onboard monitoring system, too?"

"I don't think so."

"It should've warned us of their presence when we arrived back on the ship. You keep studying schematics and fooling around with the ship's settings."

"I'm trying to improve things."

"Tell that to the captain. You're going to have to face up to this. Fortunately, the captain only has about two hours left of his shift off. He hates being awakened from his sleep but some decisions will have to be made."

The officer rose from his chair and went to the captain's quarters. He went inside but deliberately left the door open, so Grog could hear the captain's response.

Within seconds, Grog heard the captain's explosive reaction, "What!!! What do you mean we have humans aboard?"

"Take a look for yourself, captain," the officer replied.

The captain got up hastily and ran over to the screen. He saw the five bodies huddled in the corner of the storeroom. "How did this happen?" he roared.

The officer replied, "Records show that someone left the storeroom unlocked at the time. They may have entered the compartment before we entered the ship."

The captain turned red with rage. "What a series of blunders. We're not supposed to pick up human specimens on this trip. Now, what are we going to do with them?"

"I don't know," the officer replied. "We can get rid of them."

"Sure, that's an easy solution," the captain said sardonically.

The captain poked the officer to leave the chair, sat down at the panel, and stared at their extra cargo. "If we keep them, we have to feed them. Is our food system working well?"

The first officer responded, "Yes, sir. We'll have to produce food nutritionally appropriate for them."

"So, make it. Feral earthlings won't fetch much at the servant auction these days because of their state of intellectual development. They may be difficult to adapt to our needs. They may turn out to be useless. Maybe we should get rid of them. If they're so curious that they entered our ship, that's all they deserve. Of course, it was helped by a lot of carelessness by one certain individual on the ship who'll be unnamed." The captain stared coldly at Grog, who cringed at being identified as the idiot who left the hatch open.

The captain continued after some thought. "We'll take our chances with them. Number one, get our blasters in case we have any trouble. Grog, you get an auto-translator out and set it for North American English. You can also prepare compartment two to hold our new captives. Let me know when everything is ready."

The captain rose and turned to go to his quarters to wash up, while the other two prepared to meet their stowaways.

17.

Raj shivered in the cold and could feel the others shaking. The extra clothes stuffed into Roche's pack were useless in providing the insulation they needed to keep warm. Raj had no idea what the temperature was but he had never felt so cold in his life.

The minutes ticked by and hope was diminishing. They thought there would be an instantaneous response to the dropped crate but the cold was continuing to take its toll and the door had not opened, nor the light turned on.

The effort made to raise the crate had been very strenuous and draining but Raj knew there would not be another attempt at lifting it. He could not stand up if he tried and Erica and Jiao were worse off than he was. There was no way Dan and Roche could lift it without assistance. If their inadvertent captors did not detect them soon, they would die.

He and Dan pressed closely to Jiao in a futile effort to warm her but Jiao was inert and cold, her body giving up the effort to provide warmth. She had drifted off to sleep but Raj knew it was the sleep of death. Roche was in the same plight as Erica, who was still conscious but fading.

Tears began to flow down his cheeks. His one true love was in trouble and there was nothing he could do to save her. He could not even save himself. He found his mind wandering; it was difficult for him to focus anymore. As thoughts of Erica faded, he tried to have enough clarity of mind to hope that his life had been good enough for him to stand before his Lord and pass through the Pearly Gates.

Suddenly, there was a flash of light and a blast of warm air. He thought, at first, that it was death and he had passed over to the other side and soon, he would be standing in front of his maker for judgement. He forced his eyes open to notice that the lights had come on but he drifted off to sleep. There were no longer thoughts of anything.

Roche was the only one to react. He slowly pulled himself up and stood before the aliens.

The captain surveyed the scene and realised how close the humans had come to freezing. There was no point in talking to them, instead, he motioned to the other two members of his crew and each one grabbed a girl by her feet and dragged them out of the compartment and into an adjacent one.

Roche did not know what they were doing but he stiffly followed them to the next compartment. The captain stayed with him while the other two aliens left and soon returned dragging in the boys.

The captain said through his voice translator, "You'll be staying in here. Help the others regain their strength. This is what you get when you don't mind your own business." He pointed to a counter on his left. "There's food and water over there." He pointed to his right. "And you can relieve yourselves over there. Also, on the counter, is a box of tissues to wipe your noses, mouths, or anuses, if required. You push the button outside the wash area's door to wash your waste water down the drain."

The three aliens left the room and the door closed.

Roche scanned their new accommodations. Opposite the side with the door were three square cells less than two metres each side in size. The washroom near the door looked to be the same size as the other cells. All the cells had what looked like a shower head in the centre of the ceiling and a drain in the floor. The two walls separating the three cells consisted of a mesh-like material. They looked like animal-holding cells. He examined the washroom and saw that it consisted of solid plastic bars like the faces of the other cells. He grabbed two of the bars and pushed but they held firm.

There was nothing to distinguish the three cells from one another in size, so Roche guessed that it did not matter who went in each cell. Every cell had a door with a lock on it but it was open. The height of the compartment was the same as the rest of the ship, so Roche would have to continue to stand hunched over. The best thing about the compartment was its warmth.

He looked at his friends strewn about the floor and decided that the best thing he could do was to have something to drink and eat. He would have a lot to do over the next few hours. He went to the table and tasted the water. It was bland and warm but it was water and it would do a lot to rehydrate him. The food was tasteless and had the consistency of pudding but it would serve to relieve his pangs of hunger. It would also make it easier to get the others to eat as they would not have to chew to get it down.

He looked again at his friends and decided to start with the most affected. He slid his hands under Jiao's arms and pulled her into a corner cell. She felt so cold and he was wondering if he could revive her. He put his fingers to her neck and felt a pulse, though weak. He smiled to know at least she was still alive.

He went to Erica next and pulled her into the same cell as Jiao. She was cold too but her pulse was stronger. He bent down and gave her a little kiss. Until they revived a bit, he could not do much else for the girls for now.

He went over to Raj, who seemed to revive a bit as Roche pulled him into the central cell but Raj drifted back to sleep when he let him go.

Suddenly, the door slid open again and one of the aliens carrying a tray came into the room. He went to the counter and put the tray on it. He pulled a large needle from a box on the tray and placed it on the countertop. He turned to Roche and said through his translator, "You'll have trouble recovering from the cold you encountered. I would like to inject everyone with a solution that'll help to rehydrate them, provide nourishment, and help them recover their health. May I proceed?"

Roche was concerned about the alien's intent. He asked, "This'll do us no harm, will it?"

"Not at all; it'll help everyone recover more quickly."

Roche was worried but replied, "Okay, I guess I'll have to trust you. The girls don't look very well. Start with me, so I'll know if it's okay."

The alien reached over to the counter, picked up the hypodermic, and inserted it into the small container. He pulled up the syringe, went over to Roche, and injected the solution into his arm. Roche could feel the pinprick and then a surge of heat in his arm. The alien waited for a few seconds until Roche said, "I feel fine, so go ahead and do the others."

The alien pulled another syringe from the box and injected the solution into Jiao. He repeated the process for each of the other teens. He put the syringes back into the box and left carrying the tray.

Roche looked back at the others and noticed that Dan had pulled himself up into a half-sitting position against the wall next to the counter. He was in a daze, staring vacantly. Roche went over to the counter, poured some water into the only glass provided, and offered it to Dan but he did not respond, so Roche held it to his lips. Dan opened his mouth slightly and was soon gulping it down.

"Whoa there, Dan, take it easy. There's lots more here, so don't drink so much," Roche said as he pulled the glass from his mouth. He stood up and placed it on the counter. He picked up the container of food and a spoon then fed Dan.

Roche took the food back to the counter and drank from the glass. He slid onto the floor and found that the plastic material that covered it softened its surface slightly, so it felt a little more comfortable to lie on than he had thought. He saw Dan had fallen asleep, so he closed his eyes and drifted off to sleep.

18.

Dan roused Roche.

Roche, at first, seemed not to know where he was but one turn of his head reminded him this was not a dream or a nightmare. He did not even know how long he had slept. Finally, he asked, "How are the rest doing?"

"The girls don't look good but Raj seems to be reviving."

"Did you have more food?"

"Yeah, if you want to call that mush food . . . and more water."

Roche got up. "I'd better do the same. I still have such a horrible headache." He went over to the counter and helped himself to more food and drink.

Dan said, "I wish this ceiling was a little higher."

"Yeah, but the owners of this thing are short. They're not going to build a spaceship much larger than they need to run the thing."

"Did you see them?"

"Yes, you guys were asleep but I was awake and saw them come into the compartment."

"Wow, what do they look like?"

"You'll see them soon yourself. I expect they'll be visiting us occasionally while we're in here. They don't look like us at all. They resemble a lizard but their head is bigger and they only have a stump of a tail. Their arms are short and they only have three fingers on their oddly shaped hands. They're about a metre and a half tall."

"So, we have lizards to depend on."

"Yes, but they seem to be smart. Their language is nothing like ours, they used a type of automatic translator to talk to me."

"What did they say?"

"Not much, one of them said this is our room and we have food and water on the counter. We're supposed to use that cage to go to the bathroom." Roche pointed to the single cell near the door.

"Okay. I guess that's all we need for now. At least it's warm in here. Raj looks as if he's waking up. What can we do to help the girls?"

"I don't know. I hope the warmth will do it on its own. We won't be able to force water and food into them. The lizards injected something into all of us. He said it would help us get better faster."

"I guess our fears of getting killed didn't happen; we can be thankful for that."

"We shouldn't get too comfortable. I don't know how to read lizard faces but I got the impression they weren't too happy to see us on this ship. Maybe they put us here to decide what to do next."

"Oh . . ." Dan said as he walked over to the counter and helped himself to another two spoons of food and a gulp of water. He half-filled the glass with water and walked over to Raj. He bent down on one knee and held it out to him.

Raj clumsily took the glass and drank its contents.

"We'll get you something to eat a little later," Dan said, as he took the empty glass from him, "Just rest there for now."

Dan got up and put some water into the glass. He walked over to Erica and pulled her up half sitting against the wall in her cell. He shook her for several seconds until she roused a little then put the glass to her lips. "Here, drink some water."

She half opened her eyes and her mouth. Dan tipped the glass until some water flowed into her mouth. She choked on it, so he stopped.

"I'm so cold," she whispered shivering.

"I know, you should be better soon. It's warm in here."

She drifted off to sleep again.

As he got up, the door opened and the same alien who had brought the food and medicine entered. He said, "I'm glad you've improved young men. Now that you're a little better, we have a job for you to do. Come with me."

Dan and Roche looked at each other and shrugged their shoulders. They stood up and followed the alien into the compartment they had been in previously.

"See that mess you made in the corner of this compartment?" He pointed to a small pail. "Use that to clean it up. We're warming it but most of your waste is still frozen. It should thaw soon, so scoop it up and take it over to your washing area. By the time you've done that, it should be warm enough for you to use clean water to scrub the floor clean." The lizard left them to their task.

Dan picked up a small shovel that was lying on the floor and scooped as much as he could into the container. Roche picked it up and carried it to the single cell in their new accommodation. He returned for another filling. Once they had most of the mess collected, the alien gave them another container with some clean water to wash the floor. It took another two containers of water to get it cleaned. The lizard took the cleaning tools from them and put them into another compartment. He sprayed the area with some odourless material.

"You did a good job. Now, go back to your compartment."

Roche looked at the backpacks and gym clothes in the opposite area of the compartment. "Can we haul our stuff into our cells?"

"You may not. You won't need them anymore. I'll dispose of it. Just get back to where you were."

Dan and Roche shrugged their shoulders and went back to their new quarters. The lizard entered, pushed a button outside the bathroom cell door, and left. They watched as the showerhead in the ceiling of the cell washed the mess down the drain.

"Wow, that was some stench, eh?" Dan said.

"Yeah, but it's clean now."

"I've used the cell to pee so far but what do we do when we have to do a bigger job? There's no privacy."

"I guess you do it in the drain and flush as the lizard did. The lizards don't seem to be concerned with clothes, as they don't wear any."

"I can't tell if they're guys or girls."

"I think they're guys but it's hard to tell with that thing covering their privates."

"It almost looks like a beaver tail."

"That's a good way of describing it."

Dan noticed that Raj was sitting against the wall of his cell. He went over to Raj with the bowl of food and fed some of the mush into his mouth. He carried the food back and brought Raj a glass of water and held it to his mouth.

When Raj finished, he said, "Thanks. They're strange beings."

"Yeah but at least, they're giving us food and water and a warm place to stay."

Raj looked around the small compartment. "There's not much room in here."

"It's a spaceship. We should be glad they've got some place for us at all. My guess is, this is where they hold large animal specimens to bring back home. I'm glad we don't have anything in here already."

"I think you're right. I'm glad to be warm and alive."

Raj closed his eyes and remained where he was to allow his body to regain its strength.

Roche went over to where Erica was and cradled her in his arms.

"How is she?" Dan asked.

"She's still out but I think she'll be okay."

Dan went over to Jiao. "She's regaining her colour a bit."

"I checked her pulse earlier. It's a lot stronger. Maybe try to get some water into her."

Dan pulled her up and sat beside her. She still felt cold to the touch. He cradled her head in his arms and gently stroked her cheeks. "She's still asleep. I'll try the water a little later. You can't give water to someone who's not conscious. I hope that injection will help her."

The door to the room opened and one of the lizards entered with a fresh bowl of food and a pitcher of water. He walked out with the old containers. He returned shortly with five blankets. He said, "Use these to cover yourselves or roll them up for pillows." He left again.

Minutes later he was back in the room with a small bottle and five oversized toothbrushes. He said, "Take this medicine. Swallow one pill a day each until they're finished; it'll help all of you recover better from the extreme cold you've suffered. You can use these brushes for your teeth." He put them on the counter and left again. The door closed.

Dan and Roche got up and took a pill. Dan gave one to Raj then took one of the blankets, covered Jiao with it, and snuggled up against her. Roche did the same with Erica.

Raj saw them but did not move from his sitting position. He wanted to help Dan and Roche but his body ached a bit and he felt stiff. The light intensity suddenly dropped significantly. The teens took the time to relax and get some restless sleep.

19.

When the light increased again, Raj got up, did some stretching exercises, and walked around the room to get himself more limber.

Erica awoke soon after and seemed to have improved significantly.

Dan and Roche were soon up and went over to Jiao. They finally got her conscious enough to take some water, a bit of food, and the pill the lizard had given them.

The rest of them helped themselves to the pills and had breakfast.

"Hopefully we'll soon have Jiao back to normal," Dan said.

"Where do we go from here?" Roche added.

"We're at their mercy now. When we get the chance, we should ask them to take us back home," Raj suggested.

"That's a good idea but will they go for it?" Dan asked without enthusiasm.

Erica piped up. "We've got to try."

"Maybe we're on our way," Raj said hopefully.

"I hope so. We're trapped in here and live in cages," Erica replied. "It's like being in jail."

At noon, an alien entered and replaced their food and water but left the teens no time for questions.

Later that day, Jiao started showing signs of coming out of her stupor. Erica took it upon herself to look after her. She gave her water, then a few hours later, some food. Shortly after that, the lights dimmed. With nothing to do, the teens drifted off to sleep.

The next day was another one of recovery with everyone but Jiao stretching and doing light exercises to get their strength back. They said little. They had time to consider their plight.

Jiao sobbed for quite some time, while Erica held her and consoled her. Erica was finding it difficult to stay stoic.

Raj stayed by himself watching the girls. Internally, he was having a meltdown but could not show it to the girls and especially, not the other guys. They moved about like zombies until the lights went out.

With the lights on again, they woke up each in their turn.

Jiao, with the help of the pills, food, and water seemed much improved.

When their fresh food and water arrived, all three lizards entered.

The teens stood up.

The captain began to speak. "Earth people, now that everyone has almost recovered from your rather unfortunate situation, we want to get you cleaned up. Everyone, get out of your dirty clothes."

They all looked at one another and Erica said, "What do you mean get out of our clothes!"

"Remove your clothing," he ordered.

"Right now, all together?"

"That's exactly what I said."

"Our people don't do that. We usually bathe in private."

"I don't care. Just take off your dirty clothes. I'm aware of some of your social practices but this is not . . . what would you say . . . a hotel. You came here remember; you're not our guests. We have no private accommodation here. This is all we can provide. You can use this cell . . ." He pointed to the same cell as was used for their washroom ". . . to wash yourselves in the shower. It'll provide the soap you need to wash your hair and body. All you have to do is push the green button inside the cell for rinse and the blue button for soapy water."

Raj leaned over to Erica and whispered, "I was wondering what those buttons were for, every cell has them."

The captain leered at Raj and continued. "You may do it one at a time if you wish but we want all your clothes, now. We want to get rid of them. After you've finished, put these on."

The lizard that had brought them their food and water dropped a pile of brown clothes on the floor in front of them.

They looked at the pile.

Erica bent down and examined one of them then held it up. It resembled a sack. "You're not going to give us these things, are you?"

"That's it. We have the right size for each of you, so you can sort that out among yourselves."

"But what about underwear and do you have any other colours?" Jiao asked.

"That's it. Clothes are for keeping people warm. The temperature in here is comfortable for you, is it not?"

"Yes, but we usually wear underwear."

"This is all you're getting. We're not going to pander to your need for visual covering. In our culture, we use clothes for insulation in cold environments. We have no shame in our bodies as you do. Be considerate of the fact that we're giving you these coverings and do not push us for more than that."

"We can wash what we have now and reuse them," Erica suggested.

"No, you can't. Get your clothes off and drop them on the floor."

They all looked at each other and did not move.

"Now!" the captain said loudly and firmly, without emotion. "And don't touch these clean clothes until you're clean and dry. The air in here is relatively dry, so you should dry quickly. I believe you use something to dry yourselves but you don't need it here."

Roche perked up and asked, "What are you going to do with us?"

The captain responded, "That's what we'll discuss later. Right now, I want to get you cleaned up. You're dirty and stink."

Reluctantly, Dan turned toward the wall and started taking off his shirt. The other boys followed suit. The girls drifted off to their cell, undressed, and tossed their clothes out of the cell. One of the lizards picked up the clothes and the aliens left.

Erica said firmly, "Okay, boys, we're going to wash first. Don't you dare look at us? This is the most embarrassing thing I've ever done in my life and I don't want to make it any worse than it is."

Roche replied, "I'll make sure you have your privacy. Please respect ours when our time comes."

The boys went into the opposite corner and waited with faces to the wall as each girl took their shower and slipped into a sack that seemed to be about the right size. The boys then took their turns.

When done, they looked at each other.

"These look like the tunics the Romans used to wear during their empire days," Dan said.

"These are shorter and look like sacks to me," Erica said, "and in brown. I hate brown."

Roche responded, "Actually it looks good on you. I'd like to see you in another colour. It's a nice change."

Erica gave him a sneer.

"I guess soon we'll find out what happens next," Raj said. "I hope they're taking us home."

"I wouldn't bet on it," Dan said. "I don't think they're going to go out of their way to accommodate us. They'd have left us in our clothes and kept our other stuff if they were doing that."

They helped themselves with food, water, and pills. They had to take turns because they had only one glass, bowl, and spoon.

When complete, Erica and Jiao went into their cell and quietly talked about their predicament.

Erica started with a beef about their clothes. "My, I hate this new rag we have on us. It doesn't even have sleeves."

"Yes, it doesn't leave too much to the imagination, does it," Jiao responded. "We're going to have to be careful whenever we sit down. With nothing on underneath, not even a bra, it'll be embarrassing."

"I bet after a few days we won't care anymore. The boys aren't going to try anything. I think they'll police themselves."

"Dan won't try anything for sure."

"At least we're all in the same predicament. The boys are going to have to watch themselves, too. How are you feeling?"

"Good, I'm going to try doing lots of stretch exercises. I still feel quite stiff and have a bit of a headache but otherwise, I don't feel too bad."

"When we see the lizards next time, we should explain to them that we need to have something absorbent when we have our periods. I'm overdue for one, probably caused by everything that's happening right now."

"I won't have mine for a week or two, yet but we'd better get them prepared."

"If they're lizards, they won't know what we're talking about. I don't think lizards menstruate."

"If they studied humans, they're likely to know."

"I hope they do and don't try to push the idea that we don't need anything because it's another vanity thing."

"I hope they're going to take us back home. We don't belong here."

"Maybe they'll realise we're kids and should be with our parents."

"If we're already halfway across the galaxy, I don't think they're going to want to go back just for us."

"I wonder if the guys are thinking about how to get us out of here."

The boys sat quietly along the wall opposite the girls.

Raj was staring at the girls while they were conversing. "I wonder what the girls are talking about," Raj asked Dan quietly.

"Probably about how ugly their clothes are," Roche responded.

"They're not the best colour, are they? I don't care but Erica likes black and Jiao likes light pastels, so both won't be too happy about their predicament," Dan said.

"I think clothes' colours are the least of our worries," said Roche.

"Our new friends say they're going to tell us what's happening, soon," Raj added.

"New friends … that's being optimistic. The way their apparent leader was talking to us didn't sound too friendly to me," Roche countered. "Let's be realistic. They're not our friends. They're taking care of us but I'm sure they don't have our interests at heart."

"I hope you're wrong," Raj said optimistically.

"I think the best we can do for ourselves is to keep in good shape. We should do some exercises each day. Sitting around doing nothing isn't going to be good for us," Roche replied.

"I don't know if the girls are going to favour exercises, Roche," Dan said realistically.

"You mean on account of these dumb clothes?" Raj asked.

"Yes, there's not a lot of room in here to spread out," Dan replied.

Roche said, "I'll talk with them and see what we can work out. I hope they understand it's important for us to keep healthy and strong, or in a few weeks in this lower gravity, we'll be all fat and no muscle."

Roche got up and wandered close to the girls' cell and talked to them about his proposal. He returned shortly after.

"As you said, Dan, the girls aren't excited about exercising but they realise the need. They think that we should wait until we see what the aliens' plans are first."

"Well, hopefully we'll find out, soon."

For the rest of the lighted period, the group listlessly sat around and talked, ate, and drank. The darker period came as expected and they eventually went to sleep.

20.

The light brightened again. Most of the teens awakened early. Jiao slept in, so the rest of them were quiet until she woke up a couple of hours later.

They ate and drank separately. Everyone averted their gazes when someone went to the washroom and all of them were anticipating another meeting with their captors.

About midday, the door slid open and the aliens entered their compartment.

"Good morning. It looks as though everyone has recovered from your stay here. You're likely curious about what's going to happen to you," the captain said.

The teens nodded.

"Well, you're stowaways, not guests. We intend to continue our planned schedule and will be arriving at our next destination in less than three weeks. We may solicit your assistance while you're with us. You may as well earn your keep while you're here."

There was a pause and Erica took her opportunity to speak. "After your next destination, will you be taking us home?"

"No, we'll visit another planet and eventually return to our home planet."

"Why can't you take us home?" she asked.

"We're not here to waste our time and resources to take interlopers back home. You joined us; we didn't invite you here."

"We'd like to go back to our planet. Is there any way you can arrange that, maybe on another ship?"

"We don't make regular trips to Earth. We may not return there for decades."

"So, that means we're never going back?" Roche confirmed.

"Exactly, we'll eventually take you to our home planet and the officials there can do with you as they will."

"We have friends and families at home. We're just kids. We need to get back," Jiao implored with tears in her eyes. "Our parents must be frantically searching for us."

"We won't take you back. The alternative is eliminating you but I think you'd prefer your current situation to that option. Another reason we can't take you back is that you know about us. We prefer to remain undetected on the planets we visit, especially more developed ones. The primitive ones are less of a problem. If we return you to your home, you'd have quite a story to tell; a story we don't want told."

"How about if we didn't tell anyone what happened to us?" Erica asked.

"You wouldn't be able to explain your absence adequately. Your people aren't stupid. I suspect you've done a lot of damage to our intent as it is. Even if we had found you aboard our ship immediately, I couldn't have let you go. I could've wiped your minds of your short-term memory and, for one or two people, that may have worked. The tiny threads that would've remained, wouldn't have been enough to re-establish your memory of what happened to you but with five, it would've been quite likely. Together you may have had enough remaining pieces to have re-established your memories.

"The tracking technology of your people is such that your officials may be able to establish the possibility of our existence from the clues they would find in the area you disappeared. In your past, or even in many countries of your world now, police are too busy to look for missing children but, in your country, you, with our errors in judgment, may have let your people consider the possibility that you aren't lost but mysteriously disappeared. I hope their strong beliefs that you are the only intelligent beings in the universe will overpower the logical conclusion that you were taken by extra-terrestrials."

"What's going to happen to us on your home planet?"

"There are jobs that can be given to you. If you cooperate, you can live out your lives comfortably."

To the teens, that was not a good option but they had no choice.

Erica had other concerns she wanted addressed. "If you've studied our people, you'd know that we wear clothes. I don't like what I'm wearing."

"I'm sorry but I addressed that already. Clothes are a waste to us. We'll provide you with nothing further."

Erica was frustrated. "Are you aware of my and Jiao's need for . . . some type of absorbent . . ." she stumbled on how she was going to explain to this male alien lizard what she wanted to say and was embarrassed to say it in front of the boys.

The captain stood puzzled for several seconds until he realised what she was trying to say. "Ah, I'm guessing you're referring to the females of your species and your fertility cycle."

"Umm, yes, are you aware of it then?"

"I thought those tissues we provided you would be sufficient but I guess not. Yes, we can provide you with something suitable but we don't waste anything. It takes energy to produce them, so we expect you to use them only when required. If you abuse this privilege, we'll stop providing them to you."

He paused for several seconds then said, "If there's any other issue, then address it now, as we have more important things to do than cater to five adolescents."

There was only silence. No one wanted to say anything. They were stuck here and it was now permeating their minds.

The aliens turned and left.

About thirty minutes after they left, the one who seemed to be looking after them returned with a small bundle of what looked like diapers.

After he left, Erica walked over to the counter and examined the bundle. She picked up one of them and said, "These are more like adult diapers. The lizards aren't very advanced in this area."

"Maybe their women don't have periods and they never needed to make anything better," Jiao commented.

"Maybe . . . but we don't have to like them."

There was not much conversation immediately following the discussion with the aliens, as what the aliens had said had stunned everyone. They knew, that they had no immediate hope of getting back home. They needed to take the time for everything to sink in. They ambled around restlessly until they knew the end of the day was near then they settled into their cells.

Jiao's eyes quickly filled with tears. Erica tried to console her.

"I miss my family," Jiao said, "Now, it looks as if I'll never see them again."

Erica held her closely. She looked at the boys who also looked dumbfounded. "We've got to be strong, Jiao. I miss my family, too." Her eyes watered but she fought the urge to cry. "We've got to be strong not for us but for the boys. If they see us cry, they may start, too."

Even when the room darkened, they found it hard to sleep.

21.

The next day, the teens knew they had to establish a liveable regimen. By now, they realised there was a regular night and day period. Twice a day, the reptiles took out their leftover food and water and replaced it with fresh supplies. If anyone wanted a shower, they stood in the designated cell and pushed the wash and rinse buttons. They talked a lot of their time, as there was nothing else for them to do. All they had with them in their old existence like their clothes, phones, books, and packs, was gone.

Their biggest change though was they had no parents, school, friends, or siblings. When they used to meet often at school, doing homework, or just hanging out in their busy daily schedules, they now were with each other all the time. When they wished to be alone in the past, they could retreat into the sanctity and serenity of their bedroom or bathroom. Now, they had none of that. They were stuck in this one small compartment with relative strangers, certainly their best friends but people they had only known a few years of their lives. Now, they had to live with them.

They got up each in their turn when the light intensity increased and did their morning activities. After they finished eating, they sat together legs crossed in the tiny area outside the cells and stared at each other.

After breakfast, Jiao was the first to speak. "It seems dumb to sit here and not say anything."

"What's to say?" Erica responded.

"Looks as if we're stuck here," Roche added.

"It struck me last night," Jiao said, "that I'm not going to see my mom, dad, and little brother anymore." Tears were beginning to flow down her cheeks. Dan slid his arm around her shoulder for support.

"We're all in the same boat," Erica said sadly.

"But I love them. I guess I didn't know how much until yesterday. There was hope to get back but there's nothing, now. I was thinking of them a lot. They love me and must be wondering what happened to me. My parents came from China to have more children only to lose their first-born child," she responded, now sobbing uncontrollably.

Erica was now crying. The boys were trying to remain stoic but Raj was having a tough time stopping his tears. Roche wrapped his arms around Erica to try to console her.

Dan said quietly, "We might as well cry if we have to. We'll have lots of time for that."

They remained in those positions for many minutes.

Jiao finally gained control of herself. She looked at the ceiling of the cell and asked, "I wonder if they're watching us?"

"I've thought the same thing," Roche responded. "I've tried to find a camera but haven't spotted anything. Has anyone else noticed anything?"

Nobody responded, so Roche continued. "I'm sure they have something. They wouldn't leave us in here all the time without keeping an eye on us."

"Well, I hope they know why we're unhappy and change their minds," Jiao said angrily with a raised voice.

"One of them comes in two times a day, maybe that's all they need," Erica said.

"Maybe but I don't know," Dan responded.

"Watching us should give them something else to do, while they're travelling. They can't have a lot to do between stops."

"Yeah, I guess."

"Well, I hope they're satisfied," Jiao said angrily, then she wrestled her way out of Dan's arm and continued. "You're the one who wanted to come into this place."

Dan sat shocked by what she had said but it was true. He was the instigator who insisted on looking inside the ship. His head drooped in shame.

Roche looked around and tried to support Dan. "Well, if he's to blame, I'm not that far off. I was curious, too. I wanted to follow him.

I know we did something stupid but, at the time, it seemed to be okay. There was nobody around. We can't undo what we did. We're here now and we're going to have to stick together." By now he was breaking down himself. He choked out, "To survive now, we're going to have to ignore our mistake. I know we can never forget it. Let's hope that, if we're good prisoners, they'll have compassion on us and change their minds, although that's unlikely from what we've heard so far. We must move on. We can't tear each other apart. We have to keep going."

Roche paused for a few minutes to let everyone calm down then said, "We've all suffered from our days of hunger, dehydration, and the cold. We haven't done much since we've been here and we've deteriorated in physical conditioning. We've recovered our health but we're very lethargic with not much to do all day. I've started doing some exercises but we all should do something. The type of food we're eating won't make us fat but we must improve our muscle tone or our muscles will atrophy. It'll also do a lot to improve our mental health and give us something more to do than mope around and talk." He paused then continued. "I propose that we exercise together twice a day. What do you guys think?"

"How can we exercise with these stupid clothes? We're naked under them remember," Erica stated.

"I guess we can be as careful as we can. We'll do it in a line, so nobody can see anyone else. We can't sit around doing nothing."

"Well, I got to see a little more of you than I wanted to the last time you exercised," Erica added.

"I'm sorry but we'll have to do the best we can. If some of you want to do it once a day then that's fine but it'll also give us more to do together. I'm used to exercising twice a day but I miss my weight work to keep up my strength. I feel so flabby, now. I might use the bars on the shower to help with that if they're strong enough to hold my weight. If you don't like what you see, please look away but I want to keep in shape."

They sat in silence for a while. Roche got up and ate. While the others ate, he started his exercise and Dan joined in after he had eaten.

The others turned away.

Near the end of the day, Roche, Dan, and Raj did their exercises, being as careful as they could. The girls sat in their compartments and talked quietly.

"I'm starting my period. This is going to be so embarrassing," Erica said.

"I'm not due for a while yet," Jiao responded.

"We're going to have to do some exercises ourselves."

"I've never done exercises, except at school, if you don't include sometimes when I joined my mother with her Tai Chi."

"I didn't do too much myself."

"But we were active though; riding our bikes and walking to and from school or into town and back."

"I think it's bad enough we have to be careful sitting around, walking, going to the bathroom, and showering, without having to exercise. I hate these clothes."

Jiao smiled and said, "If we didn't have the boys, it wouldn't be so bad."

Soon after, the lights dimmed.

22.

The next morning, Erica put on her diaper. She had a mixed reaction to it. It looked horrible but it did cover her as underwear. She was not so fearful of exposure but it was embarrassing, as it was so large and bulky and the boys would see it red with blood. It was all she had though and its bulk made it more visible under her tunic.

They ate breakfast then the boys did their exercises.

Later in the day, Erica had to remove her diaper and place the soiled one on the counter for removal. She put on a new one and stood for a few minutes. She could see the tension in the air.

The boys were trying not to notice. It looked as if the situation was embarrassing for them, too. They did not know how to react.

She finally raised her tunic, held the hem in her hands on her hips, and said in a sing-song voice, "Welcome to the latest styles in women's undergarments. This new multi-faceted panty serves as underwear and functions as good as, or better than, panty liners, pads, or tampons. It's also good for women with continence problems. Its size is large enough to contain a hundred gallons of liquid allowing the user to keep it on for a full day, or maybe even a week."

Everyone was looking at her gyrating in front of them and wondering what had happened to her.

She continued without pause. "One of this new product's other advantages is, it comes in one colour – brown. This eliminates the need to spend hours trying to decide what colour to wear and if it matches your other clothes. It's designed for easily determining its contents when used."

By now, the boys were staring at Jiao for guidance on what to do. They were stifling laughter.

"If it's red, you know you can put it in the red bin to be sent to the Red Cross for transfusions; if dark brown, the brown bin to be spread onto farmers' fields for fertiliser; and if yellow, the yellow bin for colouring lemon and orange popsicles. If it remains light brown, you know you can use it again."

They could hold their laughter no more and when Erica was also breaking down, they all burst out in laughter.

Erica knew she had to break the tension. She knew that Jiao would have to go through the same experience in a few more days.

While Erica continued to wear her diaper, the girls sat out the exercise routine.

When her period finished a few days later, she encouraged Jiao to join the line with the boys.

The next couple of days were frustrating for all of them. With the added length of the line, the exercise routine ended up with people hitting each other. Roche was frustrated, as he had to leave out other important routines like running on the spot or touching toes.

Even sleeping was a problem, as sometimes someone would wake up with their garment twisted embarrassingly. Most times nobody could see, or would notice, when someone inadvertently exposed themselves but if someone did notice, there would be the occasional grin or snicker.

One morning, they were exercising, when Erica stopped in the middle of it and shouted out, "I've had it with this. I can't take it anymore. We can't continue this way. We can't move. We can't sleep. It's crazy. I hate this way of living together. We get no privacy for anything and these clothes are for shit. I'm bored and sick with everything."

In tears, she grabbed her tunic and whipped it over her head and onto the floor. Everyone turned their eyes from her but she yelled out, "Look at me, this is me. We've got to stop this silliness. We're stuck here. We're stuck with each other. Look, damn it. We've got to get over all this crap. The lizards stuck us together like this. We're stuck, okay? This is our new normal. We've got to live with each other as we are. We're not little kids anymore. We're just male and female humans stuck here and have to live with each other."

All eyes were on her, as she stood naked and sobbing. Jiao slowly went over to her, hugged her, pulled away, and slid her garment onto the floor.

The three boys did not know what to do. They were very nervous about what had happened. For the girls to take off their clothes was one thing; but the guys, although they were sympathetic with them, had their fears. They stood staring at the girls with renewed respect for them. They did not remove their tunics but lifted them for a few seconds then let them drop again.

To Raj, Erica looked more beautiful than ever. What she had done showed an inner strength he had not seen until now. They were stuck in these tight quarters and with all their conversations over the past days had grown to know a lot about each other but she was baring all as if this was the final wall to fall.

He knew he had to get her away from this. He didn't know how or when but vowed to get her back home. He no longer had any fear of what happened to him. He would meet the challenges that would befall him and find some way of getting her home.

Things changed after that. Somehow, they had matured to get over their physical differences and focus on what they needed to do in their circumstances. They all participated in both sessions of exercises and Roche developed a regime that included all types of exercise. They no longer bothered with one line. They had a purpose and had something else to do in the endless hours of boredom they endured together.

About a week later at one meal, Roche walked beside Erica and whispered, "I miss you; you know."

"What do you mean you miss me," she whispered back. "We're together every minute of the day."

"I mean our quiet times together we used to have."

"Um, well, you forget there are five of us here in this little room. I'm sure the lizards aren't going to give us a private room together and under the circumstances I don't think it's ever going to be a good idea. If we went into a corner together, Dan would want the same thing with Jiao. Raj would be left out of the equation."

"So?"

"What do you think? We can't pretend to have privacy. There's so much testosterone in here."

"But I love you."

Erica's mouth dropped. This was the first time he had ever said that. It caught her off guard. She wanted to fling her arms around his neck and kiss him but she did not. She could not. Instead, she said, "You tell me that. Why have you never said that to me before?"

"I don't know. I guess I always wanted to keep my options open."

"Your options open? Your options are open. What's that supposed to mean – some other girl comes around and you dump me?"

"Not really; I guess I finally saw something in you the day you threw off your clothes. That took guts you know," Roche responded.

"I took my clothes off before, remember."

"Sure, but not in front of everyone else."

"Hum, you're strange. We can't do anything alone. We've got to keep our distance."

"You don't trust me?" Roche asked.

"I don't trust either of us." She paused for a few seconds. "The last time we did it I was terrified of getting pregnant and don't want to be in that predicament again. Here there's no privacy as the lizards are watching us and we have three other teens here. You'll have to set a good example for Dan. I'm sure he misses Jiao, too. We can't even kiss."

She turned from him and went to join Jiao.

After weeks of travel, their captors came into the room one morning. The captain said, "I've got some news for you. We're almost at our destination and will be landing soon."

"On Earth, I hope," Erica told them sarcastically.

"Of course not, we haven't changed our minds," the captain responded firmly. He looked at her with an amused look on his face and said, "Ah, from the person who ripped her garment off her; the alpha female!"

He continued quickly to cut off any responses. "As I said, soon we'll be landing. You can choose to stay locked in this compartment, or help us in some way. We see that you're maintaining your physical health and may appreciate getting out and moving around. You might even get to discover new forms of life. We've only been on this planet once before a couple of hundred years ago and found a rather primitive state of intelligent life. They're not exactly like primates on earth, more of a mammal-like reptile."

"Sort of like you?" Roche suggested, as an example.

"Yeah, between what you look like and what we look like would be a fair match, however, their intellectual level is much lower than ours."

"Of course," Roche admitted. "We'll have to decide together on this, so please give us the time. If we decide not to assist you?"

"You'll stay locked in here."

The aliens turned and left them.

Roche said, "You heard them. What do you think? We can stay safely in here, or get out and get some sunshine and exercise."

"So, they've been amusing themselves watching us." Erica cut him off.

"You expected it. Wouldn't you, if the tables were turned?"

"The tables aren't turned," she said, annoyed.

Roche smiled. "My woman the alpha female."

"Alpha-female, my eye; I'll give him some alpha female. Don't ever think I'm your woman. Nobody owns me," Erica said angrily.

Roche stared at her, stunned for several seconds, and changed the subject. "Okay, I guess we have two options of what we do while we're here; stay here or accompany them on their studies of this planet. If we stay here, I guess we'll have to ask them about our food and water. If we go, how safe are we; how dangerous is it out there?"

Erica took his pause to say, "We can ask about a third option. Why can't we just stay here, and let us keep our door and the ship's hatch open, or at least unlocked? That way we can get some fresh air but stay safely near the ship."

"Maybe they'll go for it," Jiao stated. "It's worth a try."

For the rest of the day, they waited for the aliens to discuss the other option but they did not come.

When the lights dimmed, they went to sleep.

23.

When they woke up the next morning, fresh food was there for them to eat. They did their morning ablutions, completed their morning exercises, and sat idly wondering what would happen next.

Erica yawned and said, "I wonder if we've already landed."

"How would we know that?" Dan asked.

"I woke up last night but I'm not sure if it was a dream or not. I felt some vibrations in the floor."

"Hmm, well they said they were going to be landing on another planet soon, maybe it was soon," Roche said. "If so, they'll be in here any time to finish yesterday's conversation."

Erica said, "I don't want to stay cooped up in this cramped space. My first choice is to get out of here for a while. We don't know how long it'll be until we get to the next destination and it'd be nice if we could stay near the ship."

"Well, let's sit here for a bit and see what happens. Plan A is to get out of here close to the ship. If we have no choice, do you want to go with them?"

Everyone nodded.

Thirty minutes later, the door opened and the aliens entered.

The captain said, "We're making our plans. The sun will be coming over the horizon soon. What's your decision?"

Roche answered, "We'd like to get some fresh air but remain near the ship."

"You can't do that. This isn't a party. Either come with us or stay inside your quarters."

"How will we get food and water while you're away?"

"We'll leave you enough for the duration."

"We won't try to escape if you leave us the freedom to leave the ship; after all, where would we go?"

"You only have two choices, if you still haven't decided, we can come back in thirty minutes and ask you again."

"No, that won't be necessary. We'll go with you." Roche could see everyone was agreeable with what he was saying.

"Okay, you've got thirty minutes to get ready."

They left the room.

Jiao said sadly, "I guess that's it. They didn't give us much choice."

Everyone was as ready as they could be but thought they could all go to the washroom, as they did not know when they would be returning to the ship.

Just as the aliens said, the door opened punctually and they led the teens into the main area of the ship.

Roche and Dan were each given a large bag to carry then the hatch opened in front of them as they approached it. They formed a single line, with the first officer leading, then Roche and Dan, the captain, the three other teens, followed by the alien who looked after them which the officers called Grog.

They noticed the increase in gravity almost immediately after they set their feet on the planet. The ship had maintained a gravity that was a little less than Earth but it seemed to them that the gravity on this planet was higher than Earth's. They looked up to see that the sky was a glorious greenish-blue colour. They began to walk.

Within seconds, Erica stopped and asked, "Aren't we going to get any shoes?"

The whole line stopped.

The captain responded, "No, just watch your step. Your feet will get accustomed to walking without shoes. You've spoiled them during your life."

"We're going to cut our feet," Erica said, looking at all the branches and leaves strewn about the path ahead of them.

"You could go back to your cell."

The teens looked at each other and no one wanted to return.

The officer started walking again and everyone followed a small trail cutting through a dense forest. The light turned almost black from the shade of the trees. It was beautiful in an eerie way. The shade allowed many different coloured mushroom-like lifeforms to grow. Occasionally, a break in the canopy revealed the beautiful clear sky above them.

Before long, they stopped for a break and the aliens took the bag from Dan and passed out a water container. If the gravity was affecting them, it was affecting the lizards more.

Jiao looked up and spotted something above them and asked, "Hey, what's that?"

Everyone looked up and saw it, too.

The captain responded, "Oh, that's a flying reptile – this planet's bird. None of them have feathers, as you have back on your planet."

"It's like a pterodactyl," Raj said.

"I guess you could say that," the captain added.

They were soon on their way again, climbing the side of a small hill. When they reached the top, they were at the edge of a small cliff that overlooked quite an expanse of forested area and glade. They stopped again to rest. The teens were sweating and had laboured breathing. The aliens were also breathing heavily but there were no other outward signs of exhaustion.

The captain opened Roche's bag, pulled out binoculars, and looked over the scenery below. There was a stream in the distance and a large clearing in the forest. The lizards were focussing their attention on the clearing. The humans tried to make out what the aliens were looking at and soon got their turns using the binoculars.

"As you can see, there are human-like lifeforms in the clearing," the captain said. "These beings are starting a stage of settlement. For the most part, they still use caves and trees for habitation but some of them are using artificial building forms of wood, grass, sod, or rocks, depending on what's around them. This is allowing them to increase in population and move into newer environments.

"Although they look a little like you, they're quite different in many ways and their genetic structure is quite different. The last time our people were here, we captured a few of them to take back for study. We're not doing that this time. These people are generally gentle but can be quite aggressive, so I suggest we always stay close together."

They had lunch there eating the same food as they had on the ship.

"Are any of the mushrooms and plants here edible?" Raj asked.

"Like your plants, some are but some are poisonous, so if you think you'd like to eat some of the living things, I'd suggest you ask us first.

Although the food we give you is bland to you, and some of the living matter here may be tastier, you may get violently sick or die if you eat anything around you," the captain responded. "I suggest that if any of you need to go to the bathroom, do it here."

The teens disappeared into the bushes around them. When done, they packed up and followed a trail to the bottom of the cliff. They walked along it for several minutes until they reached a cave. They entered and were amazed by the beautiful drawings on the walls.

The captain recounted, "The people of this planet, used this cave for a home but now use it to paint using pigments from some of the plants and flowers found nearby. There are still many different species of human-like beings and they have their style of drawing, some of them quite primitive, and others quite elaborate as you see here."

The lizards pulled out two cameras from Dan's pack and began taking pictures of the art found on the walls.

The teens pored over the paintings. Most of them were hunting scenes. The types of animals pictured were all lizard-like but there were also pictures of aboriginals fishing along a shore and sometimes using a primitive boat, which meant there was a lake or sea not too far from the cave. Erica turned her head toward the boys and found them preoccupied with the many love scenes depicted on the wall.

Erica lightly ribbed Jiao. When Jiao turned her head to her, she nodded her head towards the boys.

Jiao turned her head in the boys' direction and grinned. She looked back at Erica with a little giggle.

"Figures," Jiao said in a whisper.

Erica quickly scanned the pictures and asked aloud, "What's your favourite picture, Roche?"

Roche turned his head to her and, with a little blush, said, "Umm, I'm not sure." Then with a big grin, he said, "I think the one with the fisherman in his boat holding up the big fish."

The teens burst out laughing.

The aliens looked toward the teens and wondered why they were laughing then turned back to their task.

In some of the pictures, Erica noted the hopefully exaggerated sizes of a certain part of the males. She leaned over to Jiao and said quietly, "I'm guessing that men drew these pictures."

Jiao knew what Erica meant and smiled shyly.

When the lizards finished, they left the cave and followed another trail, stopping periodically to take samples of animal and plant life and placing them into plastic bags or bottles from the packs. They stopped for another break and soon found themselves back at the ship. The aliens led them to their compartment and left them fresh water and food. The teens ate.

"I guess it was nice to get out. This place looks a little like Earth a few thousand years ago," Roche said.

"Yes, it was nice to get out for a walk. My legs are tired, though. We needed the exercise and for that, we needed a nice long walk," Erica said, "and we got to see a few different pterodactyls and bugs, as well as all those drawings in the cave."

Roche added. "Especially the drawings in the cave," and the teens laughed again.

"I don't mind you guys looking, as long as you don't get any ideas," Erica said seriously.

Raj stared at Erica. He turned away. Something was bothering him. He didn't know what it was but in close quarters he occasionally felt it hard to remember his promise to forget about her. Today was one of them. He wandered over to his cell, sat down, and stared at the wall almost in a meditative fashion.

Everyone was too tired to do their evening exercises, so they quickly settled in and went to sleep.

Raj had several dreams that night, only two of them he remembered vaguely; both were about Erica. In one, he pictured her walking with him then some wild man dragged her away. He fought to get her back but she always was a few centimetres from his grasp. In the second dream, he was sitting next to Erica and she turned her head and kissed him.

24.

Raj had a rough and fitful time in the early morning and woke up hot and sweaty. He walked over to the shower to wash both him and his garment. He had seen Dan and Roche also occasionally get up and take an early morning shower. He tried for the rest of the morning to stay as far away from Erica as he could.

The group decided that a morning exercise would be unnecessary, as they were too stiff from the walk the previous day. They expected today would be similar.

After they finished their meal and washed up, they sat silently in their cells.

Erica quietly said to Jiao, "I wonder where we're going today."

"They didn't say what we'd be doing. Maybe one day is all that's planned," Erica responded in a whisper.

"Maybe."

"I feel so lightheaded today. I know I'm stiff from all the walking but I don't think it's that."

"You seem a little flushed."

"I do?"

"Well, it's hard to tell. It might be all the exercise you had yesterday."

"Yeah."

Jiao thought a bit more and said, "It could be something else."

"Oh?"

"Sometimes when I felt a little like that my mom said I might be ovulating."

"Shh, the boys might hear you. You shouldn't talk about stuff like that when the boys are around."

"The boys are always here. We're just one of the team, right?"

"Well, boys don't ovulate."

"Yeah, but they have their problems, like morning showers."

"Well, we need extra showers too sometimes. Those diapers are better than nothing but they're not foolproof."

"Yeah, the problems of living, I guess."

"I hate the lack of privacy, even from the prying eyes of the lizards. Sometimes I wish I could be all by myself."

"We all do but that's the way it is. I hope it'll change once we get to their home planet."

"Yeah, I wonder what they're going to do when we get there."

"I don't want to think about it. I try to live one day at a time."

The door opened and Grog entered with two sacks. He dropped them on the floor and said, "Let's get going."

Dan and Roche each picked one up and everyone left the ship. The hatch closed behind them.

They followed a trail heading in the opposite direction to the one the day before. It wandered close to a clearing where they could see a small village.

The captain and senior officer set up a block and tackle into a nearby tall tree and assembled a small platform. The boys hoisted the platform holding the two officers to the top and Grog secured the end of the rope to an adjacent tree.

While they were there, the teens and Grog examined some of the insects around the site.

At noon, they lowered the platform and had lunch.

When they finished, the boys raised the officer, while Grog and the captain went to another area to collect more samples of insects and plants. Most of the men in this small village were out hunting and the women were working together on the other side of the village.

The teens stood at the bottom of the platform occasionally looking up to see if anything was going on. The first officer was mostly looking into his binoculars and quietly voicing his comments into a small microphone.

"We're not seeing anything," said Jiao.

"Yeah, this is boring," added Erica. "The only fun we had was watching the boys carry the bags here and pull on a rope."

"The scenery is nice and it's a chance for us to walk around a bit. We can join the boys to look at some insects or small animals."

"We could've done that near the ship," Erica countered.

"I wonder how many days we'll spend here."

They joined the boys until the captain and Grog returned. They lowered the platform and had an afternoon snack.

Erica took her turn at the bowl and drank some water then sat down next to Jiao.

"God, I'm getting tired of this food," Erica said quietly. "It's the same for breakfast, lunch, and supper. I can't see how they don't get tired of this."

"Maybe they eat this all the time, even on their home planet. At least it's something to eat."

"Yeah, if they could change the taste, colour, texture, or anything, it would make it seem different. We might even be able to use our teeth. Oh, how I wish I could have a nice hamburger or a pizza."

The boys overheard what the girls had said. Their mouths watered at the thought of real earth food. They were not happy with their situation but what could they do? They had no weapons to threaten their captors to take them back home. They could escape here by just rushing off into the forest but where would that get them? The Aboriginals could not get them back home.

They would have to survive on their own. They could not assimilate into the aboriginals, as their genetic make-up would be completely incompatible with theirs. Their only option was to go along with what was happening and keep hoping some opportunity would present itself and, so far, that had not happened. They were helpless.

At supper time, the captain and Grog returned with a bag filled with artefacts they had picked up around the camp. They lowered the platform and the officer got off. They raised it again.

Roche asked, "I guess we'll be coming here again tomorrow?"

The captain replied, "Yes, we'll spend most of tomorrow here then visit another location on this planet before we're on our way again. We may as well eat here; I'm sure that you enjoy it here more than in the ship. The plant and animal life here are different, yet like yours back home."

Raj responded, "Yes, a little; there's the odour of flowers in the air."

"Here, the trees exude that scent even without flowers."

"So, it's like this all the time?" Erica enquired.

"Well, they do get a short season of winter in the high latitudes. Their planet does not tilt as much as yours to its sun, so the polar regions are frozen with enormous ice caps and most of the rest of it is tropical. It's in an equilibrium where the amount of ice that melts is equal to the amount that freezes. Fortunately, their planet has lots of water."

They ate supper in silence.

Erica finished first and had not gone to the washroom for hours. "I'd better go to the bathroom before we leave," she said to the others.

Jiao asked, "Do you want me to go with you?"

"No, it's fine. You still must eat. I won't go far," she said, as she picked up a few tissues from a sack and started going up the path.

Within fifteen minutes, everyone had finished eating. They started to pack up to leave.

Jiao said aloud, "Erica hasn't come back yet!"

The captain stared at her for several seconds and looked around. "She went up the trail, didn't she?"

"Yes, but she should be back by now."

"If anyone gets lost, we have to leave them behind."

"We can't do that."

"Please, sir," Roche said, "We can finish packing then head up the trail to find her."

"We normally don't do that. When you came aboard, you had to face the consequences and we don't want to let the aboriginals know we're here."

"It won't do any harm to make a small detour."

The captain did a reptilian equivalent of a sigh.

Dan and Roche tied up the tops of the bags and hoisted them onto their backs. The captain led them along the trail Erica had taken. Within less than three minutes he stopped and said while he pointed off to the left, "She went into there. Grog, look in there, and see if you can find her."

Grog entered the bushes and returned a few seconds later. "She's been there but there's no other trail from there. She must have returned here."

"Good, that's confirmed then because I can see her footprints in front of us, meaning she turned the wrong way."

The captain continued down the trail for several minutes until he stopped. "We're not going any farther."

"Why not?" Raj asked.

"An aboriginal is now on her trail."

"What? That's more reason to try to find her!" Roche exclaimed.

"No, that's the reason we have to stop. If he or she has seen her, then we can't show ourselves, too. We're not supposed to let them know we're here."

"But the Aboriginals already know we're here, so it shouldn't matter anymore," Raj reasoned.

"Erica's a different-looking being but not so different that he or she might think she's another animal or species of their planet they've never seen before. If they see there are more, especially us, then who knows what they might think. We must not interfere with them – at all."

"Well, we could. We're not extremely different from them. How about we go alone then?" Roche implored.

"No," the captain said emphatically.

"But we'll come back. We don't want to be stuck on this planet. We can leave Jiao with you and go find her ourselves," Dan added.

"Or can I go alone?" Raj volunteered.

"No, we're leaving before the end of the day tomorrow. She'll have to find her way back. That's it. Our laws are clear," the captain said, as he pulled his pistol from the belt around his waist. "Don't forget that, if she can't make it back to the ship, maybe she'll find us at our research site tomorrow."

That effectively ended the conversation. The captain led them back to the ship while the other two aliens walked closely behind the four teens.

When they arrived at the ship, the captain let the hatch close. He turned to the teens and said, "In appreciation for your help so far, you're invited to dine with us rather than return to your cells. Unfortunately, you have one person missing. We'll keep the ship's computer on the alert in case she shows up near the ship, so we can let her in.

"I took the liberty to collect some edible fruit from the local plants and we would like to share it with you. What you've had so far is a defined amount of protein, fat, carbohydrates, fibre, vitamins, and minerals that you need to keep you healthy. Our dietary needs are different from yours, of course, so we have a different formulation and don't share our meal with you. Grog will help you get things set up. As we don't have enough chairs, please sit on the floor any way you'd like."

Everyone but Grog sat, with the teens doing so carefully. Grog disappeared into one of the other compartments.

The captain continued his conversation. "When in space, we try to limit ourselves to what we use, as everything is artificially made by the ship. That's why we only provided you with a common bowl, spoon, and glass. That's all you need. I know your customs are for each of you to have your implements but that's wasteful, so we don't do it here."

"Is that why we have these clothes?" Raj asked.

"Partly, our custom is different from yours in that area. We have been very deferential to you by providing you with what you have. When you get to our home planet, you may be treated to having your implements to eat but you may find clothes being a luxury you may not get; partly because they're not our custom and partly because they're generally not available, especially for humans. I've been very generous to you in that area."

"And I guess that explains the mush we get all the time," Roche added.

"If that's what you call our food, then yes. Our engineers designed this ship to recycle everything. For example, the recycler broke down your clothes and other things you brought with you on the ship to their elements and compounds to use when needed. Even your bodies' waste materials are recycled."

The teens scowled at the news.

To change the subject, Jiao asked, "What are the people on this planet like?"

"What do you mean?"

"Are they dangerous?"

"I guess that's in respect to your absent member. As I said, they're relatively benign. They do get less so concerning territory, at times, and of course in matters of mating."

"What do you mean by 'mating'?"

"Males may get aggressive to another male when a female nearby is in heat. It's all a matter of the survival of the fittest. Usually, they're gentle to the female but the male may get aggressive, if she shuns his advances."

"Not much different from on our planet," Jiao commented.

"Except, you're more aggressive, in my opinion," the captain said.

"Another distinguishing characteristic is your mating practices. You're one of the few species in nature who mate outside the female's fertile period. Most animals' males only desire to mate when they sense that females are in heat, usually by the females' scent but sometimes by sight, or sound. Your males have mostly lost the capability to sense when the female is fertile. To compensate, you mate anytime, so are aggressive all the time."

Jiao smiled slightly as her confidence in Erica's safety increased.

Grog appeared and brought the teens their large communal bowl of mush. He left again and soon returned with the smaller bowl for the aliens. They all shared the jug of water.

When everyone finished their meal, Grog brought in a bowl of fruit they had picked near the village.

"Wow," Dan said excitedly, as he finished a mouthful, "this stuff is wonderful. It's so sweet."

The teens enjoyed the pleasant change in food. When done, the aliens asked the teens to return to their compartment. Within minutes, the light darkened and they settled into their cells to sleep.

25.

Erica headed up the trail for two or three minutes until she turned into the bushes for several metres and squatted. When she finished, she headed back out to the trail and walked for several minutes along it until she realised, she must have turned the wrong way, as she should have been back at the worksite before then. She turned around to retrace her steps and froze.

Just eight metres away from her was one of the planet's aboriginals. It had grey-coloured scale-like skin. It was less than two metres tall and was completely hairless, as you would find on a reptile, yet it was not completely reptilian in appearance as it stood erect and had almost no tail. They stood silently staring at each other for many seconds. As the human-like reptile was not wearing any clothes, except for a leather belt around its middle, she could see it was a male and knew exactly what he wanted.

The male took a step toward her.

She turned and ran as fast as she could farther along the trail but, within minutes, she was tiring fast. The weeks of relative inactivity had significantly decreased her stamina. She tried to find another trail, as she realised that she was heading closer to the village.

The male behind her was closing in.

She stumbled to a halt in front of another larger male who had appeared out of the trees in front of her. She cringed in fear, as the male behind her flashed by her and crashed into the other male.

They began to fight.

She froze to watch for a time, partly due to exhaustion and

indecision. The second male smashed his fist heavily into the face of the male that had pursued her and, after a few more exchanged blows, the smaller male scurried unhappily and in pain into the bushes.

She quickly spun around to run back up the trail toward the worksite but the male quickly overcame her, scooped her up into his arms, and turned toward the village. She wrestled and squirmed to try to escape but he was too strong for her to succeed. She was soon too exhausted to continue her struggle.

Within minutes, they entered the clearing to the village and soon entered one of the huts close to the edge of it. He placed her onto a mat made from reeds and stared at her while occasionally sniffing the air.

She got up to try to escape but he caught her and dropped her back onto the mat.

Erica realised she could not escape and the male was not interested in hurting her. She sat up and stared at him for a while trying to regain her strength. If he tried anything, she was going to resist with everything she had left.

He reached for her and she pulled back. He reached for her again and she slid toward the door of the hut and dashed away to the path. He was right behind her and caught her. He pulled her back into the hut and lunged at her. She twisted onto her side and hit him with her arms several times on his head and neck.

Suddenly, he stopped and pulled himself into a sitting position. He looked inquisitively at her and grunted something unintelligible to her. It was as if he had never seen a female resist him before. He watched her for many minutes, probably to decide what to do next. Finally, he reached over and raised her tunic.

After a few seconds, she grabbed the edge of it and put it back in place.

He raised his hand again and brushed it over the mound he could see on her chest. He reached over and passed his three fingers through her hair, as he had never seen anything like it before. He looked perplexed. She did not look like an aboriginal female.

If he was hairless an aboriginal female was likely to be, too. If their females laid eggs, then they would not have mammary glands. This had stirred his curiosity. He was beginning to realise how different she was from a local female.

He leaned over, sniffed her, and grunted again. He must have decided to delay any further advances on her, as he opened a large vessel near him and pulled out some light-coloured fruit and held some out to her. He grunted again.

She was hungry, so she took it and put it into her mouth. She was amazed at how tasty and sweet it was. She finished what she had and he gave her more. It was such a treat from the tasteless pudding provided by her captors in the spaceship.

As it was getting dark, he used a flint to light an oil lamp and continued to stare at her. After thirty minutes, he put out the lamp, protectively wrapped his arm around her, and pulled her onto his mat with him. He fell asleep.

She stayed awake for at least an hour. She was apprehensive that he would take advantage of her as she slept but, exhausted, she eventually drifted off to sleep.

She woke up. It was black as pitch and, for a few minutes, she thought she was back in the compartment in the spaceship but from the slight snoring next to her she remembered where she was and there was no point in trying to escape because she would not be able to find her way back to the worksite or the spaceship in the blackness.

She wondered what was going to happen. Was she going to be stuck here? Had he claimed her as his prize and she was going to struggle with him in the morning, or would he release her? She wondered what the custom was in this society. One wrong turn on her part had resulted in this. She should have taken Jiao's offer to go with her but it was too late, now. She slowly drifted back to sleep.

A poke in her back partially awakened her. There was another one. She rolled over carefully to avoid wakening the male beside her. It was a little lighter now, so she could make out shadows around her. At first, she was excited that perhaps it was one of the boys who had found her but the dim light showed it was the first male she had seen on the path. Her hopes crashed. He must have crept into the hut and crawled over to her. He motioned her to follow him.

She was still in a half-dream-like state and was wondering what to do. Was she safer with the male who had won her in battle, or the one asking her to leave with him? If she did go with this one, what would happen when the other one woke up? Would this end up in another chase and fight? Would the larger one hurt her for escaping?

She was fully alert now and could see from the view outside the door to the hut that it was lighter than she last looked. Was it morning? If so, maybe she could get this young man to take her back to the trail near the worksite.

She carefully pulled herself away from the larger male and eased out of the hut. Her liberator followed. She saw that the increase in light was due to the sky clearing of clouds and the rising of a moon. It was much smaller than Earth's moon but the combination of light from the stars and the moon made her see well enough to see around her.

He motioned her to follow him.

She was quite sure he was not going in the right direction but she followed and found that he was back-tracking and going over obstacles and across a stream. They walked into it and followed it for many minutes until he stopped on a sandy bank.

He motioned her to stay where she was and disappeared for about five minutes. This was a great opportunity for her to escape but she had no idea where she was concerning the alien's camp.

When he returned, he was carrying an armful of different kinds of berries.

They ate.

She was happy to have another wonderfully tasty meal of something other than the crap she had eaten for the last few weeks.

When they finished, the colours of the fruit had stained her hands and face. She tried to wash it off in the stream but the pigment remained on her.

He leaned over and sniffed her.

She looked at his fruit-stained face and noticed the bruises he had received the previous day, as well as a large welt on his shoulder. He was willing to fight a larger person than he was to have her; perhaps an action a little brave and a lot stupid but it impressed her.

In addition, he had risked further wrath from the other male by helping her escape from him. Now, he had brought her fruit; perhaps his people's equivalent to giving flowers to women back on earth. Would she be able to convince this male to take her back to where he found her?

She was finding his being so close to her distracting but she cleared her mind and tried to use her hands to tell him what she wanted.

First, he seemed to be confused. He grunted something. Perhaps her response was not what he expected but she finally seemed to have gotten across to him.

He smiled briefly, then looked sad and tried, in his way, to say that he would lead her to the path near the worksite.

She smiled and asked him the direction she had to go and he pointed to his right.

He looked at her, lowered his head, picked up a branch from the ground, and brushed their footsteps from the sand. Once done, he threw the branch into the trees and started leading her down a trail.

The sun was rising and she knew the others would not be at the site yet so, when he stopped for a break, probably because he noticed she limped, she was in no hurry to begin to walk again. She was rather stiff from all the walking she had done in the last two days and more so from the mad dash the previous day.

She admired his thoughtfulness. He was not aggressively pushing himself on her. He could lead her somewhere else and keep her, or abandon her and leave her helpless and alone on this planet but she felt confident he would not do that.

This was a relatively primitive society. She had read about different animals' mating practices. She had found out from her experience here that these primitive people must respond to pheromones much like other animals. They apparently must have had the same, or similar, pheromones to people on earth. She was in the ovulation stage of her period and would have sent a chemical message to the males she encountered, so this was not unexpected, she thought. She knew the effect she had on Raj and, to a lesser extent, on Roche at these times.

She hoped he would continue to help her. He had so far, although technically he had caused her plight to begin with, even if not intending to do that.

The male left for a few minutes and returned with more fruit for them to eat. While eating, he remained very close to her, continuously sniffing her. He grunted something.

When they finished eating, he leaned over to her and put his lips close to hers.

She gave him a slight touch with her lips and found herself in internal turmoil. The baser side of her, the chemical side, was urging her to relax and allow him to get his wish, after all, he had saved her from the other male and it might be an interesting experience but she straightened up and motioned him that she wanted to resume her walk.

He reluctantly pulled away and led her farther up the path then through two junctions until he stopped and pointed ahead.

"This is where we part then?" she asked knowing he would not know how to respond. She smiled and said, "Thank you."

He grunted a couple of times. She leaned over and kissed him again lightly. She turned and headed up the trail without looking back.

26.

The morning was beautiful. It was neither hot nor cold. The sun blazed in full glory over the land. Birds were chirping and the insects loudly announced themselves to the world.

The teens on the ship were awake and unhappy but quickly ate breakfast.

The ship's crew came to get them and said nothing about Erica, which indicated that they had heard nothing from her. They exited the ship and were on the way back to their observation post. Although the boys were taking in the beauty of the planet, Jiao was not pleased. She knew the aliens would be concluding their work this morning, returning to the ship later in the day then leaving this site. If Erica did not show up within the next few hours, that would be it. She would be the first casualty of their mistake in entering the ship.

They soon reached the site. The captain and his first officer followed a small trail into the forest to collect more samples of small animals and plants. The boys pulled Grog on the platform up to the top of the tree, so he could complete their observations of the village.

Dan and Jiao sat together on a log holding hands.

"This is the first time we've held hands since we've been with these aliens," Dan said. "This is sure a nice morning. It reminds me so much of home."

"For me too," Jiao responded. "I'm so worried about Erica. She's not back yet."

"I think she'll be back. She's strong and can look after herself. I hope an aboriginal hasn't captured her. If she's with one, I'm sure she can get them to help her get back here."

"I hope so. She's been away all night and doesn't have much time left."

At the first break, the boys lowered the platform and they ate and drank. They raised the platform again.

Minutes later, Jiao heard a rustling sound behind her and whipped around in terror to face it. Dan noticed her move, sped to her side, and asked, "What's wrong?"

"I thought I heard something."

Dan reached down and picked up a tree branch. "Maybe it's the lizards coming back."

Jiao's face lit up when she finally identified the image vaguely from the darkness of the forest.

She shouted, "It's Erica . . . Erica's back."

Everyone turned in the same direction. When Erica entered the clearing all the teens crowded around her to welcome her back.

"Where have you been?" Roche asked excitedly.

"I'm okay," Erica said smiling and happy to be with the group again. "I visited the village and got to meet a couple of the locals there. Don't worry, I'm not hurt. They were quite friendly."

"Well, you're lucky to get here before we leave," Roche added. "We were all worried about you."

"I'm back and I'm okay."

"What happened anyway? You're all wet."

"I took a wrong turn to get back here and turned to retrace my steps. I saw this local guy and ran in fright. I eventually ended up near the village where I met another person and ended up staying there overnight. The first guy guided me near here this morning. There's a stream near here and I took the opportunity to get clean."

"Well, you didn't do a good job."

"What do you mean?"

"Your face is stained with a least three colours."

"Oh, that. I've been eating the local fruit. If you think that's bad, look at my hands." She held them out for everyone to see.

"I'm glad to see you're safe and sound," Jiao said happily.

"Well, I'm glad to be back."

Roche took her hand and squeezed it gently. She smiled back, relieved to be with her friends again.

They offered her some food but she reminded them about the fruit she had eaten. They filled her in about the previous evening's dinner and the discussions with the aliens. She confirmed the information the aliens had told her by what she learned first-hand from the local people.

At noon, the captain and first officer returned to provide everyone with more fruit than they could eat. The captain welcomed Erica back.

After lunch, they dismantled the platform and placed the parts of it into a sack. By mid-afternoon, they headed back to the ship.

Soon after their return, Grog brought them fresh mush and water. He told Erica that the captain wanted to speak to her.

She followed Grog out the door of their compartment and entered the captain's quarters. It was the same size as their cell but was living quarters. She saw a fixture on the wall that looked like a recessed bed. It had an enclosed washroom and a desk with three chairs. Grog ushered her into one of them and left.

"Well, well, well." The captain opened the conversation. "I guess you must have had some adventure. We're always interested in studying the practices and culture of the intelligent beings we meet. Your encounters will give us an excellent opportunity to study how well beings from different cultures and planets interact."

"I was gone for less than a day, so my encounter was not very long."

"Yes, but I'd like to hear all about it and don't leave out the details, or I'll have to ask you for them."

Erica felt uneasy about describing the encounters she had had but once she started, she provided the details he requested. He was so casual and impartial to what she was saying she found no reason to withhold details.

The captain summarised the facts and said, "This is all interesting to us. What you've told me helps us study the ranges of hormones that may affect other forms of life. You're in the fertile portion of your cycle, although not all human males would notice. It does affect the locals on this planet. The molecular structure of your pheromone is different from the beings here but still is similar enough to affect the males. As you can see, your pheromone does not affect us."

Erica commented on his findings and conclusions. "This all seems so cold and scientific."

"There's your earthly attitude showing again. Maybe seeing these other cultures will open your mind to some of the rigid notions your culture has about some things. Well, it's getting late and we have lots of work to do, so thank you for this talk. Grog will escort you back to your room."

Grog entered and took her back to the rest of the group then left.

"So, why did he want to see you?" Jiao asked.

"Just to explain my absence; it's being added to what they know about the people on this planet."

"They told us a little yesterday." Jiao then proceeded to inform her about what the lizards had told the group about the locals.

At the end, Erica said, "That's about it. They're gentle people. They didn't hurt me even though I was a stranger to them and didn't even look like them."

"I was worried about that. After you didn't return, we followed your trail until it included that of an aboriginal then the lizards wanted to go no farther, so we did try to find you. They even pulled out their guns when we said we'd find you on our own."

"I knew you'd try your best. You told me that you had fruit yesterday, well the locals have so much fruit that I think that's mostly what they eat, along with some types of vegetables I'd seen but never tasted. The pictures in the cave show they do eat some meat, though."

"Maybe that's one reason they're relatively gentle," Jiao guessed.

The rest of the evening was relatively quiet, as all their outside activities exhausted everyone.

Raj had been watching Erica from the other side of the room. He had tried to get close enough to talk to her and tell her how happy he was to see her again but each time he had to pull away. Her eyes looked so flashy and bright. He decided to lie down early to try to sleep but was too restless.

Soon, the rest of the group decided to go to bed, too and the light dimmed

Erica thought about her long busy day and was happy to be back with the rest of the gang. Her encounters with the Aboriginals were scary at first but ended up being an interesting experience. She had learned a lot about herself and the effect one person can have on others. The Aboriginals must have been like Earth's humans were centuries ago but seemed not to be too dissimilar to their current life on Earth. Males were males and females were females and they both had to do what was necessary to survive in the jungle, be it the real jungle or the urban one.

She examined herself to see if there were any bruises but she could not see clearly in the dimmed light. She smiled and wondered if she had passed up an opportunity on that planet. She rolled onto her side and finally fell asleep.

Raj had a restless sleep that night. He could not get Erica out of his mind. He knew that he would have to get up early to take a shower and wash his tunic again.

27.

The aliens had to get the teens up the next morning.

They rose quickly, ate their meals, and cleaned up for another day of adventures on the new planet. They knew they would be at another site and were eager to see more of this strange new land.

When they left the ship, they were disappointed with what they saw. They were on an island by a shore but the land consisted mostly of rocks, grass, and scrub.

Grog and the boys returned to the ship and hauled out two sacks. The lizards pulled out some plastic planks and expandable struts that would form the basis of a floating dock in the ocean. For over an hour, the aliens built the structure while the teens watched. The aliens pulled out and spread out some netting, carried it to the end of the dock, and lowered it into the water. Periodically, they pulled it out to examine the catch keeping much of it but returning most of it to the sea. What they kept, they placed into bottles and plastic bags to store in one of the ship's compartments.

"What're you going to do with all the fish you're collecting?" Raj asked the captain.

"Most, we'll flash freeze and some, we'll preserve by other means. They're for our scientists to study and people to see in our nature museums.

"Why don't you take some time to swim, or wander around the island; we'll be here all day."

"We can do that?"

"Sure, it's a long swim to any shoreline, so I don't think you'll try something stupid like that but do your swimming on the other side of the island, so you don't disturb the fish here."

The teens scurried into the ship to drink water and eat. Once done, they left the ship and gingerly walked to a beautiful sandy beach, while avoiding cutting their feet on the sharp rocks peppering the opposite shoreline.

"Wow, this island isn't very large but it sure has a great beach," Jiao said excitedly.

Within seconds, all of them were in the water. Dan and Roche were swimming farther out, while the other three enjoyed themselves wading closer to the coastline. When they got hungry, they wandered back to the spaceship to eat and drink then returned to the beach. As the sun was getting low in the sky, they decided to take the opposite route around the island to the spaceship and food.

When they arrived, the aliens already had some of the local fish frying over an open fire and had collected some limited fruit available on the island. They feasted royally. The fish was particularly succulent.

The next morning, they had one last time to play on the beach. They took the time to wander around the island and examine some of the small animals and plants.

"This little island is beautiful, except for the rocks. I almost cut my feet several times," Erica said.

"Yeah, and there's so much to see. Everything is a little different from what we see on Earth," Raj said.

"I'd rather be back on earth," Erica responded.

"Being out here reminds me too much about being home. It's nice we're together but I do miss my mom, dad, and little brother." Jiao added.

"I think we all feel the same but we have to try to bear with what we have. I have a feeling that we're going to be away for a very long time," Roche said sadly.

They arrived back near the ship for lunch and found that the lizards had prepared another feast containing the local delicacies.

In the afternoon, they all helped to dismantle the dock. As the aliens completed their work outside the ship, the five of them wandered again over to the beach.

"This is the last time we'll be away from the lizards for a while," Jiao said.

"Looks like it," Dan replied.

"They didn't say anything about landing again on this planet, so maybe you're right," Roche responded.

"Maybe we should hide somewhere on this island and escape from them," Dan suggested.

Raj quickly challenged that idea. "What, and stay on this planet forever! How are we going to get home from here?"

"Who said that we're going to get home from anywhere." Dan countered.

"Even if we did, we're on an island. We can't live the rest of our lives here."

"We can swim. You can see land at one point on the horizon. This is the last chance to escape."

"Maybe you can but I'm not a good swimmer and suspect that there are others in the same predicament. We could build a raft but there's nothing here to build one."

"We could try using grass."

"I want to go home," Jiao moaned. "What are we going to do here? The people are primitive. They have no spaceships."

"There's lots of food if we can get to the mainland. We'd have to start over on our own," Roche said, "The people don't seem to be dangerous. It'd be like Adam and Eve over again."

"Well, I don't want to be Eve," Erica said haughtily.

"Our only option then is to return to the ship and find other opportunities," Dan added.

Except for Roche, there seemed to be general agreement that staying on this planet was a bad idea. The teens took one last look at this peaceful beach then turned and returned to the ship and bed.

28.

They woke up late the next morning and were stiff from head to toe. After weeks of relative inactivity, they walked, ran, and swam heavily during their days on the planet.

Roche went to the counter first and found that the aliens had already been there to provide them with their usual meal of mush and water. He helped himself and said, while eating, "I don't know how the aliens can get up early after the heavy workout we've had over the last few days. This should remind us of the importance of daily exercise."

Jiao stuck her tongue out at him and Roche caught it but said nothing. He finished his meal and Jiao was the next to eat.

Erica said, "It looks as if it's back to the gruel again."

Jiao replied between gulps, "They could've brought in some of the food from the planet and put it in cold storage."

"I saw them bring in bags and bags of grass and other plants in here," Dan said.

"Yeah, I did, too. Notice that they brought in all the leftovers," Roche responded.

"Maybe they're keeping it all for themselves."

"Maybe; but grass? We didn't eat grass."

"Perhaps they're samples for analysis or even used to restock that recycler they talked about."

It was a slow process but eventually, everyone had their fill.

Roche did some exercises and Dan joined him.

"Anyone else going to join?" Roche asked when he noticed the rest of them idle.

"Not after all the exercise we got on the planet," Erica said.

"This'll help your stiffness."

"I'll pass, maybe your second session."

"Well, suit yourself."

The girls stayed in their cell, while Raj stayed in his. He was happy he was returning to normal. He did not have the weird dreams about Erica that he had the previous few nights. He got up and, instead of doing exercises, stretched his muscles.

In the evening, they all participated in Roche's exercises.

A shuddering of the ship awakened them early the next morning.

"What the hell was that?" Erica asked.

"Either we've hit something, or we've landed again," responded Dan.

"Well, I hope we've landed," Roche added.

They got up; everyone to eat, others to wash and shower. After they finished, they sat down and waited.

"If they've landed, they may let us join them," Roche said.

"It's too soon to be another solar system. Either they've landed some other place on the planet, or maybe another planet in the same solar system," Raj said.

"There's another planet that has life on it?" Roche asked.

"It's possible if planets are in the correct zone around the star. In our solar system, we could have had life on three planets. Venus is a little closer to the sun and may have had life if the right atmospheric conditions and planetary rotation were present but it ended up being too hot, with a negligible rotation, and a poisonous dense atmosphere. Mars was also a possibility but it's much smaller than Earth and likely lost most of the water and oxygen it had because its gravity was too weak to hold it. It's a cold barren desert with very little atmosphere."

Within thirty minutes, the door opened and the three aliens entered.

"Good morning," the captain said, "we've landed on a moon of one of the giant planets of the same solar system as the planet we landed on. Surveys of previous journeys here have indicated that there are large quantities of valuable elements on this moon, which is almost as large as your Earth. We want to verify the findings. Because it's so far from its sun, its surface is mostly ice, except around many of its active volcanos. As a side activity, we want to see if any kind of life has developed near some of the warmer areas.

"Because the surface is inhospitable, we'll have to use a surface vehicle to travel. My first officer and I will be staying on the ship as a home base to look after you and do some testing near the ship. As the vehicle can carry only two people about our size, one of you may go with Grog." He paused for a response.

Raj stuck up his hand and offered, "I'll go. I'm probably small enough."

"Good, then let's get going."

Raj got up and left the compartment with the lizards. The door closed.

Raj was excited to get out again but he had another reason. Ever since he had started listening to the garbled language of the aliens, he had tried to make some sense of it. He knew two languages well and was familiar with several other languages, including French, Arabic, and Mandarin. So far, it has proven difficult to equate what the translator was saying in comparison with the background language. This trip would hopefully give him a chance to learn some of the structure of their language.

"Grog, get him all set up and ready to go to site B. You've got to get going soon. We'll explore site A on foot from here."

Grog led Raj to another compartment that contained a vehicle with large tires. The door slid closed behind them. Grog took him to four hooks that held four silver-coloured things that looked like space suits.

"Do we have to get into these things?" Raj asked.

"Yes. We'll have to see how it fits or you might not be able to go. We're not the same shape as you are but the suit is flexible enough that you might be able to manage in it. You're still interested in going?"

"Well, I guess so. Do we need these things?"

"The vehicle is open to the harsh atmosphere out there, so yes. This will keep you warm and provide air to breathe. I'll take this one and you can have the one beside it."

"Why do you have four when there are three of you?"

"One's a spare."

"Oh. That makes sense," Raj responded with embarrassment.

Grog took one suit off the hook and Raj took the adjacent one. He watched Grog as he put on his suit and tried to follow. Grog helped him when he did something wrong.

Within minutes, Raj had dressed but found the suit uncomfortable.

In some places, it was too tight and in others too loose. He found it hard to see properly out of the faceplate, as it was too far from his face and did not follow his head's movements, so he had a very small peripheral view. It encumbered his movements, so he got claustrophobic very quickly. He began to regret he accepted this opportunity.

Grog looked at him and asked if he was okay.

He gulped and said that he was. He hoped that, in time, he would adjust to it. He would fight his claustrophobic fears.

"All right then, let's get into the vehicle," Grog said through the microphone in his suit. He helped Raj get to one side and got to the other side.

It was not too different from an earth tractor. Raj could remember being in one back in India, although that was a long time ago.

Grog pulled a security bar over them and informed the captain that they were ready to leave the ship.

Raj could hear the hissing of the air leaving the compartment.

Soon, the outer hatch opened and Grog drove the tractor down a ramp and onto the moon's surface.

29.

The instrument Grog used to manoeuvre the tractor was very much like a joystick one would use in a videogame.

Before they reached the bottom of the ramp, Raj panicked. Exiting the ship into an open space terrified him. He felt so closed in within his suit. He tried to turn his head to see around him but only saw the side of the helmet. It was as if he was looking down a long tunnel.

Grog could see the suit shaking, so he slowed a bit and cut the tractor-to-ship communications. He said to Raj, "How are you doing?"

He heard nothing in return.

"Raj, talk to me. Do you want me to turn around and go back?"

Raj collected himself enough to respond, "No, I'm okay. I have a little case of claustrophobia and I'm working on it."

"You're sure?"

Raj replied, "Part of it is the suit but I'll get used to it." He clenched his fists and thought of Erica to divert his mind to other thoughts.

"Okay, I'll turn on the communicator again, so poke me if you change your mind and want to return to the ship. The captain doesn't need to know about this."

They travelled for four hours weaving among rocks and over several kilometres of flat clear surface that must have been a huge lava flow. Finally, it was back to a rather rocky and pitted surface until they got to the edge of a huge crater.

During the trip, Grog diverted Raj further by exchanging life histories. Raj's story was relatively short but Grog told him about his life. He was a rather studious person whose major area of study was geology with a minor in palaeontology. He had done most of his studies on his planet and this was his first trip into space. He was going to use a lot of what he learned to write a paper. Between his studies and this trip, he had never married. Marriage was not a big or important occasion to them.

Raj also concentrated on listening to Grog speak but he spoke too quickly to determine his language's construction in comparison to any he knew. As their bodies were different from Earth's people, their larynx, if they had one, would have been significantly different from a human's. All Raj was hearing was a fast-paced monotonic series of snaps and pops created by the alien's teeth or something else inside his mouth.

While conversing, he learned to use the suit, so his claustrophobic feeling was still there but had significantly diminished.

The helmet had one tube close to his mouth, so he could take sips of water when he wanted and another one for food which was the same old mush, he had eaten inside the ship but was thinner in consistency to flow through the tube. When he needed to urinate, he found the suit sucked the liquid up when it contacted the material of the lining of the suit.

"We'll have to go the rest of the way on foot," Grog said as they ground to a halt.

Grog raised the security bar and they got out. He pulled out two sacks from the back of the vehicle and hooked one onto Raj's suit and the other to his suit.

"These are sample bags. You didn't think you were coming here for nothing."

They began a long and winding climb up the side of the crater. At the top, they rested for about fifteen minutes then resumed their trek down the other side into the cauldron. There, they spent several hours collecting samples. Grog was also using a test apparatus that was analysing the surface and perhaps subsurface of the cauldron's floor.

"A large meteor struck here many years ago and exposed some of the core of this moon. You may see some glistening metals along the floor. The yellow stuff you see is gold but there are many other elements in here. Take a little souvenir, if you wish," Grog stated.

Raj bent down and picked up a small chunk of yellow metal.

"There is very little oxygen in the air here, so corrodible metals like silver have not oxidised. That's why they glisten and are quite pure."

Grog added.

"Why are you doing this? Are you planning to mine these metals?" Raj inquired.

"Not for a long time. We identify particularly rich sites for that possibility but there are many places closer to our planet for now. Someday, we may come this far to mine it. We normally don't steal resources from Aboriginals. Maybe in the future, the people on the planet we visited may get into space and these resources will be theirs. Perhaps, if they become extinct and there does not appear to be any further evolution of intelligent life, we may claim this as our own."

Roche was learning that these beings were quite intelligent and considerate – certainly not greedy.

Soon, they finished their job and Grog led him back up and down the side of the crater to the vehicle. They loaded the bags into the cab, got in, and lowered the safety bar. They wound around the rocks strewn about until they reached the lava bed.

Grog stopped, turned off ship-to-tractor communication, and asked, "How would you like to drive?"

Raj's eyes lit up and he said innocently, "But I don't have a driver's license."

Grog smiled and responded. "I won't tell the police and it's a flat straight road ahead. Do you want to try?"

"Yeah, sure, wow." He felt so stupid.

"I'll release my control which will activate yours. All you do is hold the stick steady and lean it forward to accelerate and pull back to slow down. Don't pull back too far, or we'll go backwards. Maybe stay straight for a while until you feel comfortable then turn slightly just to get the feel of it. You can look out the window but look frequently at the monitor in front of you. Aim directly at the marked spot which is the location of the spaceship. The only thing I ask of you is not to tell the officers about this. I'm not sure they'd approve."

Raj looked closely at the controls. "You've got a deal. I play lots of video games which use something like this, so I should be okay." He eased forward on the stick and the tractor began to move. He practised slowing and speeding it up then tried soft turns in both directions. "Does this have brakes?"

Grog sat puzzled for a few seconds, as that word translated badly. "I think I know what you mean. It does not need brakes, the motor acts like a brake."

"Oh, okay. Pull back for brakes."

"I'm curious."

"About what?"

"When I speak, you seem to be focussing not on what the translator is saying but what I'm saying and watching my face and lips carefully."

"Yes, I know a few languages on my planet and was interested in learning yours."

"What do you think so far?"

"Well, I can't figure it out. Our languages use tone a lot but it doesn't sound as if you have tones at all. To me, it sounds like a lot of toneless chatter as if ten people were talking tonelessly at once. As far as I know, we have no language like yours on Earth."

"Which seems logical, as we're not from Earth. You're correct, as far as we know there's no spoken primate language like ours on Earth."

Raj mumbled, "Spoken, primate language. Does that mean there's non-primate talk like that?"

"The only way you might learn our language is by reading it first. Unfortunately, we have no beginner grade school books on board but I have a manual I can give you. It has some labelled diagrams and identifies the technical terms. Once you look at it, if we get opportunities, I'll sound out some of it, so you can learn some more. I doubt you'll ever be able to talk though, as you are not physically able to make the sounds properly; as we'll never be able to speak any of your earth languages . . . You're driving well."

"Thanks, I'm good at video games."

"This isn't a game."

"I know but there are some games where you can drive cars, tanks, and boats that are similar to this."

Raj began to push harder on the stick and the vehicle sped up. He continued to push. The speed had increased to the limit. He could push it no farther. The speedometer was almost at the limit of its scale.

"Yahoo," Raj yelled over the strained whining of the tractor as it sped over the terrain. He tried a few furtive turns and found the vehicle very responsive. It did not take long to cover the last portion of the lava flow. He slowed the pace as he approached the looming rough terrain.

"Have you ever gone that fast with this thing?" Raj asked.

"No, but when I was young, I used to see how fast some other vehicles could go."

"So, your teenagers are like Earth's teenagers?"

Grog laughed a bit and admitted, "Yes, I guess you could say that. I guess adolescents of many species are the same – like a young colt of your horse trying to see how fast it can run or how high it can jump. They're exploring their world and the established limits. It's part of the learning process and the parents hope they go through it quickly before they kill themselves."

Grog smiled and said, "Do you want to continue driving?"

"Sure."

"Don't stretch your limits on this next part."

"I won't. This part is going to be tricky and I don't want to get you in trouble by having an accident."

"This vehicle can be set to autopilot too but I like to do it myself."

"It's way more fun."

"Yeah, it's way more fun," Grog repeated with a grin.

Raj did an excellent job of guiding the vehicle to the spaceship. Grog turned the communicator back on, took over, and drove it into the compartment. The hatch closed behind them. Soon, Raj heard the hissing of air as the compartment filled with air again.

They left the vehicle, got out of their suits, and pulled the full sacks out of it. Raj picked up his souvenir. As they hung the suits back on the wall, the inner door opened and they entered the main section of the ship.

The captain welcomed Grog back and said to Raj, "I guess you must be very tired. That was a very long and full day for you. The rest of your friends have already been sleeping for some time."

Raj walked over to his door. The captain unlocked and opened it. In the dim light, he placed his souvenir on the counter, slid beside Dan, and almost instantly fell asleep.

30.

Weeks went by and, if the teens had not been doing exercises twice a day, they would have gone crazy. Although everybody got along well, there was nothing else to do but talk but there was nothing to talk about anymore. They knew everyone's life stories. They talked about their experience on the last planet until they exhausted that topic. It came to the point where everyone spent much of their time quietly doing nothing.

Raj was the only one to get any respite from his boring times. Grog gave him a manual to study and occasionally got together with him to learn to read their language.

Finally, the day came when the captain entered the compartment again. They knew it was important when he came to see them, so they stood up and he told them they would be landing again.

"We've only had one expedition to this planet, so we don't have a lot of information on it. We know it's more primitive and barbaric than what you've seen so far. The surveyors found its animals were quite fierce, so the most intelligent life on this planet is equally vicious to survive. Last time we picked up samples of some of its plants and smaller animals.

"This time we're going to try to capture a male and female of the most intelligent species. It should be a challenge. Again, you may come with us if you want. If you want to stay alive though, you must stay close to the group. You may not be so lucky if someone strays this time. Don't give me an answer right now. I'll be in to see you again tomorrow morning." He left.

They stood together looking at each other.

"A planet fiercer than the last one!" Erica exclaimed.

"Maybe we should stay inside this time," Jiao said uneasily.

"Don't you want to get out of here? We've been sitting together for weeks bored," Roche replied. "I know I'm sick of being in here. It was nice the last time we went out. As the captain said, we've got to stay together. We're used to being together, so there's no reason to separate. It'll also give us something else to talk about."

Erica and Jiao were interested in going; they were just a little more nervous about what the captain said about the animal life on the planet. The boys looked eager to get out, so the girls looked at each other, shrugged their shoulders and agreed to go.

The next morning, they were up and ready soon after the lights brightened. They waited impatiently for another thirty minutes until the door opened and the aliens entered.

"Are you coming?" the captain asked.

Roche responded, "Yes."

"We noted the problems you had with your feet last time and have developed foot coverings to protect them. The terrain here is much harsher on the soles. You can see we're wearing some ourselves, especially for better footing. The environment is very wet here, so the ground is considerably slippery."

Grog dropped the five pairs of boots he was carrying onto the floor. Two were slightly larger.

The teens picked up the boots and slipped them on their feet. Although the sizes did not exactly fit their feet, they seemed to adjust quickly to fit each foot.

"These are very comfortable," Erica said quietly to Jiao, "They should've given these to us last time."

The minute they stepped out of the ship; Erica realised why the aliens had given them boots. The fog in the air was quite heavy and the ground was very uneven and slippery. If it were not rocks that they were stepping on, it was brambles and sharp undergrowth. They would not have lasted thirty minutes walking barefoot on its surface.

Whereas the other planet had a constant fruity-flowery smell, this one smelled of rot and mould. It was like walking in a garbage dump. Erica turned to go back to the ship but Jiao encouraged her to stay with the group.

They walked for about forty-five minutes then stopped. It looked as if the fog was lifting, so they took a short break until visibility improved further.

The captain said quietly, "There's a village not far ahead of us. It's at the foot of a rocky rise which the villagers use as a shelter and protection from wind. Once we get there, we'll stay hidden behind the rocks to observe them. I'll be staying with you while my crew go somewhere else to set a trap to catch an aboriginal."

Grog and the first officer left with one of the bags.

"Will they get hurt in the trap?" Erica asked.

"You're probably thinking about the traps you use on your planet. No, they won't. When a person or animal gets near one of our traps, they're just stunned. It's as if it paralysed them. There's no pain at all."

"What happens if several animals are trapped?"

"We set it for one. If more than one is in the same location, it turns itself off. They wouldn't know it was a trap. We get a signal on our communicators, so we can move it to another location and reset it. We can also use our communicators to scan our surroundings."

"So, what are we going to do here?"

"The same as before; we want to collect as many small lifeform samples as we can. We intend on staying here for one day then we want to try another location on this planet to study another species of intelligent life."

"You want to capture one of them, too?"

"No, but we want to collect some DNA samples."

The captain knelt on the ground and scanned it for life.

A drizzle began to fall.

The teens stooped to see what kinds of life they could find. When they found something interesting, they called out to the rest of them to look. They were nervous about picking up things as some looked rather fierce, even if they looked small and harmless. Many of the creatures looked like insects but others were like nothing they had ever seen before. They came in all different colours and sizes. Some had four legs and others up to ten. A little digging brought many other creatures, some like worms but others were gross looking with large heads and long skinny bodies.

The first officer arrived back from setting the trap. On the way back, he had caught several odd-looking lifeforms. He showed them to the teens who looked at them with awe.

At noon, everybody but Grog returned to the ship where they had lunch and went to the washroom. Soon, they were back out. Within minutes, Grog sent a signal from his communicator to say that he had caught something in the trap. The captain stopped their progress.

"It'd be nice to get some help to bring it back," the captain said looking at the boys.

"Don't we have to stick together?"

"We can get the girls back on the ship before we go."

"What do you think?" Roche asked the girls.

They shrugged their shoulders and looked at each other.

Erica said, "I'd like to go along but if we're going to be in the way, maybe we could sit this out. You won't be long, will you?"

"The trap is about ninety minutes from here, so you won't be alone for long," the captain answered.

The girls turned and went back into the ship with the first officer. The captain waited until he returned.

"Okay, let's get going boys," he yelled.

They trudged through the brambles and into a forested area. It contained the strangest trees the boys had ever seen. The leaves were gigantic and very smooth looking.

The captain noticed their mouths gaping and said, "The leaves are large enough to gather as much sunlight as they can. Clouds often shroud this planet, so plants must adapt to this environment."

They rounded a bend into a small clearing and there, in front of them, was the trapped aboriginal.

"Ah, a female and a complication," the captain said quietly.

Grog was soon beside them. "Captain, I got her bound but I heard a noise, so I pulled away quickly. The aboriginal may have seen me, though. It's smaller in size, so it's likely a male. He hasn't gone into the clearing to get her," he said quietly.

"Yeah, I can see him through those two trees over there," the captain mumbled. He pointed to a spot almost directly in front of him. "The trap mechanism is turned off, so he may not have seen it. He can also see that she's bound, so if he didn't see you, he knows something isn't right. We've caught her but maybe we can try to capture him. I suspect that he is her mate."

The boys could not see anything near where the captain had pointed. The other two aliens seemed to have spotted him. The boys were starting to realise that the aliens' eyesight was much better than theirs.

"He's gone," the captain said. "Either he has pulled back to hide, or he might have left to get help." He pulled out his communicator and pointed it to the other side of the clearing, then from side to side. "I can't detect him, so let's move quickly and get her into the ship."

They speedily entered the clearing. The aliens picked her up and hoisted her onto Roche's back. For a female, she was tall, over two metres and she must have weighed over one hundred kilograms. Dan put his arm around Roche to help support him.

Grog reset the trap. The boys could see that it strobed a certain frequency of light. He guessed it attracted the Aboriginals who wanted to investigate its source.

"No, Grog, turn it off and bring it with you. The Aboriginals may not be returning alone. I think we're done collecting an Aboriginal at this site," the captain said only loudly enough so Grog could hear him.

Grog did what the captain said.

"I'm glad this wasn't a man," Roche said as he almost ran out of the clearing, following the lead of the captain.

Once they were back in the trees, the captain answered Roche, "Actually, the men here are smaller than the women. The men are smaller to be fast and agile to get through the tight conditions in the forest. The females must compensate for their lack of speed by being strong and powerful. They're also large to lay their eggs. You'll see a different condition when you meet the other intelligent beings in another part of this planet."

"She's not going to like being in the cramped cells you have," Raj noted.

"Yes, and she may be strong enough to cause some damage to the cells. We'll have to monitor the situation. We plan to sedate her somewhat and will have to experiment on the proper dose."

"You're not going to put her in with us, are you?"

"No, we have another compartment to put her in. We were hoping to try to capture a male, too. Let's move as fast as we can back to the ship. Those males can move quickly. I hope he has to get back to the village to get help and he's not part of a nearby hunting party."

Roche was tiring quickly, even with Dan's support. It was awkward to walk the way they were. Finally, he asked Dan to let go and he began to run faster to keep up with the fast-moving aliens. Soon, they were back where the ship should have been but where was it?

The captain suddenly climbed an invisible stairway and disappeared, followed by the first officer. Roche followed and found that he was inside the ship. Once they were all inside, the hatch slid shut.

Roche slid the female onto the floor and fell to his knees, panting heavily. He was sweating profusely.

Grog went to get him some water.

Roche had tried his best to retain his upper body strength with the use of the shower rod but his legs were not what they once were, especially because of the lighter artificial gravity of the ship. He, like the other teens, had lost weight with the light-weight diet they were on.

The captain remarked, "We can't stay here long. They'll likely track her. Our scents may mix in with hers but they'll likely end up here. As you saw, I've turned on the visual damper but once they get here, they'll be able to feel the ship, so we should move to another location. We hadn't planned this but I think we can try this again near another village of the same species." He turned to the teens and told the boys to join the girls in their compartment.

When they entered, Erica asked, "So, how did it go?"

Dan responded, "They caught a female of an intelligent lifeform. We think that someone saw her in the trap, so the captain wants to take us out of there. They're going to land somewhere else and try again. We're glad you didn't come because we had to get out of there quickly. Roche carried her back to the ship. That's why he's so tired."

"What did she look like?"

"Very much like a lizard, only nothing you'd see on earth. They're heavy looking and have a short thick tail that seems to help them stand up. They're black and have extra-large eyes. She's also large, bigger than Roche. Maybe you'll get to see her sometime."

"I'm in no hurry."

They had supper but Roche spared them the exercises, although any of them would have been able to do them on their own.

The boys told the girls about some of the things they had done and seen, showered then everyone went to sleep.

31.

The next morning, they awoke and knew they would be at a different location on that planet. They got up, ate, and the boys got ready to leave.

"Let's go this time," Erica said firmly. "It looks as if it wasn't that dangerous."

"It was bad enough," Roche responded.

"It's boring here. We have nothing to do."

Erica looked at Jiao. "What about you?"

"I guess it would be okay," she responded nervously.

"You sure?"

Jiao nodded her head.

"We're not sissies, you know," Erica said bravely.

The captain and his crew entered. "Let's finish what we wanted to do yesterday, shall we?" When he saw the girls following, he asked, "Are you sure you want to come with us?"

"Sure," Erica responded.

Everyone trooped out of the ship and followed a trail through a forest. They stopped by a stream and the first officer remained with the teens looking for and taking samples of lifeforms in the water while the captain and Grog followed another path and disappeared into the forest to set a trap to catch an aboriginal. About an hour later, the captain returned, while Grog stayed by the trap to watch it.

They were sitting down to lunch when Grog came running into their area by the stream with great alarm on his face.

"I turned off the trap but couldn't retrieve it. The trap's light attracted some large heavy beasts which are now behind me, so you'd better move fast. I haven't had time to call ahead to warn you."

The first officer quickly threw the food in the bag and everyone got up to flee but from the jungle, huge lizards closed in on them. The aliens swiftly drew their weapons and started firing at the closest of the beasts. When that was not effective, they adjusted their guns and shot again. They continued the process as Roche was under attack himself. The closest earth animal that would describe them is a rhinoceros but in reptilian form with a long thick tail.

The boys grabbed the largest branches of the deadfall around them and started hitting the closest beasts in a desperate attempt to drive them off. The girls were inside the circle of men and grabbed branches of their own to strike out when they felt the need.

The aliens' blasters began to affect the beasts but they needed multiple blasts before one would drop. What everyone was trying to do was to avoid the teeth of the beasts' massive gaping mouths and their metre-long tongues that lashed out like whips.

"We can't stay here, there're too many of them and the ship is too far away to escape, so we'll have to find closer shelter," the captain shouted above the din of battle and the roars of the beasts.

He pulled back into the battle circle to survey their surroundings. He held out his communicator and swept it in a circle. "Over there – there's a clump of trees thickly packed together. Once we're there, we can get inside and might be able to get ourselves up into the trees and out of reach of these animals."

He pointed his hand in the intended direction. "Grog and I will concentrate our efforts in that direction to create a path while the rest of you protect our rear as best you can. Everyone, keep tight and move with the front line. We're going to have to climb over the fallen animals to get to those trees."

It was torturous work. The encircled group had littered the area around them with the immobilised beasts. They could see the beasts were not dead and perhaps could revive enough to rejoin the battle if the aliens did not get to shelter quickly.

The frontline of aliens knocked down the animals as everyone slowly moved across the stilled beasts. The following beasts were having trouble keeping up with the moving circle as the huge masses of their downed compatriots were not providing a firm foothold for them. It seemed to take forever as the captain led his team forward but soon, the first officer was often providing additional support against the forward animals.

They shuffled toward their target but everyone was tiring. The walking and slashing or firing actions were taking their toll but, if they gave up, they would surely serve as food for these voracious beasts.

Roche led in the rear-guard action. Because he was the largest morsel of food to these beasts, he had been specifically targeted. They had lunged at him several times and he had lost some blood by their slashes. Erica often had stepped out of the circle to lunge with the long sharp branch she had picked up to strike at the beasts' tongues.

Once the group neared the trees, a natural gap slowly opened between the defenders and the trees.

When they were close to the trees, the captain yelled, "Run!"

Free of walking over downed beasts, the group broke their circle in a mad dash to the crotch of the trees and they edged their way through the opening into the centre. The beasts wailed loudly at the possible loss of a meal and pounded their heads against the trees in a vain attempt to beat their way into the opening and slip their long tongues through to catch a meal in its grasp.

As they huddled together in the centre of the cluster of trees, the captain allowed everyone to catch their breath and regain some of their strength but he was soon mustering his crew to see what they salvaged from the battle. They managed to drag one of the sacks with them but nobody knew where they had dropped the other one. The one they lost contained mostly their food and some of the sample bags. The bag they had, held mostly the equipment, some samples, and water.

The aliens began pulling some material out of the bag and assembling some pieces to build a small platform and pulley structure. Within a few minutes, they were shooting pins high into the trees and establishing the roping for the pulleys. Once done, everyone got onto the platform and raised themselves into the trees.

The captain said with an exhausted breath, "The beasts will soon stop trying to break their way into the trees once they realise that we're too high up for them to get at us. I don't recommend we do anything further until the light of day. You can see the sun setting, so I recommend we get some sleep."

"I see some of the animals you blasted getting up. Weren't at least some of them killed?" Raj asked.

"We first tried to hit them with a stun blast at setting four— as we don't kill living things without good reason – but they're too large and their skin and nervous system are quite different from many other animals. We ended up turning up our weapons to a strong killing blast at level ten that would normally have disrupted their nervous system so badly they should have had heart attacks but we only knocked them out for an hour or so. If they don't hang around here, we should only see ruined trees and matted undergrowth in the morning as the stunned animals wake up and move out.

"Tomorrow, we'll see where we dropped the bag and can collect it and the trap mechanism. Let's not think about that – just rest.

"As you know, we lost our food but we have small water containers we can share with you; particularly you Roche. You took a beating back there. You're quite a fighter." The captain looked at Roche and gave him a stiff reptilian smile then handed him a small canteen.

"Thank you, I can use it. I won't drink too much," Roche replied.

"Unfortunately, there's no food until we find the other bag, or get back to the ship."

"If we could hardly survive against these animals, how can the Aboriginals do it with no fancy weapons?" Raj asked.

"Remember, their village was close to a rock outcropping which not only shelters them from strong winds and rain but attacks from many large beasts such as these. The beasts can't climb things very well, as you can see in our situation. When they attack a village, the villagers could run up the steep slope. If the beasts, or any other animals, tried to follow them, they could throw an effective barrage of rocks down at them. If you looked closely at the rocks near the last village we saw, you would have seen that most of them were bare of vegetation and chipped, indicating that something had often gathered them up and taken them back up the hill."

"Wow, you saw all that in the rocks?"

"You must learn to be observant. We're here for a relatively short time, so we must learn about these people by observing clues about their lives, for example, the cave drawings on the last planet. There're no drawings here but we look for clues about how the aboriginals live and what stage of their development they're in."

Everyone had two gulps of water then, without much fuss, curled up and drifted off to sleep on the crowded platform.

32.

With the rising sun came the gradual awakening of eight very hungry beings. They finished the water while the captain used his binoculars and communicator to scan the area around them. As he had predicted, the beasts were nowhere in sight.

"Okay, it looks safe to descend our little nest," the captain said confidently. "When we're down, Grog, go reset the trap and we'll see if we can catch a male before we leave. I saw our sack on the ground near the forest where we were first attacked."

Erica asked, "You're going to try that again, despite what happened yesterday?"

"We'll take you back to the ship and set the trap ourselves. The beasts are very likely far away from here by now. Today can be a time for you to relax and heal."

They lowered the platform to the crotch of the trees and everyone got off. Grog headed back to the forest, while the first officer left to get the other sack. The rest of them dismantled and repacked the platform and ropes.

The officer returned before the dismantling had finished. They had a break to eat, completed their work, and headed back to the ship.

When the hatch opened, the teens almost stumbled in their effort to get in. Their whole bodies were still suffering the effects of the previous day. They entered their room and behind them was the officer with some fresh food and water. They gobbled up the food and took turns to shower and clean their sweaty and bloody bodies and clothes.

Before they finished, the first officer entered again and put some pills on the counter. "I've left you some pills to help you mend faster. Take one now, then another one each evening and morning until they are gone. Today you'll rest but you may be interested in getting out tomorrow to see another site on this planet. It's a more arid region and there's a different type of intelligent lifeform there; they fly."

When he left and everyone finished washing, they took their pills.

Everyone but Erica went to their cells to lie down and sleep. She entered Roche's cell, knelt beside his prone body, and pulled up the jumper on his back.

"Wow, you bled a lot on your back and there's more on your arms, chest, and neck." She got up and went to the counter for some tissues. As best as she could, she covered his wounds and said softly, "I don't have anything to tie them down but if I press them onto you, maybe that will help your blood clot better. I hope those pills help. I guess these aliens have pills for everything."

She lay down beside him, holding onto the places that had bled the most. She looked at Roche and noticed his eyes staring at her. She raised her head to look at the other cells. She said, "It looks as if everyone's asleep – Raj is even snoring lightly. It'll be good for you to get some sleep, too."

Roche kept staring at her.

"Get some sleep, okay," she repeated. She closed her eyes and tried to go to sleep herself.

Roche's hand slid over and gently stroked her waist and thigh. He slid closer to her and began to kiss her.

Roche had been a hero the way he fought yesterday and had paid the price. He had been the frontman, taking the worst of the attack from the beasts. She was proud of him but this was not the time or place for romance. She said, "Stop," a little louder than she should have but not enough to awaken the rest of the teens.

Roche gave her a look of complete despair. "Damn," he said.

She looked at the frustration on his face and his puppy-dog eyes and wished she could acquiesce but said sadly and softly, "Let's stop while we still can, shall we." She sighed deeply and sat up.

He groaned and whispered, almost angrily, "Not now!"

"I want our love to mean something. We're not ready for this," she whispered.

"This may be our only chance."

"That's not what I mean; when we're ready to be married and

committed to each other – when we're stable and have a home we can call our own."

"We may never have that now. Who knows what tomorrow brings? I love you. We might be dead tomorrow," he said quietly with passion.

She sighed and said, "I love you, too. You can't use the soldier's ruse that they might never make it home. You already got your treat in advance."

She looked again at his sad pleading eyes and sat there for uncounted seconds, now beginning to doubt herself. He was right in a way. Who knew what tomorrow or the next few months would bring but finally she said, "We have to stop. I joined you to soothe your pain, not make out." She got up and stopped at the door for several seconds wondering if she should turn back then continued to her shared cell with Jiao.

She lay down but tossed and turned for many minutes and could not get to sleep.

"You're a little restless," Jiao said quietly.

The sound of Jiao's voice startled Erica. "Oh! You're awake . . . Did I wake you up?"

"No, I'm not used to sleeping in the middle of the day. Even if I feel tired, I can't take a nap."

"You've been awake the whole time?"

"Yes," Jiao said shyly.

". . . and you heard what was said in the next cell?"

"Not much of it."

"I only went there to help stop his bleeding. The next thing I know he was . . . I guess that's what you get when you try to help. Even if he looked half-dead, he had enough energy to think of that."

"They're hard-wired that way, I think."

"Maybe I'm weird but that's not for me, and don't think it's a hang-up or something like that. My parents weren't pressuring me in any direction. They had their preferences and told me what they were. I guess that's who I am. Maybe that's why I like being a Goth; it's a way of expressing myself. I'm modern but old-fashioned, so everybody must accept me the way I am. If Roche doesn't like it, then he can leave and, so far, he's accepted it but that's not going to keep him from trying. I must accept that, too . . . Life is so complicated. Sometimes I wish there was a hole I could hide in."

"I feel that way sometimes. We're halfway between a kid and an adult."

"You've managed Dan so far."

"We don't have clothes to protect us."

"Yeah, that complicates things. You try to be one of an amorphous gang but it's hard to be that when you mix males and females. . . You know, we're all friends and we're good as a group but there are two couples, and a fifth wheel."

"Fifth-wheel?"

"Fifth-wheel – someone who doesn't fit in. If Raj wasn't here, things might have been quite different."

"What do you mean?"

"Well, how do you think we would have sorted out if he wasn't here – would we be girls and boys separate or would we have ended up coupling?"

"I don't know."

"That's what I mean. Coupling would have been more complicated for us. Raj is holding us apart – giving us a good excuse for a set-up like this. The boys accepted it more easily."

"Except Raj has a crush on you."

"Yes, he's had it for many years – maybe as long as when we first met. We got along well and I still like him and want to be his friend. He's a nice guy. I don't know why I didn't go the next step as he did."

"Yeah, life is so complicated. I guess you're an alpha female."

"Don't get going on that alpha-female thing. I don't even know what that is."

"Sorry."

"You know, you look good in long hair." Erica changed the subject abruptly and twirled a few strands of Jiao's hair between her fingers.

"I've never let it grow this long before. I hate it. I can hardly control it. We have no scissors and combs."

"Well, you'll get used to it. Think about what I must go through. My hair was long, to begin with. My hair was to my waist; soon it'll be longer than this stupid jumper I'm wearing. You've seen me spend hours passing strands through my fingers. We can't even cut the ends, and my armpits are ugly."

"The boys are getting to look very shabby, too. They're getting to look a lot like apes."

"We're all quite barbaric, aren't we?"

They stopped talking and took the time to rest until the boys finished their nap.

Nobody felt in any shape to get up and do anything in the little time before the lights went out for the day. They ate a meal, had some water, took their pills, and went to their cells then talked to each other until sleep overcame them.

Grog called the captain on his communicator to say that an aboriginal hunting party had noticed the light on the trap and he had turned it off.

The captain said that he had done the right thing. He told him to retrieve the trap and get back to the ship.

Grog had to wait for some time for the hunting party to pass but immediately after, he collapsed the trap and carried it back to the ship. They had failed in trapping another intelligent being.

33.

The boys woke up first, as they had taken a nap the previous day. They ate, showered, and waited two hours for the girls to get up. The worst of their wounds were healing well. There was no thought of exercises.

They were ready to go on the next adventure well before the doors opened and the captain and crew arrived.

The captain opened the conversation. "We're at a new site today. We're not sure how long we'll be here – perhaps three to four days. We'll be blazing a rough trail through a valley and into mountains. We don't know much about the next intelligent beings, only that they appear to live mainly in mountains, are white, and fly. Our primary aim is to find out as much as we can about them and, if possible, collect a DNA sample. If we could, we were to capture an adult but you're occupying the cells we could have put them in."

Jiao exclaimed, "Oh, they sound like angels!"

"No, more like bats, although they're white; not from feathers but from a type of fur. I imagine they'll be as aggressive as what we've seen so far. It's a tough planet to live on, with all the fierce competitors.

"Because of the dangers involved, we suggest that we leave the females behind to avoid their getting injured."

There was some murmuring among the teens.

"Now, I know you like to keep everyone together," the captain explained, "but we were in a tight situation last time and barely survived, so I'd like to propose an alternative. As you know, we've captured a female aboriginal and couldn't trap a male, so she's alone.

She's depressed and is not eating or drinking. I'd like your woman to stay here to comfort her and try to get her to eat, otherwise, she'll die."

"Why can't you let her go?" Erica asked.

"The same reason we can't let you go and our objective is to collect her."

"What makes you think we can help?"

"You may not succeed but I wish you'd give it a try. We'd like her to live and I think you do, too.

"For safety, we'll lock you in the ship and you'll have access to the food and water supplies. We'll leave you and the captive's compartment doors closed but unlocked, and her cell doors locked to protect you in case she gets aggressive. I've also rigged up our translator, so you can wear it and speak with her. However, we know nothing about her language, so the interpreter will be learning as you go along. We've created some books, so you can show her pictures and build up a vocabulary within the translator. It might prove to be an interesting and rewarding challenge for you. If you can develop a kinship with her as a female, she may start to talk and eat. She won't feel alone.

"With the girls secure in the ship, the boys will know they're safe and we'll feel confident to provide them with weapons to protect themselves. We also want to ensure there's no mutiny, so if the boys try it, they won't be able to get into the ship."

He looked at the girls. "Don't worry about being stranded on the ship. If something happens to us, headquarters will either send a ship to collect it or, less likely, will fly it home remotely. They'll have to try to retrieve our equipment – our people don't want to leave our technology with the natives. Discuss it among yourselves and we'll return in a few minutes to hear your decision."

The aliens left.

"Well, they're giving us a good excuse for not going," Erica stated.

"Yeah, you were nervous about going the last time and we got ourselves into a pickle that almost got us killed," Roche responded.

"Yeah, but I don't know if you'd have made it without us there," Erica commented. "I wish we'd be able to go out to get some fresh air, although, the fresh air outside smells like garbage. I do like looking at the different types of life we find."

Jiao added. "I like getting out too but it'll be useless for us to ask them to let us go outside. The captain would never allow it. I think it might be interesting to get to know the woman they captured. That should keep us busy. It's a lot safer and I didn't think I contributed much to the battle we had. I mostly just huddled in the middle of the circle with a stick in my hand."

"If they give us weapons, at least it'll give us a chance to defend ourselves better," Roche said assuredly.

Erica said, "Okay, I guess that's it. We'll stay comfortable here, while you sleep on the cold wet ground. You go to fight battles and get killed, while we hold down the fort. I now feel like a wife."

"Well, I don't feel like a husband," Roche said briskly.

Erica blushed, while Jiao snickered.

Their door opened. The teens turned to the aliens and Roche said, "I guess we're going with you and the girls will stay here."

Roche and Dan picked up their bags and brought them to the ship's hatch.

The captain took the girls around the ship explaining how the food and water systems worked – there was another special formulation of mush for the aboriginal. Their voices would open their door as well as the aboriginal's. He showed them a small pile of picture books they could use to help communicate with the captive and how to work the communicator; both to call if anything happened on the ship and to take a call if there were any problems with the exploration crew. He handed them a translator and showed them how that worked. He demonstrated how to use the monitor to observe her in her cell.

"Well, I guess everyone's ready. Does anyone have any questions?" the captain asked.

There was no response.

"Okay, let's go," the captain said as the hatch opened.

The boys hugged each of the girls, turned, picked up their bags, and followed the aliens out of the hatch. It slid shut.

"So, I guess that does it. We're alone for a few days – some time for us and some time to see what we can do with our new friend to get her accustomed to her new surroundings. If I had my way, I'd just let her go but she's locked in her cage and we're locked in the ship," Erica said. "I hope we did the right thing by staying here."

"To tell you the truth, I'd rather be here," Jiao said unapologetically.

"Yes, but I think we helped the guys survive in the fight with those huge dinosaur beasts."

"Maybe you did. I was terrified the whole time. You were doing your alpha stuff. I'm not even a beta, more like omega."

"Don't put yourself down. You've got more spunk than you think."

"Yeah, like I was good at hiding behind you and Roche."

Erica smiled and did not respond. "Well, we were left with a job to do. Maybe we should get at it."

"If she's as big as they say she is, I wouldn't want to mess with her."

"She's locked in her cage, poor woman. She must be terrified and angry. She's all alone. I guess I can sympathise with that, after all, at least we have each other to help us cope."

"Weren't the aliens concerned that she might be able to damage, or break out of her cage?"

"To be safe, let's see what she's doing in her cell."

"Good idea."

Erica walked over to the console in the middle of the control room and turned it on. She clicked on the camera they wanted and looked at the monitor. "It looks as if she's sitting in her cell doing nothing and nothing is damaged."

"Has she eaten anything?"

"I can't tell. Should we go in and check?"

"How about you go in first? When I get brave enough, maybe I'll follow you later."

"That's not very supportive," Erica said disappointedly. She went to the door and said, "Open." It opened. She took two steps inside.

The woman was sitting on the floor in the centre of the cell with her eyes focused on the door. She peered at Erica and did not move.

Erica moved forward and looked at the food and water bowls. The woman had not touched them. She looked at the woman and thought she was one of the blackest animals she had ever seen. There were black dogs, cats, panthers, and even humans but they all had some shine to them. This woman was jet black – flat black and was well camouflaged for life in the jungle.

The woman and Erica stared at each other for several minutes.

Erica finally ventured. "Do you want to eat your food?"

The woman got up, held the cage door, and glared at her. She yelled out unintelligibly and grabbed the netting around her cell.

Erica noticed the aliens had opened the partitions of the adjacent cells, giving her one oversized cell. She also realised she had not brought the translator with her. She turned and left to get it.

"Boy, is she angry," she said to Jiao when she entered the control room. She fastened the translator onto her, turned it on, and returned to the woman's cell. It was not translating the gibberish spewing from the captured woman. Erica was going to have to find a way to bridge the communication gap between them. She had to find some common ground.

She went to the woman's food container and looked at it. It was the normal alien fare – mush. Would this woman know this was food? Even Erica had not liked the pudding that served as their first experience of the food on the ship. If the captive was not eating, she would know that the other container was water and it looked as though it also was untouched.

The captive wailed and whined for several more minutes and then silently turned around and sat focussing on the wall behind her.

Erica was at a loss for what to do. She had hoped the translator would have given her at least a word or two but she guessed that there were no terms of reference. For now, the translator was just storing sounds without meanings.

She left the compartment and left the door open.

"What do you think I should do?" she asked Jiao.

"I don't know. She might be yelling swear words as far as we know."

"Why don't you come over here and help me?"

"Maybe she'll be intimidated by both of us. You know, she's huge but she doesn't look very old to me."

"How do you know?"

"I don't. I'm guessing from how she looks and acts."

"Maybe she keeps her age well."

"Let me go in and I'll try to communicate with her."

"Be my guest," Erica said as she bowed and waved her hand to the open door.

Jiao was not sure what she had gotten herself into but she entered, walked up to the cage, pointed to herself, and said, "Jiao."

The woman turned her head to the new voice and Jiao repeated her action. The woman yelled again for a few seconds and resumed her previous position.

Jiao left the compartment. "I think we'll have to find some common ground, so I think we should stay in her room for now and go about our day. Maybe we can do our exercises and later talk for a while. I can't think of anything else to do. Maybe if she gets to know that we're not her enemies, things will go smoother."

They re-entered the compartment and did their morning exercises. They brought in their food and water and had a meal. The woman had turned herself forty-five degrees and was now half watching them.

"I wonder what the boys are doing," Erica said for something to talk about.

"I hope they're going to have a better time than we've had so far on this planet. I'm glad we're in here this time. If I had known a herd of wild beasts was going to attack us, I would have stayed in the ship for sure."

"Let's get one of those picture books and see if we can get this woman to talk."

They went out to the central area and picked up one of the books. They looked through it.

"I don't think this is going to work well, many of the pictures in this book can't relate to her world. They're from the lizards' world," Erica commented.

"I think some of them will if we keep things general. We can try to find words like 'animal' but not 'kangaroo' for example."

They returned to the woman's compartment and tried again to introduce themselves but the woman kept rebuffing their advances and shouting gibberish. Finally, they gave up and milled around the compartment until it was lunch time and they brought in fresh food and water to drink. They ate as the woman watched them.

Erica held out the food and the woman approached but, after a few sniffs of it, the woman went back to the centre of the cell brooding.

"She must be very hungry by now," Erica said. "I wonder if she can't relate to this as food. I wish we could open the ship's hatch and smear some of their dirt on it. I guess if it doesn't smell like garbage, she won't eat it. That might be why she's also not drinking the water."

"Maybe if she sees us eat it enough, she'll catch on. It might also be that she's on a hunger strike. She's frightened and this might be a natural reaction in cases like this."

"Maybe if we eat a bit of her special formulation it'll help."

They ate some of the captive's food, drank her water, and backed off.

After an hour or so of watching her watch them, Erica said, "She probably doesn't understand who we are. She's probably never seen mammals before and she's never seen lizards quite like the aliens, so this is very strange and frightening for her. She's also never seen clothes before. Maybe one step would be for us to take off our clothes."

"What! In front of her!" Jiao exclaimed in surprise.

"Look, she's not communicating, eating, or drinking. We've got to try something," Erica said in earnest. "Maybe she'll figure out we're females like her – someone she can relate to and open up to. When we get further along, maybe we can also let her know that we're not her enemy and we're captives, too and nobody's going to hurt her. She must realise we're completely different from the aliens."

Erica raised her jumper, pulled it over her head, and tossed it on the floor. Jiao reluctantly followed suit.

"Okay, now what do we do?" Jiao asked.

"Nothing for now, let's give her some time."

Nothing happened for the rest of the afternoon. They had supper and did their exercises again. Jiao tidied up the compartment by picking up the jumpers and neatly spreading them out on the door of the single cell.

The woman said something quietly.

Erica quickly noticed it and gave the woman a puzzled look.

The woman repeated the sound.

Erica checked the translator to confirm if the two sounds were identical and told the translator to define the sound as possibly "woman", "girl" or "female".

Jiao asked, "Why do you say that?"

"I don't know but I have a hunch she realises we're women, even considering our hairy bodies. If it's not true then we haven't lost anything. I thought I'd start with that."

When the light dimmed, they lay on the floor and went to sleep.

34.

The sky was cloudy and a light chilly breeze was blowing as the males stepped onto the ground at the bottom of the steps of the spaceship which had landed on a tiny flat almost bare area of rock in a beautiful lush valley amidst two ranges of mountains.

Immediately, the boys noticed the trees were slightly different from the ones they had previously seen in the forest; their leaves were smaller and less intense green. They looked back at where they left the ship but saw nothing.

"It was difficult to find a good spot to land," the captain said, three steps from the threshold of the ship. "I wanted to find a location that was still rather temperate and where the other beings we wanted to study were at altitudes that wouldn't be too formidable for us. We're not very good climbers but soon we'll have to climb.

The aboriginals of interest dwell on the ledges of mountains. You'll see they have adapted well to their surroundings. They're warm-blooded and have a curly form of hair to keep them warm at higher elevations. Their wings are formed from skin stretching over a bone skeleton."

"The ship is locked and invisible, so let's get going," he said as he started walking through the brush near the ship toward one of the peaks. All six of them were wearing their boots. As usual, Dan and Roche were carrying their sacks.

After an hour, they could hear the light bubbling of a fast-running stream and trudged along it for some length of time, stopping at times to examine the surrounding flora and fauna, and take samples. They cut sharply up the edge of a slope and walked along a slight gradient formed by a fault in the rock. They followed this through the morning until the ledge flattened and broadened out. Here, the group stopped for some water and lunch.

It began to rain lightly as they packed up and continued along this path to another ledge that started taking them up again. The scrub was beginning to thin out. After about an hour, the gradient increased. The captain stopped for a few minutes, so everyone could have some water and take a break. He held out his communicator to determine their trail from there.

They were soon walking again. Sometimes, the path levelled out but mostly there were long periods of steep climbs. The path was narrowing, so the captain stopped them again to survey the trail ahead.

"It'll be narrow like this for only a short period, then we'll shift our route somewhat to hook up to a better trail, although it means descending the mountain for a while," the captain said.

They continued their route, following a short downward path then another steeply rising one. By the time it was supper, they were on a small ledge on the side of the mountain. They ate and drank again.

The view was breathtaking as none of the boys had been in the mountains before. They looked back and could see some of the paths they had followed and across to another range of mountains.

They walked for about an hour more and rounded the mountain. In front of them, they could see off in the distance some white creatures flying in the sky.

"Wow, is that them?" asked Raj.

The captain pulled out his binoculars and passed it to the boys. The aliens passed around the first officer's set. The boys were focussing on nests that clung to some of the mountains across from them. They could see how the creatures differed from the first aboriginals they had seen.

"On earth, birds' wings developed from their front feet. From what we see, these flying animals have arms and feet with wings above them," Raj stated with some interest. "I've never seen anything like this."

"Yes, that's right. You won't see anything like them on earth. As you saw, many animals here have a wide variety of numbers and types of feet. The intelligent being we captured has four appendages. The beasts we had to fight had six. These bird-like beings likely descended from a six-footed animal, like the beasts, and evolved their upper appendages into wings and their middle ones into arms. That makes them walk upright and they can handle things with fingers. Your birds are very limited in their capabilities compared to these creatures. Collecting genetic material will help us get a better idea of the genealogy of the animals here. We'll be able to determine who their ancestors were.

"You'll also notice that there are different sizes of fliers. The large ones are adult males; the smaller ones are juveniles or females. With these flying beings, the males, particularly when the females are nesting, must hunt and carry food home for their young, so they're larger to do this well. They're relatively safe in their nests because almost all the other animals are land-based and can't climb at all, or not very well. This means the female fliers do not have to be large. Being smaller also makes it less likely they'll crush their eggs.

"Their potential enemies would be the pterodactyl-like animals which are cold-blooded and live in the jungles to nest in lower-lying hills, swamps, or trees. They rarely travel higher into the mountains except in the heat of summer.

"You can see how well these flyers adapted to their environment. The pterodactyls are dark coloured, mostly black, to blend into the jungles, while these fliers are white to grey to blend into the snow and mountains."

The aliens spent much of their time taking pictures and movie clips of the fliers in their nests and flight. As the sun lowered in the sky, the rain petered out. They stopped their activities, unpacked their equipment, and pulled out three tents from one of the sacks.

"These were made for the three of us and storing equipment but they should fit us all if you don't mind extremely cramped quarters," the captain said. "It'll cool down quickly once the sun drops, so let's get these set up quickly."

The captain and first officer set up their tent and the smaller equipment tent, while Grog helped the boys to set up their tent. The aliens opened one of the bags and pulled out a short pole with a shiny globe on top of it. Near the top of the pole beneath the ball was a small keypad panel. They expanded the pole to a length of one metre. At the end of the pole opposite the ball, they opened a tripod base about a metre across. When done, they put the two sacks into the equipment tent. Grog pressed two large buttons on the panel. Nothing seemed to happen, except for the sound of a light hum.

"You're probably wondering why we don't use the small tent for people," the captain explained. "It's for our important equipment. We can't have it stolen or damaged. The area around our tents has a combination of forcefield and invisibility field. If anyone looks this way, they won't see us and it'll protect anyone or anything inside the field from an attack, so you can sleep in safety."

"Nothing has changed, we can still see outside," Raj noted.

"We can see out but animals cannot see in," the captain confirmed.

"Oh, something like a see-through mirror."

"That'd be a good analogy."

"Here are two large blankets you can use to keep you warm," Grog said, as he pulled the blankets from the small bundle he had and gave them to the boys.

Dan opened one of them. It was not like any blanket he had seen before. It was shiny, like aluminium foil but had the consistency of cloth. It was very thin and he wondered if it would keep them warm.

"Get a good night's sleep. We'll have another long day tomorrow," the captain said.

The boys crowded into their tent.

Roche said, annoyed, "How the hell are we going to fit into this thing."

They squeezed into it as best they could. The tent seemed to be able to take the stress on its sides.

"It doesn't have a fly, so if it rains tonight the tent is going to leak."

"I'm not going to complain about the tightness of our quarters in the ship after experiencing this," Dan said.

"I wonder what the girls are doing," Raj said quietly amongst all the rustling in the tent. They finally adjusted themselves to fit the space available.

"At least the girls have room there," Roche whispered indignantly.

". . . and the ship will be warm," Dan added. "These blankets are so thin I don't think they'll be much use to us."

Raj commented. "NASA uses blankets something like this and they work quite well. These look more comfortable than they use."

"I wonder how the girls are doing without us," Dan mused aloud.

"Probably having tea with the new lady," Roche said.

"Yeah, sure. Do you think they miss us?" Dan asked.

"I think it's going to be a pleasant break for them. They're not having tea but I'd guess they're comfortable and relaxed," Raj stated.

"They won't think of us?"

"I don't think so. They've been stuck with us for months. They could use a break. I often wish I could be by myself – not because I don't like anyone," Raj added apologetically. "I used to spend lots of time by myself. I could read books, play on the computer, or just think. Now, we're together all the time, every minute of every day. We could have the opportunity to be together; just us, to do guy things. There's a different dynamic with girls around; don't you think?"

"Well, we're doing guy stuff, now," Roche responded.

"Yeah, but the aliens are with us. That's like having parents around," Dan said.

"I guess the girls are in the same state. They have that lady there, so they're not alone."

"I'm glad we have the girls with us, although they may not feel the same way," Raj added.

"Yeah, we've become our own family," Dan said. "I'm glad we get along so well."

"Well, fighting isn't going to get us anywhere. It's a forced situation. We must stick together to survive here. It looks as if we won't get any chance to escape the way they set things up," Roche said.

"Yeah," Dan replied, "they thought of everything; the locked ship and the girls away from us. They can give us weapons when we need them but we can't use them against the aliens. We'd need at least one of them to run the ship but anyone we captured would just refuse to open it. I think we're stuck with them to their planet then we're trapped there forever."

"Trapped there forever," Raj said under his breath, "not if I can help it."

There was silence after that. It had been a long day in the mountains and they were tired, so sleep came quickly.

Raj found himself walking down the path toward the ship. He was thinking about how he was going to escape. He had to get Erica, though. If he found Erica, everything would be okay. Where was she? Would he be able to find the ship? If he couldn't see it, how would he find it?

He kept walking. The path was getting narrower; soon it was so constricted that he had to use handholds in the rock to be able to advance along the path. He realised he was in bare feet. Why had he come out here without his boots? He realised though, that he could not cross this with his boots as he was using his big toes to grip the small path he was following.

He was beginning to sweat. Was he going to make it? Was he following the same path? Was he going to find Erica? He had to find her though. He had to escape with her while he had the chance.

The path widened again and he began to run. He stopped, out of breath for a few seconds but turned around and froze. One of the six-legged beasts they had encountered the day before was before him.

He remained in his spot – afraid to move. He began to back away from it. For several steps, the beast stood like stone. It didn't blink. He was going to get away. Maybe it hadn't seen him. He backed away slowly but the beast was moving toward him; at first very slowly, unperceptively then faster. He could not run backwards fast enough, so he turned around and stumbled but he caught himself and soon was running as fast as he could.

He ran and sometimes his feet slipped. He could feel the hot breath of the beast on his back. The beast's tongue was lashing it. He was running on smooth grass. It was a sprint for his life.

Suddenly, he found the ship. He began pounding on the side of it. His knuckles were turning raw. "Erica," he cried over and over. "Let me in, Erica. Let me in. Can you hear me, Erica? Let me in."

His eyes opened and he fought to sit up but he could not because Roche was partly on top of him. It was pitch black. He could hear someone lightly snoring somewhere near him. His head started to clear, as he realised that he was still in the tent with the other boys. He lay there for a few seconds as reality slowly took hold. He tried to find a comfortable spot in the mangle of the other two bodies.

He thought of Erica. He tried to forget her, though. Why could he not forget her? She was Roche's girl. It was so hard to forget someone you were with every day. The only other girl that was there was Jiao and the aliens had taken her, too. He had no girl of his own. Erica was so close and yet so far . . .

35.

Erica had a restless night and woke up several times. She was awake when the lights brightened. She looked around the compartment and stared at the ceiling dully, trying to adjust to her reality. She could not remember the dream she had but it must have been of her family, maybe of her sister – yes, her sister at the mall, shopping but it seemed such a jumble. Was she still dreaming but with a new dream?

Jiao woke up slowly and peered at Erica. She was lying so stiffly and looked a little paler, much like a ghost. Jiao turned, raised her upper body onto her elbow, and regarded her more closely but Erica did not flinch. "What's the matter?" Jiao finally asked.

The sound of Jiao's voice startled Erica and her body twitched. Her head turned to the sound and her eyes stared at Jiao for many seconds as if she did not recognise her. Erica's mouth finally formed the words, "Um . . . I guess I had a dream, or you're one."

"I'm a dream?" Jiao giggled, trying to go along with the flow.

"Maybe, I was at the mall with my sister. All they sold were brown tunics and I wanted a yellow dress."

"You wanted a yellow dress?" Jiao confirmed in surprise. "It must have been quite some dream you had. You wouldn't want a yellow dress in real life."

"I had a yellow dress once and was quite pretty in it."

"That was a long time ago."

"It seemed real. Perhaps you're the dream . . . or nightmare." Erica looked around her and saw the woman in her cell staring at them.

"What makes you think I am?"

Erica, still in a daze, gawked at her. "You mean you're real? This isn't a dream or a nightmare?" She wanted to wake up, even if she had seen the woman in the cell as evidence of reality.

Jiao reached over and touched her.

Reality started flooding into Erica's brain. "What if we were in a nightmare – only this one doesn't end," Erica spoke in a robotic voice. "Can you imagine we're in an alien spaceship inside a compartment with another alien? It doesn't make sense. Aliens aren't supposed to exist." Erica pinched herself. "I've heard that the proof that you aren't in a dream is to pinch yourself and if it hurts, it's not a dream."

"Did it hurt?" Jiao asked.

"Yes, so I guess this is real. Have you ever thought about existence? Like . . . are we real and I'm only making you up in my mind – as if you're a figment of my imagination?"

"Maybe you're in my imagination," Jiao responded.

"I don't know."

Jiao lay on her back with her hands under her head, her eyes staring at the ceiling. "Sometimes dreams can seem very real. I had a dream when my parents moved to Germany. I've never been to that country, so I don't know why my brain picked that location. The building we lived in was multi-storied, maybe a hotel or apartment building. Behind it was a girls' residential school. I walked into the school one day, wandered around it, and later went back to where we were staying. Later, I went back to the school carrying my brother but, this time, some of the girls were not wearing clothes, so I had to cover my brother's eyes so he wouldn't see them. I went out the front door of the school and started roaming through the city. It was beautiful, with all kinds of interesting buildings.

"I strode down main streets and alleys, through shops, and restaurants but I had no money to buy anything. I carried my brother the whole time which should have exhausted me but it didn't. It was as if he was stuck to me. I began to realise that I had lost my way. I looked all around me and couldn't see anything that looked like my building; in fact, I had passed from a slummy area into a residential one. I began to ask people where my building was but I didn't know the name of it.

"Near the end of the dream, I heard the distant voice of my mother in the background, so I called out to her to help me but nothing happened. I was beginning to panic. I thought I was going insane. I opened my eyes to the real world in my bedroom, puzzled and disoriented. I wasn't sure my bedroom was real. I still thought I was crazy for many seconds until I finally got up from my bed. My mother had called me to breakfast; that was the voice I heard in my dream.

"The dream was very real to me. It was as if I were truly there, so I can relate to what you're saying. That's the only dream I can still so vividly remember. I know that we have dreams every night but that one shook me up somehow."

Erica filled in the pause. "Kind of makes you think, eh? So, the big question is: are we real? Am I only a thought in someone else's mind, or maybe God's mind? Do we create our reality, or does someone else create one, like in a reality TV show? In a way, it's like that because the aliens regularly watch us – like a big brother.

"Maybe we're only a character in a novel that someone is writing and, right now, what I'm saying is in quotation marks. UFOs are not supposed to be real. As young children, our parents told us about Santa Claus, the Easter Bunny, and the Tooth Fairy and we found out they weren't real. Aliens are supposed to be imaginary like that. I can pinch myself and feel the pain, so this must be real, even though I don't want it to be. I want to hear my mother's voice to wake me up. I want to wear a yellow dress – anything to make this dream go away."

Erica was now talking quite loudly and frantically. "It does seem unreal, doesn't it? I've tried to block out this new life from time to time. I love my family and want them so badly. I wish I could go back there but this dream goes on and on."

"You know, I sometimes can't picture my family in my mind anymore." Jiao interrupted. "I think these experiences are beginning to block them out. It's as if they died. Remember when we talked about them earlier, when they were fresh in our minds? We've gone through a mourning process and, at least for me, it's as if they're dead – or at least, I'll never see them again.

"When people die, we adapt to the fact they're gone and get back to our lives but we never forget them. My parents mean a lot to me. They raised me. They're the reason I'm here. Whenever I was depressed or needed some advice, they were there for me. They provided a link to my past and my ancestry. When we moved to Canada, they kept me grounded to who I am, as Chinese."

"Is that important?"

"To me it is. It doesn't mean we haven't also embraced Western customs but my parents are Chinese. We've adopted Christianity for instance but we haven't given up the ancient philosophies of China; we find that they complement each other."

"All I can say is, I'm European. I'm a mutt. I think my ancestry is a blend of every group in the British Isles, French, Dutch, and some Polish. With all the wars over the centuries, parts of my family are everywhere."

"China is like that, too. Many people can call themselves Chinese, from Tibet to Mongolia but I'm Han and, as far as I know, that's it. China has fifty-two groups of people, with more than ninety per cent of them Chinese who call themselves Han. They took their name at the time of the Han dynasty, even though they, at one time, lived in many little kingdoms. I'm a real Han — that's where my family name comes from. In China, we use our surnames first, so I'd be Han Jiao, which I think, sounds a lot better than Jiao Han."

"It does sound sweet . . . Your mom is not that keen on your going out with Dan, right?"

"My mom is modern in many ways but not in everything. Remember, we've been Han since before China was a dream, although, now that we've left China, she's a little more open, so she's willing to accept some change, like marrying another Chinese citizen."

"So, not so modern."

"Well, it's tough to change in many ways. In Chinese culture, for many centuries, parents arranged marriages. Also, in my country, love isn't a big factor in the choice of marriage. Being compatible is a stronger desire.

"My father's parents arranged his marriage, much like many generations before him and my parents get along well. I never heard anything about love from them. They never said it. I'd say it was more about accepting one another and mostly respecting each other.

"I never heard them argue but one day I asked my father if they ever fought. He paused for a while, as he always did, before he talked then said quietly that they had had their differences but they'd talk things out. If someone felt strongly about something and it was not that important the person with the stronger feelings got their way. If there was any doubt, and if it were something important, and they couldn't resolve it, my mother accepted his decision. They're both very traditional in that way but they realise here in Canada that they'll have to let me choose my mate. This has been very difficult for my mother.

"About a year ago, I asked my father about my going out with Dan. I knew my mother's preference but I wanted his opinion. He thought for a while and said that Dan was a fine young man. Then, he added that the old ways were gone . . . and he asked me, 'Do you love him?' I didn't answer him, as he didn't expect an answer but I got his message. My father is traditional but he's realistic and modern in some ways.

"I realised that he had said 'love', so I was puzzled about his sense of the word. A few days later, I asked him if he and Mom loved each other. He paused a long time, and asked me 'What is love?'"

Jiao paused then said, "I really couldn't answer his question. How do you describe an emotion? He continued. 'One might say it's an intense pleasurable sensation when you are around another person. It could be a physical sensation with another person. It could be anything. You're right in not providing an answer because it's only four letters but it's a big word. You'd get all kinds of meanings for it and still not describe it. It's a very personal word. Today, 'love' is in confusion – too much TV. A good relationship is a commitment and is forged through hard work and difficulties together in partnership. There's no hardship anymore in the developed world other than what people make themselves. Almost everyone has life easy. Love is giving but the modern world is focussed on taking.' Then he added. 'Two unconditional givers can endure forever but two takers, or a giver and taker are doomed to strife'. So, I never really got a clear answer from him but I know my father and mother love each other deeply by however one measures it."

In Jiao's pause, Erica said, "I never really thought about it but your parents are nice. My parents say 'love' a lot but I've heard them argue from time to time. It doesn't last long and they get over it. Sometimes people will argue over the smallest things. I guess having different opinions and voicing them are just the way it is. Roche and I argue sometimes. I even argued with my parents and sister; although my sister and mom got along very well together. I wonder if it isn't a second-child thing."

Erica paused in thought then added. "I wanted to be different from my sister . . . I wonder if things would have been different if I had been the older sister instead . . . although I can't see my sister as a Goth."

"Strange, eh?" Jiao giggled.

"Yeah . . . really. A lot of factors make up who you are, I guess.

You're the oldest and you're so sweet and kind, and quiet. You get along well with your brother."

Jiao blushed.

Erica continued. "That must come from your parents. They're quiet, too."

They sat silently for several minutes.

Erica sliced through the silence. "It sure is nice not having the boys with us for a while. We'd never get to talk like this, just girl to girl."

"It's a nice change."

"Sometimes, I can't figure boys out."

Jiao filled in the silence of Erica's thoughts. "One day, I asked my father what it felt like to be a man. I felt a little embarrassed after I said it. I thought that maybe it was a dumb question but even though he might have been embarrassed, he didn't flinch at it. He did his usual pause thing and asked, 'What does it feel like to be a woman?' He often tossed my questions back at me but never expected an answer in return. It was his way of making me think. He told me that thinking was a 'mirror to our soul', whatever that meant but then he said, 'Little Flower', that's what he called me, 'you may never find the answer to that question but you must never stop asking it.'"

There was silence then Erica began to cry and sobbed, "He called you 'Little Flower'. Is that what your name means?"

"No, that's what he called me sometimes. Jiao means 'beautiful'," Jiao said, as she started to cry herself.

"Beautiful, little flower," Erica choked out through her tears.

Jiao put her arms around her and they cried together.

It was quite some time before they collected themselves.

"I guess I needed that," Erica finally said.

"Me, too," Jiao responded.

"I miss my family. Sometimes I wish I'd never been so hard on them. I can't remember if I said goodbye that last school day morning. I never said goodbye and I'll never see them again."

"You shouldn't say that."

"It's true. I feel that I'll never see them again. It's as if they're dead. I guess we should treat each day as if it were our last. You never know when something will happen and you never said goodbye."

"My father said that we have to survive no matter what happens to us. He emphasised that. Living is important. To one of my numerous questions, he once told me, 'You must never stop learning. You may one day need to use everything you've learned to survive. If you've learned nothing, you'll not survive.' And another time he said, 'Life is a gift – a chance for you to make a mark upon this earth. It's not for you to waste or throw away. You only get to do it once. Life is a one-way street – you can't go back in time and redo it, so live it fully. Every decision you make, everything you do or say, is important. If you give consideration, kindness, and love, you'll get it back. If you give anger, criticism, and hate, it'll reflect on you.' I guess that would apply to us even now, even if we aren't on the earth anymore."

"I love your father," Erica sighed.

"Anyway," Jiao said, "let's not waste time."

"Yeah, I guess we'd better get up."

They said hello to the Aboriginal woman, grabbed all the food containers, and strolled out of the compartment. The door closed behind them. They refilled them with fresh food and water.

Erica sauntered over to the door and said, "Shit."

The door opened.

"Why did you say that?" Jiao enquired.

"Why not?"

"To open a door?"

"I was testing to see if the mechanism was responding to words or my voice. I guess we found out that we can say anything to get in."

Jiao shook her head, rolled her eyes, and shrugged her shoulders.

Erica said, "It didn't look as if she ate any food. Can you talk to her?"

Jiao went close to the cell and looked at the woman. She pointed to herself and said, "Jiao."

The woman looked puzzled and continued to squat on the floor staring at her.

Erica looked over at their clothes still hanging on the bar of the other cell by the door. "We should probably bring our clothes into our compartment." She looked at Jiao. "She still hasn't said anything yet."

"Yeah, she doesn't understand what we're trying to tell her."

"We've got to keep trying."

Jiao pointed to herself again and said, "Jiao." She then pointed to Erica and said, "Erica." She repeated the same thing two more times.

"She doesn't understand, I guess," Erica said.

They stood for several minutes looking at the woman. They noticed she had deposited her waste in one corner of her cell.

Suddenly, Erica pointed to herself and Jiao quickly said, "Woman". The translator repeated the woman's words she had said the previous day.

The woman's eyes opened wider in surprise and repeated the sound. The translator responded, "Woman".

"Our first common word," said Erica excitedly. She then pointed to Jiao and said, "Jiao", and again, "Jiao".

The woman slowly raised her right arm, pointed to Jiao, and mouthed, "Eeow."

Erica said, "That's close enough" then pointed to herself and said "Erica" then repeated it one more time.

The woman moved her arm to point to Erica and said, "Eeta". She stood, thumped on her chest, and said, "Aaootaa".

"Hello, Aaootaa," Erica said happily, "Glad to know you."

"She won't understand anything you said."

"I know but I hope this is an opening. She can see we're happy."

"I hope so."

Erica informed the translator to establish the sounds Aaootaa had made into their proper names. When done, she said, "We should get her to eat, take a shower, exercise, and flush her waste into the drain. The best way to do that is by example, so let's live in here for the rest of the day. Let's hope she catches on. Make sure she can see everything we do."

"Okay."

The girls puttered around the compartment. They brought in some picture books from the main area and spent a lot of their time looking through them to determine what they could use from them. They did their exercises, took a shower, ate, drank, and used the washroom.

"I guess we can leave now, as there won't be too much time before the lights dim," Erica said near the end of the day. They left the woman's compartment, closed the door, and returned to their cell.

They sat in their cell. Erica looked at Jiao's hair and slid behind her. She ran her fingers through it then tried to pull out the strands and smooth them out. After a few minutes, she said, "Well, I got most of the tangles out but it isn't as good as a comb would have done."

Jiao switched places and began the same process with Erica's hair. "Yours is bad, you know. It's very hard to do when it's left uncombed for such a long time, plus it's so long."

After a few minutes, she stopped. "That's about the best I can do for now. Maybe I can do more tomorrow. Sorry, I couldn't do better."

Erica turned her head and looked at Jiao, with tired eyes.

Jiao stared back for several seconds then turned away.

Erica said, "Thanks for trying anyway. It feels nice to have someone do your hair."

"I wonder what Aaootaa was thinking while we were talking this morning."

"Yeah, especially when we were crying."

"She wouldn't have known what we were saying. She was asleep when we started but awake when we ended, so she didn't see when we started."

"She must have seen us hugging, so she knows we're friends."

"Yeah, hopefully, she can be our friend, too."

The lights dimmed and Jiao lay down and curled up ready for sleep. Erica slid down and joined her.

36.

The boys had a terrible, almost sleepless night. They had started sleeping humorously tightly together in the same direction but that degenerated into a chaotic mangle of bodies often sleeping on top and crossways to each other. They all woke up in a sour mood.

"Let's get out of this thing," Roche said but as soon as he pulled off the blanket, he felt the cold draught of the morning coolness. "Whoa, it's cold this morning but I have to pee." He raced out of the tent and in seconds was back inside. The other two ran out briefly and returned.

When everyone had settled under the cover again, Dan said, "It looks as if it rained last night and the inside of the tent is still dry. There's only a small amount of water close to the stone wall."

Raj said, "I think the water was coming mostly from the side of the mountain. The forcefield must have kept out most of the water. It has to let the air through or we'd suffocate, so water vapour and some of the rain must have leaked through, too."

"I bet we won't get a hot breakfast this morning. It'll be our tasteless slop," Roche mumbled.

They realigned themselves and fell asleep again.

Two hours passed before they woke up to the stirring in the adjacent tent. They decided to remain under the cover until Grog eventually poked his head into their tent. "Time to get up. The sun has warmed the air enough to be comfortable."

"I guess you guys don't function well in the cold," Raj remarked.

"You're right. We almost couldn't move this morning but things are better now. We're still a little slow. Part of the coolness is the altitude. We'll be leaving soon."

The boys were soon out of their tent and everyone had their fill of food and water.

As Grog and the first officer were picking the things they would need, the captain said, "Today we're going to climb higher to get above one of the nests on this mountain. We'll be collecting samples of living organisms as we go along but we want to try to collect an egg from a nest, or if not, some fur, blood, or anything we can get with the genetic material of those fliers. An egg is preferable, as when we take it back to our planet our experts can study the being's morphology.

"The trip will be tough but we hope to be back here by the end of the day, so that'll be our base for tomorrow night also. We're taking what we need with us in one sack. To protect what we store here, we'll leave our invisibility and forcefield on in case some of the fliers or other animals stumble upon this camp. Is everyone ready?"

The boys nodded positively. They watched as Grog went to the pole and pressed one of the large buttons on the panel to turn off the forcefield. Everyone walked several metres from the campsite and stopped.

Grog pulled out his communicator and keyed something into it. He walked toward the campsite a few steps, stretched out his arm, and said, "The field is back on, sir." He walked over to join the group.

They continued up a steep incline and then farther along a very narrow area where they had to travel slowly. At one point, the aliens stopped to construct a bridge to get them over a very narrow ledge. The captain told them that it would make the crossing safer and speed up their descent if they needed to move quickly on their way back. After several hundred metres, the captain stopped. Grog held onto the captain while he rummaged in the sack and pulled out his binoculars. He looked down below them.

He said softly, "This nest has a female beside it and has a nestling. We'll take our chances on the nest higher up."

They continued their trek up the ledge and, at one point, had to build another bridge. By mid-afternoon, they found themselves on a narrow ridge where they stopped to eat and drink.

While they ate, the captain said, "This is about as high as we can get up this mountain without rappelling. About twenty metres beneath us is another larger shelf that contains a nest of fliers." He pulled out his binoculars from the sack Roche was carrying and leaned slightly over. "I won't let you use the binoculars this time because if you lean over, you may lose your balance and fall."

He peered down at the nest and said quietly, "We're in luck, this nest contains two eggs. If we take one, it'll impact less on the flier's family. There don't appear to be any fliers around." He put away his binoculars and began pulling out some material from the sack.

The first thing he pulled out was another device to make them appear invisible. He set it up to the side of them where there was a large enough surface for the tripod's base. He pressed only one button on it. "This should leave us undisturbed, as we're close to the nest and the fliers may attack, if they arrive back at the nest and see us."

The three aliens pulled out ropes and other materials and began assembling a small platform that would serve as a seat for an alien. Grog gave the platform to Roche to hold, while the aliens tied the pulleys around a secure prominence above them to the support ropes leading to the platform.

Once everything was set, the captain pulled out a metal box from the bag and attached it to his belt. He attached another rope to him and sat on the platform. Everyone else used the ropes to lower him down to the nest.

When he was near, he had to pull himself toward the nest, as they were not directly overhead. He opened the box, reached for the egg, and manipulated it into the box. He closed it, attached the other rope to it, and let himself swing away from the nest.

Grog began pulling the box up the mountain while the others held the captain in place.

Suddenly, a flier whirled from another location around the side of the mountain, swooped heavily into the captain and smashed him against the rocks. The flier grabbed him into his arms and pulled him from the platform. The force of the attack broke the captain's belt and it crashed heavily down the mountainside. Within seconds, the flier was off the mountain and disappeared into the direction he had come.

Everything had happened so quickly that the others had no time to react.

Grog quickly finished pulling up the box and slid it into the sack. He turned to the first officer and asked excitedly, "What do we do?"

There was silence for several seconds but the first officer regained his composure and responded, "Well . . . the fliers can't see us, so we're safe for now. I don't think the flier that attacked the captain is the owner of the nest. I'm sure they'll return soon, so we can't stay here too long. Before we leave the protection of our cover, I'm going to try to locate the captain."

He reached for his belt, pulled out his communicator, and turned it on. He swung it around slowly. "I'm doing a low-level scan and he's lower on this mountain. If he were farther away, there would be nothing we could do. We could never get to him in time to save him."

"Are you going to try to get him back?" Raj asked incredulously.

"We'll have to find out exactly where he is first."

"We can't use the ship?" Dan asked.

"Of course not. Just like on Earth, we can't expose the ship. If we're caught here, the beings would likely think we were another unknown species of this planet but using the ship is out of the question. Let's get the platform up here and get it packed up. We've got to leave."

"But once we turn your thing off here, they'll see us," Roche said.

"There's no one to see us right now."

They dismantled the platform and packed it into the sack. They had a quick slug of food and a gulp of water.

The first officer quickly turned off the device, folded up the extension and the legs, and tossed it into the sack. He dug a little deeper into it and pulled out a smaller bag. He opened it, took out three guns, gave one to each of the boys, and showed them how to use them. "Here are small belts for you to hang them on you until needed."

The boys put the belts on and attached the guns.

They quickly retraced their steps and crossed the first bridge. When they reached the other side, the first officer pulled the bridge down and everyone packed it away in the sack. He did another scan. "We're close now. Another few steps and we'll be over the captain by a few tens of metres."

They walked a little farther and stopped again. Another reading found them almost above the captain's location. He whispered, "This spot is a horrible site to do anything. This is where we saw the female flier and her nestling. This path is much too thin, hold me Grog and Roche and I'll pull out my binoculars and locate the captain."

They held him while he surveyed the scene below.

"The captain is on a ledge beside a nest below us." He tried to find a way they could work their way down to the site. "The female is still beside it. I'm guessing that the captain will be food for the nestling. There's no way we can get down there without a rope." He put away his binoculars and pulled out his communicator. He scanned the area around them.

"There don't appear to be any other fliers around. The male flier is not in the scanning range. He's probably looking for more food. The scanner indicates that the captain's condition isn't very good. If we don't get him now, we'll be bringing home a corpse."

He looked at Grog and told him to give his communicator to Dan then showed him how to use it. "Keep this on so you can hear us inside the field."

The first officer put away his communicator, pulled out his gun, and showed it to the boys. "These are set at five which would kill a human but should be sufficient to knock out the fliers. Dan and Raj, you go on ahead with the sack. There's a wider space just down the trail. Set up the device we used before and press both buttons. You'll be invisible and it'll give us a safe place to go if we're attacked. You were watching how we set it up and turned it on. Can you, do it?"

Raj answered, "Yes."

"Okay, get over there. It looks as if the fliers aren't accustomed to seeing land-based animals in the mountains, so they aren't expecting to find us here. That may change soon though, so be careful. A flier has found the captain but doesn't expect to find others. Guard that bag with your life; it's got the egg in it."

Raj and Dan carefully followed the trail and disappeared around a bend then set up the field generator.

Grog fed rope through two sets of pulleys and, as they could not find another way to support the ropes, the aliens fired a pin into the rock above them.

The first officer looked down to see the flier in the nest look up.

Everyone froze against the mountain.

After a few seconds, the first officer peeked again and saw her re-settled on the nest. He whispered, "I guess they're used to hearing noises in the mountains due to the heating and cooling of the water in the rocks."

The first officer fastened a rope around him and attached the other rope to his belt.

"Okay, now hold onto me while I lean and shoot the flier below."

Roche and Grog held him while he leaned over and fired.

"Shit," the first officer said as he quickly changed his gun's setting and fired again. "Okay, the flier is lying limply over the nest. Set your guns to eight – or for you, Roche, three notches higher, which would be the third notch from the end of the scale. Level five hardly fazed her. She almost took flight."

The first officer stood up again, so the two others could adjust their weapons.

"Okay, now lower me down, so I can fasten this other rope around the captain and we can haul him up."

The officer tested the integrity of the pin and handed his communicator to Grog.

Roche and Grog took a firm hold of the rope and the officer stepped over the edge. They had to do the job quickly, so they lowered him speedily but carefully, to the nest.

The officer fastened the rope under the captain's arms, then between his legs and back to the arms. Soon he was ready to go. He motioned for them to pull him up first, so they would have three people to raise the captain.

Grog and Roche were pulling up the officer much slower than they hoped.

The officer was almost at the ledge when Grog spotted movement out of the corner of his eyes. He turned his head to see the almost instantaneous appearance of a flier. "Hold the rope," he said to Roche as he grabbed his weapon and fired. He missed the first time but got the flier as he slammed forcefully into the first officer. "Shit," he called as a deafening howl pierced the air and echoed off into the distance.

The unconscious flier reflexively spread his wings as he coasted away from the mountain.

Grog slipped his weapon back into his belt and the two of them finished pulling up the unconscious officer. "Let's get him over to the others; he won't be able to help us pull up the captain and I don't want him to fall off this ledge."

While they were moving him, they could see fliers beginning to appear close to the nest they were now leaving. They appeared to be assessing the situation. "It looks as if the flier's howl has mustered the troops. We'd better get under cover soon."

37.

The aliens and young men were now in a precarious situation, as they could see more fliers coming toward them from other sites in the mountains. As Grog neared the area of safety, he called Raj to turn off the forcefield.

"Okay, just a minute . . . It's the blue switch, is it?"

"No, the green one."

There was a pause and Raj said, "Okay, it's off."

They slipped behind the invisibility screen and joined Raj and Dan.

"What was the horrendous screech we heard a few minutes ago?" Dan asked.

Grog answered, "We managed to get the ropes around the captain but were attacked by a flier. I blasted him but it got a call out for help. That was the howl you heard. The flier injured the first officer, so we'll have to leave him here. Raj, you stay here to help him, if he awakes. Dan, you come with us. You can use your gun to cover us while we pull up the captain. Both of you set your guns to level eight."

Roche and Dan changed the settings on their guns and slipped them into their holsters.

Grog continued. "When we leave, Raj, reactivate the forcefield. Remember, this is the same device we have at our campsite, so nothing will get through to you if you're attacked. Don't panic if a flier comes toward you. The fliers may want to investigate where we disappeared, as they can see this spot on the mountain but can't see you. Don't bother shooting, as the guns won't penetrate the field. Everybody ready? You all know what to do?"

The boys nodded. Dan pulled out his weapon.

"Okay, let's try to move as quickly as we can," Grog said, as he headed up the trail.

The three of them moved quickly to the ledge over the nest while Raj restarted the forcefield.

The hoard of fliers followed them, swooping at them from time to time to try to scare them off.

When they arrived, Grog could see that three fliers were examining the female flier and poking at the injured captain. He pulled out his weapon and fired at each of them. Two went soaring down the side of the mountain, while one of them slumped down unconscious over the captain.

"Roche, grab the rope with me and let's get him up," Grog asked.

They tugged hard on the rope but the combined weight of the flier and captain was too heavy to lift. Grog fastened the other rope around him and Roche lowered him.

The hoard of fliers began their assault. Three of them went for Grog, while another three attacked the boys.

Dan hit the three attacking him but two of the fliers lower down had slammed Grog against the mountain and were attempting to grab him. Dan fired quickly at them. Two fell away and he missed the third but he had another three attacking him.

Roche had lowered Grog by the nest. He pulled out his gun and began firing.

Dan was concentrating on the fliers attacking them, while Roche was focusing on the fliers attacking Grog. He could see that a flyer had injured Grog but Grog had managed to pull the unconscious flier from the captain. Soon, he pulled out his weapon and was firing.

There had been about thirty of the fliers originally but the squeals they had been making had attracted many more members to help with the attack. The numbers of fliers had kept climbing as the attack progressed but now the number was dropping and the fliers pulled back and flew around angrily just outside the range of the aliens' weapons.

"Pull me up," Grog said loudly. He slid his weapon back into his belt.

Roche slipped his weapon into his belt and began pulling on the rope. It was slow going.

Dan put away his gun to help but the fliers took note of it and began another attack. Dan let go of the rope, pulled out his gun and began firing again. At first, he was losing ground and it looked as if Roche would have to help somehow but the fliers pulled back again. Dan continued to hold out his weapon, while Roche slowly edged Grog to the ledge they were on.

Roche helped Grog onto the ledge.

"Now what are we going to do?" Roche asked.

"We'll have to get the captain up soon before the fallen fliers begin recovering. It also looks as if more fliers are arriving," Grog replied.

"My arms hurt so much I don't think I could even pick up a pebble," Roche said while wincing in pain.

"Okay, I'm going to have some trouble doing it myself as I can hardly move without pain shooting through me. Dan, please give me a hand. Roche, get ready with your weapon in case they try to attack again."

They got themselves ready then Dan and Grog started pulling up the captain. Occasionally, a flier ventured closer to them and Roche picked them off with the gun.

When the captain was about halfway up, the female flier that had been leaning unconsciously over the nest was showing signs of awakening. They tried to pull faster, as that meant that the other fliers they had knocked out, would also be close to re-joining the hoard of fliers just outside the range of their weapons.

The captain finally reached the top and they pulled him onto the narrow ledge. They untied him and pulled in the ropes. Grog rolled them up and attached them to his belt. They took down the pulleys and fastened them to Dan's belt.

The number of fliers was growing again but, so far, they were respecting the power of the aliens' weapons.

"Roche, do you feel strong enough to help me carry the captain?"

"I think so," Roche said, as he slipped his blaster into the holster.

Dan pulled out his gun, while Grog and Roche took hold of the captain and began a slow trek to where they had left Raj. The sun was getting close to the tips of the mountains.

Grog said, "It'll be getting dark soon, so let's try to speed up a little but don't go too quickly so you lose your footing. It's a long fall down the mountain. We're almost safe."

When they got close to where Raj was, Grog called into his communicator, "Raj, can you hear me?"

Raj replied, "Yes, I can see you. You're almost here."

"Keep the invisibility screen up but turn off the forcefield, so we can get in."

After a few seconds, Raj said, "It's off."

Grog and Roche continued to carry the captain through the invisibility field and disappeared.

Dan followed.

"This is a good place to stop, as it's getting dark," Grog said, "but it's going to be too small for all of us. To make sure none of us slip off this ledge, I'll adjust the forcefield a bit to make it a little narrower. That way it'll hold everyone onto the ledge." He reached over to the pole in the middle of them, pressed the green button to re-activate the forcefield, and punched his fingers on the small panel on its side. He tested the field by leaning into it.

"See, it'll hold you, if you lose your balance. As this ledge is not more than one person wide, I'd like to rearrange us. I want the three of you to get over to the end nearest our camp. I'll get between the captain and the first officer."

Everyone tumbled around, sometimes walking over each other to make the change.

"Will it get cold again tonight?" Roche asked.

"Maybe, we put a blanket in the sack we brought with us. We didn't expect to stay away from the campsite, so we didn't bring them all."

"The fliers are still swarming around here," Dan said. "It looks as if some are coming very close to us."

Grog responded, "Yes, they can't see us and the forcefield will keep them away if they get too close. It's keeping us in and it'll keep them out."

Some of the fliers were coming right up to the forcefield just centimetres from where they were, even pressing against it. The fliers seemed puzzled.

Grog watched them for a few minutes then took off his belt, removed the ropes, and slipped them into the sack. Dan handed him the pulleys. Grog pulled out some food and water and everyone had their fill. He grabbed a small box, pulled out some material from it, and worked on the captain for several minutes. He reached into the bag, pulled out a small object and turned it on. Light glowed from it.

"Can the fliers see us?" Raj asked Grog warily.

"No, our invisibility field will cover it."

Grog continued to work on the captain, as he was still bleeding. The boys noted that his blood was green in colour.

It took about an hour for Grog to patch up the captain. He then punctured him with a needle and injected the healing medicine. He filled a syringe with water and injected that into him. "These'll help to heal and hydrate him but he's in bad shape. The longer we stay here, the less likely he'll make it."

Grog looked out at the darkness surrounding them. "It looks as though the fliers have gone away for now. I hope we won't see them until morning."

He turned his attention to the first officer. There was no apparent bleeding, so Grog gave him a shot of the medicine. "I don't know how long it'll take our officer to revive, so we're in a sorry state right now." There was silence for many minutes then Grog said, "We still have that small bridge we made to cross over that other narrow area of our route." He shook his head dreading the rest of their journey down the mountain. "Farther along the trail we'll have to backtrack a bit lower down to try to retrieve the captain's belt. It's too far down for us to get it from here."

"You mean you want to stop to pick that up after all we've been through!" exclaimed Roche.

"It's a piece of our technology."

Roche rolled his eyes. "So now, we're going to try to sleep on this small ledge?"

"It's the largest one in this area," said Grog, trying to comfort them. Roche sighed.

Grog added. "Remember, we're safe here. You won't fall off."

"That's comforting," Roche said facetiously.

"Here everyone, take one of these pills. Even though you weren't hurt, you guys must feel exhausted, so they'll also help you with that."

Each person took a pill and swallowed it.

It was a turbulent night where no one got much sleep but even the little sleep they did get, helped heal their ills and tired muscles

.

38.

Erica woke up first. She had had a good night's sleep. The lights had already brightened. She sat up, yawned, and looked at Jiao who was still sleeping soundly.

Erica got up and went into the central portion of the ship. She turned on the monitor and stared at the screen. Aaootaa was sitting quietly staring at the door. The webbing of the cell looked sound. She zeroed in on the food and water containers and mumbled, "Hmm, I can't see anything in them."

She went to the door and said, "Open sesame." The door slid open. She waved at Aaootaa and went to the small slot in the cell. The water container was empty and the food – if anyone wanted to call it that – the container was almost empty. She smiled at her then looked over at a corner of the cell that Aaootaa had used for urinating and defecating and saw it was clean. She was also wet, so she had taken a shower – her desire to be clean must have encouraged her to try to use what she saw them using.

Aaootaa had figured out how to use the facilities; probably by watching them yesterday. Erica thought that was smart for a person who had never seen any kind of advanced technology before.

She turned her head back to the woman and smiled then went to the slot and took out the containers and spoon. She returned to the central area, cleaned the containers and spoon, and filled both containers again. She returned to the Aaootaa's cell and placed everything back in the slot. She smiled at her and left.

Erica returned to their compartment to find Jiao getting up. "Good morning," she said.

Jiao mumbled a little under her breath.

"Aaootaa is awake and finished her food and water. She washed herself and flushed her crap down the drain. I put out fresh food and water for her. I think it's going to be a great day," Erica said cheerily.

"Just give me time to wake up," Jiao half mumbled.

"Let's get over to Aaootaa's section and we can eat, shower, and get our exercises done. Then we can get on with our day."

"Are the boys supposed to come back today?"

"I don't think so."

"Oh, yes, I think it was not until later today or tomorrow. Maybe we should put our clothes on today, just in case."

"Let's wait until supper. We want to make Aaootaa feel at home. Hopefully, we can get her further along in communication so we can explain to her what clothes are."

Jiao sighed, "Okay, let's get over to her compartment and eat."

They went over to Aaootaa's compartment, ate, exercised, and showered. They went back into the central room, picked up one of the picture books and brought it close to Aaootaa's cell.

Aaootaa stood up and started shaking the webbing of the cell.

"I think, that's a universal sign," Jiao said.

"Yes, she wants out," Erica replied.

"How do we tell her we can't do that? It'd be even better if we could get across the notion that we're in the same predicament. She might think we're in league with the lizards."

"All we're starting with are our names and 'woman'."

Erica waited until Aaootaa calmed down then opened the book to a page that showed pictures of the lizards.

The woman glanced at them, made an angry face, and started pulling at the webbing again.

Erica moved her fingers over the figures and said, "Lizards."

The woman paused with her struggle and looked carefully at the pictures. She seemed enthralled that such accurate pictures could appear on a sheet of paper. She seemed very interested in the book, too. These were completely foreign to her.

Erica repeated her action.

Aaootaa looked at Erica and made a sound.

Erica linked that sound to 'lizards' and said the word to the translator. The translator repeated the woman's sound.

That astounded Aaootaa. Her mouth gaped at what was happening. Erica – or the machine – was speaking her language.

Erica pointed to a female lizard and said, "Woman." The word from the translator said Aaootaa's word for it.

Aaootaa nodded.

Erica pointed to a lizard that was male and said "Man".

Aaootaa looked at the picture carefully and made a noise.

Erica linked that noise to 'man'.

They continued the process through the day, first linking the words for child, family, mother, father, son, and daughter then learning the woman's sounds for trees, animals, flowers, and common things like food and water as well as some verbs like eat and wash. By the end of the day, they could have a very basic conversation with her. They refilled her food and water.

They returned to their room very happy with their progress.

"Well, it's been a busy day," Jiao said.

"Yes, we've made a lot of progress. We didn't leave a lot of time for ourselves. I liked having our conversations lately. We got to know a lot of things about each other and our families. We even got our hair fixed up a little."

"The day isn't over yet."

"Yes, I know. We've made some progress with using the picture books. We should have enough there to be useful tomorrow."

"As the men should be returning tomorrow, that'll be all we need."

"They said three or four days and that isn't very precise, so I wouldn't bet on it," Erica responded.

"We forgot to bring our clothes over here."

"Oh, yeah, we might as well not disturb Aaootaa just for that. We can do that tomorrow."

Erica took some time to review the remaining books, while Jiao combed Erica's hair with her fingers.

Erica finished the books, put them down, got behind Jiao, and ran her fingers through her hair.

Jiao said, "Thanks, it's hard for me to do without a mirror."

"I'll try to straighten it up as best as I can. It takes much longer without a comb." Erica commented.

"It's probably better than at any time since we entered this ship."

The lights dimmed and they went to their cell for the night.

39.

The sky was still black when Grog shook each of the boys awake.

"It's still dark, why are we getting up now?" Raj asked after rubbing his bleary eyes.

"We should get a head start over the fliers," Grog responded, as he turned on the light. "We're lucky it's not very cold this morning. The first officer has revived but I'm afraid he can't walk; he can't feel his legs but his arms are okay, so he can fight."

"Why? How can we walk in the dark?"

"I'm worried about the bridge. The fliers might have noticed it and decided to destroy it in the morning. That would be disastrous for us. We could rebuild it with the parts stored in our bag but we'd be under constant attack. We're going to have enough of a problem with getting ourselves across but we're going to have to get two injured people across, too. How we do it, I'll explain in a few minutes, so pack up and get ready to go."

The boys wrapped the blanket around the first officer and tied it with rope.

Grog passed the food and water around.

"Now, do whatever you need to, so no one will have to take a break for a while," Grog said in a low voice.

Once everyone finished, Grog continued. "The shelf is wide enough for us to turn off the forcefield and travel most of the distance to the bridge while under the invisibility shield. Keep alert so no fliers get close enough to discover that it's off. I'm hoping that all, or most, of them are asleep.

"First, we'll get everyone up against the field closest to the bridge. Dan and Roche, you put your hands under the captain's armpits and pull him along with you. I'll do the same with the first officer. Raj, you drag the sacks. When everyone has finished, one of you turns off the forcefield, picks up the generator about two centimetres then walks toward the people and sacks and puts it down. Then we'll repeat the process. You'll know we can't go any farther when the generator's supports can't fit on the ledge . . . Any questions?"

The boys looked at each other and nodded their heads.

"Okay, let's go," Grog said softly as he grabbed the first officer and got ready to pull.

The hardest part of the process was pulling the two injured aliens along the trail. It was slow going, as they could only move about two or three metres at a time. The minutes ticked by as their exhausting process edged them closer to the bridge. The ledge began to narrow significantly and they could go no farther.

Grog turned on the forcefield and said, "Our next step will be our biggest challenge because we have to haul two bodies over the bridge and to the next safe ledge which is quite a way from here. We'll leave the field generator here for now. When you're ready to go, I'll turn off the forcefield. When we get outside of it, I'll remotely turn on the forcefield again to protect the captain and our sacks. Roche, get over here, so you can help me at this end. Dan and Raj, you carry the front end of the blanket and lead the way. Try to feel your way along the mountain wall. Use this light if you need it but the bridge should give you good footing. A small section of the trail after that might be more problematic but it should be dawn by then and you'll be able to see better. Okay everyone, let's get going."

Everyone stumbled around as they got into their positions. They all grabbed the rope and slowly began the trek over the first few metres of the narrow path before the bridge. After they had gotten thirty metres, Grog called a halt, so he could turn on the forcefield. They picked up the first officer again and soon were crossing the bridge. It was slow going along it but they slowed even more while they traversed a very narrow section of the trail.

The sun had risen over the mountains to provide full light and Grog spotted the vanguard of the arriving hoard of fliers. They continued the journey over the narrow area and felt exhausted by the time the fliers arrived.

Grog shouted, "Okay, Dan get on this side and the two of you continue to carry the officer to that wider area ahead. When you're there, get him unwrapped. Roche and I will provide cover for us if they attack. Let's hope they leave us alone."

Dan climbed over the first officer and grabbed the rope. While Roche and Grog began to fire their weapons at the approaching fliers, Dan and Raj continued to struggle with their burden toward their destination and unwrapped the blanket from around the officer.

A furious battle began. The fliers must have alerted their comrades from other mountains to help in their war against the interlopers because their numbers had significantly increased from the previous day. The recovery of all their stunned fliers likely emboldened them.

Roche and Grog fired as quickly as they could but were struggling to defend both themselves and the other two.

Raj and Dan finished untying the first officer, wrapped up the blanket and rope, and placed it on the path next to the first officer. They pulled out their weapons and joined the fray.

Soon, the officer groggily pulled out his weapon and was helping.

Just as quickly as they had attacked, the fliers broke off the battle.

Grog yelled, "Raj, you stay with the first officer. Dan, pick up the rope and blanket and stay between us and Raj in case the fliers attack either one of us. Roche and I'll run over to the bridge to protect it."

Everyone moved quickly to their positions.

When the three of them rounded the corner, they could see that Grog was right, the fliers were at the bridge figuring out how they could take it down. As soon as the three of them got close enough, they started firing. One group of fliers broke off to attack them, while another worked at the bridge. At first, they were having a problem with defending themselves, let alone attacking the fliers at the bridge.

Eventually, Dan took over the battle of defence while Grog and Roche focussed their fire at the fliers busy on the bridge. The tide of the battle was turning.

Soon, the fliers at the bridge broke off the attack and flew in the direction of Raj and the first officer.

Grog shouted, "We can't go and help them; Dan, stay where you are and provide support to them. They'll have to defend themselves for now. We've got to get the bridge repaired and get across it for the captain and the sack." Grog picked up the blanket and rope from beside Dan and walked with Roche to the bridge to effect repairs.

While Grog and Roche worked on the bridge, Raj and Dan fought for their lives. The first officer was a good shot and was providing effective support.

The fliers finally decided to break off the attack and regroup.

For a while, the fliers stayed beyond the reach of the interlopers' weapons. They could see the workers repairing the bridge and moved in for another attack there but their numbers had dropped significantly and could not sustain an effective offense.

Grog soon had the bridge capable of supporting their weight again. He left Dan to defend the bridge while he and Roche travelled back along the trail, turned off the forcefield, wrapped the captain up in the blanket, and fastened the rope around him.

The fliers used this as an opportunity to attack the bridge again but as soon as any flier got within range, Dan picked them off. Raj and the first officer fired at any flier trying to get Dan.

After only fifteen minutes, the fliers backed off and kept their distance. They must have realised that their numbers were getting too few for a sustained attack and the interlopers had set up an effective defensive strategy.

Grog could see what was happening and knew they had to move quickly. He had noted that several of the fliers had flown away but they were returning with more recruits. He and Roche slowly carried the captain along the path to the bridge and onto the new site. Raj was happy to see them.

"You saw they have even more fliers," Raj remarked.

"Yes, the fallen ones will likely be starting to revive, soon. You continue to hold down this site and unwrap the captain. Roche, let's get back to get the sacks. Dan, you cover us on the bridge." Roche and Grog quickly got back to where the sacks were and turned off the field remotely. They entered, turned off the invisibility field, dismantled the device, and put it into a bag. They quickly got themselves over the bridge.

Grog gave one bag to Dan who took it to the new site. Roche stayed where he was to guard the bridge.

Dan returned to his central position while Raj opened his bag, took out the field generator, set it up, and turned it on.

Grog arrived at the bridge and he and Roche began taking it down.

The swarm of fliers had increased in numbers both by arriving recruits as well as the first group of revived fliers. Most of the swarm disappeared into the brush below the mountain. Most of the bridge was down when the fliers who had descended re-joined the swarm. Once together, the regrouped fliers headed toward them in force.

Dan rounded the corner to the bridge yelling, "Here they come," and began firing at them.

Roche joined him. They were hitting them as far as they could in the distance but there were too many of them. Roche stood in shock as a large rock hit him on the arm and it began to bleed. "Shit, they're throwing rocks at us," he yelled excitedly.

Grog finished dismantling the bridge and stacked the bridge parts in a pile. He would not have much time to pack it, so he adjusted the setting on his weapon to ten and fired at it. The rope and planks burst into flame.

Just as Grog turned his head to join the fray, a rock hit him on the side of his head from the direction of the fliers. He could see that, within minutes, the fliers would overwhelm them. It was evident that the fliers had added another element to their attack – projectiles.

Grog could see that their plight was desperate. If they did not change their tactics, they would lose. The fliers would kill the three of them and Raj, leaving the first officer, and captain, stranded on the side of the mountain where they would eventually die of dehydration or starvation. The equipment would then be vulnerable to the fliers obtaining them when the field generators ran out of power. Their entire mission was in jeopardy. He had to make a pivotal decision.

Without re-adjusting his weapon, he turned and began to fire at the cloud of fliers heading toward them. Instead of seeing the fliers knocked unconscious and gracefully fluttering down the side of the mountain, they were exploding. He was breaking the aliens' rules. They had previously used the setting of ten to knock out the giant beasts earlier in their expedition but these beings were much smaller and were having their nervous systems traumatically shocked; the aliens were killing them.

Rocks hit Roche several times but he was still fighting for his life.

Dan was in poor shape, though. He was slumped on the trail but still firing furiously.

Suddenly, Grog saw fliers falling from the sky as if someone in their new camp was killing them. That could only mean that Raj had risked turning off the forcefield to join them in their fight. From the number of fliers dropping, the first officer must also have joined him.

"Adjust your blasters to level ten," Grog yelled in desperation.

Roche and Dan paused for a few seconds to reset their weapons to level ten and were now killing fliers but they were so close that the exploding fliers were spraying them with blood. Another rock hit Dan and he was out of the battle. Roche could hardly hold up his gun anymore.

Then, it was over. The fliers retreated and resumed their flying beyond firing distance. There were still quite a few of them but they must have seen the carnage and decided their losses were no longer worth the fight.

Grog slumped onto the trail out of exhaustion and his injuries, grateful that the fliers had quit when they did. He knew Roche was exhausted and would not have lasted much longer. Perhaps the fliers had thought the interlopers had more energy left in them than they did.

They waited for a few minutes to be sure the fliers had finished their attack and were not regrouping for a final blow.

He could see movement out of the corner of his eye and turned his head. Raj had come out of the field and had his hands under Dan's arms. He was pulling him down the trail around the bend toward their new shelter.

Grog decided he had better get himself moving. There were still many unconscious fliers who would be revived soon and that may embolden them to attack again. He pulled himself upright, grabbed the bag, and slowly and painfully slogged toward Roche and his bag. He helped Roche to his feet and they slowly moved toward their shelter inside the field.

Once they were inside, Raj turned on the forcefield.

Grog moved toward the field generator and adjusted it, so it would help to hold them onto the trail as it had done earlier.

Roche collapsed where he was, while Grog sat for a few minutes to rest.

"Do you know any first aid, Raj?" Grog asked.

"Not really but I'll help you. Just tell me what to do."

"Okay, you're close to Dan, so have a look at him and feel his arms to see where he's hurt and if any bones are broken."

While Raj followed his instructions, Grog examined Roche. He had half a dozen spots where he was bleeding and, after a bit of probing, may have had a broken rib or two. He had so much blood on him it was hard to see how much of it was his but there were three or four gashes to his head.

Raj's examination showed that the fliers must have hit Dan at least three times in the head and had up to a dozen other areas in his body where he appeared to be bleeding but it was difficult to know for sure because of the amount of fliers' blood on him.

"Okay, reach into the bag and pull out the box that I used for the captain and first officer. Hand it to me and I'll patch up everyone."

"What about you?"

"Let's get everyone else done, shall we?"

Grog handed a couple of bandages to Raj. "Do you know how to tie a reef knot?"

"Yeah, I think so."

"Wrap up that bad arm with one bandage and tie it up fairly tightly then wrap up those two open gashes on his forehead. I'd have him cleaned off but we don't have much water left. Here's a bottle of sanitizing solution to pour on the bleeding areas. Give me the bottle when you're done."

Grog looked at the gash on Roche's chest, grabbed the first aid kit, and taped some gauze onto it. He put a bandage on the worst gash on Roche's right arm. When Grog got the bottle of sanitiser from Raj, he poured some on several other areas on Roche.

"Well, that's the best I can do under the circumstances. I don't know if Roche and Dan have concussions but there's not much I can do about that. We're not equipped for such massive trauma. Hand me the syringe and the medicine bottle. This'll be the best thing for them."

Grog injected the solution into Dan and Roche then leaned over, with Raj's help, to give another one to the captain and the first officer. Grog felt very faint but he wrapped up one of his arms and poured sanitizer on several other spots. He held out the bottle for Raj, who capped it and put it into the little box along with the rest of the kit.

"How about you? You got hit a few times while you were out of the field."

"I'm okay. I think it's mostly bruised."

"Get me and you a pill then put away the kit. We can all use a drink of water but let's ration it for now."

Raj followed his instructions.

Grog took his pill and slipped into an exhausted sleep.

Raj looked at everyone along either side of him and wondered what was going to come of them. It was like being in an emergency room of a hospital. There was so much blood on three of them that he was wondering if anyone would die over the next few hours. The first officer had fallen asleep again. He was not even sure the captain was still alive.

He looked out at the mountains. The number of fliers was growing again but they were keeping their distance. A few of them were occasionally wafting nearer almost as if they were testing what would happen. All of them were eyeing the area where the interlopers had disappeared, much as they did the evening before but from farther away.

He felt so helpless and useless. He wished he could do more for everyone but he could not even give them water. If everyone was so badly wounded, he wondered when and how they were going to get themselves back to the campsite and the ship.

He sat and stared at the fliers. They looked so majestic. He was sad that so many of them died, even though a few minutes ago they were trying to kill him.

Soon, the fliers were moving closer but for now, they were mainly around the corner where most of the battle had been. Several minutes later, there was a long procession of them carrying their dead comrades away from the side and base of the mountain. The blood of their fallen covered their shining white. Then they were gone.

A while later, a few fliers glided through the sky in the distance, probably observers keeping surveillance on the area where the interlopers had disappeared.

He wondered what the girls were doing. In their innocence, they would be going about their business not knowing what had happened out here. The captain had been vague as to when they were going to return, so probably the girls would not be worried yet. He thought about asking Grog to call the girls and tell them of their plight when Grog woke up but for now, maybe it was better they did not know.

He looked at the few gashes he received during the brief time he was in the skirmish. Most of the wounds had only bled lightly. There was one on his chest which was slowly oozing some blood but it did not appear to be serious. He had suffered the least. The rest of the group would not likely be able to move the next day, so they would be staying on the trail again.

He reached into a bag and took out the food containers. He

checked the alien's container and found not much there. He felt quite hungry, so decided to take a small amount of the alien's portion even though he knew it would not meet his nutritional needs. At least it would help to quench his hunger.

As the sun dipped behind the mountain tops, darkness overcame the sky and Raj drifted off the sleep.

Within a few hours, Raj woke up shivering. For a while, he lay there but could not take the cold anymore. He remembered the blanket in the sack but wondered how he could cover everyone with one blanket. He reached into the bag and felt around for the flashlight. He pulled it out and turned it on. He shone the light on the other sleepers. He noticed that Roche and Dan were still asleep but were shivering. The three aliens seemed comfortable enough.

"Find the blanket and cover yourselves," the voice of the officer said.

The sudden noise startled Raj. He thought everyone else was asleep. "What about you guys?" he asked.

"Don't worry about us, we won't freeze. I don't think it's that cold. Our metabolism will slow down a lot but we'll be okay. It's you I'm worried about. Just don't expect us to get up early in the morning."

"Thanks, the blanket will help us stay warm."

Raj searched through the bag with the light of the flashlight and pulled it out. He opened it up and put it over Roche and Dan. He could see that the blanket had worn significantly from chafing, as it slid across the rocky ledge while covering the captain and first officer. He turned off the flashlight and put it away. He crawled under the blanket with them. Despite the holes in it, his shivering stopped.

He wished Erica was under the blanket with him to keep him warm.

Eventually, sleep overcame him.

40.

Erica cheerfully got up the next morning. She replaced their water and food then went over to Aaootaa's compartment and did the same for her. While there, she picked up their clothes and brought them to their place.

By then, Jiao was awake and lying on her back staring at the ceiling. Jiao saw Erica come in, stretched, and got up.

They went over to the Aaootaa's compartment carrying their food, water, and translator with them. Afterwards, they ate, while the woman ate. After a brief rest, they began their exercises and were surprised to see Aaootaa trying to follow them as best she could for her shape. The three of them had showers.

When they finished, Aaootaa grabbed the bars of the cage and began to pull on it again but stopped her actions after a few seconds, when she realised it was futile.

"I feel so bad about cooping her up in here," Jiao said.

"I know. I wonder how we can tell her that we're prisoners, too."

"She may not know what a prisoner is. Let's keep that in mind but, for now, let's get back to the books and link more words."

They brought in another book and looked through it.

"A lot of the pictures in this book don't relate to her level of technology," Erica said.

"Didn't we see one that had pictures of scenery in it?"

"Yeah, but the plants don't look much like she'd see here and we know the general words for most of what's in there."

"Not everything, we could use it for bringing up general words like sky, clouds, mountains, streams, top, bottom, rocks, and hills."

"Okay, it's something to do. The larger the vocabulary, the better, I guess."

"Maybe we should put on our clothes."

"Yeah, I guess the guys should be coming back today." Erica went back to their room and brought in the jumpers. They slipped them on and gave Aaootaa the name for them. She made a sound.

"I didn't think they'd have a word for clothes," Erica said.

"They must wear something sometime then, I guess."

Erica linked Aaootaa's sound to the word 'clothes.

They went to the control room to get another book and began going through the pictures in it to learn the names of other terms with those of the woman's language.

By noon, they finished and had lunch together. The girls got a few more books and, for the rest of the day, they continued with their project.

For supper, they ate together again. They removed the translator, did their exercises together then took another shower.

"You know what we should do tonight?" Erica suggested.

"What?"

"Sleep in here, again."

"Why?"

"I think this is how we can let her know we're captives like her."

"You think so?"

"Maybe; I've been thinking about it all day and it's the only thing I can think of that might work."

"It's fine with me."

"You know, I still don't miss the boys," Erica said pensively.

"I guess so."

"Why do you guess?"

"Well, it's a little quieter."

"We wouldn't be able to walk around naked like we did."

"And maybe we wouldn't have made as much progress with Aaootaa," Jiao commented.

"For sure, I think she's become our friend and it's kind of cool to have no clothes on. It's like having total freedom."

"What if the boys had shown up earlier?"

"The guys have already seen us. They'd probably yawn."

"Clothes may bring some normalcy and I think sleeping in here is a good idea."

"I wonder why the men aren't back yet," Erica thought aloud.

"Maybe they're staying one more day."

"I guess so. I hope they're having a more exciting time than we are. We're imprisoned in this stupid ship."

"At least they're up and walking around doing something. It's nice having the run of the ship but I'm bored with that."

"Me, too. Maybe we could do our hair now," Erica suggested.

"Um, no, I'm tired."

The two girls went into the central room and picked up a few more of the picture books. They walked into the cell across from Aaootaa that they had used as a shower and bathroom while they were in this compartment. They looked through the books until the lights faded then went to sleep.

41.

Raj did not get much sleep. He kept having nightmares of the previous day.

He woke up in the middle of the night and peeked out from the blanket to see two eyes staring at him from the other side of the forcefield. He froze in terror then quickly ducked his head back into the blanket. He calmed his breathing. It was another nightmare, he thought. It was his imagination run amok. He slowly slid the blanket off his head until he could see again but, sure enough, two eyes were there, though not looking at him.

It was a flier who was trying to see through the invisibility screen. The flier was beating his wings to allow him to hover against the impenetrable forcefield. He must have sensed something was there; firstly, it was the place they had last seen the interlopers and secondly, he could see that he was not flat against the mountain but some distance from it.

Suddenly, several faces were trying to look through the field. Some of the fliers were trying to force themselves through it. Then they were gone and Raj could see rocks bouncing off the field and hear them tumble down the side of the mountain. If they could not push their way through that space against the mountain, they were experimenting with other means. Soon, the barrage stopped and silence returned.

Raj felt relieved and put his head under the blanket again. If the fliers were out there and he was inside, he was safe.

Raj slid back into his nightmares and one particularly unnerved him. Erica had left the ship and was trying to find them to help them but had come under attack from the fliers. She was calling him for help. She began to scream.

Raj woke up in a cold sweat and felt the cold draught of air as soon as he raised the blanket. He looked around him but it was dark. Two of the planet's tiny moons were out, so objects on the exterior of the forcefield were visible as dark shadows. He peered out but could see nothing outside. He was unsure that there had been anyone or anything out there earlier during the night. His dreams had been so disorienting.

He shook his head to wake up. Had Erica called? Sometimes dreams were a harbinger of danger. Maybe it was not a dream and she was out there and needed his help. He had to go and save her. She was in danger. He pulled himself out of the blanket ignoring the cold air. He walked into the forcefield and almost fell over. It was then he knew the forcefield was still on. He corrected his balance, reached over, and turned it off.

He walked as quickly as he could, following their trail back down the mountain. He was beginning to feel the cold and wanted to turn back but he had to save her. She was in danger and no one else was awake. He was unsure whether she was still alive but he had to get to her quickly. He travelled for hours, passing the narrow ledge as he went.

He seemed to walk forever, until suddenly, he ran into something hard and almost fell over. He corrected his step with time enough to prevent himself from falling down the side of the mountain.

"Shit, what the hell was that?" he said, as he reached out to feel what was there. There was nothing, at least nothing hard like stone. It was blocking his way down the mountain. He was puzzled at first until he realised that it must have been the camp that they had set up on the first day of their climb up the mountain. There was no way he could save Erica. She needed his help and he could not get by this point. He panicked. He had to find her. She was in trouble.

Then, he became confused. Where was he and what was he doing? He turned around to walk back up the trail when he froze in his tracks and turned pale.

Before him was a flier towering majestically above him more than seven feet tall. The flier's right hand was high over his head. Raj looked up at the hand and saw it contained a large rock ready to strike him. The flier was hesitating though, he knew not why. He looked at the face of the flier and it betrayed much anger and hatred.

Raj knew he was going to die. Interiorly, Raj was trying to stop the tears flowing from his eyes. Somehow, he wanted to display a brave face but was failing badly.

They stood staring at each other; each face remaining frozen in position. They continued for at least a minute until the flier moved his left hand over to Raj's right eye and brushed his fury finger beneath it to feel the wetness there. The flier's face softened as if he realised his opponent was not fully a man but a terrified, immature boy cringing with fear and crying.

The flier lowered his arm, dropped the rock, and flew away.

Raj stood where he was in shock. He was in a stupor walking up the mountain but he still did not know if this was real, or he was having another dream.

What was wrong with him? Here he was, halfway down the mountain and he did not even know why he was there. Erica could not be in danger; she was on the ship or should be. Had he heard her in a dream, or was it real? He had come face-to-face with a flier – or had he? Was that part a dream, too? If it was a dream, was he going to wake up now?

If this was real, he had turned off the forcefield and now everybody was in danger of attack. The fliers would not see them but could pass through the invisibility field and see them behind it. Maybe the flier realised this and that is why he left – to attack the rest of his group. Even if the fliers did not attack them, someone could roll over and fall down the side of the mountain.

"Holy shit, what have I done?" he murmured under his breath. He had to get back to the group as fast as possible but he could not run. He could lose his footing and fall off the edge.

He hurried back to the makeshift camp and was unsure where it was until he walked into the field.

"Ouch," Raj said, as he stood stunned for several seconds.

"Okay, the field's off," Grog said softly, so as not to awaken the others.

"But I turned it off already," Raj admitted.

"That's right but I turned it back on shortly after you left. Where did you go? I thought you had gone to pee or something but you've been gone for hours. What were you doing? There might be fliers out there. They've got keen eyesight. They could have seen you and killed you."

"I know, it's a long story."

"Well, the field is off now, so get in here," Grog said tersely.

Raj was happy to be back, as he stepped inside the area of the field and saw Grog with a rather grumpy look on his face.

Grog leaned over and turned on the forcefield again.

"Now get back to sleep. You're lucky I'm still functioning in this cold. It took a while for me to turn off the field and get it back on. I don't think I'll be functional until late in the morning, so stay under the blanket. You must be cold."

Now that Raj had stopped walking, he was not only cold, he was shivering. He slid under the blanket and cried for quite some time. He was not sure why; perhaps the loss of his family, or Erica, or the stupid thing he had just done, or the flier sparing him, or his current circumstances, or maybe everything. He finally drifted off to sleep.

Raj woke again a few hours later. He poked his head out from the blanket. It was still cold outside but the sun was shining; a warm inviting sun. He stared at the clouds in the sky for several minutes then looked around him. He could see a small group of fliers off in the distance. Everybody else still seemed to be asleep. He was hungry but remembered that the food container had very little in it, even the water was low. He decided to leave the food and water for the others.

He tried to go back to sleep but even though he was still tired, he could not. He was trying to remember what had happened over the night but everything was a jumble. He focussed on one event. It was fuzzy in details and could have been a dream. He cast it aside. He could never have left the warmth of the blanket and gone searching for Erica; she was safe in the spaceship. What a night of nightmares but today would not be any different – or had everything yesterday been a dream. He was under the blanket and with his best friends, so everything seemed normal.

Lying there with nothing to do; he fell asleep.

When Raj woke up over an hour later, Roche was awake, too.

"So, you're awake," Roche said.

"I've been awake on and off all night."

"I know, you almost got us killed. What were you doing freaking out like that?"

"You were awake?"

"I woke up when you got back. I heard you talking to Grog. You're lucky the fliers didn't attack us. We could've been killed."

"Sorry, I didn't know what I was doing, I guess."

"Even if they didn't attack, the fliers could've seen you, as it wasn't that dark out. They could've killed you. We'd be in a bind without your help moving us out of here. You're the only one who didn't get hurt much."

Raj did not tell him that he almost died. Just thinking about it again made him turn pale.

"Never freak out like that again. It was as if you were going crazy. You've got to keep yourself together," Roche admonished.

Raj hung his head, embarrassed.

Grog woke up shortly after that but was unable to move and said nothing until the sun warmed him enough to function properly. Then, he went around to everyone to give them a shot of the healing formula. He went into the sack and pulled out the food and water. He handed it first to Roche. "This feels rather light, there may not be much in there for everyone."

Roche opened it and only ate a little bit. He handed it to Raj.

"I don't need any. Save it for Dan when he wakes up."

Roche looked at Dan and poked him a few times. He put his head to Dan's chest and said, "He's really in a deep sleep. It might be a coma. He was quite hurt out there and lost some blood."

"I hope he recovers," Raj said

"So, do I; I think he will though. He needs time to rest and regain his strength," Roche responded.

"That was quite a day," Grog said.

"Yeah, we almost got wiped out. It was a good thing they stopped when they did. I wonder if killing them helped."

"I hated to do it. It's against our code but if we didn't, we wouldn't have made it. I think the fliers stopped because they found out we could kill them. Just knocking them out was emboldening them to continue the attack, if we knocked them out; they'd just rejoin the battle later."

There was silence for a few minutes. Grog said sadly, "I've never killed anyone before. I felt terrible doing it. I'm ashamed."

"It was the first time we've ever seen people get killed. I feel bad for the fliers," Roche added.

The day wore on.

The first officer woke up in the early afternoon and got an update on everyone. "From what I see, we won't be going anywhere today. We'll have to stay here. The fliers may forget us and make it easier for us to leave. The three of you might be able to move the rest of us out of here by then. The captain doesn't look well. I'm not even sure he's alive. When we have severe injuries, we can enter a state of suspension which mimics death. We won't know for sure what state he's in until we get him back on the ship. Dan might be much better tomorrow. I'm afraid I can't feel my legs and that may not change. Somehow though, we'll have to get back to basecamp tomorrow, as we're almost out of food and water."

Late in the afternoon, Dan opened his eyes. He was very groggy. Roche gave him the last of their food and water, and a pill. Dan tried for several seconds to sit up but gave up. He hurt too much and ended up staying where he was. Roche filled him in on everything that had happened.

Before the end of the day, Roche got up and Raj joined him in some simple stretch exercises. Grog gave the captain two injections, one with the last of the aliens' water, and the other a healing potion. The rest of them took their pills. When they finished, they noticed Dan had drifted back to sleep. They soon joined him as the sun slid down behind the mountains.

42.

The light in the spaceship brightened and Erica and Jiao awoke worried that the boys had not returned.

Erica turned to Jiao and said, "The captain said they'd be back in three or four days, didn't he?"

"About that."

Erica thought a few seconds then responded, "Maybe I should give them a call."

"The captain told us to call him if something went wrong here."

"I wonder if I should call to see if everything is okay with them. Maybe they're in danger and need help."

"We can't get out of here, anyway."

"The captain must be able to let us out remotely."

"I'm sure if they were having problems, they wouldn't want us out there."

"Maybe they're all dead."

"What, all six of them!" Jiao exclaimed incredulously.

"They're in the mountains; they could've fallen off a cliff or something."

"Now, you're making me worried. I'm sure they're okay. They've all got guns and equipment with them."

"I don't care, if they're not back tomorrow morning, I'm calling them."

Jiao did not respond; she was also becoming concerned.

Aaootaa awoke, likely due to their conversation.

Erica grabbed the translator and said, "Good morning, Aaootaa."

She grunted, not knowing what Erica had said.

They changed their and Aaootaa's water and food then exercised and showered.

They spent more time with Aaootaa with the books but they were also exchanging more information about life on her planet. She described the plants and animals on it and about her daily life. A lot of their discussion was in sign language for things that were too specific than the pictures in the books. The translator did its best to keep up with the stream of information exchanged between them. The girls found out that Aaootaa's people did occasionally wear clothes, of sorts, during some specific social activities and ceremonies, particularly during their coming-of-age and wedding ceremonies.

Before lunch, Erica said, "It's hard to tell but I think staying in here with Aaootaa has helped our relationship with her a lot."

"Yeah, I think we made a lot of progress."

"You're the language expert. How can we let her know that we're not associated with the lizards and aren't their friends?"

"That's easy," Jiao said, as she got up, sorted through the books strewn about the floor, picked up one, opened to the page with the lizards displayed, showed it to Aaootaa, tossed the book on the floor, stomped her feet on the page.

Erica giggled. "I guess that showed her." She looked at Aaootaa and smiled.

She returned the smile, the universal sign of friendship.

After lunch, the girls changed the topic and tried to describe their lives and daily routines. They had to keep it simple because it was extremely difficult to describe things like phones, electric lights, and refrigerators.

The three of them spent the rest of the day using what words they had and communicating. Aaootaa was amazed that humans bore live babies instead of laying eggs. They also had much to laugh about as they struggled with some of the appropriate words for topics they were discussing. For instance, how could you explain in some way what marriage was?

"Well, we've taken this as far as we can," Erica said after supper. "I'm very disappointed nobody is back yet."

"Are you going to call them?"

"I'm tempted to but I trust them. It must have taken them longer than they thought. Let's see how things go tomorrow."

"They should return during daylight."

"Yes, but we don't know if this planet has the same cycle as the ship."

"Oh, yeah."

They fingered each other's hair.

When the end of the day approached, the girls lay down, curled up in the empty cage across from Aaootaa, and went to sleep.

The lights dimmed.

43.

Raj was the first to wake up. He had a rough night again with many nightmares he soon forgot. Sleeping within the narrow confinement of the field and on the hard, rocky, and uneven ground of the ledge had provided him even more misery. It had been another cold night which had tried the capacity of the thin and worn blanket to hold in body heat. If they stayed out much longer, the lack of water, food, and warmth would start taxing their ability to stay alive. It reminded him of their first days on the ship.

He left to visit one corner of the ledge, where the ground under him was wet from the urine of his compatriots, to empty his bladder and hurried back under the blanket.

Oh, how he missed the warmth of his dry, comfortable bed at home and the love of his parents. He thought of the delicious meals he had eaten at home in comparison with what they had here. He even missed school.

When he eventually did get back home, he would not have finished his education. He had planned to go to university. Now, all that was gone and all he had to look forward to was many more weeks cooped up in a small compartment of the spaceship and an unknown fate on an alien planet if he could survive his current challenge. If he had not had Erica's presence to provide some hope, he did not know what he would have done by now. Life would not have been worth living.

He thought back to the night and his encounter with terror. The flier could have killed him. Why did he stop? In some way, it would have provided a way out of his predicament. He could have ended his life at once but, for some reason, the flier had spared him. Was there some meaning in that? Could it mean that the flier had seen something in him – that there was some reason for his life to continue? They somehow connected in that long period of staring at each other. Maybe the fliers were not evil. They were living beings as he was and they could also show compassion.

Right now, though, he was miserable and almost cursed the flier. Maybe he had gone on that mad journey subconsciously wanting to die. He believed that everything in life was important; everything happened for a reason. His parents had driven that into him since he was a small tyke. His parents believed in fate and so did he. He wanted to die but the flier spared him – maybe for some reason he had to endure more punishment.

At present, he did not appreciate it. He was miserable and was in no mood to accept his continued life as something good. He was cold, hungry, thirsty, and so tired and weak. He wanted food, water, and to sleep forever but had none of that. He longed for the comfort of the arms of his mother. He wanted her there to cuddle him and rock him in the big old rocking chair they had back in India when he was an infant. He wanted her to sing the little lullabies of old.

He had spent his life wanting to grow up – the faster the better. Now, all he wanted was to go back to India and be a baby again. Life was so simple then. There were no thoughts about what he was going to do when he grew up and certainly no thoughts of girls. Girls were just strange boys back then. The future just happened with the new day but that was then. He was stuck in the present, in this strange body that ruled him and made him think of thoughts he never considered then.

He was maturing while enduring and being driven by, hormones he did not understand. His life had changed but he was still a little boy who, right now, just wanted to be cuddled by someone, by his mother maybe, or by Erica – yes, Erica would do but she was not here and even if she was, it would not be him she would hug; it would be Roche. In the end, he had no one and maybe that is why his mind drove him to the edge of insanity.

The flyer spared him from death for some reason. Maybe it was so he could save Erica and escape back to earth then he would be her hero. There would be no more Roche. She would be all his and take him into her arms and hug and kiss him, and love him. That is what he wanted from the first moment he saw her, although that was before all the hormones got in the way. It was a simple form of love then, but real love was more than that. His hormones screamed out and he wanted that, too. He wanted it all but it eluded him.

Then again, maybe he was going psycho and who would blame him? The little boy in him started crying.

Roche woke up. He got up slowly and painfully and left the blanket briefly. When he got back, he looked at the whimpering Raj and said harshly, "Don't go wacko on us again."

"I'm not crying anymore."

"Okay." Roche sat and thought for a while. "Maybe you should cry. That might help you."

"I'm done with that."

There was silence for a couple of minutes then Roche added, "Don't be embarrassed, okay? I've often felt like crying. I get tired of trying to be the toughie all the time. I'm afraid if I cry, everyone will break down. Just think of how this affects me. I'm the stupid one who encouraged us to get into the ship. We have a new life and are stuck with it. I miss my family and other friends. Our whole lives have changed and not for the better. I was going to be an engineer. My dad was one and I liked what he did. Now, I have no idea what's going to happen to me. If we managed to get back to earth, it wouldn't be for quite some time. I'd have lost school. I'd have to start over again and I'd be years behind everyone we know."

Raj could hear the cracking of Roche's voice. There was silence until Dan woke up several minutes later.

Dan noticed that the other two boys were awake. "I don't have the strength to get up, so I just peed here. Sorry about that," he said.

Roche answered, "Don't think about it. I did it in the middle of the night. It was too cold to get up."

"Well, we're still alive. I thought I was going to die yesterday," Dan remarked.

"So, did I. Those fliers had us on the ropes."

Dan reiterated what the aliens had said before. "I guess the fliers were taking too many losses. They could see many of their kin were dying. Maybe the cost of lives was getting too high. Getting knocked unconscious was one thing but getting so many of them killed might have been too much for them."

"You were unconscious but everyone except the captain was still firing."

Dan looked at the others and himself. "We must have lost a lot of blood. We're caked in it."

"It's not all ours. Most of it is the fliers' blood."

"Yuk, gross." Dan looked at his surroundings. "So, we're still on the ledge where we fought?"

"Yup."

"We're still far from the tents."

"And we have to get to the tents today, if we can because we're out of food and water."

"That's a few hours from here, isn't it?"

"Not too far, if we weren't under attack and had to carry half the people along as we go. As it is, it might take a whole day to do it."

"So, you're telling me it's going to be another long day."

"Looks like it."

Dan looked a little forlorn.

Roche smiled at him and shrugged his shoulders.

They waited under the covers until it was warm enough for Grog to revive.

When Grog got up, it was slowly. He finally said, "Sorry for the slow start. We have a definite handicap to warm-blooded animals. You should realise that warm-blooded animals are a small portion of the total population of the galaxy we've seen so far, so cold-blooded animals have done very well. As cold-blooded animals evolved a high level of intelligence and developed technology, their handicap reduced, as they invented ways to keep them functional even in cold climates. Since we had you, and were in no hurry, we decided not to use our artificially-heated clothing, as they are quite uncomfortable. Also, we usually try to limit our explorations to temperate or tropical climates."

Grog changed the topic. "I see the first officer is awake. Everybody, take a pill and I'll give an injection to the captain."

There were no meals to eat, so Grog went over to the first officer and talked to him briefly. When Grog finished, he looked at the boys and said, "The first officer is not in very good shape today, so I guess my job is going to be to get us out of here and to the campsite.

"As you can see, the fliers are out there keeping an eye on us, although it doesn't look as if there are a lot of them. They may be able to increase numbers quite quickly if they spot us again. I guess our best plan is to do what we did yesterday and move under cover of the invisibility field. It's slow going but safer. I don't know if we can stand another attack, even if they're only using rocks. Before we get going, make sure you're ready for a long period of movement. I'll call the girls and let them know we're behind schedule and assure them everything is okay."

While the boys did one last pee, Grog called the girls. "Hi, who's this?"

"Both of us," Erica responded. "Jiao can hear what we're saying."

"I'm calling to tell you we're behind schedule. Things have been a little more challenging than we expected. We won't be back today and likely not tomorrow, so it might be the day after that. I'll keep you informed if our plan changes."

"Is everything okay?" Erica asked apprehensively.

"Oh, yes, the boys are fine, a little ragged and tired but doing okay. How are you progressing with the aboriginal?"

"We're doing great. We've established quite a vocabulary."

"That's good. We'd better get going over here, so keep up the good work and we'll be seeing you soon."

Grog disconnected quickly to avoid their asking too many other questions.

"Okay, it looks as if everyone is ready, so Raj and Roche, you get in front of me and carry the first officer to the edge of the field. I'll wrap up the captain. When I'm done, Dan, please help me carry the captain to the edge of the field. I'll go to the middle and turn off the forcefield and we'll use the method we used to move under cover of the fields. Dan, please drag the sacks along with you."

Everyone packed up, sorted themselves out, and followed their instructions.

For the first half hour, everything went well, until several rocks came crashing onto them from above. Grog looked up to see a group of fliers several hundred metres above them. He shouted out, "Stop, we're being bombed." He quickly reached out and turned on the forcefield.

Several other rocks began ricocheting off the forcefield. Grog stood up again and looked toward the boys. Roche was on his knees cradling Raj.

"I thought you said they couldn't see us," Roche cried out.

Grog responded, "They can't but what they can see is the field moving. Remember, we told you they can see a slight aberration when the field is moving. They're very smart. They tried an experiment to see if rocks could pass through the field when it's moving. They probably don't realise we have two fields and we turned one of them off when we moved along, but the effect is the same – they can hit us when we move. They could see the rocks disappearing into our location. If they drop enough rocks through, they know someone is bound to be hit."

"What do we do?" Roche asked.

"We'll stop for a while . . . How's Raj? Has he been hit?"

"Yes, on the side of his head."

"Any bleeding?"

"Doesn't look like it."

"Now, we have another person injured. You and I can haul my officers along. Raj was giving you good assistance. Dan is managing to stumble along behind us by using the rock face as support; now this."

After about five minutes, the rocks stopped falling.

"Is Raj still breathing?" Grog asked.

"Yes, I think he was knocked out. The rock hit him quite hard."

Grog reached for the sack and opened it. He rummaged through it and found the first aid kit. He pulled out the needle and loaded it with the medicinal solution. "Lean him over the officer."

Roche complied.

Grog injected the solution into Raj and felt his head.

"There's a slight indentation, so the skull may be damaged. That's not good. He may be out for quite a while. We'll have to keep an eye on him. He may have internal bleeding and that could be bad. The trickiest part of the rest of the trail is coming up. For several metres, the path is too narrow to support the field generator. I was hoping the fliers would have left us alone."

Grog was worried now. There were only two persons left to look after the group and they were not in good shape themselves.

44.

Grog sat down and buried his face in his hands. What was their next step? They were going to have to expose themselves to travel over this narrow area. With just two of them able to walk, it would take a lot of time to go back and forth. Now the fliers had a primitive but effective, weapon, that greatly complicated their travel plans. If they could get by this narrow section, they might be able to make it safely back to the ship but that was a big if. He could postpone further progress until tomorrow, or overnight but they had found that the fliers' sight was quite good, even at night. The next day might give Dan back to Grog as a useful partner, so that would improve things.

How long could he wait? The captain was in critical condition, the first officer was paralysed, and Raj's condition was unknown. Now, they had no food or water. On top of that, the energy level of all their equipment was low. The field generator they were using was okay for two or three days but most of their guns would only be good enough for one or two more battles and the generator at the campsite might only have one to three days of energy left. Their communicators would be good for maybe another day or two.

They were desperate. They had to get back to the tents which would give them food and water, and collect the captain's weapon and communicator on their way down. They needed a functioning communicator to get back into the ship. He did not want to think of the ramifications of failure.

Then he thought of the girls. Was there a way they could help? Would they help?

He turned to the first officer and noticed he had dozed off. He shook him a few times to wake him up.

"What? What's up?" the officer asked, annoyed.

Grog turned off both translators, so the boys would not understand what they were saying. He explained their situation to him and offered the option of getting the girls involved if they would do it.

"That's a rather desperate move, Grog. We could lose them. I don't know if they'd be any help. They have no weapons with them. They'd be easy targets. We've brought all six of our weapons here."

"They might be able to collect the captain's weapon from the side of the mountain."

"It's too dangerous and it would alert the fliers that it's there. It appears that they didn't notice it fall off the captain."

"The fliers may not expect, nor care about, people that far down the mountain."

"That's where they get their food."

There was silence for several minutes.

The officer thought of another partial solution, "Our main problem is the projectiles. We could use a blanket as a shield."

"I've been thinking of that too but we'd have to build a frame to hold it taut, so the rocks will bounce off it. We don't have long poles to do that. We could tie our short planks together but the frame would be difficult to move and we have a small portion of a narrow trail to cross. We'll be exposed for a long time as we drag people from one side to the other. I've looked at our equipment status and we don't have enough power in most of our weapons to withstand many more attacks. Our communicators and field generators are running out of power, too. Getting the captain's belt would help. There's one almost fully charged gun and communicator there."

"My communicator and gun are in pretty good shape."

"Raj's gun is not too bad but the other three are the problem."

"We have four people still able to fire them."

"Just barely. Maybe I could make a trip to the camp at night and take the field generator from there to use here."

"The fliers will then be able to see our campsite. We have our extra food and water and the samples we collected there. Some fliers also keep a night watch, so you'd be seen and perhaps attacked."

"Yes, I've seen them flying at night. We can't stay here for long, though. We've got to do something. They have the numbers, and now they've figured out how to stay out of range and bomb us with rocks."

"Okay, we're limited here. You're right, we could use another field generator. We do have one in the ship but we still have the rock bombardment with which to contend." The officer was in deep thought. Suddenly, his eyes brightened. "The cannon," he said excitedly.

"What cannon?"

"The cannon we have in the ship. I've never used it before but to protect the ship we do have a cannon."

"But how do we get it here without using the girls?"

"Maybe we have to use them."

"Wouldn't it be dangerous for the girls?"

"My main concern is not the girls – they're expendable but losing technology. If the fliers obtain any of our technology, we're in big trouble with headquarters. They'd rather lose us all than have that happen. We'd be taking a big gamble. I wish we had the captain's counsel."

"You're acting captain now, so you'll have to make the decision."

There was a pause while the first officer mulled over his options. "I don't see much of a chance for getting out of this. We might not be able to get to the captain's equipment. If we don't get the girls, our shields will run out of power before a ship arrives here, and they get our technology. If we get the girls involved and we fail, the same thing happens. If we try to get to the ship on our own, our chances are slim. If we use the girls, our chances are still slim but there's a greater chance of success.

"I'm banking on the fliers' focussing their efforts on us. They seem to live high in the mountains with deep canyons and valleys. The valley where we landed is at a higher elevation than this side. The fliers have no nests on that side of the mountain, although, they do forage outside their territory. I must rely on their staying mostly on this side and that they're not expecting anyone else to help us. If so, the girls should make it to the base camp without much of a problem. It's after that our success rate drops." He paused again and looked at the boys.

Roche was staring at him, wondering what they were talking about then he winced a bit in pain. Dan was sitting slumped, staring dully out through the field. Raj was unconscious between them.

He looked at the captain lying beside them. He looked up and knew there were fliers high above them waiting for a signal to drop rocks on them. There were several fliers farther from them outside the lizards' range of fire.

The first officer put on his translator, pulled out his communicator, and called the girls. There was a pause for about thirty seconds.

They heard Erica's voice. "If you're calling us, something must be wrong." She sounded worried because it was the first officer calling. She wondered where Grog was. He was the one who called last time.

The first officer asked if Jiao was nearby.

Jiao responded, "Yes."

"Our situation has deteriorated. We've had several battles with the fliers, the latest one was just minutes ago. The fliers seriously injured the captain. I've been partially paralysed. The fliers tossed a rock at Raj and knocked him out. We don't know how bad it is. Dan is recovering from his injuries. The only ones who are not too bad are Grog and Roche. To top it off, we've run out of food and water. There's more food and water at our base camp lower on the mountain but with all the injuries, we're hours away from it and it'll be difficult for us to get there." He paused.

"So, that's why you're late," Erica said. "Why didn't you tell us earlier?"

"We were still okay up to that point. The new battle gave us more injuries." He paused again then said, "Now, we know it would be risky for you but we'd like you to help us."

Erica looked at Jiao and pressed the mute button. "Do you want to go?"

"I don't know if we have a choice. It sounds as though the fliers injured everybody, including Dan and Raj. He says Grog and Roche are not too bad but what does that mean?"

"So, you're okay to go?"

"If you are," Jiao said with not much conviction.

Erica pushed the mute button again. "How are we going to find our way there?"

"Don't worry about that. I want to let you know that coming here is going to be very dangerous. The fliers are big, strong, and can throw rocks accurately. They got the better of us and used rocks as weapons. You'll be in a precarious situation. I don't want to scare you off but I want you to know the facts before you leave there."

"Can't we have guns?"

"We only have six guns and have five with us. The captain's gun was on his belt that fell off him when the fliers attacked him and it fell down the mountain. We might have you retrieve it on your way up. We need you to carry some equipment with you. One of them, you may be able to use to defend yourselves, if needed."

"Oh?"

"Yes, we're asking you to bring a cannon with you."

"A cannon! How are we going to carry a cannon?" Erica shouted out in surprise.

"The one we're talking about is light but the bombs deliver a heavy punch. You could also call it a missile launcher. There are a few other things to carry but you should be able to manage them. We're not exactly sure how we'll do it yet but I'm confident the trip to our base camp will be relatively easy. It's the part after that gets perilous."

The first officer paused to let the information sink in then said, "Now that you know about what we want and what the risks are, do you still want to help us?"

Erica pushed the mute button. She looked at Jiao and asked, "Are you willing to die to help the boys?"

"That's not exactly what he said," Jiao responded.

"That's the worst thing that can happen to us, so the bottom line is – we're putting our lives on the line. Are you willing to do it, knowing we could end up dead? Remember, we could stay here, make sure we're safe, and wait until someone picks us up."

"Why are you saying this? Are you unsure if you want to do it?"

"I'm willing to but I want to make sure you feel the same way. Once we leave here, there might not be a chance to turn back. We've got to be a machine out there; cool, calm, and collected."

"Right, cool, calm, and collected; I can do that," Jiao said under her breath facetiously.

Erica pushed the mute button again and said, "Okay we're ready to go. What do you want us to do?"

"First, get yourselves ready by having something to eat and drink, and leaving extra food and water for the aboriginal. Call me when you're ready."

45.

Erica was not convinced that leaving the ship was the best thing to do but they got ready for the trip and walked into Aaootaa's compartment with an overly full container of food and two containers of water then placed them into the slot of the cell. Erica turned on the translator and said, "We have to leave this place for a while."

Aaootaa looked puzzled.

Erica was not sure if it was from the translation, or if it was because she did not understand that they had to leave. She said, "Our men are hurt and need our help." She was adding hand signs, as she had done before to help Aaootaa understand what she said.

Aaootaa looked worried. She made some signs and sounds herself.

Erica got some garbled words from the translator and responded, "No, I don't think they're hurt badly. We should only be away for two or three days."

Aaootaa nodded but looked anxious. She grabbed the bars of her cell and pulled and pushed them vigorously.

Erica added. "No, we can't let you go. I promise we'll come back. We left you a lot of food and water."

Aaootaa pulled the bars of the cell again and repeated her worries.

"No, only the lizards can let you go and, right now, they need our help."

Aaootaa seemed dejected, as she turned her back on them.

"Everybody'll be back soon," Erica said and realised she might be lying to her. If their mission failed, it would be weeks before another ship came to this planet to pick up the ship, or remotely had the ship fly back to the home planet. Aaootaa would die of hunger and dehydration before that. She only had a few days of food and water there. She was trapped in a death cell.

Erica became resolved and stood as tall as her small stature would allow. She would have to make sure she did not fail. She had come to love this woman. She loved her for the simplicity of her life and because she was who she was – a kindred spirit. They were kilometres apart in culture but millimetres away as females. She was not going to let her die. She would not fail.

The girls turned, walked out of the room without looking back, and closed the door.

Jiao began to cry.

"Why are you crying?" Erica asked sympathetically. She reached out and touched her for support.

"We might not be back, right? We might be leaving her here to die."

"I thought of that. We have to make sure we get back, that's all," she responded.

Jiao dried her tears with her jumper. She had to be strong. She knew this was a serious mission and there was no room for sentimentality. She said stiffly, "Okay, what do we do?"

Erica picked up the communicator and activated it.

The first officer responded instantaneously, "Okay, so you're both ready to go?"

"Yes."

"Good, unfortunately, we don't have another belt to attach this to you, when you're not using it, so you'll have to carry this with you. Go to the centre of the room you must be in. In the third drawer from the top, you'll see something that looks like glasses. Wait for a second while I put in the code to unlock the drawer."

Erica walked over to the central control area of the room. She saw the five drawers beneath the console.

"Okay, it should be unlocked, so open it," the first officer said.

Erica opened the drawer and saw several items in it but pulled out the thing that looked like eyeglasses. It was a lot thicker than normal human glasses but she could not see lenses. Instead of eye openings, they looked like small camera lenses attached to a stretchable band that would go around the back of the head. It was like a hybrid between glasses and goggles.

"Did you find the glasses?"

"Yes."

"Put them on."

She did but all she saw was blackness.

"I'm going to turn them on and put them through some tests, so bear with me."

Suddenly, there was a bright light which finally focussed, so she could see through the glasses as she would with normal light.

"Hey, this is neat. I can see the room," Erica stated.

She looked at Jiao but the scene changed, so Erica saw Jiao as an outline in red then she changed to many other colours. The view then went back to normal but Jiao seemed to be moving away from her and soon seemed to be far away. The view zoomed back to normal but now Jiao appeared to be moving closer and closer. Erica looked at Jiao's face and soon was looking at her nose then a pore on her nose and inside the pore. Shortly, Erica saw Jiao normally again. Then Jiao's jumper dissolved and she was naked. Her skin began to peel off, so Erica saw her muscles then her organs, and finally her skeleton.

"Oh, gross," Erica cried out. All these sights were making her queasy. If this continued, she was afraid she was going to throw up.

"What's wrong, Erica?" Jiao asked. "You don't look too well."

"The officer's testing out the glasses and he's changing colours, and zooming in and out. Then he showed me your guts and skeleton."

"Oh," Jiao said disgustedly.

"Things are normal again."

The first officer remarked, "I've finished testing the device. I can see everything you can. This'll help me to help you for the next day or so. We'll be able to do things a lot quicker and I can guide you along the trail, so you won't get lost."

"Well, you didn't have to show me Jiao's guts."

The officer laughed for a few seconds in his alien way. "Sorry, I was showing you what these vision goggles can do for you. I'm going to unlock one of the doors that contain the cannon. Turn your head a little to the right . . . no, a little more . . . there. Now walk that way." She did that and the door to one of the other compartments in the ship opened in front of her.

"Walk straight and stop beside the small panel in front of you."

Erica was standing in front of a small protrusion in front of the wall. There was a small metal-like covering in the front of it.

"Okay, now reach down near the bottom of the panel and push it."

She did that and the panel popped up. Inside was a cylindrical object attached to a gear mechanism.

"On both sides of that hollow tube you see are two small pins. Pull them out."

She reached in and pulled at one of them.

"That's it. You might have to pull hard to get them out. Don't worry, nothing will break."

She pulled harder and the pin slid out. She did the same thing on the other side.

"Now, put a hand on each side of the tube and pull."

Erica did so and the tube lifted from its bracket. The tube was about one metre long. About two-thirds of the way from the hollow end of it was a seam. On the longer end was a rectangular panel with several small buttons of various colours and two larger buttons.

"You see it has two parts. The open end is the cannon. The section at the closed end contains six bombs. If you look to your left in the room, you'll see five other bottom sections on the rack. Have Jiao pick up one of them. I hope we won't need more than twelve projectiles. I don't want to load you down too much."

"The whole thing doesn't seem that heavy," Erica noted.

"It won't seem so light once you've carried it for several kilometres. Now, you can leave that room and put the cannon and refill beside the hatch."

She got instructions to find another field generator, a small box containing what he called batteries, three cloth support straps, food and water, and a small cloth bag to carry them. They also obtained a length of rope and a magnet with a loop on it for collecting the captain's belt. The officer showed her how to put cloth straps on the generator, cannon, and refill they had, to make it easier to place them on their backs for carrying.

The officer's last comments before leaving the ship were, "If you get going, you should make it to the campsite before nightfall."

They approached the hatch, picked up their equipment, and fastened it to them. The hatch opened, they left the ship, and the officer remotely closed and locked it and turned on the forcefields. He gave them instructions for where to go as they went along. Erica could see that these goggles were helping them immensely as they went.

They passed the stream and headed up the path to begin their slow climb into the mountains. Several times they had to stop to adjust their load or switch it to their other shoulder. Often, the officer asked Erica to look around and up. He also asked her to scan the area with her communicator. The officer could see the results of each scan and instruct her to change settings on the communicator when needed.

It was getting late. The sun was nearing the tops of the mountains when the officer told them to stop for a few minutes. He asked for a scan and, so far, there was not much to see. He hoped that the fliers were focussing on the stranded interlopers and not paying too much attention to a wide area around that was turning out as expected.

They were soon near the campsite which was around a bend in the mountain. They would be more visible, as the undergrowth that partially covered their advance was thinning and, for the first time, they would be entering the flier's territory.

"Okay, edge over to the corner ahead of you and crouch down. As close to the ground as you can, look," the officer instructed.

As she peeked around the corner, she could see the fliers in the distance. She looked all around her but there were no fliers nearby. Another reading with the communicator confirmed it.

He told them to crouch and walk to the campsite. The officer turned off the forcefield to let them into it then turned it back on.

The girls dumped their loads and slid onto the ground, exhausted.

"Okay, you've made it. You did a great job," the officer said. He was pleased with how the girls had handled themselves.

"Both our backs are sore, you know. I thought for a while I wasn't going to make it," Erica said hoarsely.

"Well, you did. You're safe now. They can't see you through the invisibility field and can't get to you through the forcefield. You can use either, or both, large tents, as you wish. Don't use the small supply tent. There are blankets for each of you inside the tents.

"To shut off the forcefield, if you need to leave to void yourselves, push the green button on the generator. Make sure you turn it back on when you're done. Don't touch the blue one as it operates the invisibility field. Remember, if you leave the campsite, the fliers can see you – so watch out. There's a flashlight in the bag if you need to use it. The fliers won't see any light you turn on while the invisibility field is active. Get a good night's sleep. I'll wake you up in the morning for the next step. Call me if you have any problems." The first officer signed off.

Erica removed the glasses and put down the communicator.

"I'm beaten. It looks as if we're going to keep doing this tomorrow," Jiao said quietly.

"It'll probably be worse. We got a free ride today."

"That communication with him is great. He can guide us along the trail. He helps us keep an eye out for the fliers. He can see everything you see."

"Yes, that's a blessing. I suggest we get some sleep. What do you want to do about the tents? We have two tents and two blankets."

"Sleeping together means we can double up the blankets and the body heat."

"Okay, together it is. Just take the blanket out of the tent you don't want to sleep in and let's get to bed."

"One smells like the lizards and the other like the boys, so let's sleep in the boys' tent."

"Okay."

Jiao dragged the blanket from the aliens' tent into the boys' tent and went inside. Erica followed her. They got the tent organised, put both blankets together, went out to eat and drink, and prepared for bed. To save the stock of food and water they were carrying, they ate and drank from the supplies stored in the tent.

"I think we're both tired and will have a long day tomorrow, so maybe we shouldn't talk and get to sleep," Erica suggested.

"Okay."

Throughout the whole trip, Erica had been thinking about what they had to do. She was also thinking of Aaootaa back at the ship. What they were doing, and the importance of it, terrified her. There were so many ways their mission could fail. They were safe for now but she was not sure that would be the case once they stepped out of the tent in the morning. Tomorrow might be their last day alive.

Tears filled Erica's eyes but she had to stop them. If she broke down, there was a good chance that Jiao would, too. She said quietly, "I wish we had a bugle."

"A what?" Jiao asked, puzzled.

"Well, in the old cowboy days, the troops who came to the rescue of someone in danger would have a bugler tooting out some song. That meant the bad guys and the good guys would know that help was on the way."

"Are you kidding?"

"No, that's what they did but if I had a bugle, I'd sure be tempted to do that. Maybe the bad guys would think there were a million of us coming instead of two."

Jiao started laughing and soon Erica joined in. They soon cuddled together and drifted off to sleep.

46.

The aliens' communicator buzzed. Erica opened her eyes and yawned, at first not recognising what sounded like a million crickets scraping their legs in unison. She stuck her head out of the blanket and looked outside. It was not completely light yet and the air was still rather crisp. Then, she shuddered when reality struck her.

She shivered a bit, as she grabbed the communicator and stuck her head back under the blanket. She brought it to her ear and responded.

The first officer said, "Sorry for getting you up early. You might notice that my words are a little slurred because it's cold enough to slow down my metabolism enough to impair most of my normal body functions. I'm glad it's a little warmer than we've had the last few days. I felt it necessary though to get an early start to the day.

"As I told you, one of our priorities is to get the captain's belt. We can't leave without it. I'm not sure how long it's going to take to travel the route I've planned, as you're going to swing around the back side of the mountain. It's unlikely the fliers expect anyone to save us, and more so if you're coming from the opposite direction. Please get yourselves ready, that includes eating and everything else you must do. Call me back when you're done."

Erica lowered the communicator and froze for a minute. What was a diminutive city girl from Ottawa doing on a planet outside her solar system helping aliens to get themselves out of a mess they had created? Then she remembered that this was not for them but to save three friends of hers and Aaootaa who were depending on her for survival.

She felt overwhelmed. How was she going to do anything the aliens could not do? She stared at the sun in the sky for a second then turned, woke up Jiao, and told her about the call she received. The two of them exited the campsite for a few minutes for personal needs then returned to have breakfast from the food and water in the camp. They were shivering slightly, as it was still cool outside.

"How do you feel this morning?" Erica asked.

"A little stiff and my shoulders are sore," Jiao stuttered.

"That's the way I feel, too. Are you ready to go?"

"No, I'm scared. I don't know why you're so brave."

"Ha!" Erica wrapped her arms around Jiao. "I put on a nice show, eh? I'm not brave, I'm scared, too. Jiao, remember that whatever we do is for the boys and Aaootaa."

Erica looked at the other range of mountains and watched the fliers soaring majestically through the air. They looked so at home and beautiful where they were. This was their planet; she was the interloper and had no right to be there but she had a job to do. She had to get the boys out of there.

Erica called back the first officer.

"So, you're ready?" he asked.

"Yes," Erica responded.

"Get your glasses on. Let's look around first."

Erica slipped on the glasses and scanned the area around her.

The officer asked her to activate the scanner on the communicator and she did a scan that way. He also recommended that they bring both blankets with them. They folded them up and placed them into the small bag that held the extra water and food.

"Now, look at how the field generator is set up."

They looked at it.

"Take one more look around outside before you go."

She searched the sky and surroundings.

"It looks as if there are no fliers near you, so load up your gear."

The girls picked up the items they had carried the day before. Erica wrapped the small bag onto one of the straps on the cannon, so the blankets provided extra padding between the strap and her shoulder.

"Okay, we're all packed," Erica responded.

"Good, you're going to travel an area you've already passed for a while then you'll proceed farther behind the mountain from there. Since they can see where you are, let's begin to practice how to move with the fields activated. To get out of the campsite, someone pushes the green button on the field generator and walks for a while."

Erica bent down and pressed the button. They took several steps to get away from the campsite.

"That should be far enough." He paused for a few seconds to activate the forcefield remotely. "Okay, the forcefield is on again. Tell Jiao to set up the field generator she has in the same way as she saw in the tent. Try to find the most level spot you can."

Jiao responded to the instruction. "I heard that. I'll set it up." She set it up while Erica watched.

The officer said, "Excellent, now push first the blue button then the green one. Erica, get close to the little panel on it, so I can see the readings better. I have a reading here but I want to make sure things are working well."

There was a pause while the officer examined all the numbers on the panel. "Good, it looks as if I don't have to make any adjustments for now.

"I'm going to describe a technique for travelling we used for the last couple of days with some success. The first field renders you almost invisible but when you move it against a background the fliers might pick you up if they look carefully. They won't know you're coming, so won't be looking for you.

"The other field is a forcefield that'll protect you from anything they can throw at you. However, you can't move the generator when the forcefield is on, so when we moved with it, the fliers threw things at us and hurt most of us. That's why we had to ask for help.

"Let's try the full technique for practice while you're visible to the fliers and I'll watch you as you go along. Take your time and constantly look for danger. Be ready to press the green button at any time. We'll also be watching the fliers' activities from here.

"Okay, you're standing in the middle of the protected area with all your equipment. Take your gear and take five steps to the edge of the forcefield."

There was a pause while they did that.

The officer walked them through the process they had developed.

After they had travelled the distance to the corner of the mountain, they could no longer see the fliers so, for speed, the officer told them to stop, turn off the fields, disassemble the generator, and carry it as they did the previous day. He said, "I'll guide you on this new path and might need you to do scans along the way. Keep your eyes open for fliers and be ready to set up the generator if anything happens. Good luck."

They made good time as Erica was setting a rapid pace through the light scrub in front of them. The sun was fully up and warming the air more. Instead of the cold, they were beginning to sweat.

After over three hours of travelling the first officer said, "Take a rest. You're doing a great job."

They dropped what they were carrying and looked off into the distance. The first officer zoomed in on what they saw. There was a swarm of fliers heading their way from mountains on the other side of the large valley where they had landed, likely some of the supporting fighters.

They had a bit of food and water. When they finished, the officer said, "I think the fliers are far enough away that you can keep travelling the way you are. We'll have to keep an eye on them. Keep looking up as you go."

They picked up their gear and walked for another twenty minutes when the first officer stopped them.

"They're too close, now. Stop, set up the generator, and turn on the invisibility and forcefields for a while. Let's let them pass."

The girls did it and had nothing to do but rest and watch the sky as the fliers passed by. They looked so majestic. It seemed so unlikely that they could hurt anyone.

When the fliers were beyond their sight, Jiao leaned over to Erica and pushed the mute button of the communicator.

Erica looked at her, confused.

Jiao said, in desperation, "I'm so tired, I'm going to collapse. I just can't go on anymore. Why do you have to walk so fast?"

"You've got to remember the boys and Aaootaa. I try to focus my attention on that. To the boys, every minute counts. I'm just as tired as you are. We have to keep going."

"Can't we have some water?"

"Let's save it for the boys."

Jiao shrugged her shoulders.

Erica looked in the distance in all directions and verified with the scanner that there were no fliers.

Jiao turned off the generator, folded it up, and placed it into the sack.

Erica turned off the mute button and started walking through the scrub. After an hour, she had to slow their pace as the scrub and speed were draining their strength too quickly.

After three hours they stopped to rest.

Erica looked at Jiao. Her eyes were looking dull and blank.

"Girls," the officer said through the communicator, "Drink some water and have something to eat. You haven't done that and you're no good to us if you die before you get to us. You're carrying enough food and water for all of us and there's more in the base camp."

"We've got to save it for you," Erica replied.

"There'll be enough. Eat something now and drink some water. If you're being stubborn then consider it an order from me."

Jiao opened the bag and took out the food and water then they ate and refreshed themselves. They placed the food and water in the bag and began to walk again.

"Hold it, girls. Put down your stuff and rest longer than that."

"We need to get to you as soon as we can."

"Yes, I know. I appreciate that. You're two tough young ladies but rest for a few minutes."

Jiao, especially, liked the rest the officer told them to take.

Soon, they were on their way again and, within minutes, were climbing to make their way to the other side of the mountain. Although the plants they were pushing their way through were thinning, the incline was impeding their progress.

The officer told them to take a break again.

Erica looked at the sky. The sun was well beyond its zenith.

"I don't know if I can walk anymore," Jiao cried out in pain.

Erica pressed the mute button and said, "You've got to keep going. The boys are counting on us. We would've been able to do this back home. We have no stamina because, even doing exercises, we aren't prepared to do something like this anymore."

They ate and drank lightly to preserve the food and water. They knew they were consuming the boys' food.

Minutes passed.

"Okay girls, ready to go?" the officer asked.

Erica looked at Jiao.

She nodded.

Erica pushed the mute button and said, "Sure."

They picked up their equipment and began climbing again. After a couple of hours, they rounded the mountain to the side exposed to the fliers. They crouched low and peered directly ahead. They spotted the fliers in the distance. Closer to their side of the mountain they could see a couple of fliers soaring above the peak of it. The officer adjusted her glasses to zoom in a little and she looked lower down to spot some fliers clinging to the rock on the mountain.

"Beneath those flyers is the ledge where we're located," the first officer said. "You won't be able to see it well from where you are."

"That's quite far," Erica said.

"Yes, I know. Do you want to keep going or take another break?"

Erica looked at Jiao and saw her nod.

"Let's keep going."

They kept low as they made their way onto the other side, then edged down the mountain. After a couple of hours, they took another food and water break and continued their way down until the officer called a stop.

"Before it gets too dark, we'd better find somewhere you can bed down for the night."

He had her scan the area around her until he spotted a flatter location. They carefully made their way there and made camp. After a quick meal, they set up the forcefield, pulled out their blankets, and immediately fell asleep.

The first officer looked at the energy level in the communicator and sighed. It would not last another day. He would have to use Grog's tomorrow. He looked around him. The captain and Raj were still unconscious or dead, Dan was sitting in a daze, while Roche was probably too weak to walk. Grog was giving pills to everyone and giving injections to the two who could not consume the pills. Everyone was hungry but it was the lack of water that was slowly killing them. He looked outside with his glasses and could see several fliers above them on the mountain. They occasionally tossed rocks down on the field. In the skies near the row of mountains on the other side of the valley was a swarm of fliers. He wondered if he should tell the girls to save themselves and turn back before they too succumbed to their fate but the girls were too far along. He doubted they would be able to make it safely back to the ship on their own. He had doomed them.

As the darkness slowly descended upon them, one by one, they drifted off to sleep.

47.

Despite the roughness and hardness of the ground, the girls had a sound sleep. Their exhaustion overwhelmed their discomfort.

Erica awakened first but did not move for several minutes. Her bladder forced her up. When she tried to get up though, her muscles were resisting but she turned off the field and got far enough away to unload.

She returned to camp, turned on the forcefield, and looked up at the cloudless sky. She could see hundreds of fliers along the opposite mountainside. On this side, not much had changed. She could see they were close to thicker plants and would have to plough their way through them soon. With a look at the sun, she guessed that it was midmorning. It had not been cold when she got up, so they were in for a hot day.

She sat down for a few minutes, looked at the communicator and saw that the officer had not called her yet. If she felt the way she did, Jiao would feel the same or worse. She reached over and poked her but she did not move, so she shook her a few times.

Jiao groaned and opened her eyes. She looked at Erica and said, "Leave me alone, I'm tired."

"We've got to get up. The first officer will be calling us soon. I'm worried he didn't call us by now."

Jiao looked around her and then back to Erica. "I was a little cold last night even with the blankets."

"At least it wasn't as cold as the night before."

Jiao looked at the mountains over the boys' camp and saw the fliers.

"I'm amazed we weren't seen yesterday."

"I guess it's good to be wearing these crappy clothes because the brown is helping us to blend in, although the rocks are greyish. We'll be entering the brush soon and it'll make us less noticeable. I got up to take a pee and felt like crap. We'll have to stretch our muscles to get them moving again. We're out of shape."

Jiao tried to get up but could not. "I can't move. I hurt so much when I try."

"Just try, Jiao. You can do it."

There were tears in her eyes. "I can't walk anymore."

Erica painfully got up and noticed the scratches and cuts on her formerly beautiful legs but could not think of that. There was no time. They had to get to the boys as quickly as they could. She tried to help Jiao stand up, and failed. Jiao's muscles had seized.

She had to get her mobile again.

"Jiao, you've got to get walking. I can't do this myself. We need to get this equipment and water to the boys. I need you to walk. My legs also don't want to go anywhere. I would love to lie down and go to sleep again but we can't."

She helped Jiao get up and they stumbled along in a tight circle within the field limbering up their leg muscles.

After a few minutes, Erica began to release her and soon Jiao was walking on her own. They sat for a few minutes. Erica knelt beside Jiao and massaged her legs which felt rock hard but were softening as she worked them. Jiao slumped onto her back and closed her eyes.

Precious minutes passed as the massage did its work. Erica closed her eyes and began drifting into a half-sleep state as her breathing increased. She soon shook herself from her stupor, stood, and said nervously, "Okay, get up. That should be better."

Jiao moved her legs a little. "That does feel better. Where did you learn to do that?"

"I used to massage my father's neck. My mom taught me to do it." Erica stood and held out her hand.

Jiao hesitated a few seconds still not ready to move on to their main task then grabbed it and stood.

Erica said, "There, you're better, so let's get going. We've got a long way to go today."

They went to their equipment, packed it up, fastened it to them, and began their trip farther down to the plants below them. They stopped to eat, take a drink, and take a pee. Erica's headache told her they were not drinking enough water, so she pulled out the water to drink more of it and handed it to Jiao. They would need it to survive the day.

She pulled out the communicator and called the first officer. She had to do it a few more times until he responded.

"Sorry, I didn't answer right away, I woke up only a few minutes ago and was checking the others. How are you doing?"

Erica told him about their morning.

"Good, I'm glad you've overcome your ailments and are ready to go. It's going to be another long hot day for us. Put on the goggles and let's look around."

They did an entire scan of the area. The first officer was not pleased to see so many fliers at the other end of the valley.

The girls started walking briskly through the plants but, after an hour, they slowed their pace, partly to reduce the chances of the fliers spotting them and because of the thickening scrub. They were ploughing through it while keeping a close eye on what the fliers in the distance were doing.

As they neared the desired flier's nest, the shrubbery thinned out. It looked as if there had been a landslide there in the recent past. It made walking more difficult because of the loose rock and it made them much more visible to the fliers. Because they were not close to the upper portion of the mountainside, it would reduce the possibility of the hidden fliers above the area hitting them from above.

The officer told them to stop there, set up the generator, turn on the invisibility field, and rest a while. They had something to eat and drank some water. Jiao was worried about the dropping water level in the canister.

"Beneath this area, you should be able to retrieve the captain's belt with its tools attached," the officer said soon after they had stopped. "Take out the scanner again and let's get a reading."

Erica picked it up and pushed the scan button. She moved it around from side to side.

"Okay, point it down a bit more . . . See that little blip. That's where it is. You'll have to move the field a little closer to that area. I'll tell you when to stop. We won't be able to get as close as I would like because of the configuration of the ground."

The girls used what they had learned earlier to move it where the officer wanted.

"Move to your right about four steps. You are partly out of the field and are visible but let's hope they don't notice you. Let's get to it. Take the rope and the magnet you brought along and I'll tell you how to hook it up."

The officer instructed her how to tie the rope to the magnet.

"Okay, give the magnet a bit of a toss to get by some of the rocky area and let out the rope as it falls . . . That's it. Just let it feed out more . . ."

Jiao cut him off, "I think the fliers may have seen us. Some of them are coming this way."

The girls were too far away to get any support from the stranded team.

The first officer said through the communicator, "You're right, Jiao, there's a swarm of fliers heading your way. The lower fliers will soon be over your heads to scout the area. The higher fliers are likely setting themselves up so they can drop rocks on you when you turn off your field. Keep your eye on them. Have you felt the magnet touch the belt yet?"

"How do I do that?" Erica asked.

"Just pull up the rope a bit."

"It feels heavy."

"Okay, you've likely got it, so slowly pull up the rope. Jiao, keep an eye on what's going on."

"Jiao responded, "Some fliers are hugging the edge of the mountain above us."

"You should be relatively safe from them. You're not directly under them. They're meant for us. Have you got the belt up yet?"

Erica responded, "Almost."

"The fliers are almost over you. Erica, stop pulling the rope, hold it firmly on the ground, and put a large rock on it to hold it in place, so it won't move. Move back into the field. Jiao hit the generator's green button."

Jiao did it and within ten seconds they saw rocks flying off the side of the mountain, bouncing off the lizards' forcefield, and sliding farther down the mountain. The fliers above the girls dropped their rocks but they bounced off the top of their forcefield.

After a few seconds, the rock barrage stopped and all was calm.

"Erica, look up and turn your head to the right. You can't see us but you're looking at the fliers above where we are."

She did so and the officer examined the mountain above them normally, magnified a few times, and in infra-red. Erica could see what he saw.

"You can't rely on support from us right now," the officer said. "We still have those fliers above us and we're too far from you to help. If the fliers over you see the rope move, they'll toss rocks to try to hit you without the shield. We both can't sit here all day, so let's let them see what else we have."

"Erica, look directly over you."

She looked up at the swarm of fliers over her. Soon, she also saw some symbols appear over what she saw.

"Okay, pick up your cannon, set it on the ground open side up close to the generator, and pull out the legs near the bottom."

Erica did it.

The officer said, "Put your hands on the edge of the top of the cannon. Jiao, please hold the side of it tightly. Erica, pull it up." The seam in the cannon slid up about half a metre. "Good, it's ready to go."

"Now, look at the little panel on it." The officer increased the magnification a bit, so he could see it. He instructed her on how to make some adjustments to the settings.

She could see that he was matching the symbols on the goggles with those on the cannon.

"While we were looking at the fliers, I was measuring their locations and I'm sending up a surprise at the appropriate height to knock the fliers above you out of the sky. I'll give you three 'nows'. The first one will be to push the green button on the side of the field generator to turn off the forcefield. The second will be to push the large button on the side of the cannon to fire the bomb. The third will be to push the green button on the field generator to turn it back on. Got it?"

"Yes."

"Don't mix it up. We open the field to let the bomb out and finally close it to keep the concussion, rocks, and flier guts from falling on you."

"I got it."

The first officer started the sequence, "The cannon's ready, so . . . now."

Erica pushed the green button on the generator.

He waited a second then repeated, "Now."

Erica pushed the button on the cannon. The girls heard a loud whooshing noise, not the loud bang they expected.

Then in another second, the officer gave the last order, "Now."

Erica pressed the green button again. The girls heard a horrendous bang. Immediately, red splashed body parts and rocks careened off the top and sides of their forcefield.

Once the din ended, the officer said, "No time for inaction." He had her look around for several seconds then asked her for a scan. The only fliers around them were on the mountainside over his site and the hoard at the opposite range. They all seemed agitated. He hoped this moment of shock would last long enough for them to move quickly.

He said, "Turn off the forcefield, Erica."

When she had done it, he told Jiao to pull up the rope. Within a few seconds, Jiao was holding the belt.

"Erica, take the captain's belt and put it around your waist as best you can. It's made a lot longer for our thicker waists."

It took her a minute to tie it around her waist.

Jiao picked up the cannon and cradled it in her arms. They used the cover of the invisibility screen to advance again but they soon were walking through slippery, blood-covered rocks and body parts of the downed fliers. The scent of freshly killed meat filled their lungs.

Jiao wanted to vomit and stopped to heave for several seconds but there was not much in her stomach for her to succeed.

Erica shook Jiao and urged her to keep moving. Several times, each of them slipped and fell into the mess. As the metres passed, the amount of blood and guts dwindled and disappeared. They were leaving the exposed area of the rockfall into the scrub again.

The officer stopped them. "It looks as if the fliers are still in disarray. Turn off the field generator and pack it up, as the brush will give you good cover without the field. You'll travel a lot quicker that way. I'll keep an eye out for danger signs from our location up here."

The girls packed up the generator. Jiao slung it over her shoulder and they continued their trek.

48.

While the girls walked, Erica thought about the simple pleasures of home with her parents and sister. She missed them. She thought that, if she saved the lizards, maybe they could change their minds and take them home but they had said unequivocally they could not.

Often during the walk, she looked for any signs that the fliers were going to fly above them again.

As they progressed, the ground cover thickened. They stopped briefly to see the blood that now stained them and their jumpers. The blast had done its job. For now, they travelled in silence, unmolested.

After about two hours, the girls stopped for a food and water break.

"What's your current status?" the officer asked.

"Nothing's changed," Erica responded. "The soles of my boots are almost finished. I've cut some parts of my feet. Jiao's in about the same state."

"I've been away from the communicator for a while. I had to switch to Grog's as mine went dead." He waited to give the girls some idle time before they began their trek again.

After a few minutes, the officer said, "Okay, you've made great progress today. I'm going to try to find a way to get you onto the trail we're on. It's been too steep so far. When you get up there, you'll be out of the ground cover. You'll see that the number of fliers has grown significantly. I think they have several hundred of them and there are more of them coming. The ones over us have constantly been testing our field by dropping the occasional rock. I sometimes see a few fliers not too far from where you are. I think they know you're still around and approximately where you are. They may not be sure if you're associated with us and might be afraid of you. I guess the cannon blast has not deterred them. We may be in for a good fight. If you're rested enough, let's go."

The girls got up, picked up their equipment, and began forcing themselves to keep walking through the bushes again. Each step was a torturous task.

After a couple of hours, the tired girls stopped to rest and massaged their leg muscles.

Suddenly, Erica turned her head a little and froze.

Jiao noticed it. "Is there something around?" she enquired with fear in her eyes as she looked around and saw nothing.

"Shh," Erica replied "Don't you hear the sound of water trickling?"

Jiao listened. "Maybe, is that what you heard?"

"Yes."

"I thought you heard some fliers." She sighed with relief.

Erica got up slowly, picked up the bag, took the water container out of it, told Jiao to stay there, and walked in the direction of the noise.

Within five minutes, she located a small trickle of water and cupped her hand to fill the bottle. When the container was full, she took a deep breath. There had not been much water in the container and Erica was concerned that there might not have been enough to bring the boys back to health. She drank some of the water, refilled the container then returned to Jiao.

"I've refilled the bottle. Here have some." She handed it to Jiao. "We'll have plenty for everyone; at least until we get to the camp."

While Erica reported to the officer, Jiao drank her fill.

Erica returned to the stream, refilled the container with water, and they started walking again.

After another thirty minutes, the first officer asked Erica to do a scan of their surroundings.

"It looks as though there may be an area you can climb up to this trail. It's a little steep but the slope shouldn't be too hard for you and you may be able to walk most of it transversely. We'd never be able to do it but you should."

He had them walk some distance to the area. He had Erica do another scan, then guided them to the site and left them to do what they had to.

It was very difficult for the girls to climb with the equipment they had to carry. Erica had put her communicator into the small bag she was carrying to free up her other hand. She noticed the light was waning, so she quickened their pace.

It was almost twilight when the scrub cleared and they pulled onto the ledge the first officer said was the path toward them. They looked toward the other set of mountains. They could not believe their eyes. The fliers were so numerous they looked like a cloud in the sky. The distraction caught them off guard.

As the girls began to take off their equipment, rocks began falling on them. Erica looked up to see a couple of fliers settling onto the mountainside above them.

Jiao pulled the generator off her back and set it on the trail. When she finished, a rock hit Erica in the back of her neck. She fell onto the trail in pain and lifted her head to see Jiao lying face down on the ledge beside the generator. Erica reached over and pushed both buttons then blacked out.

Erica regained consciousness a few minutes later. The fliers in the distance were moving in. She looked at Jiao who was still lying not far from her. She got up slowly and painfully. She opened her sack and pulled out the communicator. She said, "We've been attacked but I'm okay."

The first officer sighed with relief. "Good to hear you. We could see the fliers heading your way but you were too far for us to help you. Through your goggles, I could see you fall. I wondered what happened. I guessed that a rock hit you. I can see that Jiao's down, too."

"I got hit on the back of my neck. It's bleeding a bit but I seem to be better now. It hurts though. I'll go look at Jiao."

She crawled over to Jiao and lifted her head. It looked as if a rock had grazed it and then hit her shoulder. She described the situation to the officer.

"Yeah, I can see. Is she breathing?"

"Yes."

"That's good. The fliers are smart. They're using our weaknesses to their benefit. You didn't see the danger until it was too late. They set up an ambush and you walked right into it. I couldn't call you. They must have estimated where you'd be when you left the shrubs. Are you able to look up?"

Erica could not tilt her head back because of the pain, so she twisted her body around for her eyes to see up the side of the mountain. She saw nothing, even when she adjusted the focus and zoom. She automatically did a scan with the communicator.

"Yes, it looks as if they hit and ran. See what you can do with Jiao. It'll slow you down if she's immobile."

She took off her glasses, put the communicator in her bag, and returned to Jiao. She checked her more carefully. She did not see any reason she could not turn her onto her side, so she did. She leaned over to the small bag and took out the water container. She opened it, poured some water into her hand, and swabbed Jiao's face with it. That seemed to rouse her a bit, so she did it again and said, "Jiao, wake up."

Jiao stirred more and soon opened her eyes. "What happened? Why am I down here?"

"The fliers hit us with rocks. I've turned on the forcefield, so we're safe. How do you feel?"

Jiao shook herself a bit then said, "My head and shoulder hurt and I've got a headache but I seem to be okay."

"Here, drink some water. Do you want to eat?"

Jiao only took a sip of water and said, "I don't want any food. I'm okay. I'm sure the boys are starving. We should save it for them."

The communicator began to buzz, so Erica pulled it out of the bag, put it to her ear, and told the officer Jiao was conscious.

"It's good to hear she's okay," the first officer said excitedly. "Tomorrow's going to be a big day. We have a few minutes of light left. How about we give the fliers a little surprise? Get the cannon and put it on the ground. Look above you."

She saw that the fliers had returned to their perches above them. She soon saw symbols in the glasses again.

The officer quickly had her make a few adjustments to the cannon's position. He set the range. "Okay, when I say so, Erica, hit the green button on the generator then a second later hit the button on the cannon and finally hit the green button again as we've done before."

Erica did as he asked and there was a loud whoosh then a bang.

While some rocks and body parts tumbled down the mountain above them, the officer said, "Now tilt the cannon on its side facing away from the mountain. You'll have to put the base against the mountainside for support. I'll guide you on how to hold it. It's a huge swarm, so this time it might be better for Jiao to hit the button on the field generator. You can both hear me. You watched her to see how our system works, right, Jiao? There won't be much time because we're going to send out two quick shots, so you'll have to move fast."

"Yes, I'm ready," Jiao reported.

The officer told Erica to look at the swarm of fliers heading toward them. He gave her instructions to position the cannon then said, "Here are the three 'nows' for this shot." He said them in quick succession. The fliers were almost in shooting range of the guns, which was quite close to the cannon. Within seconds, he had Erica make a slight change in position for the cannon then had her send off the next shot.

When the fliers saw the bomb coming toward them, they could see that it was heading to one side and tried to disperse but it was moving too fast and was almost instantaneously in their midst. It went off.

The fliers very close to the projectile never knew what hit them. The concussion and shrapnel seriously injured others slightly farther away, and the damage graduated down to being knocked out to having no effect. Then a second shot was among them on the other side and went off with the same effect.

The immediate results were to throw the fliers completely off their plan. The survivors pulled back to help their injured comrades and survey their damage. Many of the fliers were soon trying to muster their forces for another attack because they were sure the interlopers would not be able to fire at them if they were very close to their new enemies.

The first officer, though, was already planning for another blast. He had time to get Erica ready for a new shot. When the fliers gathered for another attempt to move toward them, he hit them with another blast, with the same effect, except this time the fliers kept coming.

The officer noted that some of the fliers were heading up to the upper portion of the mountain, so he quickly set up his trap. When the fliers got close to the mountain, he blasted them up there. But his opportunities ran out after that.

The surviving fliers had enough experience with the field to realise when it was on or off and when it was off, their enemies were vulnerable to thrown rocks. The horizontal fliers stopped throwing but the ones over them started an intermittent flow of rocks.

In the silence after the blast, the first officer said, "I'm surprised they're so stubborn. This is all we can do for now. You're still too far for us to support you with our guns. You're stuck there until morning. It's getting dark and you just need a rest. It might be better to move very early in the morning.

"You know when it gets cold, we slow down but what I recommend you do is to get some sleep, then get up during the night and try to get as close to us as you can. When you do it, stay close to the mountainside to reduce your chances of the fliers hitting you. Do what you've been doing to move forward. Try to move at random times. They're going to continue to toss rocks down but you can make your move so quickly that they don't have time to throw.

"To hide your actions as much as possible, don't throw any rocks you find on the ledge down the mountain; pile them along the outside edge. The path is wide enough at your point that it won't restrict travel with the generator. You'll know you're close to us when the path gets too narrow to set it up. Get as close to us as you can but stay safe. We need you."

"Okay, we can try that," Erica responded.

"Good, I'll sign off for now. I want to save the power left in this communicator, so I'll contact you in the morning when it has warmed up. Good luck girls. You've done a great job."

Erica turned off the communicator and said to Jiao, "What do you think?"

"We're not going to get very much sleep tonight."

"Well, I think we're tired enough that we should be able to get some sleep, despite the constant sound of rocks hitting the mountain. Whoever wakes up first gets the other one up. I hope it works."

They settled down in their blankets and eventually drifted off to sleep.

49.

Erica awoke from a restless sleep. She peeked out of the blankets and saw Jiao sleeping quietly beside her. She got up and got ready to begin a very early day. She surveyed her surroundings but could not see anything. It was not fully black outside but dark grey. At first, she thought there was something wrong with her eyes and it took her some time before she realised that it was fog, perhaps with rain. The proof was the water seeping in along the mountain's edge. It was not the sun providing the light but one of the planet's moons.

She could hear the familiar sound of rocks falling off the side of the mountain like drips falling from a leaking water faucet.

She did not know what she should do. She could stay in bed and try to get more sleep or advance up the ridge toward the boys despite the current weather. Even though her visibility was negligible, the fliers could still determine when the forcefield was on by listening to the change in the sound of the falling rocks.

She had an idea. She felt around for the goggles and put them on. The officer had mostly adjusted the instrument remotely but on occasion had guided her to make slight adjustments. She felt the little buttons on the goggles and manipulated them for several minutes as she looked up the mountain's edge. She finally saw the red images of two fliers high up on the mountain. She looked horizontally toward the other mountains and noted tiny red images far off in the distance.

She lifted the glasses onto her forehead and woke up Jiao. "Get up," she whispered to Jiao, as she shook her. "It's still night time but we shouldn't waste any time. Get ready to move again."

Jiao did so, while Erica slid the glasses down again and zoomed in on the distant fliers. "It looks as if there are six fliers out there and two above us."

Jiao peered through the field but saw nothing. "You can see them? Is there fog out there?"

Erica replied, "Yes to both questions." She could see Jiao as a large red image beside her. She pulled the goggles onto her forehead. "It's weird using these things but they help me see in the dark."

Soon, Jiao was sitting beside her, ready to go.

Erica slid the glasses over her eyes and, like a military general, barked quietly, "Okay, we'll move fast at first. They won't know we're moving until a rock hits the ledge because the forcefield's off."

They loaded up and began the routine they had learned to move using the forcefield. They kept the shield on as long as possible by running while moving the field generator. They quickly realised their progress would be a lot slower than Erica wanted for the first tens of metres, as they had to clear the rubble from the previous day's blasts from the ledge. On the way back, they would have to clear the rocks from the trailing edge of this part of the ledge. Right now, though, she had to move quickly forward.

The fliers immediately realised the field was not on.

Erica could see the fliers rustling overhead as they moved forward to another perch on the mountainside but found the field on again.

The fliers settled into a new perch and began dropping more rocks and found the field wasn't there.

Erica continued to see rustling overhead as they spread out to figure out what was going on.

The fliers finally determined that the girls were moving much more rapidly up the trail than they had anticipated. They began to move farther ahead each jump to account for the girl's rapid pace. They also increased the number of rocks they were dropping.

Their speed and keeping close to the side of the mountain, helped them avoid the rocks that did fall through during the vulnerable portion of their cycle. Erica noticed that some of the distant fliers were heading toward them. The fliers above them must have alerted them to what was happening.

The girls were tiring though and the hits they were taking took their toll on them. The number of rocks had increased significantly as more fliers had reinforced those already on the side of the mountain. Other fliers were just outside their field looking for opportunities to break through it.

The girls finally had to stop to rest and sit, breathing heavily.

"We can't keep up this pace," Jiao said.

"We have to," Erica responded.

She looked at Jiao in the dim light. She could see that Jiao had some cuts and bruises on her. She looked at herself and saw her no better off. She was shivering. Their fast pace had made her forget how cool it was in the night. Now, the evaporating sweat was making her feel very cold.

Between breaths, Erica said, "I don't know when morning is going to come but we have to take advantage of the dark and the fog."

"I don't think it makes much difference," Jiao stuttered through her shivers, "but, let's keep going. Maybe that'll help us forget the cold."

"Yeah, but it might not matter. Their falling rocks are telling them where we are. We've come out here. If we don't get to the boys somehow, we'll have wasted all our effort and we'll all die. It's as simple as that, and we can't let that happen. It's up to us. We've got to save them and us. Maybe we could cut the speed and switch to randomly moving instead. That way we might get hit less."

They quickly got up and began moving again. On their third cycle though, Erica rushed ahead and had to dodge a rather large rock at the last second.

Three more cycles later, Jiao turned off the forcefield and bent to pick up the generator when a large rock hit her on the side of her head.

Erica turned to see her kneeling on the ground slumped over the generator. She raced back to the generator while dodging rocks, slipped on the wet moss that covered some portions of the trail and fell face down.

At first, she didn't want to get up. Several rocks were hitting them. She could see some of the fliers' hands reaching through the field. With force of will, she rose again and pushed Jiao off the generator. She twisted herself to face it and pushed the green button. The barrage of rocks stopped. She could hear piercing screeches as the fliers tried to pull out their hands.

Erica slumped to the ground, exhausted. She could not move. The pain was conquering her. Her strength was gone. The loss of blood and lack of food and water finally overcame her; now Jiao was lying face down on the trail, motionless. Try as she could to move, her muscles had seized. She began to cry but no tears were forming. There was nothing else she could do.

It took several minutes to compose herself. She crawled toward the small bag, pulled out the food and water, changed her mind, and put them back. She had to save it for the boys. They were relying on her.

Erica crawled over to Jiao, bent over her, removed her equipment, and could see blood running down the side of her face. She pulled out a blanket from the bag, wrapped Jiao in it to make her warmer and more comfortable, and made it easier to drag her.

Erica was not sure how many cycles more she made alone. She was trying to be as haphazard as she could about her timing.

Suddenly, during one cycle, she was moving the equipment forward when she almost slipped down the mountain, as she had no footing for her right foot. Only the forcefield had prevented it. It was the strangest feeling hanging for several seconds suspended off the rocks with nothing there but the forcefield holding her up. It felt like a huge hand along the side of her body.

She righted herself, stepped over the equipment, and saw that the ledge had significantly narrowed. She pulled her gear about two metres in from the edge of the narrow portion. She could go no farther.

She went over to Jiao and examined her.

Jiao had stopped bleeding but dried blood had caked on the side of the wound on her head. She had other cuts and bruises on her. There was a lump on her temple.

Only now did Erica check Jiao's pulse, and felt relieved when she found it. She had no first aid kit. She figured that she would not know what to do if she had one anyway. She crawled into the blanket with Jiao and went to sleep.

50.

Erica had no idea how long she had slept when she awoke again. She poked her head out of the blanket. It was pitch black. The moon must have dropped below the horizon. Water was still seeping down the mountainside. The clouds or fog blocked any starlight that may have given her some vision.

She slipped the goggles back on her eyes and looked around. She could see the red shapes of three fliers above her. She could also hear the periodic sound of rocks dropping down the mountain. She looked toward the mountains on the other side of the valley. The number of fliers had increased from the last time she looked. That meant they were gathering again, far off in the distance and out of range of anything the interlopers had to shoot at them.

She thought about what she should do. How close was she to the boys and should she wait until sunrise before she tried anything? She huddled in her blanket for several minutes and did not want to leave the comfort of it. Her muscles seemed stiff and unresponsive and hurt everywhere.

She searched for the communicator, picked it up, and tried to call the officer. There was no response. She thought it might have been too cold for him to respond, so called several more times to wake him up. She wanted him to tell her what to do. She was like an automaton and was still trying to recover from the terror around her.

Finally, she heard a voice, weak but definable.

She said, "Hello?"

Again, she heard the weak sound.

"Can you hear me?"

She heard something again.

"I can't hear you. Who is this?"

There was silence for several seconds. It seemed like hours to Erica.

"Who is this? Say something I can understand," she said in earnest.

She heard something feebly said again.

"It's Roche, isn't it?" she said with surprise. "Okay, don't say anything. I want to know where you are. You're invisible and even if you weren't, there's a thick fog outside." She tried to think of what to do. "You guys must have a flashlight. If so, can you quickly turn off the invisibility field and shine the light this way, so I can hopefully see it. The rocks will still protect you. Please do it quickly, if you can. I'll tell you if I can see it then you can turn the field back on."

She stared at the trail ahead of her with one eye through the goggles and the other with normal sight. Minutes ticked by and she wondered what was happening. Why was Roche not responding? Perhaps he was so far away she could not see the light.

Then she saw something. First, she saw feeble red images through the goggles, then a feeble light through the other eye. It seemed quite far away but if she saw it at all, it must not have been too far.

She excitedly said to the communicator, "I can see your light. You can turn it off and get your shield working again." But what should she do? The officer was not able to tell her what to do next.

The red images and white light disappeared.

Over the next few minutes, she formulated a plan.

She called back on the communicator, "If you can still hear me; grunt or say something."

She heard a sound. "Okay, I can hear you. You're going to hear a lot of loud explosions. When it stops, keep your eyes out for me and be ready to turn off your forcefield to let me in. If you understand what I'm saying make a sound."

She heard it.

She turned off the communicator. She took some time to figure out how to detach the old cartridge from the cannon and replace it with the spare. She put the spent cartridge on top of Jiao, so it would afford her some protection from the falling rocks.

She put the food, water, and batteries into the sack, put on the belt, attached the gun to it, and placed the communicator beside her.

She planned to fire two shots, one directly over her and the next one high over the boys' location.

She put on her glasses, located the red images, set up the first positional setting, and matched the settings to the cannon. She pushed the green button on the generator and fired the shot into the air above her then pushed the green button again. By the time the rocks falling due to the explosion ended, she was ready for the next shot into the mountains over the boys' site. Following the same process, she fired again and quickly looked around her. No fliers were visible. She turned off the forcefield, grabbed the sack and communicator, and walked out of the shielded area.

It was a difficult walk. She had to contend with the narrow ledge and thick fog. She had to feel her way with her foot along the trail and her hands along the mountainside. The fallen rocks and slipperiness of the path due to the rain and blood hampered her progress. She kicked the rocks away from the ledge but this made her uneasy because the noise of the rocks falling down the mountainside might attract other fliers. Several times, she thought she was going to fall but caught herself. She was intent on getting her package to the boys.

It seemed to take a lot of time and she was worried Roche was not going to be able to turn off the forcefield when she got there. He did not sound too well during the call.

As she walked, she felt ahead of her, so she would not run into the field.

Finally, her hand hit something ahead that she could not see. She eased up against it, so someone would be able to see her there. She waited but the field held firm. She took out the communicator and called into it but all she heard was a deathly silence. She knew that yelling would not help much and she was afraid of alerting any fliers that might be around. She slipped the goggles over her eyes and spent some time looking around and above her but other than some signs that there were some fliers off in the distance, none were immediately around her. She sighed with relief.

Suddenly, she felt ahead again and found the forcefield was no longer there. She took a step then another then could see a sight she would never forget.

She saw three immobile aliens covered in blood who looked dead. Raj's and Dan's bloodied heads poked out of a blanket; their eyes closed. Roche's bloodied body lay slumped over the blanket covering the other boys, one arm outstretched; his fingers only centimetres from the base of the generator. The area smelled like an outhouse.

She moved forward, climbing over the aliens to get to Roche. She grabbed his body and twisted him, so she could see his face. His eyes slowly opened and he tried to mouth some words. She bent down and covered his lips with hers.

She sat down, cradled his head, and reached for her bag. She opened it and pulled out the water container. She removed the cap, brought it close to his mouth and let a small stream of water flow into it. He choked a bit at it but swallowed it.

"Let that do its job. I can't stay here long because I don't know how to control the generators remotely, so Jiao is back there with the forcefield not operating. The fliers don't seem to be around but I can't take the chance they'll stay away for long."

Roche pulled himself up a bit and took a little more water. He tried to say something but could not form the words.

Erica put her index finger over his lips. "You don't have to say anything. Just blink your eyes if you'll be okay and look after everybody else here. I've got to get back to Jiao."

Roche blinked his eyes.

Erica took their food from the bag and said, "Here is some food for you." She pulled out the next container and said, "Here is some food for the lizards. I heard your communicators are almost dead, so here's mine. I'll keep the captain's belt, communicator, and gun. This little box contains some batteries."

She bent over him and gave him a gentle kiss. She raised her head and said, "Okay, I'll go. Turn on the forcefield when I leave and good luck. If anything happens here and you need help or anything, give me a call."

She got up and left. When she got outside the field's zone, she looked back and felt for it. It was on. She replaced the goggles on her eyes and looked around. She was sure the fliers could not see well in the fog but they must have heard the blast. There were no fliers above her but there were some in the distance. She could also see a group of them had broken off and were heading her way. She would have to hurry but was unable to.

She slowly felt her way along the trail again. There were still a few rocks on it and the rain had picked up. She periodically glanced at the fliers' progress and noted that they were within range of the gun. She had a decision to make; stop her progress and fire at the fliers to try to frighten them off, or keep going in the hope she could get under cover before they arrived. She was not sure how close she was to the edge of the field and what setting the gun should have, so she set it to its maximum setting and hoped for the best. She turned and fired.

She could see the rough forms of the fliers but could not determine how many there were. She kept firing and, with each blast, she could see a form fall away from the group. They were not stopping though and were getting too close for her comfort. She had committed herself. There was no escape. She no longer had any choice. She would either drive them off or die here as her last stand. If she did, the fliers would kill Jiao too but at least she hoped she had saved the boys. She could die satisfied with that.

They were so close the exploding fliers were spraying her with blood amongst the raindrops. One grabbed her from the side, some had gone higher and soon rocks were hitting her from that location. After she shot at the flier that had grabbed her, she could see no more fliers in that direction, she looked up and spotted several above her. She fired several times at the ones she could see clearly and they dropped away. One almost hit her as he fell. She caught another one she spotted briefly. She was still hearing rocks fall, so she thought she should become a moving target and began to move again toward Jiao and keep her eyes up as much as she could to take the occasional shot at the fliers higher up the mountain.

The rocks hit her several times. She did not know if she could bear any more pain than she already had but it was overwhelming her. Her body was trying to shut down and she was forcing herself to keep going. Several times she almost slipped from the trail. She was becoming too weak to advance anymore. Her walking became more erratic. Finally, an obstacle ahead of her stopped her. She began to force herself over it until she realised it was the field generator. She leaned down and pressed the green button.

51.

Roche lay on top of the blanket letting the water inside him take effect. He knew he had to start moving but his body was telling him otherwise, so he let some minutes pass.

As he rested, he noticed a flash of light outside the field then many others in quick succession. It looked like lightning but there was no thunder after them. He forced himself up and slid down beside Dan's head and lifted it off the ground onto his lap for support. He poured a little bit of water on his fingers and washed it onto Dan's face.

Its coldness must have startled Dan awake, as his eyes opened.

Roche said, "Here drink this but not too fast or too much."

Dan eagerly took several gulps, then slumped down again, and closed his eyes.

Roche moved to Raj and wet his face too but he did not stir.

He next moved to Grog who had his eyes closed.

Roche asked right into Grog's ear, as he could not speak loudly, "Are you able to wake up, or is it still too cold outside."

Grog shook his head and opened his eyes. He stared at Roche for several seconds uncomprehendingly then his eyes cleared and he said weakly, "What's up?"

"Erica was here and she dropped off some food and water. She had to get back to Jiao, so she left."

"Food and water! Great, she made it. Is she okay?"

"I think so."

Grog sat up and took the water container from Roche. He had several gulps of the precious fluid and looked around the site. "How is everyone else?"

"I gave some water to Dan but that's it. I was hoping you'd take over, as I don't want to risk giving anyone a needle."

"That's fine. The sun is warming us up, so I should be able to help in a few minutes. What's the flier situation?"

"I can't see, it's too rainy and foggy outside."

"Oh, that's why it's a little wet in here." He leaned over and picked up the first officer's glasses and put them on. He looked up and around. "There don't appear to be any fliers overhead but I can see quite a lot of them swarming in the distance."

"I heard two loud explosions before Erica came. I think she was shooting off the cannon. Then I saw what looked like lightning after she left."

"Did she give you the captain's gun and communicator?"

"She gave me just her communicator."

"That's okay. We must keep in touch with her. Hers should have a lot of charge in it, we'll need it. She might need to use the gun. Maybe that was the lightning flashes you saw. She might have been attacked."

"I hope she wasn't hurt."

"So, do I. I can't see anything outside without these glasses."

Grog searched the path ahead with the goggles. "If she was out there, I'd detect her body warmth. She's either behind the forcefield or fell off the ledge. I don't detect her lower on the mountain though."

"I hope she made it back okay."

"Well, I guess the cannon and gun helped to get her here. Good for her. The fliers don't seem to be dropping rocks on us."

"Yeah, it's been quiet for a while."

Grog sat building his strength. After about twenty minutes, he asked Roche, "So, all you did was give Dan some water."

"Right."

Grog leaned over to Raj and felt his pulse. "Raj seems to be still alive, so far." He leaned over and picked up the first aid kit. He took out the small syringe and gave Raj a shot of medicine then took out the larger syringe and filled it with water. He injected it into Raj's abdomen.

He took out the bottle of pills, removed two of them, and popped one into his mouth. "Here's your pill."

Roche took it and swallowed it.

Grog injected Dan with some medicine and water and then dealt with the first officer and captain.

When he finished, he said, "Take some food."

Roche opened the boys' food container and spooned some into his mouth. He had a second helping shortly after.

Grog said, "Roche, the water container was full. The girls must not have had water since they left the spring lower down on the mountain. I hope they had some of the food and water there. They'll be okay without food but going without water is taking a risk."

"I guess they were saving it all for us."

"I hope it doesn't create a problem for them though."

They had their first substantial meal in several days. Grog picked up the communicator and called the girls but no one answered. "I hope they're okay over there."

"Erica seemed well when I saw her. They must be exhausted. They had a long hard day and travelled at night. They're probably sleeping. Let's leave them alone." He spotted the other thing Erica gave him and picked it up. "Here's a box of batteries"

Grog took it and replied, "That's a box of gold right now. I can replace six dead or almost-dead batteries." He spent some time collecting guns and communicators and replacing their batteries. He put the spent ones into the box.

Dan woke up an hour or so later and had some more water and food. Another hour later the first officer woke up. They spent the rest of the day recovering.

Late in the day, Grog gave another shot of medicine and water to the captain and Raj.

Jiao began to choke. She was face down in a small pool of water. She lifted her head to get a breath. She looked at the small puddle, stuck her mouth into it, and sipped the water voraciously. It felt so good going down her throat. Her head dropped back onto the ledge and she stared at the rocky side of the mountain.

Small rills of water were seeping down the side and wetting the surface of the ledge. Where the rock had a depression, the water was filling the holes. The small tufts of algae, moss, or lichen seemed more colourful and alive.

She was glad it was raining. She drank a little more water and forced her body to turn her head in the other direction to stare at the greyness outside. She realised then that there was no sound of falling rocks. The fliers must have been taking a rest.

She tried to ascertain what day and time it was. How long had they been there? How long had she slept? It was daylight for sure but she could not determine the time without seeing the sun. She tried to get up but no matter how hard she tried, she was stuck in this awkward position with the blanket and the empty artillery shell cartridge on her.

She called out, "Erica are you here?" There was no response. "Erica, are you okay?" She tried again to get up but it was futile. She took one more mouthful of water from the puddle and passed out.

Erica awoke several hours later. She hurt so much. She hurt everywhere. She turned her head to look at the ledge and noticed the water in small puddles. She bent lower and lapped up the water like a dog. In one of the larger puddles, she could almost make out her face but it did not look like her face. It was ugly and splattered with dirt and blood. If her mother could see her now!

What had she become? Her mother used to talk proudly of her two beautiful girls but now she looked more like the Wicked Witch of the West. Her formerly beautiful long hair was matted and knotted. All she needed was a cone-shaped hat to make it real. She looked at one of her hands and saw blisters, dirt, blood, and cuts. Her nails, which started too long the day she left the ship because she did not have scissors to cut them, were all different lengths. She would have to use her teeth to cut them.

She was all cried out, though. It did not matter. Who cared what she looked like? Would anyone care anymore? She was cold, not just outside but deep inside. She only hoped that what she had achieved with Jiao would be worth it. If only she had not followed those damned stupid boys, she could be in her warm bed back at home with her parents.

To stay sane, she often told herself that somehow, she would get back home but she did not want that anymore. She did not want to go back and have her parents see what she had become and face the embarrassment of getting into a spaceship. How stupid could a person be to do that – a stupid boy thing.

No, she did not want to go back anymore. All she had been to her parents was a stupid rebel; always trying to be different and make her mark. Well, she sure had done that, all right.

She had been stupid before and she sure had proved how stupid she still was. All she could think of was that yellow dress she never got to wear. Her mother tried so hard to counter what she was doing – to try to return her to the little princess she used to be. She would have looked good in it but she wanted to be ugly. She wanted to do her own thing. She looked at her image in the water again and smacked her hand violently into it to blot it out.

She noticed the slimy green algae which had encircled the water. She guided her finger around the water's edge to collect it and stuck the green scum into her mouth. It did not taste too bad it was quite good. It was not enough to ease her hunger pangs but it would help.

She realised how far she had fallen. Here she was, eagerly seeking green scum to eat. If there had been a garbage can inside the field, she would have searched through it for fragments of food. She would have sucked the bottom of a pizza box for the grease contained in it. She could never have conceived of looking or feeling as badly as she did.

She lowered her head and licked up the water in the little puddle. Her pain lessened then, after a short time, she returned to her nightmarish dreams.

52.

Roche got up the next morning and looked outside. The rainy weather had given way to a cloudy day but it was warm and getting warmer. He could see many fliers still out in the distance and the rocks were falling on the field at irregular intervals. He thought the fliers were being extremely obstinate. The fliers had taken such a heavy beating, yet were still fighting them.

The fliers knew the interlopers had to cross the narrow part of the ledge and would have to expose themselves in the process. He guessed that they were hoping to overcome them there. This would be the decisive battle. If the aliens could pull it off, maybe the fliers would give up and let them go. If the aliens failed, it would be the end of all of them.

The food and water Erica had brought them had revived them somewhat. It would take days for them to recover fully. Their guns had fresh batteries in them and they had the cannon. Roche was ready for it. It was either fight or die.

He ate a little food, sipped some water, and waited. He was happy Erica had succeeded and was proud of her. She had saved their lives and given them a chance to make it out of these mountains.

About an hour later, Grog woke up and, shortly after, the first officer. Grog did his ministering to the ones who could not help themselves.

When Dan woke up, they ate and drank to prepare for the day which included doing some stretching and light exercise to test their capabilities. Only Roche and Grog would be able to do the hardest job of moving everything to the other side of the narrow ledge.

The officer began to plan the day. They would start by moving the bags to the other side as they were the most valuable and contained some food and water for the girls. They'd move him next, as he'd be able to get the girls into the ship if all else failed. They could carry Dan over after that. The two unconscious members would be last.

The officer looked outside to see the tactical situation. The fliers had flown to this side of the mountains and were flying within meters of the forcefields. They were so thick around them that it was difficult to see beyond the swarm but, with the goggles, the officer could also see a handful of fliers several hundred metres beyond the vanguard. He guessed they might be the leaders of the attackers. Above them was a bevy of other fliers who were continually bombarding their locations with rocks.

He considered waiting another day. Every mobile person was still weak and could use the extra day of rest. The food and water would last at least that long. He could also wait until evening and hope the fliers would reduce their strength or the lack of visibility would give them the advantage but he could see that the trail was treacherous and had many rocks, blood, and fliers' body parts that had fallen on it as a result of the cannon blasts and the rocks thrown by the fliers. That would slow them while traversing it. The visibility of the daylight would allow them to cross faster.

He decided the extra day would not give them any significant advantage, so it was do or die today.

The first officer picked up the communicator to see what the situation was with the girls. He needed their help again. They were going to be an integral part of his plan. He sent them a signal that he wanted to talk to them.

Erica awoke about an hour earlier and got ready for what she needed to do. Her muscles were stiff and sore. She still hurt everywhere and had a bad headache. She looked at Jiao and woke her up but she lapped up some of the water remaining in some of the little puddles and drifted off to sleep again.

Erica was on her own and hoped the aliens were going to give them a day to recuperate. When she saw the swarm of fliers outside, she immediately thought it was hopeless for any effort to move. When she heard the buzzing of the communicator she groaned and picked it up.

The officer said, "Good morning, we're a lot stronger today because of you. Thank you for helping us. I don't think we'd be waking up today without the water and food you brought us. How are you two?"

Erica responded weakly, "Jiao seems to be out of it this morning. She's still asleep and I can't wake her up. I'm hungry, thirsty, hurting, stiff, and weak."

"Would you be able to help us this morning?"

"This morning? What can we do this morning? The fliers are all over us!" Erica exclaimed with surprise.

"It looks as if they've changed their tactics and they'll likely not change them tomorrow. We can't wait to get going. We have to move today if you're able."

Erica sighed but knew he was right. They had to move today. She and Jiao had not eaten or drunk since they were near the spring. They had saved it all for the boys. Another day and they would be in bad shape. The little bit of water they still had in the puddles would evaporate soon by the warming sun, even from behind the clouds.

"If it's not heavy work, I can do it," she half lied. She felt so sick, she did not feel up to doing anything.

"Good, then," the first officer said then spoke a little louder, so Roche could hear him better. "We're not going to wait. I think the fliers will be sticking around us like this from now on. They're likely banking on our not being able to use the cannon very close to us and could overwhelm us as soon as we turn off the forcefield. It's a good strategy and it might work but I think we could do it with your help, Erica. Have you put a new cartridge in the cannon?"

"Yes, and used two bombs already to get the stuff over to you."

"Okay, you have four left."

"And I might have one or two left in the other cartridge. I forgot to count the shots we fired."

"I don't think there are any left. I can tell you how to check if we need to but let's see what we can do with what we have. I'll give you the coordinates for our first shot. Set yourself up close to the generator, so you can turn the forcefield on and off quickly. We're going to send a shot that will affect all the fliers out there. The blast should get most of them with the explosion and many of them with the shrapnel. After you fire the first shot, I'll set you up with another one, and maybe a third. The important thing for you is precision timing. You'll have to open the field for as little time as you must to make the shot then close it before the blast. Leave it open too long and the blast or dropped rocks will kill you. Can you, do it?"

"I'll have to."

"You've had enough experience with the process that you'll do a good job. Have confidence in yourself. Don't panic, just act precisely. I'll let you decide exactly when to do things. Okay?"

"Yeah."

"Put your glasses on and I'll set you up with the first shot."

Erica put on her glasses and grabbed the cannon.

"Cover you and Jiao with a blanket. That'll help reduce the effect of the rocks when you turn off the field."

Erica pulled a part of the blanket off Jiao and slid it over her head and body like a cowl which covered both girls.

"Look out and I'll tell you where to look." He guided her eyes to the spot and then told her to stop. Symbols appeared in the view through the glasses.

She took the cannon, used the side of the mountain as a base, and set it to the readings she could see in the goggles.

"Great, you're right on. Anytime you're ready, take the shot. Remember that the blast will go off almost as soon as it leaves the barrel, so you've got to have the field back on before it goes off. Good luck, Erica." The first officer turned off the communicator.

Erica paused to get herself ready.

"Why did you turn off the communicator?" Roche asked as he saw the officer turn it off.

"I don't want the sound of the blast to blow out our eardrums," the officer replied.

"She can get killed, right?"

"If her timing is off, that's right."

"Then she won't fail."

"I'm hoping the one blast will be enough to dissuade the fliers from further attacks. The next one or two are going to get our point across. So, if she's killed, she likely will be saving our lives because a lot of fliers are going to die with her. Let's not think of that scenario, shall we? Let's hope her timing is good."

Even through the attenuation of the sound by the alien's shield, the blast was horrific. When the smoke cleared, they could see the fliers in utter chaos. There was blood splattered everywhere. The number of them still flying had greatly decreased.

The officer looked where the girls should be. "It looks as if things might be okay," he said excitedly. "The blast would have damaged the generator and we'd see quite a mess over there but I see nothing."

Roche was excited. They heard the fall of the rocks on the field commence again.

The first officer pulled the communicator to his ear and turned it on. "How did it go?"

Erica responded, "My ears are still ringing but we're okay."

"Ready for another one?"

"I guess so."

He guided her eyes to a new spot and set the new coordinates. The blast went off shortly after with further devastation to the fliers who had settled higher up the mountain over the boys' camp.

He set new coordinates and Erica soon sent out another shot that blasted higher up the mountain over the girls' camp. Each time, there was a shower of rocks, blood, and body parts over the camps.

There was total silence after that.

The first officer looked around and up. There were several fliers left high up on the mountain but they were moving up and over to the backside of it. There soon was no sign of them at all. He smiled and said to Roche, "I think we've done it. I was wondering if they'd ever give up. Okay, let's move quickly. I see the main body of fliers lower down on the mountain collecting the dead and wounded. The group of leaders have disappeared with them. Turn off the forcefield and grab the sack; I think the girls would like some food and water."

Erica watched the red-covered rocks tumble over the forcefield after the last blast. The amount of blood was enormous. It covered everything outside of it. She gazed out at the ledge strewn with more rocks. She stared at the decapitated head of a flier among the rubble. Its eyes were open and staring at her. She had seen more than a hundred fliers reduced to blood, guts, and body parts. She was responsible for this. The sickness within her churned her stomach and heaved its contents onto the ledge beside her. The fliers would never see their families again, as she would never see hers. She wanted to cry but could not. She was again in her robot mode.

53.

Grog heard the conversation between Erica and the first officer and was quick to react. He looked at Roche who knew what to do. He fastened his weapon onto his belt, packed the bags, and slipped them under his arms. He turned off the field. They exited the camp and he remotely turned on the forcefield. Grog grabbed a gun and led the way. As he progressed, he cleared the debris from the ledge with his feet. The stench of death was everywhere. It was like being in an abattoir.

Roche was getting sick. At one point, he turned his head away from the mountain and retched over the side of it.

Grog looked back and said, "I guess you guys aren't used to all this. It must be quite a shock. I've never seen anything like this before either. The battle with the beasts was horrifying but there was little blood there, except for some of ours."

Roche replied, "I've never seen so much blood in my life. It's sickening. Just think of how many fliers we've killed." He was now in no-mans-land.

"Well, I guess it was better them than us."

"I wish there was another way. We don't belong here. This isn't our planet and it isn't yours either."

"We study life on other planets. We don't usually take life, though. It's a rather high price to pay for science but this is an unusual situation. The fliers are thriving here. This planet has hundreds of thousands of them. It won't take long for them to recover from this."

Roche gave him an angry look. "You use that as an excuse?" He almost slipped on some of the slime underfoot.

"Watch your step. Focus on what we've got to do," Grog cautioned.

"Why do you need to study other organisms?"

"To advance science; study other lifeforms. We can understand the many varieties of life under different conditions. We can apply what we learn to better ourselves and life on other planets."

"I'm sure you're not thinking of them."

"We think well of every being. All life is important. Here, we have a dilemma – a clash of priorities – that of damaging a lifeform by interference by our presence or staying alive ourselves to ensure we don't give them our technology. Sometimes there's a price to pay."

"Killing is a high price, here."

Grog gave no response.

They walked very slowly and carefully over the narrow ledge.

When they got to the other side of it, Grog held out his hand and felt the field still on. He reached for his communicator and turned it off remotely.

Roche walked around Grog and went inside. He could smell the strong scent of fuel, explosives, and vomit. His eyes froze on Erica. She was staring outside at the opposite end of the trail. He looked beyond her and saw the flier's head. He looked over at Jiao. She did not seem to notice him, as she was looking at Erica. Both girls looked as if they were in another world. He did not know what to do. Should he say something or go over to them to break them from their stupor?

Roche was blocking Grog from entering, so Grog soon poked him and said, "Well, get in. Let's get moving. We've got the opportunity to get things done, so let's do it."

Roche took a couple of steps in so he was almost beside the two girls.

"What's up with them?" Grog enquired when he entered the field and could see inside. He took the sack from Roche.

"I don't know. They were like this when I came in."

"Well, here are the food and water containers," Grog said, as he opened the sack and took them out. "Get them to eat some food. Try to get them to move over to the other end of this camp, so I can move the things they have and the sacks over there, too. I want to move this camp a little farther up the ledge, so we can move ours behind this one. We can't get everyone and the equipment under one field, or we might affect its integrity. Also, the generator would require much more energy and drain its stored energy too quickly. We should use two fields. Since it might take you too much time getting the girls straightened out, I'll squeeze by the equipment and clear the trail ahead."

The jostling of Grog's effort to get by the equipment and the girls finally brought them back to reality.

Erica's eyelids closed.

Grog left to clear the trail ahead and nudged the flier's head from it with his foot to let it roll down the mountain.

Jiao sadly looked at Roche and said, "I'm glad you're here."

"How are you?" Roche asked without moving.

"I'm not in great shape. I don't know if I can walk."

Roche responded, "I've brought food and water for you."

He handed the two containers to her. "What's wrong with Erica?"

"I don't know. I was asleep or unconscious and a lot of bangs woke me up. I only saw her near the end. She was staring out the other end of the camp. It's been a very gruelling two days for us. As you can see, a whole bunch of rocks hit us. I think one of them knocked me out. I can't remember exactly what happened." She began to eat the food and had a swig of water.

Roche responded, "We're really happy you made it. I don't think we would have progressed this far without you. The cannon turned things around." He turned his attention to Erica but she was not responding well.

She looked at him dully. The head on the trail was not there to distract her anymore. She mumbled, "I killed them. I killed so many of them. Did we have to kill them?"

"You saved us, Erica. You got here and saved us." When she was not responding to him well, he grabbed her shoulders and shook her gently.

"Why are you doing that?" she demanded, annoyed.

"What's the matter, Erica? Is there something wrong with you?"

"I killed them," she muttered.

"Look, I've brought food for you," Roche said. Jiao did not want any more food, so he took the container and put it in front of Erica.

She did not move.

"Aren't you going to eat?"

"No, not hungry," she said so quietly that Roche could hardly hear her.

Roche looked at the vomit on the ledge beside her and knew she was lying.

"How about water?"

"No water," she responded similarly.

"Okay, have it your way then. It's here if you want it. We'll have to move you then we're going to leave and be back soon."

"Move us?" she asked quizzically.

"Yes, Grog wants to make room to set up another forcefield behind this one."

Roche looked at Jiao and asked, "Are you able to move?"

"With help."

"Okay, let's go to the edge of the field."

He put his arm around Jiao's waist and guided her there. He went back and got Erica. He wrapped his arm around her too and guided her beside Jiao. He moved the equipment beside them and returned to the centre of the forcefield. He turned off the forcefield, gently raised the generator slightly above the path, and walked to where the girls were. Grog returned and moved the equipment forward while Roche did the same with the girls. They did this for five cycles then stopped.

"Okay, let's get back for the first officer," Grog said to Roche. "This part is a little wider, so it'll make it easier to walk around things."

Grog brushed by the girls, turned off the field, and walked outside. Grog turned on the field then they walked to the other site.

Grog turned off that field, wrapped the first officer in a blanket and they carried him to the other site. Once inside the field, they got him settled, picked up the other two blankets and returned to pick up Dan. They dropped the blankets there. Roche guided Dan to the other site while Grog wrapped the captain and Raj in their blankets.

They suddenly realised that several fliers were already close to the site. Just before Roche entered the field on the other side of the trail, a large rock hit him on the back. He dropped Dan inside, raced to the generator, and turned on the forcefield.

"What the heck is going on? What hit me? Did you see it?" Roche asked Dan.

Dan responded, "It looked like a rock. It seemed to come from above us."

Roche looked up and thought he saw one flier high in the sky. It was almost a dot but it was moving back beyond the top of the mountain. He picked up the communicator and called Grog.

Grog responded, "What's up?"

"I just got hit by a large rock."

"Oh, that was the noise I heard." Grog paused as he scanned the sky. "They appear to be trying a new approach. There's one flier high above the mountain. They might be thinking that we wouldn't send up a bomb for one person and, if we did, we'd only kill one of them. It's a good move but from that distance, their accuracy shouldn't be very good. I recommend that we vary the pace of our activities a lot. That way we'll throw off their accuracy even more. Are you hurt?"

"It's only pain, so I can still walk okay. Luckily, the rock didn't hit my head."

"Never walk with a regular pattern and it'll be good. We have the forcefield on over here, so we'll be okay. Get over here and help me carry Raj over."

Roche turned off the forcefield and left. Jiao turned it back on immediately after. When Roche got to Grog's location the field was off. Three rocks had dropped on Roche during the walk. Roche said, "It's getting very cramped in the other site."

"I imagine it is. Let's get Raj over there."

They went to Raj, picked him up and carried him to the edge of the field. Grog put his side down and turned off the forcefield. He picked up Raj again and started walking. Once they left, he turned on the forcefield and continued over the treacherous part of the trail, dodging rocks as they went.

Grog noticed that there were three filers. At a wider part, Grog asked Roche to stop while he took potshots at the fliers with the gun to force them higher. He hit two of the fliers which tumbled down the mountainside almost hitting Roche as they fell. Grog picked up his end and they made it to the other side safely. They entered the camp and placed Raj so he would fit into the tight space within the field.

"Let's pause and have something to eat and drink. The last chore is going to be the hardest as we'll be exposed for quite some time," Grog said.

They rested inside the cramped protected area and kept on the lookout for the fliers. They could see some of them flying low over the ground hauling bodies and body parts across the valley.

After a few minutes, Grog said, "Okay, let's get going, Roche."

On the way, Grog had to fire a few more times to remind the fliers above them to stay high. Another flier tumbled to his death. When they got to the other side, Grog turned off the forcefield and entered.

"Okay, Roche, turn on the generator." They rested for several minutes.

Grog said, "Okay, let's get going quickly, so we can set up this generator on the other side of the trail. Remember to vary our speed as we cross. Just follow my lead."

Roche turned off the generator and folded up the legs. Grog took the holding strap and showed Roche how to fasten it to the generator. Grog had to fire a few shots at the fliers as they were trying to take advantage of the two exposed interlopers.

Grog took hold of the end of the rope around the blanket holding the captain. Roche slung the generator over his shoulder and picked up the end of the rope. They were keeping their eyes open for falling rocks.

Roche spotted a flier above him and soon saw a rock plunging toward him. He quickly released the rope and stepped back a couple of paces. The rock hit the trail, chipping a piece out of it as it continued down the mountainside.

They quickly resumed the perilous journey across the narrow section of the trail while dodging the sporadic bombardment of rocks.

Before they got fully across, Grog said, "When we get over, set up the generator as quickly as you can and get both fields going."

They reached the wider ledge but, before Roche could set up the forcefield, the fliers hit Roche's arm with another rock. He bent down in pain favouring the arm with his other hand. Grog quickly reached over, picked up the generator, set it up, and pressed both buttons.

After they settled in, Grog looked at both of Roche's wounds. "They must be dropping large rocks because both have damaged your skin on your back and arm."

Grog put his communicator to his ear and sent a signal to the other tent.

Jiao picked it up and responded.

Grog asked, "Would someone over there bring me the first aid kit, one container of water, and our food."

Dan offered to do it and ran over there with them.

Grog opened the first aid kit, worked on Roche, and managed to stem the bleeding. He gave him a pill with some water. He confirmed that Roche was going to be able to carry the others and equipment along the trail. As they had to proceed with two generators, he decided to keep the teens together as one team and they would be responsible for themselves and all the equipment. Grog would be responsible for moving the lizards inside his generator's field.

Roche was not as confident as he wanted to have been. Fortunately, only Raj needed carrying. He felt that, with everyone's cooperation, they should be able to keep moving.

To get things set up, they did the same manoeuvre as done for the last move. Roche helped Grog move the first officer and captain to the alien's site then Roche returned to his area.

While the teens rested, the first officer opened their field briefly, so Grog could fire on the fliers over their sites. Between each shot, he prepared it well before the field opened. The gun was still set to kill.

Grog managed to hit most of the fliers he aimed for but the result was that the fliers stationed themselves even higher in the sky.

Grog had to think ahead. He had one bomb left. If he kept one in reserve, he could use it if he needed it. However, with the change in the flier's tactics, they were using very small groups of them to reduce their losses. The fliers were very aggressive. It was very apparent that they did not give up easily and Grog had to deter them from any further significant attacks on them. They had a long way to get to the ship and he wanted to come up with one last sign that would send them a message. The fliers did not know that the interlopers were almost out of missiles. Grog wanted to make good use of this shot.

He put on the glasses and scanned the area. There were three or four fliers high above them. One or two fliers would disappear to load up with rocks, while the rest continued to drop them. There were only a handful of fliers at the other end of the valley. He turned up the scanning sensitivity, so he could peer through some of the rock of the mountains and noticed a large hoard of fliers a few hundred metres behind them.

It gave him an idea. He discussed it with the first officer and got his approval. He raced over to the other site to the cannon, set up the shot, and fired it toward the small group across the valley. He could see the fliers begin to scatter. When the bomb was about to strike them, it swung a tight curve and headed behind the mountain to where the larger group was hiding. Soon after that, a distant bang reverberated through the mountains.

He looked through the glasses in the same area and found no signs of an organised group there. He smiled to himself. He hoped the fliers were getting the message that he could see and hit them at any distance anywhere. They did not have to be in his line of sight.

He told the teens to begin their process to move toward the main campsite. He returned to his group, let them get a lead, and began to advance, too.

Occasionally, he would take a shot at a flier above them who tried to get too close and was often successful in shooting one down.

Within an hour, the bombing stopped, the fliers disappeared, and the aliens continued their trek unimpeded.

Grog did not want to take the chance of delaying their progress by taking a break. They kept going until they reached the campsite. There was no sign of the fliers, so they shut down the forcefield at the campsite and set up two campsites. Inside the lizard's area was one large tent, their food and water, and all the equipment. In the teen's site were a large and small tent and their food and water. The girls had the first choice of blankets.

A field generator was set up for each site and the fields were turned on.

They ate and drank heartily, as the sun began to dip below the mountains. The boys settled into the large tent and the girls in the small tent. It was not long before everyone was asleep.

54.

It was still dark when a twitchy muscle jolted Erica awake. The stars provided enough light to see a little inside their tent.

She was shivering and tried to move deeper into their blanket but could not because it had become a straightjacket. When they had opened their neatly folded blanket in their tent, they saw that it was no more than an old beaten and holey rag.

Now, it was posing a problem. It did not provide much insulation and, with her rolling around during the night, she had become so entwined in several holes she could not get out. She struggled a while trying to get out without success.

She heard a giggle. "Jiao, is that you?" she whispered.

"Do guys giggle?" Jiao responded.

"Instead of laughing, why don't you give me a hand?"

"You've grabbed the entire blanket and I'm freezing over here."

"Why didn't you get me up?"

"I didn't want to disturb you and I certainly didn't want to miss this."

"Are you going to leave me like this, so you can keep laughing?"

Jiao could sense that Erica was getting annoyed, so she crawled over to her and looked at the mess. It was quite dark, so Jiao located the small lamp inside the tent and switched it on.

"Do you want me to tear it more and pull it away that way?" Jiao asked.

"Then we'd have nothing at all to keep us warm. I think that we should try to keep it the way it is if we can."

Jiao looked closely at how it had strung around her. She poked at one arm and pulled at the blanket a bit to loosen it then grabbed Erica's arm and pulled at it.

"Hey, that hurts."

"Well, if I can get your arm out, that would make it easier to get it off your neck."

Jiao went back to pulling, while Erica winced in pain. Soon, Jiao slid Erica's arm out and unwrapped the blanket from around her neck. She pulled out one of Erica's legs next then the rest of it went easier.

"I don't know what you did to get it like this but you did a great job, Houdini," Jiao said. "You know you have a rip in your jumper that exposes your breast. When did that happen?"

Erica looked down at herself and said, "I haven't a clue. I hurt so much I wouldn't notice." She paused. "What a mess. Did you know if this happened before, or did it happen when I was entangling myself in the blanket?"

"I think it was torn before but not as much."

"So, the boys saw me?"

"Probably but they wouldn't care. I don't think, at this point, that it matters. We've seen so much of each other these past few months."

Jiao tried to pull together the torn pieces. "If I had some thread, or even a few clips or safety pins I'd be able to close it up." She removed her hand and the end of the tear slid back off the breast. "It looks as if it's going to stay that way."

"Thanks for getting me unravelled." Erica picked up the blanket and held it up. "Do you think we can still use it as a blanket?"

"Not like that. Let's double it as we did before and see if we can."

Some of the holes were even larger than before but it was better than nothing. They also found that being in a tent was warmer than without one. It was providing a little insulation. They slipped under the blanket and snuggled together for warmth.

"I hurt so much," Erica said.

"When I saw you yesterday, you didn't look so well."

"Neither did you. You're all banged up. I hope we don't get scars?"

"I hope not."

"It's been a nightmare ever since we got on this damned spaceship. We almost froze in the ship's compartment. I turned the wrong way and almost didn't make it back to the ship on that other planet. We had to fight those beasts and now, the fliers. I had the two worst days of my life. I'll never forget the fliers I killed. I kept killing and killing."

"You'll have to put that out of your mind. You had to do it. We'd be dead if you hadn't done that."

"I'll never forget it. It was as if I were Lucifer killing angels. We had no business being there to begin with . . . Let's get back to sleep."

The sun rose and a bright sunny day greeted the awaking intruders of this world. Grog was surprised to see that he was the first one up. He quietly had his breakfast and ministered to the captain. He pulled out the glasses and put them on. He could see no fliers overhead and could not hear rocks tumbling down the mountain. He looked at the other side of the valley and saw three fliers flying high over the mountain tops. There were no others around, even behind some of the other mountains. The lone fliers might have been sentinels to scout the interlopers' activities at a distance.

Grog smiled. He guessed that, since they were over the narrow point of the ledge, the fliers had decided to pull back. The interlopers had come up the trail and were leaving by the trail. The distant fliers must have been there to make sure that these strange and dangerous new beings left their territory. Did they think they had won the battle and the intruders were retreating?

Grog did not care. No alien would be visiting their planet again for many decades. He wondered how long the stories of these battles would pass by word of mouth to future generations. Would the fliers still be talking about it the next time their people saw the aliens?

He hoped this disappearance was true, or were they setting a trap farther up the trail? He looked in that direction and found no evidence of that.

Roche dragged himself out from under the cover to start his day. When he finished eating, he shut off the forcefield and poked his head through the invisibility field, so he could see what the plans were for the day.

Grog could see him, so he shut off his forcefield and stepped out to talk to Roche. "Are you the only one up?"

"So far," Roche replied.

"Well, don't disturb them. Let them sleep. If the fliers don't attack us, we should be able to get back to the ship today."

"When they get up, I'll get everyone ready. I don't see any fliers. Should we leave the fields off?"

"Leave the invisibility one on for now. We don't want them to see us getting ready to go. They might find out how weak we are."

"Okay, I'll see you later," Roche said as he turned around, walked to his area, and went back into his tent.

Roche rested a while, left the tent and did some stretch exercises but found his body too sore to do many of them. He was afraid of pulling open a healing wound. It was going to be hard trying to be the strong man of the day. He knew Dan was not going to be very useful.

Erica got up a few minutes later and popped her head out of the tent.

Roche saw her and held out the food for her. "Here's some yummy food for you."

She walked over, took it from him, and ate in silence.

"The water container is by our tent."

Erica said nothing in response.

Jiao left the tent next. She remarked, as she bent backwards to stretch her back muscles, "Boy, how I hate sleeping on a rock. It's so hard and uncomfortable." She picked up the food and water and sat quietly next to Erica. She could sense tension in the air, so she ate in silence. She noted that Erica had repaired her jumper but there was no seam visible. She casually leaned back and discovered she had merely reversed it.

Dan was out about twenty minutes later. He stumbled over to the food and ate his fill then drank some water.

Grog walked in and noticed that Raj was alone in the tent, so he took the opportunity to enter it and give Raj his injections. When he finished, he left the tent, and said, "The first officer is awake and we're ready to go. Are you ready to start? The earlier we get going, the sooner we get back to the ship."

The four teens nodded.

Grog looked at them and shrugged. "I'll help you pack the tents."

Within a few minutes, they had emptied and packed the tents and put them into the large sack. They had already packed the equipment and wrapped the captain in a blanket but Grog and Roche wrapped the first officer and Raj into blankets and tied them up with ropes.

Grog checked their surroundings with his goggles and did not see any signs of fliers in their vicinity. They kept the invisibility shields on while they walked the first part of the journey moving the people and equipment as they went along. Once they rounded the bend leading down the back end of the mountain Grog stopped, did another scan, and found no fliers in sight.

He turned off his generator and told the teens to do the same. He conversed quietly with the first officer and more loudly said, "It was very slow going, wasn't it? At the pace we're going, we won't get to the ship before nightfall. I figure it would be faster to leave the gear and captain behind and carry the injured to the ship first. We're almost certain the captain has died but even if he's alive he could survive another night out here. We can return later today or even tomorrow to carry the rest to the ship. I've already discussed it with the first officer and he agrees. Since there aren't any fliers around, we'll also go without the shields but take one with us to set it up, if we have to."

He looked around at everyone and did not get any disagreement.

Grog folded up one of the generators and added it to the large sack with; the small sack, other sack, the cannon, the spare canister, and the captain. They placed the existing generator in the centre.

Grog strapped the other field generator to his back and, with Roche, lifted the first officer. Erica and Jiao picked up one end while Dan took the other end of Raj's rope. They walked away from the site. When they were far enough, Grog stopped and remotely activated the fields.

They began their trek once more. They walked slowly and took frequent breaks. When they reached the stream, everyone wanted some water, so they had a prolonged break where the boys washed off most of the dirt and blood collected over the last few days. The girls wanted to wait for a nice hot shower on the ship. They were soon back on the path and, by nightfall, reached the ship.

Grog suggested he keep Raj in the control room overnight, so he could examine and monitor him. The rest of the teens shrugged their shoulders and proceeded into their compartment. They knew Grog would take good care of him.

It was strange for the teens to welcome their return to the ship and prison. After their last ordeal, even the hard floors were comforting to their feet and tired bodies.

Dan and Roche collapsed on the floor of their cells and went peacefully to sleep.

55.

Erica and Jiao waited until the boys were sound asleep then headed to the shower. There, they stripped and washed themselves and their jumpers. They too were ready to sleep but the door to their room opened and Grog hurried in.

"It looks as if we have a little job for you," he said quickly. "The aboriginal woman has not eaten much of her food but the main problem is, when I walked into her room, she went into a rage. I tried to calm her but she got even more upset. She's pale and thin and I hope you can help her. We've got to keep her healthy. It's a long way home and she's key to the success of this mission."

Erica stared at him in silence but Jiao, reading her mind, said, "So, you want us to do your dirty work for you? What happened other times when your people had something like this occur?"

"We sedated them. We could do that and, who knows, maybe that's the best thing to do but we would prefer she gets used to us now rather than later."

"Maybe she'd rather die."

"Then we'll have to sedate her, at least until she gets to our planet."

Jiao cut him off. "To be studied by your researchers. That's a nice thing to happen – to feel as though you're an animal. Is that what you're going to do with us?"

"No, we've studied humans quite extensively. Remember, we didn't plan to collect humans from your planet. I'd like you to help her get used to us."

Jiao looked at Erica but there was no response. "What do you think?" she asked.

Erica shrugged her shoulders.

"You're being a big help," Jiao said exasperatedly to Erica. She looked back at Grog. "Okay, we'll try. We look and feel like hell though."

"Just do your best," Grog replied, as he held out the translator.

They put on their wet jumpers. Jiao took the translator and led Erica to the open woman's door. The moment they walked in, Aaootaa became very excited. She calmed down significantly when they got closer to the cage. She eyed them carefully, and asked, "Fight?"

The girls looked at each other. Jiao said, "We went to help our men."

"You fight your men?"

"No, we fought fliers."

Aaootaa looked puzzled.

"We fought the white birds," Jiao clarified.

Her eyes lit up. "White birds in mountains?"

"Yes. They attacked our men and we went to help them."

She nodded knowingly. "Dangerous go in mountains. Aaootaa family no go in mountains. Aaootaa tell you that. White birds are very dangerous – attack animals on the ground and eat animals. Nestlings eat the meat of animals and fish like the Aaootaa family."

"Yes, they wanted to eat our men, too. We went there to help them get away. We're here and all of us are hurt."

"Aaootaa tell you that."

Jiao smiled. "Our men are not as smart as Aaootaa."

Aaootaa smiled back knowingly, "Men like to fight. If no animals to fight, they fight other men."

Jiao smiled back without response. What else could she say? Men were men and she was finding out that behaviour seemed to be almost universal.

Aaootaa pointed to Erica and said, "She no talk today?"

"I think she's been hurt a lot. She's tired and has seen much death."

Aaootaa looked sad.

Jiao continued, "Erica had to kill many white birds. It was very sad. It's the first time we saw so much blood and death."

"What is 'blood'?"

"I guess we didn't cover that yet . . . um, I guess we could call it the red liquid that flows out of you when you're cut."

"Oh, there is much of that. Yes, I see."

Then she said a word that Jiao linked to 'blood' in the translator.

"You no kill much food?"

"No, in our culture, special people do that, so all we have to do is cut it into smaller pieces, cook it, and eat it. 'Cook' means to hold it over the fire for a while to get the meat hot before you eat it."

"Meat taste good after?"

"To us, yes."

"Aaootaa no try burn meat before, except by accident." Aaootaa stared vacantly across the room.

Jiao broke the silence. "Talking about food, we're here again and see you have not eaten much food."

"Aaootaa think strange women no come back."

"Well, we're here again," Jiao said, as she spread her hands out.

"Bad lizards come back?"

"Yes, they were with our men. They're not bad."

"Lizards stick Aaootaa in cage. Aaootaa no go to Aaootaa people."

"It's hard to explain."

"Aaootaa no want to go to lizard people."

"I don't think that's going to happen."

"Why?"

"Because the lizards want to keep you."

"They have no women?"

"They have women back at their home. Their home is very far from here."

"Why do lizards takeaway Aaootaa?"

"Because you're different from them and they want to know you better. They want to know about your people."

"Aaootaa take lizards to Aaootaa people."

"That's not the way they work. They want just you."

"How lizards know Aaootaa people from only Aaootaa?"

"Good question."

"They bad lizards. Aaootaa no like lizards."

"They'll not hurt you. They'll keep you safe."

"Aaootaa people keep Aaootaa safe."

"They're not so different from you. They like you and want to take you to their place, so you'll get to know them."

"I know lizards if lizards take Aaootaa to Aaootaa people."

Jiao smiled. Aaootaa was a shrewd woman.

Aaootaa looked carefully at Jiao and poked her hand through the bars.

Jiao was going to pull away but decided to hold her ground.

Aaootaa's hand touched her face and some of the welts. "You have soft skin. You have many hurts. The lizards hurt you?"

"No, the white birds did this with rocks."

"White birds like to throw rocks. My people throw rocks, too. They hurt you and Erica?"

"Yes, and our men, too."

"Did they hurt lizards?

"Yes."

"Good. They are bad lizards. If Aaootaa tells lizards to go to Aaootaa people, lizards no do that?"

"Correct but you might like being in a new place. You will learn about other people and how they live. They built this hut that travels to the stars and they can show you other things they've made, too. You might be very surprised at what you see."

"Aaootaa want go to Aaootaa people. Aaootaa no want to see lizard things."

"We'll be going with you," Jiao said consolingly.

"Eeow say to go to Jiao people?"

"Yes, but like you, we cannot go back, so we will visit the new home. You can visit with us."

Aaootaa did not look pleased but she could see that she was not getting anywhere. "Maybe Aaootaa talk to lizards and lizards take Aaootaa to Aaootaa people?" she responded hopefully.

"Do you want me to call one in here?"

"Yes, Aaootaa want go Aaootaa people."

"Wait."

Jiao left and was soon back with Grog.

Jiao said, "Aaootaa, this is Grog." She turned to Grog and said, "Grog meet Aaootaa."

"Aaootaa wants to go Aaootaa people," the woman said through the translator while glaring at the lizard. She could see that she was not too different in appearance from this other being.

He reached over to Jiao and switched the translator to English. He said, "Wow, you did quite well with this woman. You seem to be conversing well. Unfortunately, I did not know what she said."

"Well, you have a good translator. It seems to fill in the gaps, at least in English. Sometimes it cannot do as well in her language. She said that she wants to go home and wants you to answer her."

"You know I can't let her go. We're taking off soon."

"I know but she knows you're the boss and can make the decisions. She would like to go home. You're on her planet now, it would be easy for you to drop her off near her home, or if this isn't too far away, maybe she could find her way back from here."

"We've already sent a message home saying we have her."

"Just tell them she died."

"You know I can't do that." Grog raised his voice slightly.

"Then you tell her that."

"I don't want to argue with a captive. We'll treat her well."

"I know you will but that's not her home. This is not our home."

Grog sighed in a way that only a lizard could. Rules were rules. He did not always like them but rules had to be followed. He leaned over and switched the translator from his language through English to Aaootaa's.

"I'm very sorry, Aaootaa. We must keep you with us. Your home is very far from here. We'll care for you and keep you safe. There are no dangers there like with your people. You'll have a much longer life."

That was not what Aaootaa wanted to hear and she shook the cell's bars aggressively.

Grog glanced at Jiao, reset the translator, returned it to her, and walked out.

Jiao spoke softly, "We'll see you often. Take this as an adventure."

Aaootaa glared at her.

"Aaootaa no want to eat. Life here no good."

"Please Aaootaa, we want you to stay with us."

Aaootaa slumped down in her cell and turned toward the wall.

Jiao tugged at Erica's jumper and led her from the room. The door closed behind them.

Grog had Raj on the floor hooked up to a lot of equipment.

Jiao walked over and asked how Raj was.

He said that he had finished the scan of the first officer and had hooked Raj up only seconds ago. He informed them that the first officer's spine had broken. He had done what he could but doctors on his planet might be able to use sensitive equipment to regrow that part of the spine.

The girls watched as he examined Raj.

"It's a good thing we kept giving him the medication. It probably saved his life. He does have a concussion but what's affecting him is pressure on his brain. I'm going to have to do a little operation."

"Are you a doctor?"

"No, but this equipment is set up so anyone can be a doctor. It does most of the work. I don't know if you want to stick around for that."

"No, I guess not. Is he going to be okay?"

"I think so."

"He'll be his normal self?"

"I know what you mean. As far as I know, yes but only if I get on with the operation to release the pressure."

Jiao was tired, so she turned and led Erica into their cell and under their blankets to sleep.

56.

Erica walked along a trail filled with heaps of the fliers' dead bodies. She climbed over them to return home but the piles were getting higher and she kept slithering backwards.

Suddenly, she fell into a pool of blood and began to sink. She turned her head and saw one of the corpses staring at her accusingly; his eyes bore into her as if he were living. She tried to close her eyes, or take her eyes off him but could not and now had sunk to the level of her neck. Soon, it covered her mouth and nose. She could not breathe and was going to drown.

Erica woke up trembling and sweating profusely. She jolted up in the tent, her eyes now peering at Jiao who was staring at her. Erica talked to her but she did not respond. She reached over to her and shook her.

Jiao's eyes remained frozen in place.

Erica reached over and began to shake her. "Wake up Jiao! Wake up! You're not dead!" Erica screamed.

"Shush, Erica. You're going to wake up everyone. I'm not dead. I'm here with you. Calm down," Jiao said to her as quietly as she could so as not to wake the boys. She was shaking Erica trying to wake her up.

Erica opened her eyes and turned away from Jiao.

Jiao pulled up behind her, wrapped her arms around Erica's waist, and held her tightly. "It's going to be okay, Erica. Just take some time to heal. It's going to be okay."

Erica was shaking violently but slowly her muscles relaxed, her eyes closed, and she fell back to sleep.

Jiao relaxed her hold on Erica, lay down again, and closed her eyes.

Grog was looking at the monitor and saw what had happened. He could not sleep. He wanted to. His body wanted to but he just could not go to sleep.

The operation on Raj had gone well. The pressure on his brain had diminished and the instrument was keeping him sedated to let him heal.

Grog thought about how he would feel in the teens' situation and sympathised with them but there was nothing he could do. They should not have stepped onto the ship. It was different for Aaootaa as they had seized her from her planet but that was necessary. They needed her for important research. Their people had learned a lot about other intelligent beings in the galaxy and, as some of the civilisations matured and travelled out of their solar systems, had formed relations with them.

The teens had been through a lot over the last several days. He was glad they were aboard. The teens had saved their lives and he felt he owed them something but there was not much he could give them. He could not give them their greatest wish – to get home. All he could hope for was that they would go to good homes on his planet when they arrived.

He felt a little homesick. This had been his first mission. He had learned a lot about himself and other intelligent beings. He had learned about surviving, too. When you come close to death, you learn how much you love life. He was glad to be alive but could not sleep.

Roche woke up. The lights in the room had brightened. He did not want to get up but knew the lizards would be getting them up soon to pick up the rest of the equipment and the captain. He yawned and slowly dragged himself out from his blanket and into the shower cell. He was glad to be back and have a nice shower. He felt clean afterward but his achy body reminded him of his experiences over the last few days. He looked at his stomach, arms, and legs. There were few places free of scabs or bruises.

He felt his face and could feel through the thick beard the scabs hidden underneath. A beard he had spent his early teens removing now covered him like thick fur. He felt the long hair over his shoulder. How long was it going to be before he would be able to cut it? He tried to picture his appearance and could only think of the pictures of the hippies of the sixties, or the long Middle Eastern beards. No, this was a state he had never foreseen for himself. The lizards had no shavers, combs, or scissors. With the boys' enthusiasm in the stream, he forgot to look at his reflection. On their trip by the stream later that day he would remember to look.

Dan was stirring under the blankets. He stretched, stuck his head out, and looked at Roche. In the light, he could see his injuries. He stood up unsteadily and looked at his arms and legs. He tried to bend down and was unable to. He tried to take a couple of steps but realised he was no better off than he had been the previous day. He had hardly pulled his load. He was using the rope attached to the blanket more as support than as help to the others. He tried again to walk and tumbled down to the floor. His equilibrium seemed to be terribly off. He got up to a sitting position and sat against the wall of his cell.

Jiao and Erica got up and soon were ready to go.

All of them ate and waited for the lizards to get them going on their next task.

Roche stared at Erica. She seemed so solemn and sad. She stood as if frozen, staring at the floor. That was not the Erica he knew. He stared at the floor himself for a while. He lifted his eyes and looked around the room. All through the meal and during this waiting period no one had said a word. He lowered his eyes to the floor again. What was to become of them? He saw no eagerness in them. He hoped these sad moments would pass.

Grog entered about twenty minutes after they had eaten. He made some announcements. "We told the girls yesterday but they may not have said anything to the rest of you. It looks as though the first officer will not be walking for the rest of the trip. I did an operation on Raj yesterday to remove some pressure on his brain. He seems to be improving but I'm keeping him sedated until he's well. I got him rehydrated and gave him some nourishment intravenously.

"I'll need some help from the girls for a few minutes to replenish the food for the aboriginal. I think it'll be best if they can look after her for a while. So, if you can do that right now, I'd appreciate it."

Jiao poked Erica a few times until she looked up to join her. They left the room.

Grog examined Roche. "You're healing well. You may end up with some scars. The medicine is working to heal you but it can't perform miracles."

He bent down to Dan, "Would you stand up, so I can check you out." Dan struggled for several seconds. Grog braced him with his arm and Dan rose unsteadily onto his feet. Grog examined him briefly. "I think I had better take you over to our portable medical centre and check you over. While I'm away, you can rest for now, Roche. You guys need it. I'll see if I can help Dan."

He guided Dan out of the compartment and had him lie beside the medical instrument. He hooked him up to it and examined the readings. He had Dan go through certain exercises such as raising a hand or foot then looked at the results.

"Well, Dan, you have some damage to your left ear. I can guide the instrument to fix that but you have some minor neural damage that only convalescence can heal. I'll set up a physiotherapeutic routine that your friends can help you do. It may take a few months to recuperate. For now, I'll get you back to your cell. When the girls finish, we'll have to leave to pick up the captain and equipment but you can stay behind."

He helped Dan back to his cell and returned to the central control centre to wait for the girls.

Jiao talked to Aaootaa for a few minutes while she ate.

"You know we cannot be here all the time when you eat. You should get to know the lizards. The one you see the most is not a senior member of the crew. He's a scientist who is interested in life on other planets. During the battles they had with the white birds, the captain, who leads them and the other officer under him were badly hurt."

Some of the words Jiao used could not yet translate properly but she sensed that Aaootaa got the gist of what she said.

Aaootaa asked, "Are there three lizards?"

"Yes, only three."

"If two lizards hurt, good; lizards no take Aaootaa back to Aaootaa people. Lizards very bad."

"Well, they have their rules, I guess."

"Why do you no stay here?"

"Maybe we can some time but we also like being with our people."

"You no like Aaootaa?"

"No, we like you very much. Aaootaa likes Aaootaa's people and

Jiao likes Jiao's people. Aaootaa likes Jiao and Jiao likes Aaootaa, too."

Aaootaa nodded her head.

In this short time, the women got to understand each other.

"Jiao think Aaootaa strange?"

"No, just different. People are people no matter where they live. We must seem different to you too but we'll stay with you sometime." Jiao knew they could not stay very long. "Um, we should be leaving soon. We must pick up some hunting stuff we left behind. Maybe we'll see you before the end of the day. Eat your food. You should always keep strong and healthy."

Aaootaa made a face that seemed as if she did not agree but Jiao poked Erica and the two girls walked out of the room. The door slid shut behind them.

Grog greeted them.

"Let's check you over to see if anything needs fixing. Get your clothes off."

Jiao looked at Erica but she did not respond. Jiao led her by removing her jumper. Eric dropped hers mechanically.

"Erica is acting strangely, so let's start with her," Grog said as he attached a few probes to her, near her heart, on her arm, and a few on her head. He looked at the screen watching the symbols scurry across it. Well, she's lost a lot of blood, so is low in iron. She's had some damage to her head but nothing serious. Her other vitals are fine."

He checked her over physically. "The rocks did a lot of damage to you but everything looks as if it's healing okay. I suggest drinking lots of water to get your body back to normal and, although we've got iron in the food you eat, I'll see if I can generate a few iron pills we can give you."

He removed the probes on Erica. He waved to Jiao to come closer and attached them to her. After he finished the readings, he said, "You're in the same condition as Erica but your head and brain have been more affected by the rocks. I suggest the same course of action as for Erica. We'll monitor you regularly to ensure your brain is healing properly."

He paused for a few seconds and said, "I've never had any dealings with humans. They aren't rare on our planet but our family, relatives and neighbours didn't have them around. I only learned about you when I went to university. I find it amazing that you can nurture a baby inside of you. As you know, our women lay eggs and, when they hatch, we used to chew plants and meat and spit it into the babies' mouths as food. Now, we give them the formulation we eat. I understand you give the infants liquid milk that you make in your bodies and the babies suck it out of you. That's amazing. I guess it comes out of here." He touched one of her nipples.

Jiao flinched a bit but stood her ground. She had acclimatised to these conditions. She had lost her shyness months ago.

Grog continued. "Your skin is also very soft. Amazingly, your race survived in the wild. That's why you're so badly hurt by the fliers. If you were wild on this planet, I don't think you'd last long. You'd end up as good tasty warm meat for those giant beasts we encountered."

"Well, if we were so weak, we wouldn't have been able to save you, would we?" Jiao said aggressively.

Grog smiled. "You're right young lady. We owe you a great debt of gratitude. There's no way I can ever repay you for my life. I'm sure the first officer feels the same. I even wish we could take you back home but that's out of the question. I feel so sorry for you." He took her hand, raised it to his lips, kissed it, and released it. "I believe your men do this to their ladies as a show of respect."

"They used to but only dorks do it now."

Grog smiled again. "My translator knows what a dork is, you know. We have a word like it. It's not exact but I get what you mean. I guess I saved you from the worst event – kissing you on the mouth."

Now, it was Jiao's turn to smile.

"Well, join Roche and get ready to go. I think you're fit to help us pick up our captain and the equipment we left behind yesterday. I'm not telling you but inviting you to help us. I won't be disappointed if you decide you want to stay here. Dan's staying here, so you'll have company if you remain."

Jiao did not know what to do. Erica had always taken the lead in things like this but she was standing there doing and saying nothing. She looked at Erica to see if there was any reaction from her.

Jiao finally said, "You won't be able to get everything back here in one trip with just two of you."

"It's going to be difficult even if you help," Grog responded without emotion. He did not want to influence them in any way.

Jiao looked back at Erica. "Why are you acting like this?"

With no response from her, Jiao said to Grog, "Well, I'll go and help you. I'm not going to push Erica. If she stays here, she's staying, if she's coming, I guess she'll follow us."

Jiao gave Erica an annoyed look, slipped her jumper back on her, and helped Erica do the same. She went into their cell to get herself ready. Erica followed.

Soon, the three teens were waiting at the control room hatch ready to go.

Grog decided they would not take a generator with them. The probability was low that the fliers would see them.

They headed out and after several hours reached the protected site.

They stopped and rested under the protection of the forcefields. They pulled out the food and water from the large bag and had lunch. Grog pulled out the first aid kit and gave the captain a shot of medicine and water.

After about thirty minutes, Grog turned off the forcefields and folded the legs of the generator. They stuffed the food and water back into the large bag, which was full. Grog pulled the carrying straps that were in the small sack and attached them to all the loose equipment. Grog did a thorough scan of their surroundings and found no signs of any fliers. He slipped the large sack onto his back. Roche grabbed the other bag and slipped it on his. With the straps, Erica carried the small bag, cannon, and canister; Jiao took the two generators. Grog and Roche picked up the ropes tied to the captain and they headed back to the ship.

The journey was slower going back. They had to stop three times to rest. Twice they saw solitary fliers in the sky but either the fliers did not see them or chose to ignore them.

When they reached the stream, they took a longer rest to drink some water and cool off.

Roche took the opportunity to look at his reflection in the water. He did not recognise himself. He looked all bedraggled with a thick beard covering his face. He only recognised his eyes. He looked so . . . old. He sighed and realised that he felt old, too.

So much had befallen them over the last few months. He looked at the two girls sitting quietly by the stream. Their backs had hunched over, their old smiles were absent. The old sparkle in their eyes was gone. They looked so dejected. He was partly responsible for that.

Before all this, he had not thought much of his future and whether he would get married or not. He knew he wanted to go to university but what teen thinks of much else, except having fun? This was not fun. All that ended, now.

He had seen Erica more as company and maybe a curiosity but he had seen so much of her that he had come to appreciate and respect her. He had come to . . . love her but down deep somewhere he felt she would never be a part of his life – that all ended with those few steps into the alien's spaceship. His heart ached.

Grog stood up and slipped the sack onto his back.

They knew this was the signal to go, so everyone got ready.

By supper, they were back at the ship.

From his chair in the captain's cabin, the first officer had readied the ship for its return trip. Grog and Roche made several trips outside to haul in some vegetation for storage as food or fuel for the ship.

They had supper and the teens returned to their cells while Grog attached the captain to the medical equipment.

Later in the evening, the girls visited Aaootaa.

On entering, Jiao praised her for eating her food. She told her where they had gone and what they did. They managed to link several new words. When the lights dimmed, they decided to stay in the cell inside her compartment for the night.

Shortly after, they heard the light rumbling of the ship taking off. They had begun their journey to the aliens' home planet.

57.

The next day, Roche got up first. The lights were already on, so there was no way to tell how long he had slept. He used to complain about how hard the floor was in their cells but last night it felt so soft, he fell asleep immediately and completely.

Their food was already on the counter, so he went to it and helped himself. It was so nice to have fresh food and lots of water – even if it was tasteless and at room temperature.

Now, he only had to deal with boredom. Nobody could ever say that the days on the last planet were boring. He thought of doing exercises but looked at the shape he was in and dismissed it. When he did start them again, he would have to start slowly. He noticed the girls were not in their cell and guessed that they had stayed with the Aboriginals.

He finally went into one corner of his cell, leaned on the wall, slid down, and sat quietly.

Dan woke up about an hour later. He yawned, looked over to the next cell, and noticed Roche sitting in his cell. He got up uneasily and stumbled to the bathroom. He soon headed to the food counter using the wall for support and had breakfast.

Roche came over to him and said, "Hi, it looks as if you slept well."

Dan looked at him and said, "Yeah, for once."

"How are you doing?"

"Well, I still don't feel too well but I'm better. I still have a bad headache and am wobbly on my feet."

"I'm glad to be back though," Roche responded.

"I never thought I'd say I am, too. At least we're safe here unless we run into problems with the ship."

"Don't bring us any bad luck by saying that." Roche paused for a few seconds. "I've been thinking. Have you noticed anything different about the girls, I guess Erica the most?"

"I don't think so. I've been a little out of touch for the last few days, so maybe I didn't notice."

"Erica is so quiet."

"So, she's been through a lot. Maybe she's tired. The last couple of days have not been good for them. Their experiences must have been horrific. Did you see them? They had cuts and bruises all over the place and were covered with fliers' blood."

"Yeah, maybe that's it. I hope she's okay."

"Maybe go easy on her for a while and she'll go back to the old Erica."

"I wonder how Raj is doing? He was badly hurt," Roche asked.

"You haven't had an update on him yet from Grog?"

"Not since yesterday."

The two boys sat down in their cells.

Aaootaa was the first one to awake in her compartment. She had had dreams of her life back home. She had felt the slight vibration in the ship in the evening but had thought perhaps it was a minor earthquake far away. She was wondering about her life. Her family was gone and so was her new husband of less than a year and she was pregnant.

She glanced at the girls sleeping in the next cell and thought of them, too. She liked them, they were good companions but they were not from her people. They were strange in many ways but at least she could talk to them. What she considered almost magic was she heard strange gibberish out of the girls' mouths but heard her language out of that little tube one of them was holding. She was thankful for that. Life would have been worse without it, but she was lonely for her people.

When nobody was on the ship, she stopped eating and drinking and hoped to die. The girls' return had been bittersweet, it broke her hopes of dying in this cage and being rid of all this or living with these friendly girls. This was not her world. These were not her people and her life was not worth living anymore.

Then she started to wonder about her thoughts. She had never been, nor thought, like this before. She was without family and peer support and her thoughts were contrary to her people's customs and beliefs. No one thought of dying. Their culture celebrated life – when you were old enough to marry, or a woman laid an egg, or when the egg hatched, the whole village celebrated. There were no birthdays, as they cherished each day and one more day was the celebration of a longer life. When someone died, they did not mourn the death but cheered the life that was and the person's contributions to the tribe during that life. There was no suicide, nor thought of it. They did not even have a word for it.

She scanned the room. She was here. She did not want to be here but she was stuck here and she was alive for another day. She had met more and different beings than she had ever experienced before but it was life and she would live it as it was and even better in the hope that she would get home one day.

She sighed and looked at the girls sleeping in the cell across from hers. She looked at the slot where her food and water sat. She got up and ate breakfast.

When the girls finally woke up, they looked at her and smiled. They went to her cage and greeted her. She returned the greeting. They went over to where her food was and noted that she had eaten some of it and drank some of the water sitting beside it. They smiled at her and left the room to join the boys.

As they crossed the central control room, they noticed Grog was busy in another compartment. They thought of going over there to ask how Raj was doing but thought better of it. They entered their compartment, as the door was open.

Jiao greeted the boys as they went directly to the counter to have breakfast. When they finished, they went to their cell.

It appeared that today was going to be a day of mending.

Around noon, Grog came in and gave them each a pill to take. He checked over Dan. When he finished, he informed them that the captain was dead. He had probably died soon after the flier had crushed him. Of course, the first officer was the new captain of the ship. They would not be seeing him much, as he would be staying in the captain's cabin, looking after the affairs of the ship, and updating the log of the events of the past week or so. He added that the egg had survived the trip to the ship. He would incubate it a few more days to let it mature a little more, then would cryogenically store it until they got back to their planet.

Grog gave them the good news that Raj was healing well. He was keeping Raj under sedation while he continued to improve. He was unsure when he would be able to join them. Grog left the room but returned shortly.

"I brought you new clothes," he said. "The ones you have are in tatters. Put your old ones by the door and I'll pick them up later." He put a package by the boys' cells and another one by the girls' cell. He left again.

Nobody moved for several minutes until Roche got up and picked up the boys' package. He slipped off the little band that was around them and pulled one out. "Hey, these are longer," he said as he held one up. "Not a lot but more than we had before."

Jiao got up, picked up the girls' package, and undid the band. She began to pull it apart but found that the top part was wrapping for another layer inside. She opened the package a bit and looked in. Her mouth opened and she instantly closed it. She opened it briefly then closed it again. She walked over and sat beside Erica who had been staring mostly at the floor all morning. Jiao nudged her to get her attention then opened the cover again.

Erica glanced down and looked at its content with shocked disbelief. Jiao, wide-eyed, pulled out one of the tunics and stood up.

The boys watched as Jiao pulled it open and held it up to her. It still had no sleeves and was still like sackcloth but had a pleat in the middle, a flare at the bottom, and was . . . a bright yellow. Their jumper looked more like a yellow dress. Erica stared a Jiao for many seconds before she took hold of the packet beside her and pulled out the other dress. She held it in her hands, stared at it, and began to cry. She wanted to stop herself but all the pain and suffering of the last few days rushed out of her.

Jiao sat beside her, wrapped her arm around her, and joined her.

Grog entered shortly after that, glanced at them then started to work on the lone cell that served as their combination toilet and shower stall. When he finished, a brown sack material covered it. The teens had privacy. He walked out.

It was many minutes before anyone moved but Roche finally decided to change his clothes. He looked at the two jumpers and found them to be the same size. He took one, went into the private cell and came out wearing it. Its length was about thirty centimetres longer than before. He tossed his old one by the open door. Dan soon changed his.

Roche said quietly but loud enough for everyone in the room to hear, "I wonder why it took so long for them to do this? They could have done this from the start."

He and Dan sat down in their cells.

Jiao gathered her resolve and collected herself. In a way, she did not want to change. They had gotten used to wearing the other ones, it was such a bother to change. Who cared if it was longer or a different colour but her old one was so torn, it was not worth wearing. She got up, went into the covered area, and put it on. She looked at herself and held back the tears. She had to be strong about this and already had her cry. She pulled herself together and stepped out of the cell.

Both Dan and Roche smiled. They saw all the black and blue, the red, and the scabs on Jiao's skin. They saw the scraggly and knotted hair. They saw the sunken darkened eyes but, for the first time in a long time, she looked . . . beautiful. Dan gave her a little whistle and she blushed.

Erica remained quietly by herself.

Jiao sat beside her and said nothing. She knew Erica had to deal with this in her own time.

Erica pulled up the dress and looked at it. She had no smile. She wanted to look ugly and this was not going to make her look ugly. In a way, she wanted it to be brown again, or maybe even . . . black. She reminisced for a while. When she was small, she wore whatever her mother put on her. When she got a little older, she was always stealing her sister's clothes. Then she wanted her clothes – different clothes until she drifted into black. She was very different then. Was she ready to wear a yellow dress?

What was going to happen to them when they arrived at the alien's planet? What were the aliens going to force them to wear there? It looked as if these people wore very few clothes, if any. They had no hair either so would they have scissors or combs around? She lowered the dress and closed her eyes. She was in no hurry to do anything.

Later in the afternoon, Grog walked in with what could serve as a comb. He put it on the counter and said, "I'm sorry, that's all I could come up with. I shouldn't be doing this. I hope you can appreciate it."

He left as quickly as he entered.

Jiao waited to see if the boys would react. When they did not, she got up and pulled Erica to her feet. Jiao grabbed the dress and led the struggling Erica to the counter, where she picked up the comb and went to the covered cell.

When there, Erica sat down humbly and Jiao kneeled and used the comb to work on Erica's hair. There were many painful tugs but Jiao eventually got Erica's hair into order.

Jiao said, "Well, it's not perfect but it's the best it's been since we got on this ship. Okay, now you do me." She sat down.

Erica reluctantly got up, grabbed the comb, and worked on Jiao's hair.

After about twenty more minutes, Jiao's hair was in order.

"I'm not sure why we're doing this. We're not going to a party," Erica whined.

"Look, we got a dress and we got a comb, so it makes sense to look nice at least once on this tub."

"But if we have them, we have months to bother to look nice."

"So, let's start now."

Erica just sat there.

"Are you going to put the jumper on, or what?"

With no sign of Erica doing anything, Jiao stood up, bent down, grabbed her arm, and hauled her up. She picked up the hem of the old brown jumper with her other hand and whipped it up and over Erica's head. Jiao then grabbed the new yellow dress, tossed it over Erica's head, pulled it down, and stepped back.

"You know, you look good in it."

Erica looked down and the tears began to flow again.

"You can let loose now, there are no boys around," Jiao said, as she grew close to her and hugged her in solace.

They held tightly to each other and cried to say goodbye to their old lives.

It was several minutes later when the girls left the cover of the cell. Roche smiled when he saw the transformed Erica. That was the first time he had seen her in any colour but black and he liked what he saw. He dared not say anything, though. He knew this would be a touchy subject for Erica.

The girls walked to the counter, replaced the comb, and went to their cell. They sat down and rested.

Roche stared for a while. Erica's hair flowed gently over her back with a large swatch flowing over her left shoulder over the mound under her dress and down to her waist. He sighed and turned away. He thought he should try to think of other things.

After a few minutes, Roche went over to the counter, grabbed the comb, and returned to his cell. He combed his hair and beard as best he could. He handed the comb to Dan. When he finished, Roche took it from him and returned it to the counter.

After supper, Grog entered and asked if the girls would visit Aaootaa. They welcomed the relief and walked with him over to her cell. Grog gave them the translator and left.

Aaootaa had a big smile on her face. "Girls look nice."

"Well, the lizards gave us new clothes because our other ones were all worn out," Jiao responded.

"Your . . . what you call on your head looks beautiful."

"We had it here before. It's called hair."

"Yes, but is long and smooth and black. It was not smooth before. Aaootaa has no word for that. No animal at Aaootaa home has hair. White birds have covering but no hair like girls. I use a girl's sound for it. For girls, it looks nice. It no look nice on Aaootaa. Your men like hair?"

"I guess so. It's hard to tell. We came here by mistake. The lizards took away our old clothes and gave us those brown jumpers. In our culture, we always wear clothes in public. For a while, they seemed to think it was amusing but adapted to it. Now we're in dresses that don't show too much skin and I can tell they're very . . . well . . . interested. It's hard to figure them out."

"Aaootaa no have problem."

"Yes, you wear no clothes."

"Oh, Aaootaa wear clothes on the wedding day. Clothes make Aaootaa . . ." The translator had no word to match the sound Aaootaa made.

"Maybe you mean 'alluring'."

"What means alluring?"

"Ah, appealing; tempting."

"I not know if Aaootaa has a word."

"Maybe you do. I could explain it more in detail and you would have a word. It's a little embarrassing to talk about."

"What word 'embarrassing'?"

"Maybe it's a little beyond our need right now. All I want to say is men are strange."

"Maybe girls have strange men."

"What do you mean?"

"Men no strange. Men bring food and protect family."

"Men don't bother you?"

"Men no bother Aaootaa. Why do men bother girls?"

"I guess we think differently and they seem to want only one thing."

"Only one thing?" Aaootaa asked, puzzled.

How could she explain it? In her world, males were only interested in the female when they were in their fertile period. It would be impossible for her to understand how humans evolved so intercourse was performed for procreation and recreation.

Jiao finally said, "Our men are more complex than yours, so it might be hard to understand."

This did not resolve Aaootaa's confusion but it was a way to avoid trying to explain it.

Jiao said, "We should get going. We'll see you in the morning."

Aaootaa thanked them for visiting her.

The girls walked out of Aaootaa's cell and returned to their own.

While Jiao and Erica were with Aaootaa, Grog asked Dan to join him with the medical equipment. He looked again at his ear and recommended that he do an operation. To keep Dan still during it he sedated him. The operation went well. Grog disconnected him from the equipment, carried him over to his cell, and left him in Roche's care.

Jiao and Erica joined the boys. They asked about what Grog had told them.

They spent the rest of the day quietly in their cells.

At the end of it, the lights dimmed and everyone slept.

.

58.

The brightening of the lights heralded the morning. Some people slept in and others got an earlier start to the day. Roche was the latter. He thought he would start slowly on exercises to keep him in shape. He was quite certain no one else would want to start that early. He could not do anything too strenuous because of his wounds.

When the girls got up, they had breakfast and left to see Aaootaa for an hour or so. Jiao returned before Erica and went into the shower area, removed her dress, and washed and combed her hair. Dan entered before she finished and startled Jiao.

"What're you doing here?" she whispered.

"Um, I wanted to say good morning. We haven't talked for a while."

"Can't you wait until I'm finished? I thought I had some privacy in here. You can see I'm not dressed, or haven't you noticed?"

"I guess we've been separated for a while and are too busy to talk."

"Yeah, it's nice to have a little area like this," Jiao said as she slipped on her dress. "That's why I came here; to be alone." She emphasised the last word. She picked up the comb.

"Even without me?" he said, as he lowered his head.

She looked at him. "I don't know. Maybe today is okay. We can't talk loudly though; this area isn't soundproof."

"I know," he said quietly.

He gently took the comb out of her hand and began combing her hair. "I want to know if everything's okay between us," he said.

"Why do you think it wouldn't be?"

"I don't know. Roche is worried about Erica. He thinks she's mad at him."

"Right now, I think she's mad at everyone and everything. I can't talk to her either. Roche will have to go slowly and let her heal in her way. It's you and Roche who got us into this, to begin with."

"I know, that's why I was worried about us."

"Well, we're both pretty pissed off with how things turned out. Erica took the brunt of all the bombing and, I guess, she's in a rather big slump right now."

Dan caught a rather tight snag and pulled a little too hard.

"Ouch, watch it! If it gets tight like that back up and take a smaller chunk of hair and tease it out gently."

"Okay, sorry." He did what she suggested. "So, you aren't mad at me?"

"A little but we're here and there's not much we can do about it. Brooding over it is not going to help and there isn't a long line of other guys to take your place."

He had gotten rid of all the tangles and was combing her hair gently. He said, "You've got beautiful hair."

"I don't usually grow it this long. I like to keep it short."

"Well, I like it this way. Keep it like this, or longer and I'll comb it for you. It looks beautiful."

"No, my hair is too straight. It must be longer or shorter. This length can't look nice."

"Well, let it grow longer."

"It looks as if I don't have a choice. Grog hasn't brought us scissors. Maybe I should ask him."

"Please don't."

She let her head fall back to let her hair fall freely on her shoulders. He leaned over and kissed her then resumed combing. After a few minutes, he stopped.

"It's done," he said.

"Feels like it." She turned around to face him. They embraced and kissed. "You'd better go."

They pulled apart.

"I'm glad you're not sore at me."

Jiao leaned into him again and gave him another kiss. "There, that means I'm not sore at you." She smiled.

"Maybe when we get to Grog's planet, we can get married," he said, as he pressed close to her.

"Let's take one step at a time. We don't know for sure what's going to happen when we get there."

"I love you so much, Jiao. I can't wait for you forever."

"I love you too but let's cool it okay? I'll go but maybe you ought to stay here awhile to cool down." She left the cell and he left it a few minutes later.

Erica was sitting in their cell when Jiao returned and sat beside her.

"Why did you stay so long?" Jiao asked.

"I stopped to see how Raj was doing."

Jiao whispered to her, "Roche is worried about you."

Erica turned her head to her but said nothing.

"I wanted to let you know that I'm worried about you. I don't like what's happening to you. You're not yourself," Jiao said quietly. "I hope you can pull through this slump you're in. I'm here if you need to talk to me. Maybe you can do it when we're with Aaootaa."

Erica sighed then turned away.

"How's Raj?"

"Grog says he's doing well."

At about noon, Raj walked in uneasily wearing a new jumper. Everyone got up and swarmed around him with all kinds of questions.

"Okay, not everyone at once," Raj said. "I'm glad to be back. Grog told me that I'd been in a coma for a couple of days. I'm glad everyone else is okay. It looks as if the aliens took the worst of it."

He noticed the girls' jumpers. "Is that what Grog gave you?"

"What do you think?"

"Wow, you girls look great."

"Jiao spun around so her jumper flared a little."

"Hubba, Hubba," Raj said enthusiastically.

He looked at Erica. "My how that dress makes you look beautiful." He took his eyes off her so as not to embarrass Erica, or him.

He wandered over to the counter to eat and have some water.

Jiao asked, "Do you remember anything about what happened while you were unconscious?"

"No, I don't even remember the rock hitting me. It's as if I was walking along the trail and woke up here. I remember nothing else."

Except for Erica, each of them took turns updating him on what happened during the gap in his memory.

Raj finished eating and said, "Grog said I'd be a little woozy for a few weeks, so I should take it easy. I'll sit down for a while."

Jiao took the opportunity to pull Roche into the central control room. When they were out of sight, she asked, "Have you noticed that Erica is acting strangely?"

"Yes, she's a lot quieter than she used to be."

"Dan noticed it too."

"You know what she had to do out there was horrific. I saw a lot of it. I hated fighting the fliers and knew we had to do it to save our lives but many people can't take it, they get traumatised and do things they wouldn't do normally. They may get angry and lash out at people, or get moody, some even commit suicide. All we can do is give her time and love to heal."

Jiao sighed and they returned to their compartment.

About two hours later, Jiao got restless and suggested they all visit Aaootaa. Roche helped Raj and Dan get up and they all walked into the control room through the open doorway.

Roche asked, "Are they leaving the doors open for us?"

Grog appeared at the open door of his cabin. Now that the first officer had taken over the captain's cabin, he had it to himself. "Hi, is everything good with you guys?"

Jiao answered, "Sure, we thought we'd go and visit Aaootaa."

"That's fine, she could use the company. I think she's a little lonely in there. Too bad we couldn't catch another of her kind for her.

"Roche, you asked a question and I should fill you in. You know that we locked your door before. We didn't want to take the chance that you would hijack the ship in some way. I made a deal with the first officer to give you more freedom. He's well sequestered in the former captain's cabin and has effective control of the ship. Also, he's the only one who can open his door. Even I can't get in. So, I'm supposed to tell you that, if you try anything, for example, try to take me hostage, he won't care. I'm responsible. He doesn't think you'd kill me but you needn't try because it won't do any good, just lose your increased mobility within the ship. The only places you can go are your compartment, this room, and Aaootaa's compartment. So, you could do your exercises in here as it has more space; whenever you want."

"Thanks," Jiao said.

"You can also boot out other people if you want to kiss and cuddle, or anything."

Jiao turned red and responded, "I don't think we'll be doing that.

It's not so much the kissing and cuddling part. I'm worried more about the 'or anything' part."

Grog smiled but said nothing more.

The teens went on to Aaootaa's door, which opened for them and entered.

Aaootaa had been sitting on the floor in her cell. As soon as she saw them, she stood up.

Jiao picked up the translator from the counter and said, "Hi, we thought we'd all visit you. Raj joined us a few hours ago, so you can see the rest of us."

"These girls' men?"

"Yes, that's Roche," she pointed over to him then presented the other two.

Aaootaa looked over the boys with great interest. "Men no good for Aaootaa but Aaootaa think good for girls. Men look the same but different. Lots of hair on faces. Hard to see eyes. Aaootaa think big man good for Erica."

Erica smiled.

"Aaootaa think other big man good for Jiao. Little one good for girls when big men tired."

Jiao could not figure out whether Aaootaa was expressing her humour, or being serious but Jiao was trying to stifle a laugh. The boys did not know what to think. They looked embarrassed more than anything else.

"Well, thank you for your kind comments," Jiao said. "You're right but the little one may be good for you."

Raj's mouth flew open and his eyes bulged from their sockets.

"Little one too small for Aaootaa," she said with a big grin on her face.

Raj cut her off excitedly. "What're you girls doing? Did you bring me in here to mock, or something?"

Jiao replied, "I guess Aaootaa doesn't understand our culture. In her culture, it's survival of the fittest. They do get married of sorts but when they're in their fertile periods other males can vie for them."

"Well, thanks for the explanation but why are you talking about this anyway?" Raj enquired.

"Aaootaa was the one who started it. She's trying to understand us."

Aaootaa changed the subject. "You have different colour hair?"

"Yes, black is the most common colour but people can have

different shades of colours grey, brown, blonde, white, and even red."

They spent another half hour in small talk then the teens left.

The trip to the aliens' planet was long and boring. The teens picked up their regular exercises again. The girls got Aaootaa involved in some of their exercises. There were some that she was not anatomically capable of doing. Aaootaa tolerated Grog who was the only alien she got to see. She never got to like him. He was forever her captor.

Grog got along with the teens. He particularly enjoyed Raj's company and his insatiable interest in Grog and his culture and language. They became friends.

Erica took months to heal her emotional wounds. Until then, she remained mostly in a world of her own. She had had many burdens to carry. So much had befallen her. Her guilt over the slaughter of the fliers remained with her. She always reminded the boys about their insistence on getting aboard the ship. She also knew she would never see home.

Jiao looked after Erica. She too brooded a lot. She also kept busy talking to Aaootaa and taking care of her.

Dan slowly healed and his walking and balance returned. He tried to spend as much time as he could with Jiao. Sometimes the two of them would get together behind the screen to talk. He was ashamed of what he had done that fateful day on earth. Even though they had made up, he still felt it had strained the close bond he had with her. He hoped that, once they got to the lizard's planet, he could try to make a life with her.

Roche could see the damage done to Erica. He tried constantly to break through the shield Erica put between them. He hoped, that once they got to the aliens' planet, he could work with her to heal the divide between them but down deep, he still doubted his success.

Raj spent most of his time trying to learn the lizards' language and some of their technology. As the picture books were not good enough, Grog helped him by bringing him some technical books and he found he could learn to read their hieroglyphic-type alphabet. Grog had some recordings of their speech and slowed it down for Raj to show how it broke down. Their voice box did not give them the capability of varying tones, so their language consisted of a series of clicks and pops. Once he heard it in a slowed-down form, he could make out the individual clicks which made him think of Morse Code. He learned to speak it in a slowed-down way and could understand what Grog was saying if he spoke extremely slowly.

He was amazed at their technology. The power source for the ship was a fusion reactor. Their basic fuel was hydrogen and they derived it mostly by decomposing water and carbohydrates. That was why they brought in fresh stores of plant and animal matter each time they visited a planet. The ship's drive was fast because it took advantage of the natural warping of space to travel at what appeared to be a speed faster than light.

A machine in the ship resembling a three-dimensional printer used basic elements obtained from waste materials to prepare food, equipment, and other required materials. This allowed the ship to be able to travel for years in space without needing to refuel. However, a small ship like this had limited on-board basic material for frivolous things like clothes. It required a lot of energy to fly in space.

Raj viewed what was going on with the group with trepidation. He was unhappy with Erica's state of mind and tried to help look after her and strengthen his friendship with her. He was free of the stigma of the other two boys. Now that Roche was not a powerful influence, he thought he could get her to love him. Although Raj was forming a bond with Grog, he was always preparing for the opportunity to get back home; and when he got the occasion, he would take her and love her all to himself.

59.

After more weeks of travel which no one had bothered to count, Grog walked in one morning to say that, in a few hours, they would be landing on their planet. He brought the teens out to watch the monitor in the main control area to see it. They saw a planet with splotches of grey or white clouds much like Earth, with blue skies, oceans, and land. The only difference was the layout of the continents.

They could see other spaceships circling the planet either preparing to land or waiting to break orbit. They also saw large objects orbiting it that looked like space stations.

As the minutes ticked by, the planet got noticeably larger. Soon, the planet filled their view. Grog told them they were getting into orbit until they got approval to land. More minutes passed.

Grog told them they had started their landing sequence, so they should get into their cells, as the padded floor would protect them if the ride got bumpy. The teens left and sat down in their cells.

It was about an hour later when Grog walked in and told them they had landed. They got out of their cells and waited with Grog.

Within minutes, the ship's hatch opened and four husky-looking lizards stepped inside. Grog handed Roche a translator, so they would understand what they said.

Two of the lizards went into a storage compartment with a gurney and quickly hauled the captain's body out of the ship. One opened one of the doors of the main control area and started bringing out the sacks of equipment and sample containers and loading them onto a large cart outside the portal of the ship. The last one brought a wheelchair for the officer and wheeled him off the ship.

Grog said, "Okay kids, I guess we leave. Your ride is ready."

He led them out of the ship and down a ramp. They looked around at some of the buildings. They were rather plain in comparison to Earth but did not look very different. The only interesting thing was hundreds of flying things that looked like flying cars.

Grog noticed their interest and said, "It probably looks not extremely different from what you're used to. After all a building is a building. Cubes are very functional structures. Most civilisations have similar types of buildings. Those things you see in the air are like your cars which would cram our streets if we couldn't have most of our vehicles in the air. A control computer runs everything, so there are no accidents. Pedestrians use the surface roads."

They reached the end of the ramp and there was a small van-like vehicle at the end of it. Its back door was open.

Grog turned to them and said, "I guess this is the end of the line for us. Our headquarters will be investigating how we handled things during this trip. I hope they won't lay any charges against us. You can keep the translator. I wish you the best of luck. You're going to be taken to a detention centre until they decide what happens next."

Two large lizards appeared behind the teens. One of them said, "Get in the van."

Raj held out his hand to Grog and said, "I'm not really glad I'm here but I learned a lot from you, and you've taken care of us, so I thank you for that."

Grog shook it and said goodbye, as they walked into the van.

A lizard entered the van with them and showed them how to fasten themselves in. The door closed.

The teens could not see anything outside of the back of the van. They felt a slight acceleration and were not sure how long their journey was. It was likely about thirty minutes. They hardly felt any motion, so either the aliens had very smooth roads, or they were in the air. They felt a deceleration and soon the door opened.

The lizard helped them undo their security straps and get out of the van. They were in the middle of extremely high buildings where they could hear a lot of hubbubs from the street but were behind a gated area.

The lizard led them into a building and an elevator. They watched as the lights on the viewer were changing symbols. Soon, the elevator stopped and he led them down a long hall to a door. It opened before them and they entered a very large boardroom.

Three lizards were sitting behind a large desk. Roche's translator sounded, "Welcome, please be seated – anywhere you like."

Each of them picked a chair and sat down in a row on the other side of the three lizards.

The centre lizard spoke, "I see you were left with a translator. That's good." He paused for a few seconds.

"Welcome to our planet. I see your wounds have healed well from your last expedition. We're investigating several actions of our officers taken during this trip. As you know, the captain is dead and the first officer is paralysed. You're the only witnesses in the investigation. I must thank you for the valiant actions on your part to help them escape from the flying reptiles. They might not have escaped without you." He paused again.

"We're going to be taking you out for questioning about what happened on Earth and how you got into the ship, then what happened while you visited the white fliers. Please don't discuss what each one of you said while you sit here. We want your impartial stories. It should take about twenty minutes each."

The three interrogators left the room.

A lizard led each of them in their turn into another smaller room and returned them to the boardroom. The three interrogators asked them questions about what happened during those two events. When everyone had their turn, the three lizards entered the boardroom again and sat down.

The centre lizard said, "Thank you for your help." He looked them over. "I know your trip here is due to curiosity on your part and carelessness on the part of our exploration team. I believe the captain told you that you can't return to your planet. He was right, you'll have to stay here. Our planet is pretty and a good place to live. We'll treat you well and you can lead useful lives here. I wish you well."

Another lizard entered the room, ushered them out to the van, and hauled them away to the parking lot of another large building. He led them up a set of stairs to a large room that appeared to be a medical facility where one of the three lizards told them to take off their clothes. They took turns examining them.

When they finished, one of the medical centre's lizards said, "It looks as if you're in good health. You have a few wounds that left small scars. We're going to give you an injection. It might hurt for a few days."

One by one they got their injections on the left side of their necks, although they thought it was a strange place for it.

The medical lizard was right. It did hurt.

"This person will lead you to some showers where you can get cleaned up then he'll take you to another room, so you can get something to eat."

"Can we get our clothes on?" Roche asked meekly.

The three medical lizards looked at each other. The lead one answered, "Sure, okay."

The teens dressed and followed the new lizard out of the room.

Roche asked the new lizard, "What's going to happen to us after we eat?"

"Well, it's getting late in the day, so we'll get you somewhere where you can get some sleep then I'm not sure where you'll go next. I'm only a nurse, so once you leave here someone else will look after you."

The lizard that brought them to the medical centre entered and led them down some halls to a large room with showers in it. They cleaned up and washed their clothes. Once they left the showers, they were air-dried and the lizard led them to a large eating area. A small human male that looked thirteen served them their food and water. They looked at the food and each other.

Roche said, "This is the same crap they served us on the ship. I thought when we got here, we'd get real food."

Their driver overheard him on his translator and said, "This is what we eat all the time. Many centuries ago, we used to eat meat and plants but when this type of food came, it replaced what we used to eat. It saved our planet which was severely farmed. Now our planet is like a paradise and we like to keep it this way."

"But it doesn't taste like anything."

"Some people add spices to it to give it taste but most people eat it the way it is."

"So, this is what we're going to get for the rest of our lives?"

"Depends what happens to you."

"What do you mean?"

"Tomorrow, you're going to the job market."

60.

Roche's mouth dropped open when he heard about the market. He could hardly believe what he heard. What did that mean? Was it equivalent to providing resumes and getting a job based on it? Or, was it like a slave market? The aliens had been nebulous about it.

The lizard could see the look on his face. "You look confused. We treat our workers well. You need not worry."

"What happens at the market?"

"Many people who need help, bid on you and the highest bidder wins."

"For what jobs?"

"It could be for anything, working around their home, in the garden, childcare, anything."

"Do we get paid?"

"Not usually but maybe. The buyer must treat you well and give you room and board."

"Are we going to be split up?"

"It depends on who wants what tomorrow. Sometimes buyers bid on a group and sometimes they only buy one. You also have the disadvantage of being new here. People prefer your kind already trained. If you're new, sometimes it doesn't work out."

"What do you mean?"

"They might try to escape or kill themselves. To compensate, the government covers the loss, otherwise, no one would buy them."

"What happens to humans who escape?"

"As far as I know, they get found and sent to detention centres. The

313

authorities don't give workers a second chance to escape."

The teens were sullen.

The lizard asked, "Have you finished eating?"

They nodded their heads.

"Okay, follow me."

He led them out of the eating area and down more halls to an elevator. They entered and the door closed. After several seconds, it opened into a large room with many cages. A lizard inside approached them and led them to a cage. He opened the door and told them to get inside. They got into the cell then the lizard locked the door and left.

They were familiar with the cell, as it looked very much like the ones on the ship. They looked around and noted that earthlings or other planets' people occupied most of the cages. There were children and older adults. Some wore brown jumpers but most of them wore nothing. They all looked clean and healthy Almost all the earthlings had extremely long hair whether they were male or female and the ones with short hair were very coarsely cut.

For long minutes, they said nothing.

Roche got up and pushed the door but it did not open.

There was a wall behind them and an empty cage on one side of them. Roche looked across the aisle and noticed three naked boys about twelve years old. They were pale-looking. All three had very blond hair and blue eyes. He leaned close to that cell and said, "Where are you from?"

All three of them looked at him puzzled.

Roche spoke louder, "Do you speak English?"

They still looked puzzled.

A boy in another cell across from them who wore a brown tunic like Roche was wearing called out. "I speak English."

Roche could hardly understand the way he said it as his accent was very thick but it was clear. "Oh, good," Roche said. "So, a lot of you don't speak English?"

"There are not too many who do. You can see many races here. I'm not too sure where I came from, except my family has been here for many years. The only information we know is what our mothers or fathers told us. They were the ones who taught us how to speak. It's hard to speak like our owners, so we learn our language from our parents."

"Are you treated well?" Roche asked.

"You must be new here."

"We are."

"If you mean that we get food and good work, then yes."

"That's good."

"Where did your females get such pretty clothes?"

"They were given to them."

"I've never seen clothes in that colour before."

There was silence for a while. The teens soaked in what he had said.

"I couldn't understand everything he said," Jiao remarked. "He spoke too quickly and I can't understand the accent."

"He said his family's been here for a long time and the lizards treated them well. He says he likes your clothes," Roche said.

One of the boys in the cell next to them said something but no one could make it out.

Jiao whispered, "It sounds almost like German or maybe one of the Scandinavian languages."

Raj said, "There's a variety of races here. There are Caucasians, Africans and Orientals." He looked at Jiao. "Maybe you can talk to the Chinese girl in the other cell across from us."

Jiao looked in that direction. "I see but she doesn't look exactly Chinese, she may be a mix. She's not Japanese. Even if she was Chinese, she may not speak Mandarin or Cantonese. There are lots of other languages in China, and even a lot of dialects, especially if the lizards brought her here hundreds of years ago. Languages change with time."

"You can try."

Jiao said something to the girl in Mandarin but she did not respond.

Jiao switched to Cantonese. The girl's eyes lit up but in a rather puzzled way. She said something back.

"Wow," Jiao said. "It sounds like very old Cantonese but, on top of it, her family has been here so long that it has moved even farther away from modern Cantonese. It's as if they developed their language."

"Can you understand it?"

"A bit, I think she's having a hard time understanding me too."

Jiao asked her very slowly how long she had been there and how she ended up there.

The girl also spoke slowly back to Jiao for quite some time.

"So, what did she say?" Roche asked.

"They've been here a long time – many generations."

Jiao and the girl started another conversation and Jiao told her that she had just come to this planet. Jiao filled her in on what was going on in the world, especially in China. The girl told Jiao about her life here.

"Well, you two had a long talk, so what else did she say?"

"I filled her in on what's going on where she comes from and something about her old country. She said she was born here and an alien took her away from her parents when she was quite young. The aliens educated her. Now, she's old enough to work, so the officials brought her here for someone to buy her and she'll work for them. She told me that the population of humans is highly controlled because they don't want too many, to keep their price under control."

"So, that's what they're going to do with us," Dan stated.

"Looks like it," Jiao said.

"I hope we're bought together."

"We'd be lucky if they did. We'll have to wait and see. The others seem to be fairly well treated from what I can see."

The lights dimmed and, for the first time, Erica slept by Roche and Jiao by Dan.

Raj understood though. He realised this may be everyone's last night together and he was alone. It had been a long day and they wanted to stay awake but one by one they drifted off.

The next day was busy. A lizard awakened them as soon as the lights came on. Their food was ready for them. They ate and awaited their fate. They milled around their cell. There were no exercises that morning.

It was not long before the big door at one end of the room opened and some lizards ushered everyone into a large holding room.

The lizards pulled out several adults and left the room. When the door opened, they could hear a lot of commotion outside. Soon, the lizards removed more adults, and then the last of them.

They started pulling the youths out in their turn until they were the last five. The teens had been holding hands during the whole process and, now that they were alone, they closed in together into one hug that they hoped would give them luck for one alien to buy them as a group. If that did not happen, this might be their last contact, their last goodbye, and they wanted to show their love for each other.

Two lizards entered, grabbed Erica and Jiao, and tore them from the group. They led them into a large arena with a large gallery of benches along one side. They stopped the girls in the centre of the arena. The auctioneer began saying something but Roche had the translator, so they did not know what they were saying.

The auctioneer began his process and there were several people in the gallery raising their hands then it stopped and two aliens pulled Jiao away and out of the room. There was another flurry of activity then they came to lead Erica out.

The boys stood watching the girls disappear behind the door.

Dan had tears in his eyes.

Roche stood stoically silent. His head hung, as he stared at the floor. His worst fears seemed to have occurred. Their team was breaking up. The people he had known for so long in his life would soon be gone. The girl he had come to love was no longer there. They gave him the ultimate punishment for his hasty stupidity.

Raj could only feel anger. Anger about what was happening but anger also because it seemed so unfair. The love of his life was gone for now but he vowed that he would find her again. He had hoped they would be able to stay together but that would not stop him. He would get her back, then she would be all his.

The door opened and two husky lizards led the boys to the auction arena. One of the lizards took away Roche's translator. Roche was the first one off the block. There seemed to have been quite some activity for him. The two lizards led him away.

Dan was next and they soon hurried him away.

Raj soon stood alone. He felt they had destroyed his whole life. When kids were picking teams, he was always the last one standing. It even seemed the same with Erica when Roche won her over. Someone else was always better than he was. So here he was again, the last one.

The auctioneer began his babbling and stopped. There was silence in the room for almost a minute, until one lizard finally raised his hand – only one hand. Only one lizard was interested in bidding for him.

He raised his eyes and looked toward the area of the bidder. All he saw was a sea of faces. To him, all the lizards looked alike. All the faces looked stone-faced and business-like but this one was different. This one had a smile on his face and Raj recognised – Grog.

ABOUT THE AUTHOR

Michael has had the bug to write since before he reached his teens but rarely got much time to do it. Now he is retired and trying to catch up on his life's dream. It is never too late to start. He lives with his family in Canada.